Praise f

C000134693

'Wow! Just w(

Raw, gritty, an absolute masterpiece'
Confessions of a Bookworm

'Tenderly written...a story never to be forgotten' - ***Misfits Farm***

'*The Silent Brother* is an absolute triumph with all the makings of
a prize-winning novel' - ***GraceJReviewerlady***

'Better than Shuggie Bain. You are going to love this'
Mrs Loves to Read

'Left me speechless, breathless and completely stunned'
The Book Magnet

'*The Silent Brother* is a beautifully written story of life in a rundown
northern citythat exposes the empty rhetoric of levelling-up. The
quality of the writing and character development are superb. This is
the best crime fiction I have read for a long time'
Henshaw Press

'A gritty read set in the metropolis of the north-east where no one
can be trusted, and childhood friendships become adult obsessions'
A Knight's Reads

'A heart breaking story. Very real too' - ***Els Reviews***

'I devoured this book, and my heart is both full and broken'
Dee's book Blog

'A heartbreakingly powerful read that will suck you in & hold you'
Beverley's Reads

'A touch of brilliance' - ***Dawn's Book Reviews***

'Annie is a wonderful character...
full of ambiguities, as real people are' - **Olga Núñez Miret**

'Powerful and emotional with shades of Shuggie Bain'
Reshma Ruia Reviews

'Emotionally hard…the words sometimes feel too real'
Grumpy Old Books

'Chilling in places, but with a humour that made me laugh out
loud. Tommy and Annie's friendship is truly beautiful'
Books in my Opinion

'*The Silent Brother* is tense and harrowing but never without hope.
Van der Velde writes with such skill.'
Sarah Clarke, author of *A Mother Never Lies*

'Bloody marvellous. I need to sit and
stare into space for a wee while' - **Sarah Faichney**

'Unpretentious, raw and unapologetic' - **Davina Banner**

'An emotional masterpiece' - ***Bookworm Blogger***

'A compelling and gritty thriller set in a time of devastation and a
city where hope has been extinguished'
Sally Cronin, *Smorgasbord Blog Magazine*

'An in-depth insight into the redeeming power of love'
Airborn Press

'A gripping story of loss, loneliness and a dark, unforgiving world'
Laura Besley author of *The Almost Mothers*

'Sharp and totally gripping with brilliantly authentic voices'
Emma Christie author of *The Silent Daughter*

SIMON VAN DER VELDE was born and educated in Newcastle upon Tyne where he trained and practiced as a lawyer. Writing was always his real passion however, and Simon has since left the legal profession to concentrate on his writing. Simon is the founder and chair of Gosforth Writers Group and author of the widely acclaimed, Amazon bestseller, *Backstories*, 'the stand-out most original book of the year' 2021. *The Silent Brother* is his debut literary crime novel.

Having travelled throughout Europe and South America, Simon now lives in Newcastle upon Tyne with his wife, labradoodle and two tyrannical children.

Follow Author on Twitter: @SimonVdVwriter

THE SILENT BROTHER

SIMON VAN DER VELDE

Northodox Press Ltd
Maiden Greve, Malton,
North Yorkshire, YO17 7BE

This edition 2022

1
First published in Great Britain by
Northodox Press Ltd 2022

ISBN: 978-1-915179-07-4

This book is set in Caslon Pro Std

TO
Catherine

For my sons

Lovely to
meet you
today

Best wishes,

Simon

"The past is never dead. It's not even past."

William Faulkner

1990

Chapter One

Italia '90

I know straight away that Benjy's going to miss, cos his foot goes back too soon, so he's wobbling on one leg, waiting for the ball to float down, and then he falls over. His head thumps on the rug, but Mam picks him up. She cuddles him and tells him he's as good as Gazza. But it isn't fair, cos I'm better. I look at her face. She smiles over Benjy's shoulder and winks at me with her sparkly eyes. I run and join the hug.

'Come on, Benjy,' I say, and kiss his squidgy cheek. 'Let's play some more.'

The ball is a pink balloon that's gone small and wrinkly, and the tasselly rug is the pitch. There aren't goal posts, but if you do a really big kick then Mam shouts. 'Goal!' and everybody cheers. Me and Benjy are the players. Mam says she's the referee, but then she keeps tickling us when we're trying to do a kick, which isn't allowed.

We should have been in bed ages ago, except Mam said we didn't have to cos England were going to win the World Cup. But then we watched on telly, and they didn't. Mam said it was such a shame. She turned the telly off and Benjy started crying, even though he didn't properly understand. That's why we're playing so late. So in our game, I can be Gary Lineker, and England can win. I let Benjy be Gazza, even though Mam said he was too beautiful, and I told Mam she could be Bobby Robson, which made her laugh.

'I'd rather be Dolly Parton,' she said, and put the music on, singing along with that song about Jolene that we all like.

Well, us three anyway.

Benjy's got the ball, sort of floating up around the train on his jarma top. I'm gonna do a tackle, but Mam's got me. Her fingers are right up in my tummy, so I'm just lying on the rug, really laughing when Benjy does this massive kick, and his eyes open wide like he can't believe he's done it and Mam's shouting. 'Go… go… goal' and the balloon's nearly high as the light and Benjy's squealing and jumping so his blond hair flops over his face.

Then the front door slams, and it's like pressing pause on a video. Everything stops: There's just the curls bouncing on Benjy's head, the balloon floating down, and Dolly Parton singing about eyes of emerald green.

'Chris fuckin Waddle.'

The door swings open. Daryl is in the space. His lips are wet under his manky tash, and his Sunderland shirt's torn wide open across his chest. There's a fag in his hand. He takes ages, putting it in his mouth, holding up that long gold lighter with the red triangle shining like a jewel on the back. The flame waves across the end of his fag. He sucks so hard it looks like it hurts.

'Never trust a fuckin Geordie,' he says, pointing right at me. The snake-bitch tattoo stretches along his arm. 'Useless cunt.'

He stamps into the room. The buckles rattle on his boots.

I need to get behind Mam, but I'm not properly up when I try to run. I do a giant step but I can tell I'm going to fall. I can't stop myself. A pudgy arm comes out to catch me. I grab it, but I shouldn't have. Benjy's too little.

We go crashing into Nana's old cabinet. Benjy's okay though. I can see him watching my face with his eyes all round and green, like he isn't sure if he should cry. Like he wants me to tell him. But then he looks up over my head. This golden bottle is wobbling on top of the cabinet, like in slow motion, like when there's a goal. There's letters on the bottle, big ones I can read.

'Bells,' it says, but it doesn't ring. It crashes.

There's wet on Benjy's jarmas, and sparkly glass in his hair.

'Bastards,' Daryl stomps towards us.

'No,' Mam shouts.

'Quick, Benjy, quick,' I say, and crawl into the kitchen.

My knees thump on the lino. I think its lucky cos the cupboard's open under the sink. I scramble in over bottles and cloths. It's only when I go to close the door that I realise Benjy isn't there. I'm too scared to wait. I close it anyway.

'Daryl,' Mam shouts. 'Get your hands off…'

All I can see is a yellow line of light between the doors, but I can hear everything. There's a thud that makes the doors shake, and Mam's voice changes, shouting sounds that aren't even words. She's crying.

I should get out of the cupboard. I should help, but I don't. I stay very still, breathing a smell like wet dog with a pipe pressing down on my neck and wishing, like always, that Nana hadn't died.

'Keep the fuck still!' he shouts.

Benjy screams, louder and higher, then there's a crack like a firework.

Everything goes quiet for ages, longer than I can hold my breath. There's only Dolly Parton still singing in her happy voice like nothing bad has ever happened.

'*Nine to five…*'

Benjy screams again, worse than I've ever heard.

'Benjy?!' I push the door and crawl back through the kitchen. I'm too late.

At least Mam's got him. She's kneeling on the rug, holding him close. I can see his face over her shoulder. Benjy's mouth is wide and dark. His arm makes me think of our broken Pinocchio, and there's purple coming out of his head, thick, like Ribena straight from the bottle.

That's how it all gets started, why we have to go to the hospital. Cos of Nana being dead and leaving her cabinet in our house, cos of her not looking after us anymore. Except I know that's not true. It's cos of me breaking Daryl's whisky. Cos of me hiding and letting Benjy get caught. Cos of me not helping, even when I knew I should. Cos of me being a coward.

Chapter Two

Hide and Seek

Benjy's arm is warm on my neck, my thigh on his, our bodies tangled together like always, with me on the outside, the first to go. I suppose that's why things happen like they do. Sometimes Mam is with us, curled around me like a shell with her fingers turning in Benjy's hair until I wonder if she loves him more than me, then I feel the beat of her heart on my back, soothing me to sleep. But not now. Not while He is in the house.

It's day outside. I can see the shape of things in the light through our Rainbow Blanket. The torn-off edge of our Italia '90 wall chart that never got finished, and the hole in the wardrobe door, jagged as a dragon's teeth.

We had Mr. Men curtains. Nana got them for our birthday when we were really little. That was before she died, and they put her in a hole. Before Daryl tore the curtains down.

Mam went into Sunderland to get us more curtains, but she got this blue stripy blanket instead, from the Scope shop. He said she was a bloody nutcase. We hated him for that most of all. Cos we knew he was right. Mam smiled at the chimney pots across the street and pinned the blanket over the window.

'Now isn't that pretty,' she said, pressing us in against her softness. 'Like a rainbow.'

We said it was too, but it was just a bobbly blanket hanging where the Mr. Men curtains should have been.

I'm looking at the blanket now, with the light from outside

turning the wool blue, like the sky in summer when it's just getting dark, and the stripes are gold and fiery orange, red like Mam's party dress, and green as the grass in the garden at playgroup. It's beautiful, and what makes me smile is knowing that she was right. He was wrong.

Benjy snuffles and a hand moves against my leg, mine or his. The same. His breath changes, quieter, and I know he is awake, watching the light, thinking about Mam. If she'll come soon. If it's time to get up. I know because it's what I'm thinking, and together we bring her to us. But it's not right. The stairs squeal. She's moving too fast, and I can hear Daryl down there, shouting. Not the words, just that dry bark, like a dog.

The door swings back and the handle crunches. Bits of stuff fall behind the wall. The light clicks. I close my eyes and wait for her to speak, so I know if it will be a bad day. I know already. Benjy does too. His body tightens against me.

The duvet's gone. Mam's hand pushes between us, lifting me away. There's cold on my arm where Benjy's neck touched, and the new heat from Mam against my back. I grab at empty air, and my eyes open.

She's holding me tight, ciggy burnt to nothing in her hand. Benjy's face is white, mouth open, sucking in air. I see his scream on its way.

'They're coming for yous,' Mam says.

And then we're gone, out onto the landing. I blink up at the big yellowy cupboard that reaches all the way to the ceiling. There are long doors with two short slidey ones above, and it doesn't make any sense cos Mam gets one of the slidey doors open and lifts me up, high over her head. My legs hit something hard. I kick against the door.

'Please,' Mam says. 'Be good for your mam. Be a good

boy, Tommy. A good boy.' Her face looks broken. There's red blotches on her cheeks. Wetness in her eyes.

I let her put me in the cupboard.

'Burrow in now, burrow in,' she says, and pushes me away.

I roll back over blankets and coats, stuff that smells like Nana. The bottom of the cupboard clanks underneath me, long plasterboards piled up from when Daryl was going to fix the punch-holes in the wall. From the time when he still said sorry after. From when all he hit was the walls.

My head thuds against the back of the cupboard, stopping me with a ridge of plasterboard digging in my arm. I'm lying across the gap between the edge of the boards and the wall. That's where I need to be, down there. A safe place, like the burrow where Buster would be living if he wasn't in a cage in the yard.

I pull out a pillow and a scratchy blanket, making room. But I'm a big boy, at big school now, and my shoulders are too wide. I turn sideways, sliding down, wedging myself into the space. The boards are tight against my chest. The dusty smell of them itches in my nose.

'Tom-mee, Tom-mee.'

Benjy is screaming. I see his face in the open door like he's taller even than Daryl.

'Shhh, baby, shhh,' Mam says, talking hissy fast with big breaths between, scared even before the bang that shakes the whole house.

Benjy stops screaming. He crawls towards me over the rattly boards.

Mam reaches in. She touches Benjy's face. Not mine.

'It's alright. Just be quiet like little mice,' then she laughs too high, stopping like a question, and slides the door across.

It's black dark, the same with my eyes open or shut.

'Benjy,' I call, pretending it is for him, but really because I am scared.

He comes to me, and his breath is warm on my face. I find him. His arm, his hand, and I hold on, tight and quiet. I can't see his face, but I can feel his lips on my cheek, and together we listen to Mam out on the landing.

'Babbies, babbies,' Mam says, shushing us through the cupboard door. 'It's alright, babbies. Don't fret,' but I can hear the shudder in her voice, like when Daryl is in a radge.

The crash comes again, but this time it's different, with a crunch at the end. There's men shouting. Heavy feet, like Daryl's on the stairs, and Mam's running down to meet them.

Benjy's chest presses on my shoulder, burrowing in where there is no space. The boots on the stairs are closer. The shouting gets louder. But it's alright, cos Benjy is with me. That makes everything alright. Except I know that it's not.

'Go on, Benjy,' I whisper like a shout.

I'm stuck down in this narrow gap, but it's long as the whole cupboard. Benjy could easily slide in at the other end, with his head against my feet. I point in the darkness.

'Down there.'

I push him away from me, but he clings to the neck of my jarmas cos he knows that really; I want him to stay. So I can hold him. So his fear can make me stronger. He knows that I'm only a coward pretending to be brave and that I need him, like always. So he stays. Even when the voices are booming just outside, and if they open the doors, they'll see him up on top of the boards.

'Down there,' I hiss, right up close in his ear.

I pull his hands off my neck and push him away from me. The plasterboards rattle and lift. A gap opens between them, scraping against my leg.

'Nuh,' Benjy says, rolling back towards me, closing the gap.

The boards snap down on the thinnest pinch of my thigh.

I jam my hand in my mouth and bite, trying to balance the pain. I'm nearly fast enough. There's only a squeak, like the sound Buster makes when he's angry. But it's too loud.

The voices stop.

The pain in my leg burns hotter, up through my chest.

Steps come thumping. I push Benjy back, harder, and rougher, but he holds tight to my neck while my leg swells, big enough to fill the world. Then the door judders back and there's light all around us.

I see a hand, black hairs curling around a gold ring. The sound of fingers moving through cloth. Searching. The feel of them closing on Benjy's back, making my heart scream. Benjy doesn't scream. Just a gasp and he lifts away from me. There's a moment when I could reach him, hold him to me with my one free arm. But all I want is for the burning to stop. I let go and the pain changes. There's a draft of air at the neck of my jarmas, and Benjy's strange silence that sets the shame burning under my arms because deep down, I know. I made a noise when I should've been quiet. I let him go when I should've held on. Benjy's gone, and it's my fault.

I huddle deeper in my burrow and listen to fast footsteps down the stairs, slower ones coming back up. Doors open wide. Clothes and blankets are pulled away. Bright circles of torchlight dart across the walls. I try not to breathe. But it's stupid, cos then I have to take a big breath.

The voices save me.

'He's not been well,' Mam says. 'He's up at me mam's,' and I feel embarrassed, cos she means Nana, and Nana's dead.

A woman speaks, closer and louder, with a sad sing-song voice that's hard to understand. She's the one I saw at the hospital. The one Daryl calls "the shagged-out darkie".

'What kind of ill, Mrs. Farrier?' She means what Daryl did to Benjy.

'Well, you know him and Daryl don't get on,' and I can hear the slyness in Mam's voice.

A man answers. 'He's five years old.'

'Aye, aye, and I've told him,' Mam says. 'No more hitting the bairns, else I'm leaving.'

'Well, it's too late for that now,' the woman says in her strange voice, and all the time the lights are moving around me.

I keep my breath quiet and even, but I can feel my chest press in and out against the boards, see the mushed-up bits of them, crumbly, like old Weetabix.

The hand comes again. Hairy knuckles rap on the wall above my head and disappear. Clothes and sheets are thrown back in. The doors close, but not quite. There's a sliver of light to see the jumbled shapes, to hear the steps, slower now, going back down the stairs.

No one comes to find me, not for a long time. Not until I'm crying for the feel of Benjy's hand. Not until I've forgotten the smell of his breath against my face.

Chapter Three

Dragon's Teeth

I can hear boxes thumping, him moving around downstairs, killing more of our house, pulling out the stuff that makes it alive. The cowboy painting on the landing is gone, and that picture of when Sunderland won the cup, and him on his motorbike from ages ago, from before we even knew who Daryl Boyle was. There's another white square on the wall outside Mam's room too, but I can't even remember what used to be there. As if it never was. As if things can just get rubbed out and forgotten, like Nana.

I think about her, sitting in her velvety chair with her upside-down glasses and that big white fuzz of hair round her head. She was the one who told me about my dad. It was last New Year's Eve, the first night that Mam brought Daryl back to our house. Nana was babysitting. She turned the fire up as soon as Mam went out and held her finger to her lips, so we'd know it was our secret. Then she smiled and picked up the crossword. She never wrote in it. Well, hardly. She just smoked her ciggies and watched me and Benjy playing cars, with her eyes all giant behind her glasses.

There was this stuff on the telly about people knocking a wall down in Germany. Benjy fell asleep. His eyes opened when the fireworks went off, but he never stopped snoring. He should've been in bed. I should too, but Nana didn't make me, not even when I asked about my dad. If I asked Mam she'd frown and say something stupid, like wasn't I growing up fast. Nana just lit another ciggy.

'Your dad's name was Jack Farrier, and he wasn't a bad boy,' she said, as if my dad was just a kid. 'He had a good job too, driving one of them big wagons, but he was a dreamer, same as your mam. Spent every penny on his music, the daft bugger. That's all he had to talk about; the song he was writing, where the band were playing. The band,' she laughed and did her rattly cough. 'Him and his gormless mate. Didn't even have the sense to sing what people wanted to listen to. I mean, your Nana's not exactly got her finger on the pulse, but even I know kids don't want to hear those old country songs from back when I was a girl. Bet you didn't know that did you? Your Nana was once a girl?' Except I did, cos she told me all the time. 'Go on, Tommy, indulge your old Nana.'

She meant for me to get the picture down off the mantelpiece so we could look at it together. It was heavy, in this round, silver frame. There was a lady with a long white dress and Princess Leia's hair. She was holding a bunch of flowers and smiling, a bit like how Nana does, but with her mouth closed.

'Quite a looker in my day,' she said, like always, and I said. 'Yes, Nana, quite a looker,' which made her laugh until she coughed.

'I could've had all sorts, but I chose your Grandad Benjamin, and I'll tell you straight, Tommy. I married badly. I've better things to do than waste my time on regrets, but there it is. You just be careful who you marry, my little soldier, because it's a marathon, not a sprint.

'My mam, God rest her, told me as much, but I was eighteen and I knew it all, and I'll say one thing for your grandad, he had a smile that could light the whole street.'

'Does Mam? I mean, does she know it all?'

Nana smiled. 'Your mam's young yet, and she's angry. She's still too busy fighting with your grandad's ghost to know anything at all.'

I remembered Grandad's picture from Nana's house and tried to imagine him with a sheet over his shiny head, and Mam fighting like she does with us, blowing raspberries on his tummy.

'So that was that,' Nana flicked the ash off her ciggy. 'He was a good-looking man, but he was a drinker from the start and it took every good thing out of him; his looks, his warmth and his wit, until all that was left was a nasty, bitter drunk.

'Your dad was a better man than that, but the truth is you boys were never in the plan. Not the two of you, so close together. Don't get me wrong,' she said, putting her hand on my forehead, stroking my hair. 'He had a good heart, and he loved you, but he was only a lad himself. I remember him in this very room, holding you up in the light through the window, singing one of his soppy songs. They were only going on a two-week tour to Holland on the boat, but he was crying when he let you go. Any fool could see he wasn't coming back, even your daft mam, if she's honest.

'You see, Tommy, your mam and dad are the sort of people that'll always be kids, even when they're supposed to be grown up, and little Benjy, God love him, he's the same. But you, Tommy, you're like your Nana, and it's up to the ones like us to look out for those others,' she said, meaning her and me, and Mam and Benjy. 'The thing is,' she said, stabbing her ciggy into the ashtray. 'I won't be around forever.'

She didn't say anymore, just kept banging her ciggy down, even when you could tell it was out. I pressed my hand on her arm, but that just made her mouth go tight, like in the photo. So, I was glad when the front door went, and Mam came in, giggling and holding hands with him.

'Happy new year,' she said, in a screechy sort of voice. Her kiss was slobbery on my cheek. 'Say hello to my new friend, Daryl.'

I could tell straight away that Nana didn't like him cos she did that squinty thing with her eyes. I didn't like him either, even though he had a white jacket on so you couldn't see his snake-bitch tattoo.

'It's good to see you laughing, love,' Nana said.

'We're just popping upstairs to look at the view,' Mam said.

Nana pulled another ciggy out of her crinkly box. 'You'll burn in the fires of hell for all eternity,' she said, but you could tell she wasn't really angry.

'Goodnight, my little girl,' Nana said, just to herself, after they'd gone out into the corridor. But then Mam stuck her head back in and did big eyes at Nana.

'Mop with a tash,' Mam whispered, with her finger across under her nose.

Nana shook her head, 'child,' she said.

Mam giggled and shut the door.

'Your mam needs a man,' Nana said, after they'd gone. 'Someone to take care of you. Especially now.'

'Stupid,' I say, staring at that white square outside Mam's room. As if Daryl would take care of anyone. And I think of Nana when I punch the wall, like it's her fault that Daryl's here instead of her. My hand hurts. There's a crumple of skin on my finger and a drop of blood growing out.

'Sorry, Nana,' I whisper.

Our room is next to Mam's, with stickers on the door, Tommy in blue, Benjy in green, my name on top. I push the door, and try to be ready for empty spaces. Our mattress that filled nearly the whole floor is gone, and the drawers too. There's just round footmarks pressed into the carpet, like the drawers haven't gone at all, just turned invisible. Everything else is the same; the jumble of clothes on the floor, the fire truck, and Panda, and Nana's old wardrobe with the broken door, its spiky edges sharp as a dragon's teeth.

Even Rainbow Blanket is still hanging in the window, blue and gold and fiery orange in the light from outside. That makes me feel like everything'll be okay, cos we can't go anywhere without Rainbow Blanket. But I don't understand where I'm supposed to sleep, and I'm thinking so hard I don't even realise that Mam is standing behind me in her shiny boots and long velvety coat.

Her face is better now, with the make-up back in the right place. She shakes her soft black hair that makes the men stop and look, even the posh ones with suits. My beautiful Mam.

'I'm sorry about Buster,' she says. 'But we couldn't take everything,' and I hate it, not cos of Buster, but cos her voice is slurry and sort of vague. 'I tried to get him back.' She kneels down and puts her hand on my cheek, cold and shaking. 'I tried so hard.'

She goes quiet. She's waiting for me to look, but I know she's not talking about Buster anymore and I don't want her to say anything else, especially not in that slurry voice that makes her seem like a different person.

I stare through the broken wardrobe at the top from Benjy's Noddy jarmas.

'He's alright,' she says, which can't be true cos we're not together. 'He's in a safe place, just for a little while.'

I stretch up and pull the jarmas through the gap, holding them out to Mam. She presses them into her neck. I touch her cheek, and she smiles at me while she's crying.

There's a bang from downstairs. Mam's eyes open wider, sparkly, like Benjy's.

'They're going to come back for you,' she says, and we listen to boots thudding up the stairs.

Daryl fills the doorway, staring down at me with that stupid tash on his ratty face. He stomps towards us in his rattly boots.

Mam holds up her hand. She stops him, like magic.

'We have to go now, baby,' she says. 'We can't stay in Sunderland anymore.'

'But we can't go, cos…'

Daryl sighs like a growl. Mam's magic isn't strong enough. Not today. She can't even speak right. She made Sunderland sound like shush, like shut up, and Nana's dead and under the ground so there's only me left. I have to keep talking.

'Cos how will Benjy be able… he won't know where to find us. We have to stay. We have to wait. Please, just a little while.'

Mam says something, but I can't understand her cos Daryl's moving round behind me, messing up the air. I keep talking as fast as I can, telling her about the wall falling down on the telly and Nana saying that everything was going to be alright, and how we have to wait so Benjy can find us. Mam nods. She strokes my hair, but there's something wrong about her eyes. Her fingers are too tight on my wrist.

I pull back against the wardrobe and get my hands through into the dragon's mouth. I hold tight and call Benjy's name. And I won't let go. Not ever.

I shut my eyes so I can't see Daryl's face turn red, or the snake-bitch tattoo slithering up his arm. But I can smell his burny smell, feel his hands on me. Rings dig into my arm, sharper than the dragon's teeth against my fingers.

'Benjy,' I scream. 'Benjy, Benjy.'

'He's not fuckin here, you mental case.'

My fingers slide through the broken door, scratching and burning. Then I'm up over Daryl's shoulder. My head bangs on the bedroom door, but there isn't enough air in me to cry. He runs downstairs, out into the cold.

We're at the van. Just him and me. He holds me up in front of him. His mouth opens, so close that I can see the brown bits in his teeth.

'Your name's Boyle,' he says. 'Boyle. Say it.'

'Farrier,' I say, looking past him at the house across the street. It's got silver metal instead of doors and windows. That's what they'll do to ours, cover up the windows. Make it blind. Make it dead.

'Ya cunt,' he opens the back of the van. 'Boyle,' he shouts, so close I can feel his bristly tash on my face. His eyes are a long way back under his forehead. His hand is tight on my neck.

'Boyle,' I say, pushing the word through my throat.

'Right. And you haven't got a fuckin brother.' He throws me into the van and slams the door.

It's dark and I'm lying on something saggy and smooth. I feel along till I can tell it's the bottom of the furry sofa. I crawl up onto the next thing, our mattress, right at the top of the van. My back is tight under the roof. I press my face into the mattress's springy softness and try to breathe Benjy's smell, but there's only cold and damp, and the petrolly rumble of the engine carrying me away from him.

Boyle. I think of a huge spot with yellow in. I don't want to be Boyle. I want to be Tommy Farrier like my dad, like my real dad, but mostly I just want Benjy. Benjy Boyle. It makes me laugh, even though I'm crying. I touch my lips and slide my fingers in, tasting blood and bean juice. I push against them with my tongue and pretend that my fingers are Benjy's.

'Benjy Boyle, Benjy Boyle,' I say it like the prayers in Nana's church, holding my face in the mattress until the van rocks me to sleep and Benjy comes for me, holding me tight as I hold him. Loving me. Trusting me.

'Don't trust me, Benjy,' I push him away, but he won't let go. 'Don't, Benjy,' I feel my hands slipping through the dragon's teeth. 'Don't, Benjy, cos I'm a coward.'

The van stops and we're there, where The Social won't find us, and I'm Tommy Boyle, age five-and-a-half, and I don't have a brother and I never did. And Daryl's got a piece of paper to prove it.

But Daryl doesn't know everything, and later, when it's dark and he says he's going to "check this shithole out," Mam carries me up to my new room. She lays me down on the mattress and asks if I'm okay. I shake my head. I don't want to talk to her.

'Well, you have a look in that wardrobe when you're ready,' she says, and she goes out and closes the door.

I roll over and stare at the lightbulb. My eyes blink shut, but the light comes through, orangey in the dark.

The room's rubbish. There's a red carpet with a space cut out where something's been taken away, and pink walls with black stuff growing under the window, and nothing else except this big homemade wardrobe. This is where we live now, here in this rubbish house in Newcastle. For a second I want to be sick, but then I smile, cos if we live in Newcastle it means Daryl's going to be a Geordie, and Daryl hates Geordies.

That helps me get up and do what Mam said.

The wardrobe groans when I open the door. It's dark, with a scratchy blanket spread out inside that makes me think of Benjy in that yellow cupboard. You can tell from the shape of the blanket that there's something big underneath. I pull the blanket till it's in a pile on the floor and I can see this wooden box, the kind they sell fruit in at the market. There's loads of things inside, old clothes, and tapes and papers. I suppose it must be stuff that the people who used to live here didn't want, but then I hear Mam's feet on the stairs, carrying things, making this into our house. That helps me realise. The box is ours.

There's a black shirt with silver swirls on the front that feels silky smooth in my hands, and a red one nearly the same. I pull things out as fast as I can, tapes and videos, a belt with stars on, and these amazing boots. They smell like Daryl's biker jacket and the bottom's hanging off one of the feet, so it looks like an open mouth, but they're still brilliant, and that's when I know for sure.

'Look, Benjy,' I whisper, feeling the scaly-smoothness on my fingers, watching the boot change from silver to blue in the light, like the skin on a magic crocodile.

'You can come back, Dad, when you've finished your adventures. Anytime you want.'

Chapter Four

Sick and Blame

I'm lying on our furry sofa watching Rugrats on the telly and nearly weeing myself laughing. That's why I don't hear the big door. I don't know anything about it till Mam walks in and trips against the sofa. I'm halfway up, kneeling on the cushion with my arms out, laughing.

'You needn't work yourself,' she says. 'I didn't come for you.'

The smile aches on my face.

Mam sways against the telephone table, scowling at me with the make-up smudged on her eyes, so she looks like an angry panda. She's been on the drink. Not new drink that makes her feet tip-tap on the lino, but old drink that smells of sick and blame. She jams her fingers in the Simpson's mug on the table. There's no money in. I don't say anything but Mam spins round as if I did. Then she goes out with her long coat swishing behind her, and stamps up the stairs.

I don't get up; it doesn't feel safe, but I crawl into the passage, following. I'm on the third step when Mam screams. It's just a short sound, but it makes my face feel cold. She's crying, worse than normal, big thuds with little screams inside. It makes me think of Nana stabbing her ciggy down into the ashtray like she was trying to kill it. Except now I know, it was the other way around.

'It's up to the ones like us to look out for those others,' she said, meaning her and me, and Mam and Benjy.

I want to go up and cuddle Mam, to stop her being sad, to get the bad feeling out of my tummy. Or just say the right thing and make her happy, like that time in church when I told Benjy off for picking his nose in the Lord's house and Mam and Nana laughed for ages. It was easy to make Mam laugh then, before I let Benjy go.

I press my hands on my ears like if I can't hear her, it'll make the bad thoughts go away, but it doesn't work and I don't know what to do, so I sit at the bottom of the stairs and look up at Daryl's pictures on the sloping wall, just like in our old house. There's him sitting on this black motorbike with his biker jacket unzipped so you can see he's got his Sunderland shirt on underneath. He might be smiling, but you can't really tell cos he's got all this long hair blowing over his face.

The other picture is from when Sunderland won the cup. There's all these men with big hair and stripy shirts. One on the end is ginger, but he hasn't got a tash. There's seventeen altogether, well, fifteen with stripy shirts, and two with green. I count them out loud, over and over, for ages, until my mouth gets dry and I'm sure that Mam's stopped crying. She's moving about, coming out onto the landing. I run back into the living room.

When Mam comes in, her cheeks are red with lines down them like she's been crying black tears. She plonks herself on the end of the sofa and that's when I see she's holding a carrier bag. There's a ginormous card inside. Mam unwraps the crinkly paper and puts the card on the coffee table, then she just stares at it.

'Alright now, Mam?' I slide across the sofa in tiny movements, like I hardly know I'm doing it. 'Alright?'

Mam sniffs. Rugrats are still on the telly and I wish they'd just shut up. I'm close, leaning in, smelling Mam's hair. I let my head tip towards her arm. I know how good it'll feel. But then my head touches and she jumps up like an electric shock.

'A pen,' she says. 'I need a pen.' She pulls the drawers out of the sideboard. Action Man's head bounces on the floor, and a letter with red writing comes floating down on top. 'Aha,' she says, holding her pen in the air like it's the F.A. Cup.

There's a racing car on the front of the card, and a big blue five. That's how old I am now, except only till soon, cos I'm nearly six. Mam's made a mistake. I smile anyway, and Mam starts writing.

I'm good at reading, cos of school and Nana. Sister Sofia said I'm as advanced as anyone in my class, but I still can't read Mam's scratchy joined-up writing, and it's green, which makes it harder. I can tell some letters though, and then I see Benjy's name and I know I'm stupid and mean, cos it's August today, and that means Benjy's birthday. It makes me think of how it's been ages since Mam said he'd definitely be coming home soon, and there's all these questions jumbled in my head, but really, only one, and I know I'm not allowed to ask.

I'm really quiet and careful not to touch Mam. I wait till she puts the pen down.

'Please, Mam. Can I write too?'

She sort of gasps like she'd forgotten I was here, but she gives me the pen.

I'm not sure about the spelling, but I write as neat as I can. I use my name that just Benjy calls me, and I put five kisses on the bottom, one for every year.

Sorry, Benjy, love from Tom-Bomb xxxxx

Mam puts the card in the envelope, then she gets this scrunchy bit of paper from her pocket and starts copying it onto the envelope, in capitals. I think she's going to write Benjy's name, but she doesn't.

'Mrs' means missus. Then she writes some letters that don't make a name at all.

A-B-U-T-O-P-A-L-A-C-I-O-S, it says, and I wonder what that means. I don't ask.

Mam's crying again, not in a noisy way, just being still with tears following the black lines on her face. She writes more words that fill the rest of the envelope, then she holds up the crinkly bag till a stamp falls out. She licks the back and sticks it on the envelope.

I know what happens next and I want to go with, but I'm scared in case Mam says no. She gets up and wipes her face on her sleeve.

'Can I come, Mam? Please.'

'It's too far,' she says.

'Please, Mam, I'll be good.'

She doesn't answer, just does that sigh like before she gets angry, and walks out into the street. I follow. Her hand is hanging there, right near my face. I don't hold it, not straightaway. I wait till we're up at the top of Belmont Street, past Atwal's shop and onto the Walker Road. Then I do, and we walk along together, straight past the postbox, right into town. It's hot and sunny, and everything's perfect except for the bits of black still smudged on Mam's face.

We go all along the Quayside, past the old warehouses and up to Central Station, which is as high as the sky. There's a ginormous clock with both hands pointing at the ceiling, and an electric board with all the places written on.

'Platform three,' Mam says, to no one, and we go into this big glass office to buy the tickets. 'Sunderland,' Mam says, which is where we used to live, where we're not allowed to talk about in case The Social find out and come for me too.

I press my fingers over my mouth, just to be sure, cos when I think of the gold ring on that big hairy hand, I'm so scared that I'm glad it was Benjy they got instead of me. But we don't talk about that either. Not about The Social, and not about Benjy, not until today, so I can hardly believe it cos we've got a card with Benjy's name on and we're really going, just me and Mam, on an adventure.

There's a whistle, and the train jerks forward. Mam gets these sweets out of her velvet coat and passes them across. They're wine gums with two left in. I take the green one and give the red one to Mam. Red's her favourite. I suck mine to make it last longer, and watch the houses go past the window, but then I feel Mam looking at me with one side of her mouth turned down, like she did on the sofa. Like she does all the time. She sees me watching and turns away, but it's too late. This horrible feeling thumps in my tummy. Mam hates me. I look at the cows through the window. But I know it's true. She hates me cos I'm here instead of Benjy. Cos it's my fault they found him. Cos I screamed when I should have kept my stupid mouth shut.

I reach down under the plastic table. The inside of my leg feels fat through my jeans. I hold the tiniest bit between my finger and thumb and nip as hard as I can. The wine gum squeezes tight between my teeth, but I put my fingers over my mouth, and I don't scream. I don't make a sound. I nip harder. There's sticky sweat on my forehead, and my head feels fuzzy, like I'm not sure if I'm awake or asleep. The nails on my finger and thumb are nearly together, and I feel better. The bad feeling in my tummy is just a tiny dot, much smaller than the pain in my leg. I hold on right till we pass the sign that says Sunderland, and it's time to get off the train.

There's a throbby feeling in my leg when we come out of the

station, but it doesn't really hurt. Anyway, I'm not thinking about that. I'm looking out for our old house. I can't see it. Maybe it looks different now, if they've taken the windows away? I try to remember what it was like, but all I can think of is that blind house across the street, and Daryl throwing me into the van.

"You haven't got a brother," he said. But I do, and we've got his birthday card, and I didn't even scream.

I keep looking around, but there's just shops, and then we're right beside this shiny red postbox. I'm tall enough to reach, to put the card in. Mam doesn't say that she's going to. She just puts the card in the slot. But I'm quick. I reach up and touch the envelope, so it's like we've posted the card together.

'Happy birthday, sweetheart,' Mam says, and I think she's going to cry again, but she doesn't.

'Happy Birthday,' I say, too.

'Haway, Tommy,' she says, and we walk back along the street.

We hold hands all the way to the corner. I don't let go, but when I look back at the slot where the card went, that wide shiny mouth makes me think of Daryl. I don't look again.

'I should've done more,' Mam says, on the train back, which is sort of like talking about Benjy.

'Yes,' I say. 'I should've told more things in his card. About wearing his Noddy jarma top even though it's too little, and sometimes-'

'Next time,' Mam says, and looks hard out the window.

We get sausage rolls from Greggs on the way home, and neither of us says anything to Daryl when he gets in from deliveries. I love it cos me and Mam have got a secret, and I know what I have to do to make Mam love me again. I give my leg a little squeeze, right on the bruise, and that's when I decide I'm going to be brave. I'm going to be as good as Benjy.

Chapter Five

Dance with the Devil

I kick my robot duvet off and blink at the sunshine through the window. There's no one in the house. I can tell cos the telly's not on, and there's no shouting. Still, I push my bedroom door till it clicks, then I reach under the bed and pull out Dad's secret box. I take his crocodile boots off the top, tied up in an orange carrier, and look at what's underneath.

There's six videos, four with Clint Eastwood and two with John Wayne. I keep Clint and John separate to make sure they don't shoot each other by mistake. I mean, I know they won't really, but that's just how I've kept them since I was little, with the tapes piled up neatly on the other side. There's lots, but I know all the singers; Johnny Cash, The Eagles, Bob Dylan, and others without boxes, just with scrawly writing that's nearly faded away, and names like Nashville Live, and the '79 sessions.

I tip it all out, everything, onto my furry brown rug. I'll organize it again in a minute, but first I pull out the yellow paper on the bottom. That's where the most special things are, underneath.

There's a card with a big sparkly tower on the front and writing on the other side. It's sort of hard to read, but I've had it since I was five, and I'm eight now, so I've probably seen it about a million times.

Baby,

Crossed another day off the calendar this morning. Six nights on the road until I see your pretty face.

Love and dirty kisses,

Jack

That's not the best though. There's a picture too, a photo of one of those big pointy cars like from Nana's films, with a man standing beside it. He's leaning against the car with his elbow on the edge of the roof and his face in his hand. He's smiling really wide like he's laughing, and the way I know for definite that he's my dad is cos he's wearing those blue crocodile boots that are wrapped up right now in the carrier bag on my rug.

The bag crinkles against my fingers. I feel the leather ridges through the plastic and stare at the photo like if I wish hard enough, the boots can take me inside.

'Good one, son,' Dad says, still laughing, and I know it's cos of something funny that I've said. He takes his arm off the big old car and ruffles my hair. 'Six nights on the road,' he says, and we climb in.

The door's heavy, but I know to pull the handle with both hands. It bangs shut. Dad stops laughing. He disappears. There's only the door's echo vibrating up through my bedroom floor.

I press Dad's photo against my jarma top and listen hard. There aren't any voices, just shoes slapping on the stairs. I don't breathe. The steps aren't anything like Daryl's jangly biker boots, but they're too slow to be a normal person's. It's him. I get this dizzy feeling like back when I was little. Like that night at our old house in Sunderland when England lost the World Cup, and the whisky broke, and everything turned bad.

I can feel the fear, see that golden bottle wobbling on the cabinet and the question in Benjy's eyes, but I'm moving too, throwing Dad's stuff back in the box, listening to Daryl's slippery shoes slap across the landing. I push the box under the bed and jump onto my duvet, then I blink up at Daryl in the doorway.

He doesn't wear his biker gear anymore, just whitish jeans and this silvery jacket he copied off Crockett on Miami Vice.

'Morning, Crockett,' I say. He likes that.

'Alright, Mr. T,' he grins and turns his collar up, so I think maybe he's in a good mood, but then his mouth goes tight.

I stare at the robots on my duvet.

'Aw, shit man, look at that,' he says, but he isn't angry, more sort of confused.

There's a wrinkle in his forehead, like Mam when she's worried. He kneels down so his face is just near mine and looks straight at me for ages, then down at my bedroom rug. He stretches his hand out just above it, extra white in the sunshine.

'He's been,' Daryl says, 'for definite.'

Dad, does he mean Dad? But how can he know?

The rug looks the same, brown, and furry, with orangey bits at the end, and that baldy patch from one of Mam's special ciggies. Please come back, Mam, I'm thinking, but I know she's down the market with Moira and she won't, not for ages. There's just me and Daryl, and Dad's box about a millimetre away under my bed.

Daryl reaches out with his finger and touches an orangey spike of fur on the rug. He pulls his hand away fast. His lips stretch, like maybe he's scared, but he still doesn't say.

'Who? Who's been?'

Daryl shakes his head.

'Don't ask,' he says, staring at the rug. 'Better not to know,' but his eyes keep flicking up to mine.

I can tell he wants me to ask again, so I press my fingers over my lips.

'Alright,' Daryl says, like I've persuaded him. 'But you better not tell your mam, right?'

'Right,' I push the word through my fingers.

'See how the rug's all flat over there, but this bit's sticking up?

'Yeh.'

'Well, that's where he's been dancing while you've been asleep, with his spikey toes and his fork jamming down.'

'But who?'

'Him,' Daryl says, kneeling down with one hand on my pillow, staring at me with his bright blue eyes. 'The Devil. He's been dancing beside your bed in the night, saying his rhymes and casting his spells.' He leans back away from me. 'Looks like it's the first time though. Three times, and he's got you.'

'Got me how?'

But I see where he's been. The rug's all spiked up with orange tips like the fires of hell, and the goose bumps come shivering under my jarmas.

'Two more times, Mr. T,' Daryl does his smile where his eyes don't join in. 'Two more,' his head sways backwards like he's praying. 'And then you belong to the Devil.'

'Shut up, shut up,' I scramble off the bed and run into the bathroom and lock the door. I stay there for ages, till I hear the front door open and Mam's voice shouting up the stairs.

Daryl's gone, and Mam's got me four purple Teletubbies. They're only for little kids, but there's no one to see, so I line the Teletubbies up on my window, beside my wriggly worm. I make them move in a sort of dance and talk to each other in cowboy voices like on The Lone Ranger. I don't think about Daryl and the Devil for ages, not till it's late and I'm back in bed watching the yellow streetlight slide in through the curtains and creep across the rug, turning its pointy strands from brown to fiery orange.

I'm too scared to think about anything at first, but after a bit, the thoughts come into my head. I wonder what it would be like to be taken by the Devil, and if that's what happened to Daryl in the Falklands? If that's why he's like he is?

It makes me think of this other Sunday, ages ago. We were in church waiting for the priest, with Benjy in his new blue suit and his finger turning up inside his nose, and Nana hissy whispering over the top of our heads.

'On her own with two kids, then that bugger comes along. Made the last one look like a saint, but of course, she welcomed him with open arms, the poor, stupid girl. I'm to blame for encouraging it. I mean, I thought he'd at least look after her. Some chance. Now where is she, caught between the Devil and the deep blue sea?'

Then the Priest came in and everyone stopped talking, and I suppose Mam must've chosen the Devil.

Mam goes back to the market with Moira next Sunday. I'm fast asleep when the light comes on in my room. I can tell it's early. My eyes hurt. Daryl's standing over me, looking down at the rug. He shakes his head, and the goose bumps go tingling up my arm. I know what he's going to say. I press my face down and pull the pillow up around my ears, but I can't help hearing.

'Second time,' he says, walking away. 'Last fuckin chance.'

Chapter Six

The Finger Game

I was sitting on the step outside our house last Sunday watching this weird-looking girl move into number six when this amazing thing happened. Some bloke I'd never even seen before came up and gave me a brand-new video recorder, still in the box and everything. Daryl says it's his, even though it was Mam that bought it, from Mickey Cassidy at the Black Boar. Daryl says I'm not allowed to touch it. He says I'm not to go within a hundred fuckin yards of it, but I've watched all of Dad's videos already, and it's about time really, cos I've had them for years.

John Wayne's pretty cool, and I like the gravelly way he talks, but he's a bit old and fat. Clint Eastwood hardly says anything at all, just chews his cigar and lets the bad guys go on talking till you almost feel sorry for them, then he fills them full of lead. Clint's the best, easily, and The Good, The Bad, and The Ugly is the best film, and this bit I'm watching now, that I've already seen about a hundred times, is just brilliant.

They're in the cemetery where the gold is buried, standing in this big circle with rows of gravestones and scrubby hills behind. Blondie, that's Clint, puts this yellow stone down on the cracked ground. He walks backwards with his eyes darting between Angel Eyes and Tuco, and all the time there's this music that goes tingling right through you. They're ready for the final shoot-out. Blondie throws his poncho up over his shoulder. Tuco's fingers twitch. The music gets faster, like

- Dunununununuh, du-nu-nuh, and even though you know Blondie's really cool, Angel Eyes and Tuco are super-fast too.

I stretch out from the sofa and press pause. The music stops. I can hear Mam and Daryl upstairs. His crappy music's playing; the ace of spades, the ace of spades, the same words over and over. I get up and shut the door. There's no story in Daryl's songs. They're just loud and angry and boring, like Daryl.

I play the film, just for a few seconds, to feel that music tingling through me, then I pause it again and sit back on the sofa with the sound still going in my head.

Dunununununuh, du-nu-nuh.

Blondie and Tuco and Angel Eyes haven't moved, they're in the same position in the circle as they are on my pad. I shade in a bit of the scrubby hills, then I pick up my special H2 pencil, which is best for drawing. Mr. Corcoran got it for me. He says I'm good. Talented, he says. Daryl says Mr. Corcoran's a pufftaaarhh. He says it like that, doing his stretchy smile and making the *aaarhh* go on for ages.

I've already drawn that; Daryl's stretchy smile, his face on Angel Eyes' body, staggering back with the gun falling out of his hand and his sleeve pulled up so you can see the tail of the snake-bitch tattoo winding down onto his wrist. Blondie's easy too. That's Dad, with his blue crocodile boots and that billowy shirt like in the photo. He's got Clint's poncho thrown over his shoulder, and there's a wisp of smoke rising from the barrel of his gun. You can tell that in the end he'll take his share of the gold and ride off into the distance to have more adventures, and then he'll come back to Newcastle and shoot Daryl dead, and we'll be bounty hunting partners together. Maybe we'll let Mam come with us. Maybe not. It depends.

Tuco's more difficult. I'm never quite sure who he's going to be. In yesterday's drawing, he was Brendan the school caretaker who yelled at me for spilling his bucket, even though it was a total accident. I drew straggly hair round his bald patch and turned his gun into a mop, but that spoiled the drawing, so I started again.

This one's better, and I know it's cos I keep rewinding the video to make the music stay alive in my head. That's what I'm concentrating on, and letting the pencil go where it wants. I don't even hardly know who I'm drawing till it's done. I do big eyes and a little nose, and some lines across her cheeks until her brown face is so scrunched-up it's like she's sucking it into her angry mouth. Her hair is spikey as a hedgehog. I've drawn that ugly kid who moved in across the street. I saw her again yesterday, standing outside their red front door with the silver mermaid knocker, and her Mam shouting out the window in a voice like someone off Brookside.

'Angie, get back in…'

I didn't hear the rest cos we were in Daryl's new Mark II, driving fast. A shit brown Ford Capri is what Moira calls it. Only Daryl says, "The Mark II," like it's a rocket or something. So anyway, I didn't hear much, but I saw her scrunched-up face exactly like I've drawn it, and I don't even know if that tingly feeling is from the music in my head, or cos I sort of know, this is the best thing I've ever done.

The stairs creak. Someone's running down, but all I care about is the music in my head. I don't even feel the door open or hear Mam's voice calling down from the bedroom.

'Daryl, Daz. It'll be alright. It's just the booze.'

'Haway then, spread the fuckin joy.'

I hear that.

Daryl's standing between me and the telly, just wearing jeans and his gold chain. He's got a can of lager in his hand, and I know that something's going to happen cos he's doing that thing where his lip sticks out all wet and red so you can see the brown lines between his teeth.

I don't want to say about Tuco and Angie, so I don't say anything. I just stare at his snake-bitch tattoo till Mam comes in. You can tell she's drunk. And she's not wearing anything under her dressing gown, which is disgusting.

'What is it, baby?' she says, leaning over. She's so wobbly that she has to put her hand on the sofa to stop herself from falling on me.

'Nothing,' I say, but I turn the picture cos I want her to see.

'That's lovely, that is,' she says, but her eyes sort of slide across it.

'Fuckin hell,' the can cracks in Daryl's hand. At least his eyes still work. He knows his own face, his own tattoo.

Mam puts her hand on his arm. He stares at Mam's hand like he doesn't know what it is. The bottom of the snake's tail winds down through her fingers, curling around the word 'bitch,' just the way I've drawn it. His can falls on the floor. I jam my picture under the seat. A dribble of froth slithers towards me. I press myself back against the sofa. I know he's going to lose it, but then he belches and grins.

'Alright, Pet. Get some tea on. Tommy here can come up the Paki's with me.'

'Why don't I take him to Fosses,' Mam says. 'Get us some chips. And I'll get a bottle…'

I don't know what she's going to say next cos Daryl takes her hand and presses it over her mouth. She sounds like a baby for a second, till she stops talking.

'Get the tea on,' Daryl says.

'Don't, Mam. Don't go.'

She doesn't even turn around, just walks through into the kitchen on her wobbly legs, but with her head really still on her neck. That's how I know she's heard, and she's leaving me with him.

'Haway then,' Daryl says, like we hang out together all the time, but you can see the muscles stretched tight on his neck.

He makes a grab for me, but I can still feel the bruises from the last time, and I'm up and past him, and out onto the street. I expect him to be right behind me, but he's not. I know better than to run away, so I just wait by the car, reading the stickers in the back window. The old one that was already there: *If you can read this, you're too close,* and the new one that Daryl got: *If you can read this, you're not a fuckin immigrant.*

I write my own message underneath, then jump when the front door slams.

Daryl comes down the path, still pulling his flowery shirt on. He only does one button, and that's wrong.

I look at my message on the back window and make sure I'm round the other side of the car.

'Get in,' he says, and unlocks the door.

I do what he says. He gets in beside me and takes this dry cloth that's called a chamois leather from the inside of the door and wipes the windscreen super-slowly, the way Sister Josepha strokes Noah, the hamster at school. I try not to look. He puts the cloth back in the door and presses his hands together like he's going to pray, then he starts the car. We drive for about five seconds and stop.

'Stay,' Daryl says, like I'm a dog or something, and he goes into Atwal's.

It's boiling in the car. One of those sweaty days when the sky's really white and so close it feels like you could reach up and touch the clouds.

'Needs to rain,' Nana would've said, and I don't know if she makes it happen, but the first big drop splodges on the bonnet, and about five seconds later it's rattling on the roof like a machine gun.

I pick at a loose bit of leather on the steering wheel cover and think about Dad's video, still in the machine. I have to get it out before Daryl finds it. But then I get distracted, cos if I can make the hole a tiny bit bigger, I'll be able to get my finger in. Daryl takes ages. The car gets all misted up inside, so I reach across and wind down Daryl's window. I stop picking and watch the big drops splat on his seat. I wish I was at home finishing my drawing.

They come out together, Daryl and Mr. Atwal, pointing and shouting at each other in the doorway. They're too far away for me to hear at first, but I can see Daryl's neck is red. He's walking back towards the car and I'm thinking how he looks smaller outside of the house, pretty scrawny really, for a grown-up. That's what Martin from the key cutting shop called him, "a scrawny-arsed runt". Daryl didn't even say anything, not till we got outside.

'You change prices. Is theft. I call police. I call police right away,' Mr. Atwal says. His head nods so fast I'm sure his turban's going to fall off and splat on the soggy pavement. It doesn't, and he doesn't call anybody either. He just stands there shouting through the rain.

'You're mental, you, ya Paki cunt,' Daryl stops pointing at Mr. Atwal and points at his own head instead. 'Round the fuckin twist.'

'You are barred from my shop. Go now. Come back, I call police for sure.'

'You think I'm coming back to this Paki shithole when I can go to a decent white man's shop?' Daryl pulls the car door open so hard the edge bangs against his leg. 'Ya cunt,' he says.

'Tight arsed fuckin Paki,' he hisses, with both hands white on the steering wheel, and his thumb just touching the hole.

I sit back in my seat, trying not to be there, listening to the rain on the roof and the engine roaring. Daryl doesn't even notice. He keeps talking, calling Mr. Atwal a dirty thieving Paki for charging thirty-seven pence for a can of lager, and driving up Walker Road at about ninety miles an hour, then skidding to a stop with two wheels up on the pavement so I have to hold myself back from leaning on his shoulder.

'Go on then,' he slams some money on the dashboard. 'And I want the fuckin change.'

'What?'

'Get the fuckin chips.'

I look out through the back window at the chip shop sign a whole row of houses away, and I think about Daryl's hand on Mam's mouth, making her sound like a baby, and how we always have to do what radgy Daryl says.

'But Mam's got the tea on.'

'Aye, some manky shite. Get the fuckin chips.'

'It's raining.'

'Who are you, Michael fuckin Fish? I don't want a weather report. I want chips.'

'But we're miles away. I'll get soaked.'

'Will I call you a taxi? A fuckin limousine?'

I look back towards the chip shop, just staring, reading the signs, backwards in the back window. I can feel Daryl reading them too, the two stickers and my finger writing underneath, standing out against the condensation.

'Daryl is a Geordie.'

This time I don't get any warning. Daryl grabs my hand. His face is red, right up close, his fingers tangled up with mine.

'You think your fuckin smart, do ya? Do ya? Ya cunt.'

I don't answer. It doesn't matter what I say now.

He's got my hand pressed flat on the dashboard, and he's holding my middle finger, squeezing so his ring digs into my knuckle.

'Answer when I ask you a question,' he says, bending my finger back towards my wrist.

'Yes,' I say. 'I'll answer.'

'You think it's smart to cheek me?'

'No, Daryl, I won't cheek you.'

Daryl likes that. He belches and sighs. I can smell old cheese through the booze, and it's like the car is the whole world and there's just me and Daryl left.

'No, you fuckin won't,' he says, and I can feel him thinking what to say next. 'Cos I'm the hardest fuckin bastard in the city.'

'You're the hardest bastard…'

'Ya cunt?' He jerks my finger back. 'What are you calling me?'

'No, nothing.'

'I'm the biggest stud in Newcastle, that's what I am.'

'You're the biggest stud in Newcastle.'

'And the Mark II is the fastest set of wheels in Walker.'

'Yes, the Mark II is brilliant.'

I'm answering whatever he wants, but I don't even care, because the finger game makes Benjy real. From the beginning, if I said his name or the things he did, then Daryl would grab my hand. Sometimes he'd twist my arm, but mostly he'd press my hand flat like now, and bend my finger till I screamed.

"Your name's Boyle," he'd tell me, making me say it. "And you don't have a brother."

I shut my eyes and remember Benjy's open mouth lifting away from me in the dark. I screamed when I should've been quiet. I let them take him, and this is my punishment. The pain burns up through my wrist. It feels good.

'You going to get us some fuckin chips then?'

I wait until it burns as hot as I can stand.

'Yes. I'll get the chips.'

He shakes his head and presses on my finger.

'Too late, son, too late.'

He grins at the mist on the window, and its strange, cos I realise there's no one who's helped me remember Benjy as much as Daryl. He knows it too, that this is Benjy's game. That's why he goes back to the old questions.

'This is where you live right, where you've always lived.'

'It's where I've always lived.'

'Here, in Walker.'

'In Walker.'

'And you haven't got a brother,' he says, but I can't say that.

I was a coward when I let Benjy go, but I'm not a little kid anymore. I'm almost nine, and I know that wherever he is, Benjy's watching me with those sparkly eyes and he's seeing that I'm not a coward anymore, and that if he comes back I'll take care of him.

'You haven't got a brother,' Daryl says, 'and you never–'

My sweaty finger slips through his hand.

'Little shite.'

He punches my head, so it bounces off the window. I snatch my hand away, but he catches my wrist and presses it back on the dashboard.

'Don't fuckin move,' he says.

I look at the pink cracks in his eyes. I'm not sure if I should answer, if the game has started again.

'I said, don't fuckin move.'

'No, I won't. I won't.'

'You don't have a brother.'

I don't care how much it hurts, but this feels wrong, frightening. My nail's nearly touching my hand.

'You don't have a brother.'

I look at the shapes through the misty window, and I wonder where Benjy is, what he's doing right now.

'You don't have a brother.'

My hand burns hotter.

'You don't have a brother.'

The rain drums harder.

'You don't have a brother.'

'I don't. I promise, please.' But like always, I'm too late.

There's that crack again, like a firework. I don't even realise I'm screaming till I feel Daryl's hands on my face. I taste the dry lump of chamois leather in my mouth, and I know I'm still a coward.

Chapter Seven

Rumpelstiltskin

Karma Chameleon's playing on the radio, and Mam's feet are tip-tapping on the kitchen floor like when we were tiny. I stand in the doorway and watch her dance. She's singing into her can like it's a microphone, swaying with her hair swishing around her, slow and vague and dreamy. Her eyes are nearly closed, but then she sees me and smiles, and it's warm, like toast. Daryl's gone, and Mam is dancing again.

She opens the fridge and stops dancing, even though the song isn't finished. She comes towards me and kneels down, putting her hands on my cheeks, making them hot. Her eyes are looking right at me, so I can see the baggy bits underneath and the black stuff sticking on her eyelashes.

'Here.' She pushes some money in my hand. Even without looking, I can tell it's hardly anything.

'Go on, Tommy. Run up to Atwal's for me.'

'But EastEnders'll be on soon and –'

'I only want a couple of cans. Tell her I'll settle up on Thursday, like always.'

'Like always,' I say, and look at the two ten pences in my hand. I want to throw them at the window, so hard that it breaks. I imagine the noise, like a can of coke that's been kicked down the street before you open it.

'Please, Tommy.' Her face goes saggy as her old jumper. 'They never say no to you.' She nudges me out of the kitchen. 'Don't be long,' she says, and the coins dig into my fingers.

Even when I get outside, my cheeks feel like they're still hot from her touching, and all I can think about is the way her face sagged. I know why. It's cos sometimes when she looks at me, she can't help seeing that I'm not Benjy. That it was me who let them take him. That's why she hates me. I've known for ages. But it's like now I understand something new. That deep down Mam's too kind to hate anyone. That's why she needs the booze, to make the bad feelings go away. And it really works. Sometimes, when she's had just the right amount, she might even laugh, with her eyes twinkling as bright as that star in the song.

Atwal's blue sign is just over the other side of Walker Road, and by the time I get to the corner, I'm hoping that it's Mr. Atwal in the shop. He just says, "alright, alright," even before I've finished explaining, and writes the numbers on his list. He even let Daryl go back in the shop after all the stuff he said. But Mr. Atwal is hardly ever there, and I'm only half-way across the road when I see Mrs. Atwal through the window, in her black Araby shawl. She's turning tins around, so the labels all look the same.

At least it's not nighttime. When Atwal's is shut I have to go up and ask Mickey Cassidy at the Black Boar. That's a pub. It's long and thin with all these dark-brown tables, and crumply old men standing at the bar. It kind of feels like Sunday mornings at Nana's church. I'm not even supposed to go in, but Mickey Cassidy doesn't care. I hate the way he grins at me over the bar and scratches his rashy face.

"Tell your mam Mickey says it's no trouble," he always says, and he does that stupid laugh for no reason. "Tell her we'll sort it next time she's in."

The bell jingles when I open the door, and Mrs. Atwal goes

back behind the counter. She smiles at me, making the gold tooth flash in her mouth. I look away, getting one of the green baskets from beside the door. I wish there were other people in the shop, but there aren't.

At least I don't see anyone.

'How can I help you, young man?' she says, just like always.

I remember to keep smiling.

'I just need two cans of Diamond White, for my mam.'

'She sends a child for this.'

I'm not sure if it's a question, so I don't say anything. I slap the money on the counter as noisily as I can, trying to make it sound like loads, but Mrs. Atwal leans across.

'What is this?' she says, pointing, even though it's obvious. There's two ten pences.

I feel hot again, looking at the lines on her crinkly face, smelling her spiciness.

'Foolish woman,' Mrs. Atwal says, loud enough for me to hear.

She shouldn't be talking about Mam like that, but I'm scared to say in case she doesn't let me have the cider. So, I just have to stand there while she puts the cans in a carrier and writes the numbers on a card, shaking her head till I really hate her. Then the worst thing is that she takes a green jelly chew from beside the till and holds it out.

'Take, take,' she says, flashing her tooth at me like we're friends.

They're bad for your teeth, I nearly say, but then I take the chew, and grab the bag off the counter before she can change her mind.

I turn around fast and practically trample over this weird girl who's crept up behind me. She's got this scrunchy face and sticky-out hair. That's all I see cos then she's darted past me and snatched a Cadbury's Caramel off the rack. She stuffs it in her pocket like she thinks Mrs. Atwal's blind or something. But Mrs. Atwal isn't blind, and she's pretty fast for an old lady. She grabs a handful of sticky-out hair.

'Thief, thief,' she shouts, pulling the girl halfway over the counter, and the girl's screaming for her to get her, "old bitch hands off", so I have to really shout as loud as I can and bits of green chew go spraying across the counter.

'It's alright, Mrs. Atwal. I forgot. We need a Caramel. It's alright,' I say again, quieter. 'She's with me.'

Both of them look at me weird. Mrs. Atwal's still holding the girl's hair, but she's not pulling anymore, and the girl isn't trying to get away, she's just staring at me with her giant eyes. She reminds me of someone, but I don't know who. My hand presses on my jeans, nipping at the top of my leg, and then I realise. She's that girl I saw standing outside the house at the top of our street, with her mam shouting out the window.

'Angie's with me,' I say.

Mrs. Atwal's fingers open and the girl runs past me, out of the shop.

'Sorry,' I say, and shrug at Mrs. Atwal. She writes another number on the card and lines up all the Caramel's in the rack. 'Bye, then,' I say.

The door jangles shut, and I've just stepped out of the shop when I hear this little kid's voice behind me. She's talking really fast, with the words all joined together.

'It's Annie,' she says. 'Not Angie, and I know who you are. You're Tommy Boyle from Sister Theresa's class at St Vincent's. Laura Corey's brother Kevin's in her class too, and she says that he says that you're weird, and you talk funny.'

I carry on along the pavement and wait to cross the road, pretending like the voice isn't talking to me. I'm thinking about

Mam, about us sitting on the sofa together while she has her cans. I'll drink that Cola from in the fridge. I won't care that it's flat and tastes like chemicals cos we'll lean in against each other and watch EastEnders, and maybe she'll laugh, properly laugh like she used to, so her head shakes and her hair tickles my cheek. I'm thinking hard, making it real. I can nearly feel Mam's hair on my cheek, but the girl keeps on talking.

She follows me when I start to cross, skipping right up near my shoulder with her feet flip-flopping on the road.

'I don't think you're weird, though,' she says.

I turn just a bit, like I'm looking for cars, which I am anyway. The edge of her spikey hair touches my cheek, and she stops right in the middle of the road.

I keep going, faster. I have to get back for Mam. She'll be walking up and down the kitchen, picking the skin from beside her nails and not even knowing she's doing it. I'm all she's got. The man of the house, Mam says, since Daryl's gone. And she won't let him come back, not this time. She promised.

I'm thinking all this stuff, but I'm still sort of seeing the girl in my head, this little spikey creature like a chimney sweep from a story, with her weird ruffly skirt. And she is really little. I shouldn't leave her standing in the road. I look back from the pavement and it's like she's been waiting for me, cos she comes running across the road without even looking.

'Anyway, Laura Corey pee'd her pants in the park last week, like for no reason at all, so I don't see how she gets to call anybody weird,' she says, talking again before she's even off the road, and I can see that she isn't wearing a skirt at all, just these giant shorts that could be her dad's or something, if they weren't covered in red flowers.

'God, that cow practically pulled all my bloody friggin hair out,' she says, rubbing at her head. 'I'll smash her face in if she does it again, the old Paki,' which is a really stupid thing to say, cos anyone can see that she's one too.

I want to say, but there's bits of chew stuck on my teeth, and anyway, I don't want her to think my voice is funny, even though hers is too and she just keeps going on, saying other pointless stuff that I'm not even listening to. I start walking, but she steps across in front of me, so I have to stop. The cans bang on my leg.

'I've seen you outside your house, getting in that car. You've got a bag with white stripes on that looks like it's about a million years old,' she says, like I don't know what my own bag's like, and I just want to make her stop talking.

'What you wearing your dad's shorts for?'

'I haven't got a dad,' she says, like she wants to fight, but then her voice changes and she does this thing where she moves her head up and down like she's nodding, but sideways too, so she's sort of wiggling her face at me. 'Anyway,' she says, pointing at the red door across the street. 'We're nearly neighbours.'

'So?' I shrug, but she doesn't even notice, just keeps wiggling her face and going on about crisps or something.

'A family pack. All the flavours. They're in the cupboard on top of the wardrobe, but I can easily climb up. You can have whatever one's you want… and some Cadbury's Caramel,' she says, holding up the Caramel that's gone squidgy in her hand.

'I don't want any,' I say, but I haven't had crisps for ages and my tummy makes a gurgly noise.

I don't even realise I'm smiling till I see her laughing back. It's like she's turned into someone else, cos all the scrunchiness has gone and there's just these shiny teeth surrounded by three big dimples and a sound coming out of her, like our dodgy kitchen tap.

'Come on.' She's got my arm, and I don't really mean to, but

I'm letting her pull me across the street. 'This one's ours,' she says, pointing to the old red door with its giant silver mermaid knocker. She opens her swirly brown gate, and it's weird cos she's bossy as a teacher, but so little she has to lift the gate up with both hands to open it.

'Got Worcester sauce?' I say, nearly tasting the tinglyness on my tongue, but that makes me remember the old baked beans from yesterday, all hard and black in the pan, and how Mam left the gas on till they turned into a crispy lump and there was loads of smoke and the pan was ruined, and Mam was coughing for ages.

'I have to get back.'

'Ah, haway, man.'

'I have to,' I pull my arm away from her.

'Nah,' she says, stamping her foot, but I keep walking, back across the street.

'You bastard,' she shouts at me in this screechy voice, with her face scrunched-up, and those big shorts, and this tight green jumper that doesn't even cover her tummy. And I can still hear her shouting how I'm a weirdo bastard spastic, even when I take the key from round my neck and open our front door.

Mam's waiting on the sofa. She takes the bag off me and opens a can. She glugs a long drink and smiles at the space beside me. EastEnders has already started. I don't even care.

'What are you laughing at?' she asks.

Nothing,' I say, but I can feel that I'm smiling.

I'm thinking of Annie on the path outside her house with that long grass growing up round her sandals, and her pointy knees and elbows, and her hair all sticking up on top of her scrunchy old man's face, stamping her foot like an angry elf. I don't say, but that's why I'm smiling. Cos Rumpelstiltskin lives in our street.

Chapter Eight

A Warm Place

Daryl's back. He always comes back. I can see his shit-brown Capri from all the way up the street and hear his creepy sing-song voice as soon as I close the front door. Him and Mam are on the furry sofa. They're drinking and laughing till Daryl sees me, then he does that thing with his bottom lip sticking out, like when we play the finger game.

Mam's watching the telly, really staring like there's something great on, except the telly's turned off. I wait for her to see me. She knows I'm here, but she doesn't look. Daryl does. He stares at me and crushes the can in his hand, then he drops it in the pile on the carpet.

'Rock on, Tommy,' He makes this gargly noise in his throat, then he belches and grins.

I sort of smile back, which makes me want to be sick, then I close the door and go up to my bedroom. The drawers are all open a different amount, like steps, so you can see in without having to move them. It saves energy. The bottom one came out too far, and now it won't move. I reach into the back, feeling for the smooth shiny paper of the Cadbury's Caramel I got last week, and then I run back downstairs trying not to hear him laughing on the sofa. It feels good to let the front door slam. I kick his stupid car and run back up the street, crossing over towards Annie's swirly gate.

I've seen Annie twice since Atwal's. The first time was on the way to the station for Benjy's birthday. She was sitting on the wall at Sandy Crescent with her chin on her hand, like she was waiting for something. I would've said hi, but I was with Mam, on the other side of the road, and anyway, Annie didn't see us. Or she pretended not to.

The other time was just last week. I had to walk past her house on the way to Sunday morning football. She was standing there in the big front window, staring through the gap in the curtains, looking strange and faraway. She might've smiled at me, but maybe it was just her mouth opening. I wasn't sure, so I kept walking, but I could feel her eyes itching my back all the way to the corner.

That was when I got the Caramel. I bought it from Atwal's. I could have gone round straight after football, but I was all muddy and had to get home for a bath. Except that was just an excuse. I'm scared now, in case her Mam answers, or in case she does. I knock anyway, but just with my hand. Up close, the silver mermaid's bare boobs are too big for her body, and I don't see how people can just put their hands there. Annie opens the door in about a second, still wearing those giant shorts and scowling like Rumpelstiltskin.

'What do you want?' she asks.

'Hiya,' I say, but no more words come, so I hold out the Caramel.

Her nose wrinkles right into her eyes. She looks at me like it's a trick.

I open my fingers, till the Caramel nearly falls.

She snatches it out of my hand, then spins around like a ballerina and walks down the corridor and off into a room.

I'm not sure what to do, but she's got the Caramel, and she's left the door open, so I follow her into the room.

The curtains are nearly shut, with a triangle of light cutting down across this giant red bed that practically fills the whole space. I touch the covers, feeling the silkiness. The carpet's red too, and fluffy under my trainers. Even the wallpaper's got these red velvety swirls on. There's a picture of a lady above the bed. She's got no clothes on, just a sheet around her shoulders that doesn't cover anything. She makes me think of the silver mermaid, and Daryl's snake-bitch tattoo.

There's the sound of crinkly paper, and sticky chewing. I look away from the picture, feeling the redness in my cheeks. Annie's standing in front of this big old wardrobe with her mouth full of brown.

'Is this your room?' I ask, even though I know it's stupid.

She shakes her head. 'Mam's,' she says, except you can hardly hear cos of the Caramel.

My eyes get used to the light. There's purpley patterns like flowers painted on the wardrobe. I try to concentrate on them, but the naked picture keeps watching me, making me talk.

'Got any crisps then?'

Annie doesn't answer. I wish she'd say something cos it feels so weird, but then I can see she's shaking her head.

'That Paki bitch grassed on me,' she says.

'Mrs. Atwal?' That's all I say, but I don't understand why she keeps calling her a Paki.

'Mam went mental,' she says, lifting the side of her shorts up, and even in the purplish light, I can see that her leg looks sort of green, all down to her knee.

'God,' I say, and touch her leg with my middle finger, the lumpy one that Daryl broke, and Moira set with lollipop sticks at our sitting-room table. The one that doesn't even feel properly. I want her to notice how it's twisted, but she doesn't.

'I don't even care,' she says, and then we both just stand there with her holding the Caramel in one hand, and her shorts in the other, picking at the material with her bitten-down fingernails.

She stops chewing and looks away from me, staring at the sharp bit of light through the curtains. I can see the chocolate in her open mouth and the shininess in her eyes, so I put my hand flat against her cheek, like Nana used to do with me. It's the wrong thing.

She makes this gulping sound and a tear splats on the silky duvet. The Caramel falls on the floor, the bit that's left, anyway, then she sort of head butts me in the chest and stands there with her forehead pressing against me. My hands feel hot. I look at the naked lady's orangey eyes and don't even want to be here, in this weird room with this crazy girl. But her shoulders are shaking, and my arms come up around her.

'It hurts,' she says, and I know she means her leg. At least I think I do.

I squeeze her in, but when I try to let go, she holds on tighter, pulling me back until we're lying on the silky duvet. I start to laugh, but then I stop. She burrows in, warm against my chest. Her face is hidden in the shadows. Her breath is chocolaty sweet. We stay like that for ages, and I let myself imagine that her cheeks are rounder, and her hair curly and blond. I put my arm under her head. My other hand goes together with hers in the warm place between our tummies, where you can't hardly tell whose hand is whose, and it's so perfect that my heart starts thumping.

'Shhh,' I say, 'Shhh,' even though she hasn't said anything, and after a bit her breath gets louder.

I close my eyes, but I don't go to sleep. I just lie there with my face touching her hair and pretend that I'm five years old and there's a rainbow blanket instead of red velvet curtains, and together we're listening for Mam's step on the squeaky stair.

'Benjy,' I whisper, and there's a bang like a gun going off, and we're both standing, staring at each other in the purpley light, before I realise it was just the wind, blowing the front door shut.

Chapter Nine

Cadbury's Caramel

I didn't even realise what Annie was doing at first. At least, not for sure. I was walking up Belmont Street on the first day of term when I saw her run down the path and open her swirly gate.

'Hiya, Tommy,' she said. But she's in the year below me, and she's a girl, plus I knew there'd be loads of other kids walking up to school, so I just sort of grunted and kept going.

She doesn't say anything now, just comes out when I'm passing, and we walk up to St Vincent's, separate but together. I know that she's been waiting for me, but I can't stop her from going to school. We cross at the top of Belmont, like always, then go along Walker Road. We're just at the corner of Sandy Crescent when we see that little kid, clicking his tongue and kicking his soggy plastic ball against the crumbly wall.

'Hiya,' she says. He doesn't even look, just keeps clicking his tongue and kicking his ball in this endless game of spot.

'He never speaks,' I tell her, and it's true, he never does.

'Yeh, he does,' she says. 'When there's just me.'

'Yeh?' I don't believe her, or maybe I just don't want to.

'Yeh,' she says, and stops to watch.

Anyone can see he's good, brilliant really, for a little kid. He's only about four, with this wavy blond hair that his mam should've cut, and the buttons all gone off his too big shirt, so you can see the shininess of his ribs. I want him to miss, so I can pass the ball back, do something fancy to show that I'm good too, but there's just the thud of the ball on the crumbly wall, the scrape on the road, the click of his tongue, and the thump on his raggedy trainers. The same four sounds over and over, like some weird ticking clock.

'He looks like a girl,' I say, still thinking about him talking to Annie when I'm not there.

Annie's nose crumples into her eyes.

'Shut up, Tommy,' she says.

I shrug like I don't care. 'Don't you go to school,' I say.

'Lou won't talk to you,' Annie says, and it makes me want to kick his ball all the way across Walker Road.

'So,' I step away from her, like I'm in a big hurry to get to school. 'Hey, short-arse. Annie Cherani fancies you.'

He looks up with his mouth open so I can see the freckles in a wave across his nose, and Annie scowling behind him. The ball comes spinning off his foot, right at me. I pass it back, and he nods at me, like thanks, like I haven't done anything wrong. But I can see his lip start to wobble.

'Sorry,' I mumble, and walk away, fast.

That's how we get started, me and Annie.

She catches me up before I even get to the corner, calling me a bastard and saying how we have to get him something, like a present. But I don't have any money, and neither does she, so we go back to Annie's and get her mam's big coat, then we walk all the way up to McCleary's on St Anthony's Road.

It's pretty big, with two rows of shelves down the middle, as well as stuff all around the walls. There's milk and bread and tins, and manky old fruit that would be easy to get, but the sweets are stacked up on the counter, right in front of Mr. McCleary. It's my job to get him talking, which is pretty easy.

'It's brilliant how good Newcastle are,' I say, looking at the back of the *Evening Chronicle*. 'Three goals against Arsenal.'

'Aye,' McCleary says. 'Not bad like.'

'Not bad?'

'Well,' he says, and does this long rattly cough that reminds me of Nana. Then he starts saying how football's changed, and how there's no atmosphere anymore, now that only posh people can afford to go. Then he's telling me about some lad from round here called Shola, who he reckons is going to make it at Newcastle, but I tell him there aren't any lads round here called Shola. He laughs at that, and then he's going on about this lass called Cheryl who comes in his shop, that he reckons is going to be famous as well.

'A voice like a nightingale,' he says. 'And a face like Helen of Troy.'

'Troy,' I say, thinking of that guy on the wrestling.

'Aye,' he says, looking at his arm like he knows what I mean. 'A scratch like a tiger, an' all.' But by then I'm not really listening, just watching Annie's bitten-down fingers stuffing a big fat Mars Bar in her mam's coat pocket.

'Yeh, brilliant. Sorry, like, but I've got to go. Late for school.'

'Aye, best get to school. You don't want to waste your chances,' he says, while I'm backing out the door. 'Good to talk to you, son,' he says, and I pull it closed behind me.

I feel bad about his rattly cough, but then I reckon it's a sort of fair deal, a Mars for all that listening, cos it feels like no one's even spoken to him for like a hundred years. Probably cos of all the crazy old man things he says.

'Hey, Tommy,' Annie says, with this huge dozy smile on her face, and opens her coat like flasher. She's got loads of stuff.

'Bloody hell, Annie,' I say, and a broken flake falls out of her pocket.

She grabs it and jams half the bits in her mouth and half in mine, and then we're running hard all the way back down to Walker Road, laughing our heads off through a mouthful of chocolate and crinkly yellow wrapper. We don't stop till we get to Sandy Crescent, and even then Annie just slaps a Mars down on top of Lou's wall, and we're running again, right up till we push through her swirly metal gate.

I'm breathing fast with the chocolaty taste of Flake in my

mouth and all these sweets laid out between us on her mam's bed; three Mars, a Dairy Milk, a red Bounty that neither of us likes, loads of crisps, and a Cadbury's Caramel. The Caramel is what makes me remember that first time at Atwal's. I've been meaning to ask for ages, so now I do. I mean it's stupid, Annie calling Mrs. Atwal a Paki when she's one as well.

'My dad's Indian,' she says.

'Indian?' I imagine John Wayne galloping across the plains, shooting at a man with a tomahawk and feathers in his sticky-out hair. I know that isn't the kind of Indian she means, but the picture's in my head.

'He's called Surinder Cherani,' she says, twirling her finger through the packets on the bed. She bites down on her lip. 'And he's a Prince.'

I pretend she said chief, and the Indian gets a whole head-dress blowing out behind him, and Annie's scrunched-up face. That makes me smile.

'It's true,' she shouts, and a drop of spit lands on my cheek. 'He's the Prince of Mumbai.'

Mumbai. It sounds like somewhere from a story, but I don't say. I let John Wayne ride away out of my head.

'That's why you're sort of brown?'

'Yeh,' she says, and her lip looks liked it might burst.

'Want some crisps?' I say, cos she always does.

I open a packet of salt and vinegar, tearing along three sides and spreading it out to make a silver tray, shiny in the line of light between the curtains. We eat them together, taking turns, one crisp each. I wouldn't mind if she had more, but that isn't what we do. Afterwards, I wipe my fingers on my t-shirt.

'I never saw my dad,' I say. 'Well, only in a photo, and when I was so little, I don't even remember.'

'I saw mine once,' Annie says. 'He was dark-brown, and he talked fast, like a song. There was a man there watching us, and bars on the door. Mam said it was a prison for crazy people, but he wasn't crazy, just, y'know…'

'Yeh, sort of,' I say, even though I don't.

'At the end, he gave me a Cadbury's Caramel. He said that's what I was like, with "a glass and a half of milk in every bar."' She looks up to the ceiling to say it, then shrugs and brushes the crisp crumbs off the bed. 'Mam laughed. She said he'd got it wrong.'

'No, Annie, he didn't.'

I might've said that anyway, but when I look at the line of light on her scrunchy face I can see that he was totally right. She is just that soft brown colour, like caramel, with eyes like the darkest chocolate you can get, and little bits of gold sparkling inside them.

'Mam says I'm like the Milky Bar Kid,' I say, even though she never did, but I'm thinking of my dad and all those films, and how maybe he would've wanted me to be like that.

'No way,' Annie says. 'He's got yellow hair,' and I can tell she's thinking of that kid, Lou, and I wish he didn't even exist, cos it's like when Mam looks at me, and I know she's thinking of Benjy.

Chapter Ten

Secrets

No more Sister Theresa with her boring Bible stories. No more Sister Helena twisting my ear. No more Mr. Mizon shouting at me for no reason at all. St Vincent's Primary is finished forever. It's the last day of term and I'm walking back down Belmont Street in the sunshine, and I know Annie's mam's not in cos the blue vase is in the window. We copied it off a film.

I might as well call round. I mean, I have to walk past her house anyway and the truth is I don't really have any other friends, and neither does Annie, which is crazy cos she's really cool to hang out with, especially for a girl. Maybe we'll go nicking sweets from the newsees, and if Louis' out, then Annie'll put something on his wall to make it alright, like Robin Hood. Really though, I hope we'll just stay in her mam's room and lay together in our special way and tell our secrets in the purple dark.

I go through the swirly gate, but I don't even have time to knock. Annie answers in that weird way she does, not saying anything, just walking back into her mam's room. Except this time, she's got to push past all these cardboard boxes piled up in the corridor.

I follow her in and sit on the silky bed. She doesn't speak, just lies back, so I know something's wrong. I'm pretty sure it's to do with the boxes, but I know that she'll only tell me when she's ready, so I lie back on the bed beside her and wait.

Real friends don't have secrets, Annie always says. That's how I know her dad's in this special prison for mental cases that'll probably never let him out, and that her mam does tricks for money, which still makes me think about rabbits and top hats, even though I know what it really means, like obviously.

I've told her about my dad too, and Mam and the drink, and Daryl and the finger game, and even about running away from Sunderland and changing names. Everything really, except Benjy. I've never told anyone about him. Sometimes I think he's just someone I made up, like a little kid's imaginary friend. But that can't be true, cos me and Mam send that card every year, on his birthday.

I close my eyes and think about Mam in her velvet coat, and Benjy's card in a crinkly brown bag. How we have to get to the station at twelve o'clock and buy wine gums from the shop so we can share them on the train and write Benjy's card and talk about what we've written. Just for that time we can make Benjy real, and then we put the letter in the postbox together, to Mrs. Abuto Palacios.

That's our special thing. It's all me and Mam have got left. But that's not why I haven't said. It's that if I told about when they came for him, how we were cuddling in with Benjy's head on my arm and our hands mixed up together in the warm place between us, then Annie'd know; why I'm turning her head now, so her face is flat on my arm, and putting our bodies together the way I always do.

I can still feel that Annie isn't right, but I'm not thinking about her, so it's just sort of irritating when she takes her hands away.

'Mam's getting hassle,' she says.

So what? I say in my head. Like I don't even know what hassle she means. Except I do.

"You going round that hoowah's again," Daryl always says.

'We have to move. Mam's got a flat off the council, just near St Mary's…'

The words float around me like the dust in the purple light. They make me want to pull the curtains down and rip the stupid duvet off the bed, but I don't even move. Annie's house is the only good thing in Walker, and now her mam's taking it away. I lean across and push the door hard, so it slams us into darkness.

'At least we'll see each other next year,' she takes my hand again, and snuggles in. 'You can come over after school.'

'Yeh, I'll call in after school,' I say, even though it isn't true. It's ages till September. I'll be eleven by then, and anyway, I'm not going to St Mary's.

I'm not sure if it's cos of telling Sister Helena that God was just made up, or cos of that fight Mam had with Mr. Mizon, but I'm not going. Maybe I'll go to Benfield, or Heaton Manor, or some other place where there aren't Catholics, and they don't know how bad I am. I don't care, anyway.

I listen to the springs squeak on her mam's big bed, where she's probably done it with like a million people, and wait for Annie to stop shuffling around, to stop talking, so we can just lie here and be still. But she won't. She keeps moving and sighing, and going on about how boiling it is, even though it's just a normal day.

'Sheesh, it's just so damn hot,' she says, which is stupid cos she doesn't even talk like that, then she's kneeling up above me and it's so dark you can hardly tell it's her.

The curtains are really properly closed without even the tiniest light, but I can still tell what she's doing, lifting her t-shirt up, pulling it over her head. She's wearing this ginormous bra. I feel myself smile in the dark. I nearly laugh, but then I stop myself cos I know Annie would go mental. She'd probably kill me, but it isn't really that. I just wouldn't laugh at Annie Cherani. I hold my breath while she lies back down with her sticky-out hair touching my face, just like that first time on the road.

'Shhh,' I say, even though she's still and quiet, but you can tell it's a waiting sort of quiet.

'Let's be naked,' she whispers, so low I pretend I didn't hear.

I look at the shape of the lamp on the table and the big black square of the curtains.

'Let's be naked,' she says again.

'That's disgusting.'

'No, it's not.'

'Shush, Annie,' I say, and put my arm around her neck.

'Not shush, Tommy,' she says, pulling away. 'We always do cuddling just like you want.'

'You like it too.'

'We have to be naked, or I'm not doing it.'

My teeth press against each other. I want to say something mean, about her bra, about the knobbly bit of material I can feel on her back where she's tied a knot, about how her angry face looks like Rumpelstiltskin. But I want to cuddle too. I want to lie down in the purple dark like always and feel us tangled together and think about stuff until the thoughts stop and there's just the warm fuzzy feeling that isn't being awake or asleep.

I turn towards the door and slide my feet over the edge of the bed. I bend down and pull at my laces and listen to the sounds of Annie moving behind me. There's the mattress squeaking, Annie breathing, clothes crumpling. That's what sets my mouth going. I'm just saying anything at all.

'There's a double knot to stop them coming undone. I always do one, but if you pull before it's properly untied, then it gets tighter.'

I make a noise like I'm pulling hard, then there's two thumps close together, Annie's trainers falling off the end of the bed. The mattress moves. I can tell she's sliding her jeans off and it makes me remember that time when I saw her leg, all green and grey with that bruise, right up to her bottom.

I undo my trainers, loosening off the laces all the way along, then I take them off and look at their shiny whiteness, grey in the dark, pressed together at the edge of the bed like Daryl's tasselly loafers, always neat and clean at the side of the sofa. I kick them so they fall sideways, like a normal person's shoes, then I pull off my socks and jeans and everything and turn back around with my knees and elbows touching in front of me.

I can see more now, the shape of her face, and the whiteness on the side of her cheek, and her bottom. I know she can see me. My elbows press harder, digging into my knees, but then she takes my hand and lays my arm out flat on the quilt. She puts her head down against my shoulder. Her breath is warm on my neck, and her knee slides in between mine, just like always, just like Benjy.

'You can touch my bottom if you want to,' she says.

'What for?'

'Cos that's ecstasy.'

I don't do anything, but I feel her hand creep around my leg like a spider, and it is tickly on my bottom. I touch hers, just the edge near her leg, and look over her head at the shape of things. I'm sort of sorry when her hand stops moving. After a bit I feel her head get heavy on my neck and I start thinking about what it'll be like next term, and how it'll be weird not seeing Annie at school even though we never talk to each other, and how her hand feels on my bottom, and if I'll still get on the football team, cos it'll be at like a massive school, so it's much harder, and if Mam'll really not have any more booze in the house like she promised, and if she'll not let Daryl come back this time, and that makes me think of the finger game, and him killing our house, and what happened in the yellowy high up cupboard.

"Go down there," I'm saying. "Let go Benjy," and this time he does. He scrabbles down behind the wobbly plasterboards and there's this warm feeling all inside me, cos I know he's going to be okay. "I love you Benjy," I say, "I love you so much," and then they pull the cupboard open and there's that hairy hand, and Benjy's gone, and Annie's kneeling over me, shouting at me with her Rumpelstiltskin face all yellowy brown in the lamplight.

'Who's Benjy,' she says. 'Who is he?'

The warm feeling inside me turns hot and sick and I don't know what to do, cos I should have said. I should have told her, cos me and Annie don't have secrets, but I can't tell her now cos it's too late, and she just keeps on shouting.

'Who is he? Who is he?'

'Shut up,' I shout back. 'Just shut up.'

She hits me on the chest, and that's when I realise, I haven't got any clothes on, but she has, her t-shirt and pants, which isn't fair, and she keeps on hitting and shouting.

'Bastard,' she's saying. 'Bastard, bastard,' just like Daryl.

I hit her back. It's like my hand swings out on its own and bangs into her forehead. Her eyes go wide, and she topples right off the bed. Her head thumps on the table. The lamp goes crashing out, and I grab my clothes and run.

It's six days later when I go back. I mean, I've been back every day, but it made me angry seeing those big red curtains in the window and that silver mermaid on the door and knowing what they meant. I never went past the swirly gate. Anyway, I had to wait till today for Mam's giro, so I could borrow some money from her bag. She won't notice. I don't care if she does, anyway. There was loads. I got enough for twenty-seven Caramels.

I push them through the letterbox one at a time, as slow as I can, and wait for Annie to open the door. She doesn't. I want to knock, but I don't. I mean, she's bound to call round once she sees the Caramels.

She never does.

On Saturday the curtains have gone. I hammer on that silver knocker, but no one answers. There's metal boards on the windows, like that blind house when we ran away from Sunderland. I keep banging anyway, but Annie's gone. I don't even know where. My fingers nip and twist at the inside of my thigh. My leg burns and I deserve it. I've lost Annie like I lost Benjy, cos I was too scared to do the right thing until it was too late. Cos I'm a coward, and all I've got left is my punishment.

2001

Chapter Eleven

The Quarter-Final

The ball slides off Frogga's shin and lands right in front of me, spinning in the mud like that picture of the Earth on the telly. I should howk it onto the road. That'd waste a few minutes. The ref'd probably blow straightaway. The ball's there, and I can hear Mr. Jobson screaming from the touchline.

'Put your foot through the bastard,' but I don't.

I've been sitting on the bench for eighty-five freezing, boring minutes. I'm only on the pitch cos Carl Burns twisted his knee. At least he pretended he did, after he took out their centre-forward and Jobba Jobson did a two second substitution before the ref could fish the card out of his pocket. So, my job is to stay back, keep it tight and play for extra time, except that practically the whole of both teams are behind me, in our penalty box. There's masses of space, and my legs are running.

I push the ball ahead of me but the adrenalin's pumping. I over-hit it. One of their lads comes piling in out of nowhere, legs scissoring at my ankles.

I can feel Carl Burns' eyes on me from the touchline, and I can still hear Jobba, but not what he's saying. I don't need to. If I get caught in possession, here, on the edge of our box. If they score cos of me...

The fear is cold on my face. The lad slides in. I get both feet off the ground and run this one giant step. The scissors snap, but I'm away, up towards the centre-circle. He never got close.

He's knackered. They're all knackered, except me. Something breaks loose in my chest, like my lungs are massive, sucking in all the smoggy air in Middlesbrough.

Jobba is screaming so much his comb-over's fallen across his purple face. I still can't hear what he's saying. The roaring's too loud in my ears. I can't tell if it's from the wind or just my lungs pumping. I don't give a toss. I'm sick to death of doing what I'm supposed to; scraping green fur off the plates in the kitchen, telling Mam to stop drinking, to stop crying just cos Daryl's pissed off, and trying to be mates with Carl and them when all they do is take the piss. Anyway, everyone knows Jobba's a twat who only does football cos he's too thick to teach a real subject.

I'm past halfway, close enough to see their keeper do one giant clap and step forward off his line. No way is that kid under sixteen. He's not even under sixteen stone.

Chrissy Collins is up with me, the greedy goal moocher, standing where he always is on the thick white line at the corner of their penalty box.

There's one defender left between me and their keeper. This lanky black kid, up on his toes, swaying like a boxer. He's going to stop me. If he has to kill me, he's not going to let me past. And so what if he gets sent off? It's ones each in the quarter-final of the 2001 Inter-Schools Cup. Two more games and we're champions, and that means a play-off with the southern champions at the Millennium friggin Stadium.

I know what I've got to do.

'Give and go,' I shout, and slide the ball out to Chrissy Collins.

The boxer's feet land flat in the mud. He frowns, wide eyes following the ball. I get round the other side of him, through and clear. I'm sprinting in on the keeper, this massive pizza-face kid with long ginger hair, arms out, crouching there like

Chewbacca.

Sure, the keeper's big, but the goal's bigger. Plenty of space either side. All I'm missing is the ball.

'Penalty spot,' I scream. 'Penalty spot.'

Come on you greedy git. It's so easy. One touch. Lay it back into this big muddy space.

And he does, the beauty. A decent ball, flat along the ground. Maybe a bit heavy-footed, nearer the keeper than it needs to be, but I know, I friggin know, I'm going to get there first.

He's fast though, Chewbacca, charging out, closing the space, narrowing the angles. I can hear his growling breath, see the puss on his cheeks, spikes of ginger hair pushing through. I want to let it go. I could cut my stride, let him get there first, jump over him. They won't know I've bottled it, not for sure.

The ball rolls over the penalty spot. The ground is grey, then white, then grey. The ball slows in the mud. Laces swing across my boot. I want another stride, to steady myself, take it on my right. But Chewbacca's in the air, arms and legs spread, throwing himself at the ball, at me, like we're one thing.

My breath stops. This isn't for me or the school. This is about being scared and not letting go.

I could slide the ball underneath him, but I won't. I've known what I'm going to do for ages. Half a second, at least. I've seen it in my head. But I've stretched too far. My right foot slips. My left jabs under the ball, like a spade into soft sand, following through just enough, pulling my punch.

Chewy doesn't pull his. A gloved fist pounds into my stomach. His knee cracks against my leg, and the rest of him piles in behind.

I'm lying flat in the mud and all I can hear is this sound like a creaking gate. My throat's closed tight. I can't breathe, but I can see. The ball, grey mud on white leather, disappearing into the clouds, falling back, slow as a wrinkled pink balloon.

Chewy's head turns, blocking my view. The last thing I see is the pus oozing out of his chin, then his plastic palm fills my face. He pushes down and jabs a sly punch at my kidneys. It doesn't connect, not really. He has another go, but then Chrissy Collins comes flying over the top of us, taking Chewy with him.

I roll onto my side and get a breath, half a breath, enough so I know I'm not going to die, and listen to all these boots thundering towards us like they're running up through the ground. I lie there, thinking of old cowboy films, a squaw wrapped in a blanket, Mam on the sofa with me and Benjy cuddling in.

'Paleface, bring many horses.'

The ball bounces and rolls, settling snug in the back of the net.

There's fifty thousand people roaring, a full house at St James's singing my name. Except really, it's just Jobba and Maxi, the bus driver, cos the rest of our team are in the fight that started with Chewbacca and Chrissy. I sit up in time to see Carl Burns, who's supposed to be off injured, smack some kid's head off the goal post. There's a crack as loud as Clint Eastwood's 45, and the kid goes down like he's been shot.

I'm watching Carl, not looking behind me, that's why I don't see them coming. Someone's got a hold of me. There are hands on my arms, and my feet, lifting me, carrying me high on their shoulders, right across the pitch, lowering me down on the touch-line.

'Maybe you're not such a cunt after all.'

I look up at Carl Burns' stubbly chin. The hardest kid in school grins down at me, and I'm glowing like there really are 50,000 people cheering.

Their ref plays about ten minutes' extra time, 'for no fuckin reason,' Jobba says, throwing his arms up so his arse practically bursts through his camping stool.

'Cheating twat,' Carl says, talking to me like I'm someone. One of the lads.

'Aye, he's a cheating twat,' my voice jumps on the last word, but no one hears cos Jobba is up off his stool again.

'You fuckin cheating short-arse bastard,' he screams.

Maxi grins at me under his Toon Army baseball cap. 'That's the way, Big Jobba. Spirit of the game,' he says, but not loud enough for Jobba to hear. 'R.E.S.P.E.C.T,' he spells it out, whispering that tune that Mam likes, except he only gets to 'C'.

Then he stops.

There's about fifty kids stretched along the opposite touchline, where last time I looked there was one bloke in a shiny tracksuit, and the linesman. The bloke's still there, arms folded across his tracksuit top, with loads more kids piling out of this long brick building behind him, spreading out between our goal and theirs. They stand there watching. Not even shouting. Just staring. They don't look much like they're in the spirit of the game either.

Jobba must've seen them too, cos he stops slagging off the ref.

'Get the bus,' he says, not looking round.

'Eh,' Maxi says, looking from Jobba to the car park behind us.

'Get the fuckin bus, Maxi,' Jobba says. 'Here. Up on the pitch.'

'Right,' Maxi goes off in that fat people's run, like a normal person walking except with his arms really going.

I get up, testing my legs, and edge away from the pitch. I'm hardly even seeing the game anymore, just this mass of radgy kids pressing in like there's an invisible force-field holding them back. The ball bounces at the edge of our penalty box and Peeler does what I should've done and belts it over the fence. The ref looks at the fence, then at all their kids. Not one of them moves. His shoulders lift and fall. I can see him giving it up, putting the whistle to his mouth, sending Heaton Manor High School through to the semi-finals of the inter-schools cup.

Carl grabs my hair in both fists and presses his forehead onto mine.

'Yah fucka,' he says.

Our lads come sprinting off the pitch, ducking past Jobba who's trying to pat them on the back. We're two games from the Millennium Stadium, but the force field's broken and their whole school is walking across the pitch towards us. Jobba stops patting everyone. There's sweat running down his cheeks. He waves at Maxi like a traffic cop on speed.

Maxi grins down at him from the driver's cab, taking his time, trundling across the car park in our crappy green bus. He leans forward and turns the big black wheel. The bus swings around. Two wheels bounce up onto the grass, and the doors fold open.

'Haway lads. Don't hang about,' Jobba says, with one hand on the silver pole. He gets himself in first.

Their kids see the bus, and they're not walking anymore.

'Many buffalo,' I think in my Indian voice, and watch them stampede towards us, for about a millisecond, and then I'm there with everyone else, thirteen lads all trying to squeeze into a space meant for one. Even Carl Burns is sort of edgy. He isn't pushing to get on, just standing with his lips shut tight, looking from the bus to the stampede, with his fist opening and closing, and his eyes narrow and black.

My leg's still numb, and the other one won't stop shaking. I've got no chance. Frogga's elbow bangs against my cheek and a load of bodies scramble up ahead of me. I can hear them closing in behind. I don't look round. There's only me and Carl left. The bus pulls forward. I get a hand on the silver pole, but I'm too slow. A hand grabs my hair.

I cling to the pole, but the bus is really moving. I try to run, but my feet drag on the ground. The fist tightens in my hair, yanking me loose. I scream. I can't help it. But the fist pulls me forward, not back, and then I'm inside, lying across the plastic steps with Carl Burns' scratchy bulldog face close up against mine. And the doors pump shut behind us.

There's a sound like we're inside a drum, all this shit battering against the bus. They're kicking it, throwing mud and stones. A window bangs and shatters into a giant spider's web. No one cares. Everyone's shouting and holding up their fists, or else giving the finger out the back window. The bus jolts over a speed bump, and out through the school gates.

'We're in the semi-finals,' Carl shouts. 'And we're getting the fuck out of Middlesbrough.'

Things are a bit more chilled by the time Maxi starts shouting that we have to sit down, cos we're on the motorway and he can't afford to lose his licence, cos then we'll never get to the semi's, 'which'll probably be in some even worse shithole than that,' he says, just to me and Peeler.

We're about the only ones already sitting down, up at the front, beside Maxi. Jobba's halfway down the bus behind us, trying to make out like he's one of the lads.

'I think Jobba forgot his stool,' I say, trying to rub some feeling back into my leg.

'That's a shame,' Peeler says, sucking his cheeks into his dorky face.

If you didn't know him, you'd think he was serious. But Peeler's not as thick as he looks. No one could be, not with those stupid, sticky-out ears. Anyway, Maxi's been driving us around all season. He knows straight-off that Peeler's taking the piss.

'Hey,' Maxi says, grinning out the window. 'Have some respect for the coach.'

'Yeh, right,' I say. 'My mam knows more about football than him.'

'Oh aye,' Peeler says, even though he's never seen her. 'Your mam's brilliant.'

'Maybe he's got a better handle on the offside trap than our goldfish,' I say, thinking about what if I had pets, and what if Mam knew anything anymore, except where she's hidden the vodka. But Maxi and Peeler are laughing, and so am I, and just for a minute I feel like I'm joined onto the world.

'Tommy,' someone shouts from the back of the bus.

We stop laughing. I know who it is, but he'll just be shouting Tommy Stratton.

'Haway, man.'

I hear the edge in his voice. I have to look round. Carl Burns is waving me towards him, calling me Tommy in front of everyone, not twat or wanker, or retard. I lift my hand.

'Tommy, man,' he says again, and I go wobbling back along the bus. 'Come and have a drink with the lads,' he says, elbowing Frogga off the seat beside him.

'Piss off, Frogga,' he says.

Frogga slides his lanky body past me in the aisle. He puts a single stud on the toe of my boot and presses down, staring at me with his bulging eyes, just like that time in biology where Mr. Hollins had this dead frog pinned out on a board and I had to scrape the slime off its back.

Carl pats the seat beside him, and I sit in Frogga's still warm space. Carl's got this can with a picture of a woman on it. You can see her tits and everything. He pops the can and grins at me over a long frothy drink, and then he hands it to me and puts his arm round my shoulder. I tip the can back, feeling the weight of his arm on my neck. The bus brakes and a mouthful of lager splashes on my leg.

'Don't fuckin waste it,' Carl says.

Sorry, I think, but my fingers come up over my mouth, stopping me saying it. Cos that'd be gay.

'And pack that in,' he says.

My knee is bobbing up and down. I press my foot on the floor and take another drink.

'Cheers, Carl,' I say, and he laughs like it's a joke and passes the can across me, to Chrissy Collins.

'You like a good drink, eh, Tommy?' Carl says.

'Aye,' I shrug, wiping the foam off my lip. 'The odd pint, like.'

Carl laughs again, and I can feel Chrissy and Klepto and them, all leaning in, grinning, and waiting. All except Frogga, who's scowling at me from a couple of seats further down.

The bus hasn't moved for ages. Maxi says there must've been an accident, but nobody gives a shit. Carl keeps pulling these cans out from under the seat and giving me a drink before anyone else, and laughing at everything I say, like I've suddenly turned into Ross Noble.

'Simmer down, lads,' Jobba calls from way down the bus.

'Simmer down, yourself, Big Jobba,' Carl says, loud enough for him to hear.

Jobba says something to the kid beside him and looks out the window like he hasn't heard, like he hasn't seen the cans going along the back seat.

'Pussy!' Frogga shouts.

'Carl's uncle had a word with Jobba,' Klepto says. 'After he tried to drop him for that match at Blyth.'

Carl's bottom teeth push forward. He looks at Klepto. It's obvious he wants him to shut up, but Klepto's too into the story.

'You should've seen it,' he says, even though we all did. 'There's Eddie Burns standing on the school field like a giant hairy bear, probably with a gun in his pocket, and Jobba's head bobbing up and down like he'd suck his cock if he asked him to,' Klepto laughs, and takes a pull of beer. 'Big Jobba practically shat his pants.'

'Eh?' Carl leans across and sniffs, like he's got about a bucket of snot of up there.

'I mean,' Klepto says, talking fast, pushing the can into Chrissy's hand. 'Carlo's the best centre half in the school anyway, so Jobba should never have dropped...'

Carl sniff's again and Klepto's voice trails away. He picks a flake of mud off his spindly leg.

'Aye, he never should,' a couple of the lads say, and I join in.

The bus rolls forward, stopping and starting, chugging along like Daryl's shitty old Capri. It's dark outside by the time we pass a load of flashing blue lights and get going properly. We've drunk all of Carl's cans, and these miniature bottles of vodka his Mam got him from Spain. Our boots are off, mixed up in the aisle with a load of flat cans, and it really stinks cos Klepto puked all down the window and Carl made him wipe it up with his shirt.

Everyone's stopped talking. There's tiny lights on in the aisle, and I'm sitting in the middle of the back seat, dizzy, wishing I was down the front talking to Peeler, even if I have to listen to him going on about wanting to be a copper, again.

Chrissy's leaning away from me, doing this gargly snoring.

Only Carl's still awake. A truck comes past. Carl's face glows white in the headlights, lighting up a dark square on the side of his forehead, like someone's poked him with a square-shaped stick.

He sees me looking, so I ask.

'What happened?'

'What?'

'There,' I almost touch it, but Carl jerks his head back.

'Fuck off, man.' He sits up straighter and folds his arms.

'Right,' I press my hand over my mouth and stare at the headlights flashing past.

'Mam gets radgy sometimes,' Carl's eyes flicker in the dark. 'With her stiletto.'

I think how my mam gets radgy too, but she'd never do that.

'Even Uncle Eddie's scared of her,' Carl grins, and the light goes out in his eyes. 'Hard as fuckin masonry nails, my mam.'

I try to imagine Carl's mam sliding out of her Range Rover in her white leather trousers, and swinging her spiky shoe into his head.

'What about your dad?' I say, knowing that his dad's gone, like mine, and wondering if he ever comes back.

'My dad? Haway, man, I'm fuckin sixteen. Dads are for puffs.'

'Eh?'

I wait for him to say something else, but there's just the smell of sick, and Carl's breath, and the press of his shoulder against mine, reminding me that he's the hardest kid in school. But I can't help thinking, maybe he's the stupidest too. I lay my head back and let the rumble of the engine rock me to sleep, just like in Daryl's van a million years ago.

The dream is the same as always, with me and Benjy together on our mattress, looking at the light through the Rainbow Blanket, listening for that squeak on the stairs, the sound of Mam coming to take him away. Except this time, we're not little kids. We're as big as she is, stronger. My arms are tight around Benjy's shoulders, cheeks pressed to his, holding on. But Daryl's there, hitting us, making us scared and small again. He pushes his bony hand in my face.

'Please, Tommy, don't let me go,' Benjy's cries and kisses me. That starts me crying too. I hold tighter and press my lips to his. 'I won't Benjy, I won't,' but even in the dream, I know it's a lie.

Daryl's fist smashes down on top of my head. He swears at me, jabbing his thumb in my eye. I can't help it. I let Benjy go.

'You fuckin puff. You dirty fuckin bandit.'

My head bounces off the seat in front. I see the shine of my spit on Carl's face, his sleeve wiping it away. The bus stops. The lights go full on and there's all these white faces staring back at me. I feel the air from the open door, and see them, kneeling on the seats, standing up, getting a good look.

'Get the fuck off me!'

I snatch my arm off Carl's shoulder, and he stomps away over the pile of boots. He stops halfway down the aisle.

'Haway lads,' he says, and then he looks right at me with his narrow black eyes, and I feel my knee start going again. 'Heaton Park, after training tomorrow.'

'It's not…'

He sniffs like he did at Klepto, and this silver lump stretches out of his mouth. I hear it splat on someone's boot. I look at Klepto and Chrissy, but no one looks at me, except for Carl and Frogga who want to kill me, and Peeler useless bloody Kaminsky way down at the other end of the bus, with his cheeks sucked in under his dorky ears.

'You're fuckin dead, arse-bandit,' Frogga says, and he follows Carl down the bus.

Carl gets off, but Frogga stops at the door. He shouts back at me in his screechy, radgy voice. 'And you better be there, Bandit Boy; else we'll find you, and we'll jump you, and we'll cut your little baldy balls off.'

Chapter Twelve

Heaton Park

I walk through the playground, past the silver slide and the little kids' swings with iron bars around the seat so that whatever happens you can't fall out, and I wish I was three years old, holding tight to that bar, with Nana pushing us and Benjy beside me screaming his head off, and me laughing, swinging high, showing him how brave I am. But I'm not brave. The slide turns from silver to grey in the dusk, and there's nothing I'd rather do than lie on the bench underneath it, hidden and safe. Except I already know, there's no such thing as safe.

"We'll find you and we'll jump you..." Frogga's radgy voice screeches in my head.

The gate clangs shut behind me. The slope is so shallow I could easily walk straight up the path, but I circle round, through the trees. My feet get slower. The branches pull at me, like they're trying to hold me back. And it's not Benjy I'm thinking of now. There's another kid I used to know. I imagine her walking beside me with her skinny brown legs sticking out of those stupid flowery shorts, yabbering away like she's still nine years old.

'I know where you're going,' she says, in her bossy, know-it-all voice, 'and he's going to kill you. He'll mash your friggin' brains in. But then I suppose you probably haven't got any anyway,' and it pisses me off how she's still always right.

'Okay, Annie, shut up will you,' I say, under my breath.

'No, Tommy. Stop.'

She grabs my arm. I feel her holding me, scratching through the goose bumps on my skin. My face goes numb. It takes ages before I can look. There's a branch snagged on my denim jacket. I snap the little wooden claw.

'Stupid bloody bastard,' she says, with her nose scrunched into her eyes.

I don't stop again till I get to the edge of the trees. It's nearly dark. The lights are on in the park, but not the ones round the bowling green. There's just this grey square of grass with the pavilion over the far side, like a witch's castle in a story.

Carl Burns is standing in front of it with his arms folded.

There's a load of people sat on the pavilion steps. Alan Burns is there. He's the only Burns who was ever in sixth form, till he got excluded for head-butting Mr. Rington in chemistry. And there's other kids, too old for school, drinking cans and passing joints. Two orange lights hover over the steps like something magical. A lighter flares and then there's three, one hardly moving up near the top, and the other two sliding past each other in a jerky sort of dance.

'Haway then, Carlo, where's this fuckin poofta?'

'Aye,' one of the lasses shouts. 'Ah'm missing Easties for this fucka.' They all laugh at that.

I don't hear Frogga coming. He pushes me in the back, and I go staggering out of the trees. My shin bangs on a low metal fence. A cheer goes up from the pavilion. Carl steps onto the green in this cut off t-shirt. I pull my jacket tight around me and think of that wooden claw snapping in my hand.

'Carlo, Carlo,' a man's voice chants.

The others join in, stamping their feet on the stone steps.

'Go on, Bandit Boy.'

Frogga leans in behind me. He puts his face right up close to mine, just like he did in assembly when Lurch was going on about our "great achievement", making a big deal of things. Stupid moron. I'd been keeping a low profile till then, letting them forget about me. And they might have, if he hadn't gone rattling on.

'Well done, the lads,' he said, sounding like a twat with his posh southern voice. 'And a big thank you to Mr Jobson for all his hard work.'

Lurch started clapping, and then Klepto shouted, 'yes. Wank you, Big Jobba. Wank you.'

Everyone was shouting, but Lurch just cleared his throat about a thousand times.

'And of course, to the hero of the hour, our very own Roy of the Rovers, Tommy Boyle.'

That shut them up, and I could see Lurch staring off all over the hall nodding his head like a chicken, like he'd got no idea what was going on, and then Frogga turned back towards me with his fast lizard smile.

'Arse Bandit,' he sang, loud and slow as Pavarotti, so even Baldy Hughes looked up and turned a finger in his hairy ear, checking what he got.

'Ban. Dit,' Klepto chanted back.

I stared at Baldy's shiny finger and watched Lurch cough into his hand, but I couldn't hear him.

'Tit-ban, tit-ban, tit-ban, tit-ban.'

All these faces turned towards me, lips stretching and pouting like they were blowing me kisses, and that echoey whisper, getting louder and louder.

Like now, all of them on the pavilion, staring across, with their mouths going and their feet stomping, and the noise filling the park.

'Tit-ban, tit-ban, tit-ban, tit-ban.'

'Go on,' Frogga raps his knuckles on my head. 'Fuckin chicken-shit.'

'I don't have to do anything cos of you,' I say. But we both know, it's not cos of him.

He presses his fist into the back of my neck and I step over the rail.

The chanting stops.

I'm standing on this giant snooker table. Every blade of grass is perfect, like the turf at the Millennium Stadium. Carl must be thirty yards away, but we're the only players on the pitch. His head comes up and he looks at me with those black slit eyes. His arms fall, dangling down. He takes a step and stops.

My legs shake. I press my foot hard into the ground and clench my teeth.

We're through to the semi-finals. The semi-finals. The thought keeps running round my head like one of those crap songs you can't get rid of.

Carl's just standing there, like those Middlesbrough kids on the edge of the pitch, held on this invisible string, waiting for the whistle. I can hear Frogga's raspy breath behind me, in and out, in and out, and then Carl Burns is coming. He's running, sprinting at me, getting bigger and closer. I see the chain bounce on his neck. I need to lift my hands, bend my knees, like that black kid. The boxer. Give and go, I think, give, and go, but Chrissy Collins isn't on my team anymore. No one is.

Carl shouldn't be wearing jewellery, not on this perfect pitch, not at the Millennium Stadium. But it's there. The flash of a gold ring pumps up in front of his face. There's an engraving I've seen before. This man on a horse. He's killing some creature, like a giant bird, with flapping wings and a serpent's tail.

'St. George.' Suddenly, I know, watching the ring zoom towards my eye. 'It's St. George.'

The scream comes like puke, spraying up from deep inside me. I'm lying on the ground with this burning down my face and I know there's something really wrong. I grab at my cheek, but that only makes it worse. Carl's up above me, panting, swinging his shiny boots into my stomach, and my head. I hear them thud. What's funny is I don't feel anything. But still, I know, this is what I deserve.

'Go on, radgy lad,' someone shouts, from about a million miles away.

I grab at a swinging boot. He kicks me off, and stamps on my hand. That's when I feel the vibration, footsteps running across the grass.

'Many Buffalo,' I say, so quietly even I don't hear.

'That's it. You've sorted it,' a voice shouts, with the kicks still landing through the words.

'Enough.' The kicking stops. 'Haway man, Carlo, we'll get a pint.'

I look up at Carl Burns, with his cousin's arm around his chest.

'Fuckin puff,' Carl kicks me again, in the side of the head, and stamps away across the perfect Millennium turf.

Spikes of grass jab in my face. Someone bends over me. I stare up at them, but all I can see is this blurry shadow.

'Right,' the shadow says. 'You keep your fuckin mouth shut.'

'Uh?' I lift my head and the ground lurches.

'You got jumped. Didn't see them. Fuckin right?'

'Right,' I say, and I'm sick on the prickly grass.

Chapter Thirteen

Hospitals

There's a pain in my head, a needle wrapped in cotton wool hot behind my eye. My mouth's dry. I try to swallow, but it's like there's a slimy stone jammed in my throat. I can smell that chemical, hospital smell, and hear people moving about, talking. One voice is closer. Mam.

I imagine her cool hand pressing down on my forehead, telling me everything's going to be alright, in that slow, certain way she used to have. I wish for her to do it, like when we were here with Benjy. The last time, after that whisky bottle burst into a thousand pieces, and Daryl went mental.

I remember Mam stroking Benjy's cheek, telling him it would be okay, and him just looking at me with his round eyes and his arm in a cast, and both of us nearly believing her, till that woman came, with the name we couldn't say.

We had to go into another room, away from Benjy, with bright lights that made your eyes sting, and the woman kept asking questions in her singy voice that made Mam angry, and then they made her cry. My fists clenched so hard that my nails made four slivery moons on my hand.

'Shut up, darkie,' I screamed, 'just shut up and leave us alone,' and she did. She stopped talking. I knew she was going to give me a slap, and that I deserved it, but then she knelt down and gave me this big hug. 'Shut up, shut up and leave us alone,' I said, hugging her back and crying into her neck.

Mam's voice wakes me up. She's hunched over my metal bed with the lipstick in the wrong place on her sad, bloaty face, and black roots growing through her yellow hair.

'Can I have a glass of water?' My lips crack, but no sound comes, at least none that Mam'll hear, not when she's talking in her jumpy voice where she stops in weird places and then carries on again, just when you're going to say something.

'He's a lovely man, mind, that Ed… Eddie Burns,' she says. 'Paid for me tax… me taxi, and your grapes.'

Something rustles on the table. I close my eyes, but only one eye moves. There's this weird itchy pull on my right eye, and the cotton wool starts to unravel from the needle behind. The pain gets hotter. My hand comes up, touching the tape on my cheek, the crisscross of material over my eye.

'I mean he apologized and everything, for the… gave us a couple of quid… for the trouble, but like he said, "lad… lads are lads," and he'll be having a word with Carl en all. We just hope you've both learnt your lesson…'

I hum in my head, one long sound like a broken telly, and try not to think about the bandage and how I can only see out of one eye, and how Mam's been off the drink for nearly a whole month, till now. My fingers dig into my hands. Shut up, darkie, the words are just there in my head. But she won't. She keeps going on in that stuttery, half-drunk voice, so I couldn't even say anything if I wanted to.

'I've brought you some… some stuff, like they said. Your favourite jeans. Of course, you don't want to go talking to the polis. He's a real gentleman, that Mr. Burns, but they're a fam… family like to sort things out themselves. Don't like grasses, and ah mean, who does? Re… remember that Kieron Wilson what grassed on Mary Booth just for doing a bit of cleaning, well he deserved what he got…'

I hum louder, but the words keep getting through. My nails dig deeper and the voice in my head is different now, slow, with a bite at the end. Daryl's voice.

Shut-your-fuckin-yap.

I press my fingers to my lips, holding it in, letting it go, like I'm blowing her a kiss.

'No,' I say out loud, even though it hurts my throat. 'No Mam. I'm not a grass.'

'Good… good lad,' Mam says, and she's going to say something else, but this bloke walks over in a long white coat.

'I am Dr Banerjee,' he holds out his hand, and Mam stares at his chest like he's talking Martian.

'And how are you, young man,' he says.

'My head hurts.'

'He's alright, doctor,' Mam says, and her forehead wrinkles into her – "don't start any trouble", frown.

'We feel the operation was reasonably successful,' he says, puckering his lips. 'There was a clean break of the cheekbone. That should heal well, but the bone was forced back into the eye, tearing the ciliary muscle, twisting the ligament. The lens may be damaged…'

He goes on, not even looking at me, just talking in this weird doctor language, about bleeding and complications. And it's confusing, cos he sort of looks like Mr Atwal, but he talks as posh as Lurch. I wait for him to say something about Roy of the Rovers, but he doesn't. He just coughs and walks away, past the line of metal beds with their lumpy sheets, like mummies coming back to life.

'But doctor… wait, 'scuse…' I lift my head up and gasp at the pain. I need him to say that I'll be alright for the semi-final, but he's away past the mummies, and out the door.

'There you go, Tommy,' Mam takes my hand in her sweaty palm. 'Noth… nothing to worry about.'

We look at each other, but I can't think of anything to say. I wish she would just go. For once, she does what I'm wishing, but not before she leans right over me with her hot vodka breath and smacks her sticky lips on my cheek. She pats my leg through the blanket and waddles away, chuntering to herself with her shoulders hunched and the black roots on her blond head, like a giant clumsy wasp.

I'll never end up like that. Never. I snatch the grapes off the table. I'm going to throw them at her, but I let them fall. I look down at the brown paper bag on the white tiles, feeling the itchy bandage and the hot needle digging in behind my eye.

'Ah'd eat them grapes if I were you.'

'Eh?'

The bed beside me creaks, and this old guy leans towards me wearing red pyjamas and a black eye patch, like a pirate.

'Ah said, ah'd eat them grapes if I were you,' he grins through grey stubble that's almost a beard. He hasn't got any teeth.

Piss off. You dirty-old-fucka. Daryl's voice bites in my head, but my fingers come up and I hold it in.

'You want one?' I say, and he cackles like a witch.

'Let's say we share them,' he says.

I reach down, gripping tight to the big bed, and pick them up, holding a grape across towards his purpley hand. We only just reach. He takes the grape in his lumpy fingers, but it drops and bounces under his bed. The old guy sort of shudders. I pretend like it hasn't happened.

I get out of bed in this stupid white gown thing that's open at the back, sit on the edge of his bed, and give him another one.

He doesn't say thanks or anything, but he gets it in his mouth and makes this sucking sound.

'Ah, sweet and seedless,' he says, and I give him some more.

'You en all,' he says. 'You need to eat if you're going to get better.'

'What do you know about it?'

'A've got ears,' he says.

'Yeh, massive hairy ones.'

I feel myself go hot, but he just cackles again, and I laugh too, except my throat's too dry, so I bite down on one of Eddie Burns' grapes. Juice squirts in my mouth. I take another one, a handful, shoving them down, about four for every one the old man gets, and we keep going till every one of them's gone, and then a very little nurse comes round with short black hair and a face like a boy. She shows us a menu card and asks what we want for dinner.

'Cod's back on tonight, Frank,' she says.

'Lovely,' he says, winking, so you don't know if he means the cod or her.

'It's alright, this place,' he says, and cackles again, gripping my wrist in his sandpapery fingers.

I read for him in the afternoon from this old book he's got that doesn't even have a picture on the front. The story is about a girl and her granddad. They get thrown out of this old junk shop and don't have anywhere to sleep. It's sort of long winded, but you want to know what happens, and after a bit I don't even notice that I'm just using one eye. I'm really getting into it when I hear the old guy start snoring. I read a bit more, just to myself, but it's not the same.

When I wake up in the morning, his bed is flat and empty, and there's a new nurse who says his daughter took him home.

'Right. No bother,' I say.

'He said to tell you goodbye,' she says, but she's obviously lying, and there's nothing to do except lie in bed and try not to think about complications and damaged lenses, and the shape of that doctor's mouth.

Maybe it'll be alright. Four weeks is ages. Even if I don't get much training, Jobba'll have to let me play in the semi's. He'll have to put Roy of the Rovers in the team, whatever Carl and them say.

It's nearly dinnertime again when the nurse with the boy's haircut comes back. She tells me I should really be in the children's ward, and that they'll move me when a bed comes up.

'Oh, by the way,' she says. 'Frank left you this.' She gives me the old book.

'Right, thanks,' I say, and I have to blink when I take it out of her hand.

It's the longest book I've ever read, by miles, and with only one eye, but I've nearly finished the whole thing, up to when Little Nell gets buried, plus I've eaten everything on the hospital menu by the time they come to take the bandage off. They never did move me, and Mam hasn't been back. I don't think about it, but I know she'll be on the drink till the money Eddie Burns gave her runs out.

The nurse with boy's hair has changed the bandage every day, but this is different. This time a giant, boney man comes and makes me get in a wheelchair, which is stupid, cos there's nothing wrong with my legs. He wheels me out past the mummies and into a lift to a whole different floor. We go along miles of green corridor to a little room, where he tells me to get into this leather chair with buttons on the arm.

'Wait there,' he says, then he goes out and leaves me, lying back on the chair, looking at all these weird machines. The one in front of me could be a robot off Dr Who, with metal eyes on a big stalk.

Exterminate, exterminate, I say in my head, then I look at the buttons on the chair and wonder what they do, and if there's one that could just make everything alright.

'Hi.'

There's a girl in the doorway, smiling at me. She's pretty, with long red hair and just like a handful of freckles across her nose. She reminds me of someone. I don't even notice the white coat until she tells me her name is Dr Tiverton, and she's the ophthalmology registrar.

She sits in the chair beside me and presses one of the buttons, sitting me up until I'm close enough to kiss her. Her eyes are green, but with little grey speckles. She scrunches her nose up and pulls the sticky-tape off my face in short fast movements, much more carefully than the nurse.

'So' she whispers, lifting the bandage off my eye, and I gulp a massive breath.

I've got used to seeing through one eye, so it's weird seeing on both sides at once, like there's a line down the middle of the world. One side's normal, and the other is like looking at lights through a wet window, with the colours all bright and blurry.

'Close your left eye, please,' she says, and looks right into my eye. She smells of oranges. I think of the way her nose scrunched into her face.

'Hmmm,' she says, and writes something on her clipboard.

I'm still just looking through one eye, so her face has turned into a blob of rainbow and the robot machine looks like a spindly tree with glasses on. Exterminate yourself, you mental, metal muppet. I laugh, but it's not funny. I wish she'd hurry up and do something, get the weirdness out of my eye.

'Sit back, please,' she says, and it's like she's read my mind.

She presses the button to tip my chair back, then holds my eye open and puts in two drops of stuff. I blink and look, but it hasn't worked. Not right away. She leans over me, looking through this sort of telescope, seeing how the medicine's working.

I want her to say something, but she doesn't, and I'm thinking, okay, if it's not better for the semi's that could be alright. Carl and Chrissy and them can beat some crappy Carlisle school. Just so long as I'm okay for the final. That's what really matters, and the final's not till May. I'm bound to be okay by then. So, I don't see why my hands feel so sticky on the leather chair.

'Are your mum and dad coming in today?' she says, pressing the button, sitting me up.

I open my other eye and swallow before I speak.

'My dad's not around.'

'Oh.' She looks away, at this picture of a red boat on a sparkly sea. It's pretty crap.

'And my mam's at work. You can tell me. I'm not a kid.'

She makes a tutting noise with her tongue.

'Just tell me. Dr Banerjee did already, after the operation.'

'Well,' she coughs and starts again. 'Well, Mr. Boyle, as Dr Banerjee told you, the damage was caused by your cheekbone being forced back against your eyeball. There was a lot of internal bleeding which made the operation particularly difficult, as well as damage to the ciliary muscles…'

I watch her face while she goes on in her doctor's language, just like Dr Banerjee. She's so close I could reach out and slap her. Her lips open and close so I know she's still talking, but I can't really hear, just feel my hands going numb on the chair's leather arms.

I reach down between my knees and squeeze the thinnest bit of skin through the papery gown.

'It's okay,' I take this massive breath and practically shout at her. 'It's alright. I'll wait till the final. That's when the scouts are there; from Newcastle, and Liverpool, and everywhere.'

She looks at me with her serious elfy face, and pink lipstick that fits exactly on her lips, then she takes my hand and lifts it away from my leg. I know now; she reminds me of Annie Cherani. But that just makes it worse. Both my eyes go blurry, and it's not fair cos doctors are supposed to be old men with hairy noses, and they shouldn't be allowed to wear make-up.

Haway man, ya cunt, Daryl barks in my head. *She doesn't know what she's fuckin on about.* My fingers try to press against my lips, but she's still holding onto them.

'I want to see the real doctor,' I tell her, pulling my hand away.

'Please, Mr. Boyle, I know this is extremely…'

'Shut up, darkie,' I scream like a moron, and she just looks at me with those bright green eyes, like the grass at the Millennium Stadium, like the other grass on that bowling green, with Frogga's raspy breath in my ear.

I jump when she touches me, but she's not hitting, just rubbing at my shoulder, and there's shininess in her eyes too, a drop balanced on her eyelash. Cos of me.

'Sorry,' I say. And I think of Benjy when he was in the hospital, how he didn't cry at all, and how he said thank you when they brought him one of those crappy red lollipops that cost about two pence, even though his arm wouldn't move, and he had to reach over and take it with the other hand.

"Thank you, Mrs. Bulu," he said, and everyone laughed.

'Thank you, Dr Tiverton,' I say. 'I mean, for telling me,' and

I want to kiss her pink lips, and hit her, and hold her with my face in her soft white coat and cry until all the badness comes out of me.

'I'm sorry,' she says, with her hands folded across her coat. 'But that's how it is.'

'It's alright now,' I say.

'No,' she says. 'It's a terrible thing, but you're a bright boy, and you're charming,' she smiles at me, 'and there are other things besides football. Listen at school. Learn things. Give yourself a chance.'

I think about Mr. Spungin saying I could get an A for art if I did the coursework. But I don't care about art. I nod and try to smile.

'I wasn't always a doctor, you know.'

That makes me really smile. 'You don't even look like one now.'

I'm not sure if she'll be annoyed, but she just laughs for ages, like it's the funniest thing ever.

'I won't be playing in the final, will I? I won't be playing football anymore.'

She squeezes tight on my shoulder, and a big shiny tear comes down her cheek. She turns away fast and wipes it with her sleeve, like a kid.

'At least...' I wait till she's looking at me. 'I suppose I could be a ref. They can't see for shit,' and that makes us really laugh, till a big bubble of snot bursts out of my nose.

Chapter Fourteen

Shark Boy

I'm lying on the hospital bed with my art pad flat on the crispy white sheet and eleven pencils lined up in their box. The twelfth is in my hand. I'm drawing Emily Tiverton, trying to get the curve of her neck where it goes in at the front, the bit that moves like a tiny creature when she talks.

She never said, but I know it was her who sent me the art stuff. She gave me a tissue and we talked some more, after that bubble of snot came out of my nose. Proper talking, about stuff you think but don't know if it's right. I kept waiting for her to laugh, or try to make me say about Carl, but she just held my hand and let me talk. It was nearly like talking to Annie.

I told her that, about who Annie was, and how we used to hang out all the time, and how we had a fight, but not why. I couldn't tell her about being a coward. But I told her about how I went back with twenty-seven Caramels and how Annie was gone, and I don't think she ever got them, and how I've never seen her for five years, except for once on Grey Street, but I was on the bus, and by the time I got off she was gone. Anyway, I'm not even sure it was her. I told about Mam and Daryl too, and Mr. Spungin saying I could get an A. I might even have told her about Carl, but a red light bleeped through her pocket, and she had to go.

The pad and pencils were here when I woke up the next day, proper drawing pencils, not kids' stuff. So, I've been mostly drawing for the last three days, pictures of Emily Tiverton, and trying not to think about all that sciencey stuff she said about my eye, which makes me want to be sick. I've got this sort of dream I think of instead.

I'm older, standing in this posh bar in Jesmond with silver chairs and high shiny tables. I'm wearing this cool leather jacket that cost about a thousand quid. The barman knows me. He doesn't hassle me for I.D., just smiles and pours me a bubbly drink in a long glass, like something out of a chemistry experiment. I lean my elbow on the bar and look across to this purple lamp in the corner. Emily Tiverton smiles back at me.

She looks the same as now except one side of her face is lilac, moving with the lamp light. There's something shiny across her throat, a silver chain, with a tiny pendant disappearing into the dark space at the top of her velvet dress. She watches me with her speckly eyes, but I can tell she doesn't know who I am. She smiles like she wants to cry.

I lift my elbow off the bar. I'm walking towards her, past a row of empty chairs, when the hair prickles along my neck. There's this raspy breath, just like in the park. Frogga's hand is on my back. He hisses in my ear, trying to make the dream about him, and I know if I turn around, he's got me, so I don't look, and I don't listen. I take my big bubbly drink over to Emily's table and smile at the popping sound of Frogga disappearing behind me.

'Don't you remember me?' I ask.

'Oh my God,' she says, and the candle flickers. The tip of her tongue is as pink as her lips. 'You're that brilliant artist.'

I smile and watch her while she goes on about the flying ship I did at Wallsend, and the seven little miners at Durham, and all these other things I'm going to paint for my G.C.S.E.

I stop drawing and hold the paper out across the hospital bed. I've done about a million versions of her and thrown them all away. This one is the weirdest, like two pictures squashed together. I only kept it cos I'm on the last page in the book, and I've sort of got to like it. There's Dr Tiverton on one side, with her red hair blowing out behind her, and three freckles and one speckly green eye. The other eye came out funny. It smudged where I kept rubbing it out. That made her cheek go saggy, like there was a load of rotten sweets in there, and you can see Mam's brown teeth inside, and her waspy black and yellow hair.

I was doing the yellow last night, just before tea, when the giant man brought the wheelchair. I knew he'd come for me. I closed the pad and slid it down behind my locker, and then he wheeled me back to that room with the robot thing and told me to get into the big leather chair. I waited ages till Emily Tiverton came. She didn't say anything about the pencils, just nodded, and told me to lie back in the chair.

I could hear my heart banging inside me, trying to get out of my mouth, but she didn't even notice, even though she's supposed to be a doctor. She took off my bandages faster than last time. I nipped at my leg, but she didn't stop me, just looked at my eye through the stalk robot and told me to look in different directions.

'Alright, Tommy,' she leaned back, taking her orangey smell away with her, and wheeled the robot back from my face. 'We'll send you a check-up appointment for a fortnight's time. You'll have to be careful to avoid sudden impacts, but aside from that,' she smiled at me, like she was saying something good, 'I don't see why you can't go home tomorrow morning.' That was it. She was leaving me there.

'Am I going to look like a weirdo forever,' I said, wanting to make her stay.

She stopped in the doorway. 'You don't look like a weirdo,' she said, and even through her hair I could see her neck turn pink. 'It's pretty sexy, actually,' she laughed, and pulled at the ring on her finger. 'Like the gods spilt a tiny jar of honey across your eye and sprinkled it with moonlight.'

Her shoes clicked away down the corridor, and a minute later the wheelchair came squeaking back to get me.

I called Mam after tea and listened for sixteen rings. She never answered. I even went out to the lobby this morning and stared at the silver phone, then I came back to the ward and pressed my face into the pillow. There was no point. If she wasn't answering last night, she definitely wouldn't be answering now, so I got the pad out from behind my locker, laid out the pencils, and pulled the sheet up over my shoulder.

That's why I'm still here, trying to draw Emily Tiverton's throat, the bit that moves when she talks. My feet kick the covers. I could just do jewellery, a gold heart, like in my dream, but that'd be wrong. Cheating. I think about it anyway, but really, I'm just trying to get back to my dream in the silver bar. I've nearly got the taste of that long frosty drink when the nurse with the boy's hair comes round with the cards for dinner. I take one right out of her hand and tick the box for chicken and rice.

'My Mam can't come till after dinner,' I tell her.

She says to get dressed and makes me tell our phone number, but she takes the card, and when they come round with the food, there's some for me. Afterwards, this other nurse comes, and I have to get up while she takes the sheets off the bed. She says to get dressed too. I feel stupid in this papery nightie anyway, so I get the orange carrier out of my locker.

The sleeveless t-shirt on top is one of Daryl's with a picture of a shark across the front. There's a pair of my trainers, but no socks. Then I pull the jeans out of the bottom of the bag and this groan comes out of me, like one of the cows on the moor. They're my blue Levi's, worn sort of grey across the front.

"Your favourite jeans," Mam said, and they were, once.

I squeeze the cloth in my hand and remember when we got them. There was snow on the pavement, but it was sunny, and I was sweating in my duffel coat. We'd gone down to the posty for Mam's giro, then into town to meet her friend from Australia who she hadn't seen since school. She just had two drinks, then her friend had to go, and she took me into the shop without me even asking.

'The state of those trousers,' she said, and her voice sounded sort of Australian.

I chose the Levi's, and they were exactly the right size, which hardly ever happens in Oxfam, and Mam didn't even complain about how much they were. I got this Indian jumper too, red with gold bits. Even then I sort of knew it was weird, but I was only in year eight, and when I tried it on Mam stroked the silkiness on my shoulder.

I lean back against the metal hospital bed and pull the jeans on, but I can't do the zip, and they stop halfway down my leg. Summer fashion, I think, but I know I look like a dick. At least Daryl's t-shirt is long enough to cover my pants. I pack my stuff in the orange bag and walk out past the mummies.

'Hang on.' The nurse with the short hair steps in front of me, ticking things off on a clipboard. 'You can't just go off on your own.'

'Yeh, but my Mam's waiting outside.'

'Well, she'll have to come up,' the nurse says.

'She can't. I mean,' I say the first thing that comes into my head. 'My baby brother's asleep in the car. We've got a Range Rover.'

The nurse shakes her head, and that's when one of the mummies starts thrashing about under his sheet. You can tell it's a man cos of the noises, and the bony leg sticking out.

'Mr. Curry,' the nurse calls. 'Go and wait in the dayroom,' she tells me, over her shoulder.

I go out into this pukey green corridor, past the desk that's called the nurses' station, to the next door along. That's the dayroom. I know cos they sent me there yesterday. It's just the same, with the news on the telly, and two rows of shiny plastic seats and no one inside. Except today there is. This man is hunched on the end chair, rocking backwards and forwards with his face in his hands.

'Baby, baby, baby,' he says.

I look down the corridor, but there's no one around, so I close the door and walk along. I check all these complicated signs for a way out, but I can't help thinking about what might have happened to the baby, and Mr. Curry screaming under the sheet. I feel bad about them, but sort of good too, cos it makes me realise that I'm okay, lucky to be getting out.

There's a lobby with a silver lift. The giant porter's already inside, with a super-thin woman in a wheelchair. We go down to the reception hall. I'm ready to say that Mam's waiting outside, but nobody asks, so I just walk out of the lift and through the tall glass doors into this weird lop-sided world.

I must've got used to the ward, with all those beds on the shiny floor and people that hardly moved, but the world outside is huge and twisted, like everything is wrapped in wet cellophane. I look back through the glass doors. The giant porter is taking his wheelchair back towards the lift, and I feel like a little kid watching his Mam walk away from him. I want to run back in, to pretend my eye is exploding, anything, so they'll let me stay. I watch until the porter's saggy pants disappear round the corner.

I put my foot on the edge of the curb, but it slides onto the road. I fall forward. My hands slap against the side of an ambulance.

'Excuse me,' this posh bloke says, like someone has a tight hold of his balls, but I can't see the expression on his face.

I shut my right eye, and his face jumps across the back of the ambulance, scowling. I concentrate on the ground, and walk out of the hospital like a zombie, with my arms held in front of me and my bad eye winking open and closed.

The hospital's up in the west end, so I have to go right through town. There's millions of people, and I feel like they're all looking at me, except I can't really tell. I get away from them as fast as I can. I walk for miles, down to the river, past the bridges and the Baltic, and the posh flats, up onto Walker Road. Atwal's is open and I can see Mrs. Atwal straightening the tins inside.

The thing isn't to shut my bad eye, cos then I only see half of everything, but to open them both and concentrate on the good one. I can see stuff, but with this blurry rainbow around one side, and everything is in a different place to where it looks. I keep away from the edges of things, and don't look too far ahead. By the time I turn into our street, I'm walking along with both eyes open and my hands in my pockets. I've got it sussed.

There's a blue transit down near ours. That should be enough to warn me. I mean, I know the Capri's knackered, and he needed something for his deliveries. Still, I don't really think about it, not till I get down as far as Annie's old house and hear Mam's voice through our open window. She gets louder and screechier when I cross the road, then there's a bang, and Mam screams. It isn't even dark.

'Bitch,' a man's voice shouts, and the heat burns up from my stomach.

Daryl's back. I knew he would be. I knew that however much Mam cried and promised, we'd never get rid of him. As soon as there was money, she'd be back on the vodka, and he'd sniff it out, like a pointy-faced Smirnoff rat.

Maybe it takes half a minute to walk along the street and get the spare key from under the stone. Long enough to be ready for the mess of cans and bottles, the stink of piss and overflowing ashtrays, and the noise of them, like a car's brakes just before the crash. I only open the door wide enough to slide through and shut it without a click. My hand is on the banister when Mam looks up through the living room door. She stops screaming and puts her hand across her chest. She tilts her head to one side.

'Tommy. Baby.' She waddles into the lobby, with Daryl at the far end of the living room, staring at me over his tash.

Her hand slides down my arm. She holds my wrist and presses against me. I turn my face away from her pukey breath.

'We're just sorting out, getting cleaned up,' she says, and it makes that heat burn through me so fast that I'm scared to turn around. I nip my thigh, not hard, cos the bruise is still ripe, just enough to settle me. Then I get away up the stairs.

The bathroom's disgusting. I flush the toilet and open the window as wide as it'll go, then I stare at my face in the mirrored cabinet. There's a line down the middle where the doors open, cutting through my nose. It's like there's Tommy on one side, and this weird boy on the other, looking back at me with his shiny eye.

'Moonlight,' I whisper, 'and honey,' but it feels stupid.

I shake my head, and my face and hair and the yellow tiles over the bath all streak together, like the Road Runner. Just the shark on my t-shirt is still, with a thousand teeth under its silvery eyes.

'Shark Boy,' I say, and open my mouth as wide as I can. I stretch till my jaw aches.

My teeth snap shut, but I don't hear them, cos Daryl comes clattering through the door behind me. He starts pissing. Spray bounces off the seat. He doesn't even know I'm there, not at first. When he does, it breaks the flow. He stretches his cock and looks at me in the mirror, pointing from his eye to mine.

'You want to get one of them every week,' he says, 'three hundred quid for nowt. Happy fuckin days.' He zips up. 'You can get that fuckin t-shirt off en all.' He belches and slaps the back of my head. 'And cheer up, ya cunt,' he says, walking out of the bathroom. I stare at Shark Boy and listen to Daryl's voice from the top of the stairs, 'it might never happen.'

Chapter Fifteen

Getting a Job

I'm walking up between the science block and the AstroTurf chomping on my canteen pizza, when someone shouts, 'Shearer,' and a football rolls across in front of me. There's a load of little kids stopped on the school field, watching. I step over the ball, get my standing foot beside it, weight balanced.

'Aye, man, give us it,' one of them shouts.

'Aye, man, aye,' they all shout. 'Eye, eye; eye, eye,' but by then I'm past the ball, up towards the high back gate with the pizza turning to plastic in my mouth.

I try to make out like it's no big deal, like every day for weeks now, when they've been waiting for me at the school gates, and in the hall at assembly, even in the corridor on the way to the art room at dinnertime. But whatever I pretend, everyone can see the shine in my eye, and even the little kids know that I can't see them if they come up on my right side.

The gate is shut like always, with the wire mesh fence running all around the school, but up close I can see that the padlock has gone. I pull the gate towards me. The loose chain rattles. I step out into the line of trees, and push through a clump of dried out bushes.

My feet stick in the claggy ground. I stand back against a spindly tree and press my head against the bark until it hurts enough to balance the bruised feeling behind my eye. The leaves look like a painting with the colours all running together.

Impressionist, Mr. Spungin would call it.

I close my eyes and stand there for ages with this warm fuzziness in my head, and the cheesy taste in my mouth. I open my good eye. Maxi's bus, that should be taking me to Carlisle, is in the car park. My other eye opens, and the bus splurges into a watery blob.

A branch creaks over by the gate. I step away from the tree and peer through the leaves and shadows. Some part of me already senses that it's him, even before I hear his tight, screechy voice.

'Aye, aye, Bandit boy. Playing today, are you?' Frogga steps out in front of me. I jump, not realizing he was so close. 'Why aye. Course you are,' he grins. His hand lands flat on my chest, knocking me back against the trunk. 'You gotta come, so you can have another snog with Carl.'

Frogga's hand slides up around my throat. I try to pull away, but his fingers tighten. A branch digs into the back of my neck.

'You waste of fuckin space.' He slaps me, slow and careful.

My fists clench, nails tight in my palms. But I don't move.

"Avoid any sudden impacts," she said.

'You're a piece of shit loser. Right?'

I stare at the blue lines on my trainers and try to act like Frogga isn't even here, but I know he's right. Tears sting in my eyes. I want to tell him that I'm not even crying cos of him, but that'd be pathetic. I try to think of Emily Tiverton's face in the candlelight, but my legs are shaking. Frogga's hand is the only thing that's holding me up.

'Right, Bandit?'

"That's how it is." I see her hands folded on her white coat, going on like she knows everything in the world.

'Right, Frogga,' I say, not even caring what he's asking.

'You alright, Tommy?' Maxi's standing in the open gate with

the metal padlock bulging through his fist.

'We're just having a chat, shooting the breeze, giving it a bit of the old chin-wag,' Frogga grins and pulls me towards him. 'Aren't we, Bandit?'

'Is that right, Chester?' Maxi says.

The name comes out with a sneer on it, and two red blotches come up on Frogga's cheeks. He lets go of me and stares at Maxi, spitting through his white lips.

'You mess with me, bus man, and Eddie Burns'll fuck your fat arse for you.'

'Oh aye?' Maxi gets a handful of silver chain off the gate and comes towards us with the chain ticking off the metal frame, slithering through the bushes like his pet snake.

'Going to fuck my arse, is he? You saying Eddie's a puff then, are ya?'

'Nah, but…'

'I've known Eddie Burns since before you were squeezed out your mam's sorry cunt,' Maxi keeps walking, till he's right up in Frogga's goggly face. 'And I'll tell you what he really hates. Hanger-on wankers like you. Now piss off.'

Frogga looks down at Maxi with his eyes bulging out of his head. Maxi must be six inches shorter, but he's solid, and twenty years older, with a chain wrapped around his fist.

'Go on, Chester,' Maxi says, and laughs out loud at Frogga's name. He waves his arm at the school. The chain rattles.

'Fuck off, fat man,' Frogga snarls, but he rushes it, and stomps way too fast, back through the gate.

Maxi watches him go.

'D'ya want a job, son?' he says.

I wipe my sleeve across my cheek.

'Haway then,' he says, and I follow him out into the car park.

'Ah'm pressed for time. Got to be away to Carlisle for... well, you know what for.'

He gets in the driver's cab while I stand there with one foot on the road and one on the bus, not sure what he wants me to do. He sits with this notebook on the steering wheel, hunched over, so all I can see is his Toon Army baseball cap and the top of a chewed pen. Then he pulls these brown envelopes from the pocket in the door. They're small, but fat and bulgy, like him. He writes a number on each of them: One, two, three.

The envelopes go into a crumpled Morrison's carrier. He ties the top and chucks it at me, then he holds the piece of paper out in front of my face. There's three addresses. They're all places down in Walker, one just near our house, and each address has got a number beside it in red felt tip; one, two, three.

'Got it,' Maxi says.

'Eh?'

'You can read, can't you?'

'Yeh.'

'Right. It's not bleedin difficult. You take each envelope to the address on the list, ring the bell, tell them it's from Maxi, then you tear that list into little pieces and bin it, right? No littering.' He grins again.

'What if no one answers?'

'What's that? Get your fingers out of your mouth.'

I press my hand flat against my leg.

'What if no one answers?'

'They'll answer.'

He leans forward and gets this thick wad out of his back pocket. His hand stretches around it, then he holds out a twenty, so new and crisp it doesn't look real. 'Here.'

I take the money, quick, before he changes his mind.

'Do it right and there's plenty more, but if you screw this up,' his face sags, like all the muscles just snap. 'Don't screw it up.'

I wait to see if there's anything else.

'Go on then,' he says, and I scramble down off the bus and back towards safe, boring maths revision.

'Oy,' he shouts, poking his head out of the bus. 'Where the fuck are you going?'

I point at our brand new, state-of-the-art school.

'Nah, nah,' he comes plodding towards me. 'Not with my gear, you're not. This is work, son. You can go to school tomorrow.'

'Right, Maxi.'

'Right, Maxi,' he says. 'Now go on. Do Welbeck first, and you don't stop, you don't get chatting to anyone till you're done. I'll be ringing the lads in an hour, and they better be happy. And you don't open my fuckin envelopes.'

He's still shouting things at me when I walk away out the front of the school car park with his crappy carrier swinging against my knee. I might not be playing in the semis, but I'm free, out of school with a twenty in my pocket and Frogga out of my face. Except that isn't true, cos somehow Frogga's bulgy eyes can see the truth about me, that I'm a screwed-up loser, with my alky mam, and no dad, and no brother.

I shouldn't look back, but I do. The lights are on in the art room. That starts me thinking, about Mr. Spungin and Emily Tiverton's pencils. I get a good grip on my thigh and squeeze till it burns. The pain clears my head. Right. I look at the first address on the list. Welbeck Road. This is a real job, not like doing homework and drawing pictures. Anyway, it's just till things get sorted, till my eye gets better. And it will, whatever she says.

Chapter Sixteen

Happy Birthday

Benjy is pressed against me, so little I can feel the papery brush of his nappy on my thigh. He mews like a cat and throws his sticky arm across my neck.

'Tom-Bomb,' he says.

'Benjy,' I whisper, balanced on the edge of my dream.

My legs stretch and tingle under the duvet. The Rainbow Blanket hangs in the window with its colours blurring, red and green and gold. My eyelids flicker. I hide from the light, but I can't stop the coldness of the wall against my foot, or the sickening thud of reality in my stomach. Benjy is gone, and those swirling rainbow colours are what I will always see.

My watch is balanced on the bedside table, like a mini version of the station clock with the pointers already high on its face. Shit. It's after eleven. Mam still hasn't come. I bet she isn't up, even though I reminded her about a million times. I pull my jeans on and stomp as loud as I can across the landing. I push Mam's door so hard that it thumps back against her bed. Daryl might still be here, but I don't care. I step into the smell of old cider. My foot hits something hard. A bottle clangs against the radiator, spilling frothy wetness under my toes. I click the light on.

'Mam.'

She groans but doesn't move. The duvet's right up over her head, but at least there's just her. I pull the duvet off her head.

'Fuckin hell, Tommy.' She rolls over and presses her face into the pillow, just like I do. That makes me stop. I sit on the edge of the bed and put my hand on her raggedy hair.

'Haway, Mam, it's Wednesday.'

She pulls the covers back over her head.

'Are you not at school?'

'School?' I slap the pillow beside her. 'Wednesday the 1st of August, like I've told you about a thousand times, and you didn't even listen.'

'No, Tommy,' her head comes out, eyes wide under her witch's hair. 'I did. I've got the card and everything. Just slept in, that's all.' She sits up and rubs at the grey smudges on her face. I can see that I've made her scared.

'It's alright, Mam,' I look out through the window, at the old freezer in the yard with its door hanging off. 'But can we go soon?'

She grunts in a good way, and I leave her there. I've just filled the kettle when I hear the shower running. Brilliant. My hand stops on the tap. I'm smiling, thinking of that time when Daryl was in there and I turned the cold on as far as it would go. Daryl went mental, but so what? He's always in a radge, and anyway, it was worth it.

I click the kettle on and check the fridge. Jam, but no margarine, and two bits of cardboard bread on the shelf. I put them in the toaster. For me, not Mam. She doesn't eat in the morning. I don't much either, except it's nearly half eleven and I'm starving. I put loads of jam on.

I stand by the sink watching bits of last night's fish fingers float in the water, and it's like my hand goes on its own, turning the cold tap just a bit. I wonder if Mam'll even notice, but I don't want to think about that, so I remember sitting on Annie's mam's shiny bed telling her how Daryl had come thundering down the stairs. 'Bollock-naked with this purple blotch across his chest.'

What really got her laughing though, is how stupid I was, still standing there, right by the sink. She pressed her hands in against her tummy and made that sound she did, like a dodgy tap. If anyone else had laughed, I would have hated it, but maybe it's cos she always had worse bruises than me, or maybe just cos it was Annie Cherani making that crazy noise, but I started laughing too, till we were both rolling around on that silky bed, practically wetting ourselves.

'What are you grinning at?'

'Hi, Mam,' I put the coffee down in front of her.

She takes a sip and makes a face. It's cos I've put cold water in with the hot, so she can drink it quickly, so we still might get to the station in time.

She puts the cup down, then she picks the kettle up, shakes it, and holds the spout under the tap. She fills it up to the top and presses the button. We watch it boil.

'Come on, Mam, please.'

She puts her hand on her forehead and sighs.

'I wish I'd put the tap on full,' I say mostly to myself, then I walk through to the front room and throw myself back on the furry green sofa.

Mam hates that, says it knacks the springs. They're knackered anyway. My knees are up nearly level with my face, but the pad and pencil are still where I left them, under the seat. I get them out and stare at the blank page. The kettle clicks in the kitchen. I hear the cupboard open and close. At least she's not just standing there. She's really making coffee, even if it is only for show, to make me wait.

I put the pad on the rickety brown table and go out to the

cupboard under the stairs. There's no light. The ceiling slopes down to nothing, so I'm on my knees in the dark, feeling through jackets and shoes till I find the soft velvet of Mam's long green coat, jammed under the hoover. I pull it loose and touch the velvet to my cheek, and a hook digs into the top of my head.

'Fuck,' I let the scream come loud.

I crawl back into the light, shaking out the dust and crumples, and smooth the coat with my hand. The belt's lost and there's dark patches on the shoulders where the softness has gone, and a long stain, like an arrow down the front. I want to go in the kitchen and put it on her, but I know she won't let me, so I hold the coat against the sloping wall and smooth it down, over, and over.

The doorbell goes. I stop with my hand on the coat. I can't turn round in case it's him. I'm not scared. Well, not much. If I was thinking, I'd know it wasn't. Daryl won't come back now. This is Mam's skint week, till giro day tomorrow, and anyway, Daryl's got a key. I turn the latch and Moira Kennedy's skinny pink arm shoots through the door with a two-litre bottle of Strongbow clutched in her scabby hand.

'See, Kazza. I never let me mates down,' she says, then she sees me, and the grin slides off her face like mud in the rain. 'Oh,' she says, and steps past me as if I don't even exist.

Mam's coat is tight in my fist. I make my fingers relax, and hang the coat over the cupboard door, then I wait till my breath gets normal before I follow her in.

They're both sitting at the rickety table, so I can see the back of Moira's electrocuted hair, and Mam's face, and that big bottle between them, on my art pad.

'Get us a couple of glasses, will you, love?' Mam grins at me like a brown-toothed kid.

My head goes fuzzy, so I can't think, so if they asked me my name, I wouldn't even know.

'Right, Mam.'

I find a glass and an Abba mug and take them through. Mam slops fizzy gold onto my pad.

That's all Mam wants. Her three quid bottle of cider. Three quid. I've got forty pounds in my back pocket, plus a tenner more in shrapnel, and I'd give her all of it just to get her out of the house. But then she wouldn't be coming for Benjy. Anyway, if she knew I had money, she'd only hassle me for it, and then she'd get pissed and tell Daryl.

'Haway, will you, Tommy.'

'Eh?' I look at Mam.

'Don't just stand there staring.'

'Right Mam,' I have to lift the bottle to get my pad, and I can feel Mam's eyes on me, see the tightness of her lips. I put the bottle down. Her lips relax.

'That look,' Mam says to Moira, talking like I'm not there.

'Like a wet weekend,' Moira says.

I press my hand over my mouth and stamp up the stairs.

'Enough to give you the creeps,' Moira says.

I lie on the bed and stare at the cider stain on my pad, smelling its stale sweetness. I draw a mouth around it, lips stretched wide, eyes narrowed to slits, then I rub them out and let them open wide with fear. I do soft blond curls, light as angel dust, and a pudgy chin sloping down to the neck of Benjy's Noddy pyjamas. There's an oblong of chipboard underneath him, and I'm doing this other hand, reaching out from the bottom of the page when I hear Moira's voice in the passage.

'I cannot, Pet, I cannot. Ah'm meeting our Michael at the Turbinia.'

The front door slams. I don't even care. I want to stay up here and draw, but I can't. I run down and get Mam's coat off the door handle and hold it while she puts it on. The buttons won't do up. She looks even more lumpy than normal, and I wish I'd just given her that baggy coat she always wears. At least it looks sunny outside. I've actually got the door open when she scuttles back through to the living room. I watch her through the doorway, necking the last half glass of cider, then she grabs her leopard skin handbag of the sofa and I pull her out of the house.

'You've got the card, Mam?'

'Don't hassle, man, Tommy.'

'Have you got -'

'Aye, aye, I've got it.'

She's a bit clumsy, but not really pissed, and we get all the way into town before she has to stop for a pee, at this posh pub called the Pitcher and Piano. I go in with her. The pub's about ten times as big as our house, and there's this hard-faced cow staring at us from behind the bar. Mam doesn't care. She goes round to the toilets while I stand at the far end of the bar and look through this massive window, at the new Millennium Bridge, and out across the river. Mam takes ages, like always. I find her, eventually, sitting on a bar stool with a glass in her hand.

'Just a quick one, Tommy. Just a half.'

I go to squeeze my thigh, but my fists are clenched tight. I press my fist over my mouth. Today especially, I know it's my job to take care of her. I try not to look at my watch, but it's gone three, closer to half past by the time we finally get to the station. We're still out in the bit where the taxis are when Mam goes off ahead.

'I'll just nip and get some wine gums,' she says, wobbling away from me. 'You check the trains.'

I don't see why we can't get them together, but at least she's remembered about wine gums. Maybe everything'll be okay. So, it's not twelve o'clock, but Benjy won't know. We'll have wine gums and write the card on the train, then we'll post it together and let go at the same moment. I think of when I was a little kid, with me and Mam pushing the letter through the slot together, and her explaining how we have to post it in Sunderland so The Social don't know where we are, so they don't come for me too. That felt so scary, thinking that they might get me. But now, I'm trying not to wish, more than anything else in the world, that they had.

"Back at the Star Wars Café," Mam used to say, and it made me laugh every time, walking in under the big arches and seeing all the weird sorts of people that you'd never see together anywhere else. Like this woman with a little round hat and a matching dress as if she's the Queen, and all these lasses in 'Hayley's Hen Weekend' t-shirts coming past her, so it looks like she's with them.

One of the lasses trips over this trampy bloke sitting against a pillar. He's really old, with a pointy beard and a squashy hat, like Guy Fawkes or something. He doesn't look at me, but he rattles his cup. A tankard, that's what you call it, with *Northumberland Fusiliers* written across it, and this big gold emblem underneath. .

'Spare a few shillings for an old soldier,' he says, with his fingers all twisted and purpley around the metal handle, like Frank in the hospital.

I don't even know what a shilling is, but I know there's a load of pound coins jingling in my pocket. I jam a handful in his silver cup. He stares at them, then looks up at me with these watery eyes, so pale I can see right through to the light behind them.

'You sure, son?' he says, but the tankard's already gone, hidden under his crappy coat.

I nod anyway, and walk on into the station, and I'm thinking, fuckin hell, I've just chucked a tenner away, and I don't even care.

'Spare a few shillings for an old soldier,' I hear his voice behind me, and I can't help smiling. I bet he's got a thousand quid stuffed away in that coat.

The next train to Sunderland is from platform one, which is right in front of me. I stop where I am, in the middle of the station, and wait for Mam to come out of the shop. For once, she doesn't take ages.

'Mam, over here,' I walk towards her, smiling, and then I see the cellophane shining on the card in her hand. I run the last few steps, but by the time I get to her the card's gone, in her bag or her pocket, and she's looking at me with her eyes wide open, like she's never done anything wrong in her life.

'Where's the wine gums?'

'Eh?'

'The wine gums you went to get.'

'Whah? Where's the train?'

I look at her for ages, but she just looks right back, and I can't help seeing how blank her eyes are, how there's nothing behind them at all.

'Platform one,' I say, walking across towards it and sitting on this wooden bench.

Mam sits beside me. I turn my face away, but I can hear the crinkle of the cellophane in her hand, then she's got the biro from her bag, and I know she's going to start writing it, like she's too pissed to remember we're supposed to do it together, on the train, after we've talked about what to say. Or like she just doesn't care.

'Stop,' I'm thinking, trying not to hear the pen scratch. But I can't say. My finger and thumb are tight on the inside of my thigh. I keep my eyes on the metal tracks till she puts the card in my lap.

There's a boat on the front, and a man inside with a long stick. *Venezia*, it says, on the front, and inside she's written: *Happy birthday. Love ya. Loads of love, Mam.* She hasn't even put Benjy's name, or that he's fifteen today, but that isn't what makes me feel sick. There's two words already printed on the other side of the card in big curly letters: *Happy Anniversary.*

I stare at the words, breathing like I've just sprinted the four hundred metres. Benjy's fifteen and she doesn't even care. I think of him cuddling in and try to find that glow inside me, like when I woke up this morning. But Mam's right. The real Benjy doesn't exist anymore. He's got nothing to do with some fifteen-year-old lad that I don't even know. Some kid who's probably got his own PlayStation, and a normal Mam and Dad that only get pissed and radgy on Saturday nights.

I give the card back to Mam and watch her pen scratch across the envelope. That weird name: c/o Mrs. Abuto Palacios, at Social Services, then she puts the card inside, not even looking at it, not even seeing that I haven't written anything.

The tannoy announces that the next train arriving at platform one is the 3:45 to Sunderland. I can hear it coming with this echoey rush that makes me want to scream. Mam gets up, holding the envelope flat across her chest. It's that noise that makes me do it. I snatch the envelope out of her hand.

'You fat fuckin piss-head,' I rip the envelope in half. 'You let him do whatever he fuckin likes,' I tear it again.

The third time it won't rip properly, just bends, and I throw the pieces out across the track, and watch them floating down.

I could jump after them, fall in front of the train, and make all the noise stop. Or push Mam instead. Maybe she feels it cos she steps back, and the train comes roaring in before the bits of card have even hit the line.

Mam says some crap that I can't even hear.

'Ya dirty cunting liar,' I scream with the noise of the train, and stamp away through the giant arches.

The tramp's still there against his pillar. He looks up at me, and I think he's going to say thanks or something, but he just rattles his cup in his filthy hands.

'Spare a few shillings for an old soldier,' he says, like I'm no one, like he's already forgotten me, the greedy, ungrateful piece of shit.

I stare at his cup with that fizz like shaken up coke in my head, and a plastic cheesy taste in my mouth. '*Northumberland Fusiliers*,' it says, in gold on the silver tankard, and there's this unfuckinbelievable picture underneath. A man on a horse, pushing his spear into a dragon. My left foot lands on the slippery tile floor, level with his cup.

'Get a fuckin job, you lazy twat.'

My right swings down. I catch it perfectly, following through, sending the cup spinning up under the domed ceiling with coins clattering down, ratatatat, like a machine gun on the tiles.

He shouts something behind me. I walk faster. There's other people shouting. I look round, casual, like I'm not scared, and I'm fuckin not. There's money all over. A couple of charver kids in white trackies race around trying to pick it up. So what? It's not his money.

'Ya hairy scrounging cunt,' I bite down on the last word and my blood roars like that train. I'm not scared of anyone. I'm buzzing, hard as fuckin masonry nails, with the plastic taste of the future sweet in my mouth.

Chapter Seventeen

A Bad'n

We're all in the sitting room with ten cans of Strongbow lined up on the carpet, still held together in their plastic rings, and three empties, bent over like worn out old men. The telly's on, but nobody's watching. Daryl's lying on the sofa with a can on his chest, and his ugly long toes that look like fingers, hooked on the arm of Mam's chair. I'm sitting at the wobbly table behind them, so all I can see is the top of her waspy head, and the hunch of her shoulders when she bends to take a drink. She's about halfway down the second can, just getting to that stage where she knows everything.

'There's some people you don't want to be getting involved with,' she says, shaking her head at the telly.

You should know. You stupid cow. That's what I want to say, but the glistening red on Daryl's lip helps me hold it in. I press the can to my mouth. My weight goes back, tilting the wooden chair up on two legs. The chair creaks. I keep it balanced, with one hand on the doorhandle, and take a long drink.

'How d'you think I got the money for the cans?' I tell her, like an idiot, even though I'm supposed to keep my mouth shut.

'I don't care,' Mam says. 'He's a bad'n, that Maxi Blair.'

'He works at school,' I say, like it makes any difference. 'And he's never been done for anything.'

'Right,' Mam says. 'He's never been done. But what about the lads that work for him? That Paul Conway got six months in

Durham. His Melanie was in the Black Boar, crying her eyes out, eight months gone and big as a balloon.'

'Mam, he's got nowt to do with Maxi, and he's twenty, at least. I'm not sixteen till Thursday. Even if I did get done, I'd just have to paint the underpass or something.'

Aye,' she says, 'but once you get a record ...'

Daryl belches for about five full seconds. Mam stops talking. Rain spatters on the window, and the man on the telly says we should get down to Allied Carpets while stocks last.

'Here we go,' he says, talking to the cracks on the ceiling. 'Mrs. fuckin know it all.'

'Well,' Mam says. 'He should be going to college.'

Me and Daryl both laugh at that.

'It's August, Mam,' I say.'

'Well, you should be applying. Somewhere that'll let you do your exams again.'

I stare at the ridges on the table.

'Fuckin exams, blah-de-fuckin blah. Ah've looked after that bairn since he was a babbie. Tret him like my own. And now he's bringing a few quid into the house, you want to fuck it up.' Daryl taps his finger on the side of his head. 'Are ye fuckin stupid,' he says, biting down on the last word.

'Yeh,' I say, thinking about Daryl, and my eight failed GCSE's. 'Fuckin stupid?'

'Good lad,' Daryl says.

'Least I'm not ignorant,' Mam says, in her pathetic sulky voice.

'And I am?' The can cracks in Daryl's hand. 'Think you're something special? Miss Evening Chronicle 1983, with you five fuckin "O" levels. But where's it got you, eh? Look at yourself. You stupid fuckin alky.'

Daryl grins at me like he wants me to laugh. I take a long

pull from my can. He does the same, like we're mates, then he pushes his feet against Mam's chair till he's sitting up, with his finger pointing at me. I can see his tattoo, that snake tail winding down his forearm, and I can tell. He knows everything too, and he wants to share.

'They're not like us, lasses.'

I let my chair thump down onto all four legs. He doesn't even notice.

'You can't trust them, but I'll tell you what. It's not their fault.' He shakes his head like I'm arguing with him, like I give a toss what he says. 'Nah, it's not. Like imagine if you were the wimpiest lad in school, which you practically fuckin are, right?' He laughs, and I do a super slow fake laugh right back. 'Haway, son, I'm kidding. But say if you were, then you'd have to be sly. Wouldn't have a choice, would you? Eh?'

'You shouldn't talk like that,' Mam says.

She's slid so low in the chair it's like she's disappeared. And she has, the real Mam, the one who danced in the kitchen and had that magic power in her eyes. He's beaten it out of her. Now I understand that's how real life works. Like if the Slytherins had given Harry Potter a good enough kicking at the start, that would've been that.

'Ah don't mean being fast, like when you were a bairn,' Daryl says, 'reminded me of myself, to be honest, always getting into things, slipping away before shit hit the fan. Not like that other one, sat there like a tart. Aye,' he says, sucking at his drink. 'I did you a favour there. I mean a dead weight…'

My can goes down. Cider froths over the table. I'm out of the chair and round in front of the telly with Daryl still shitting on, and Mam staring at this half-eaten Jaffa cake under the radiator. I get down on my knees and pull a new can out of its plastic loop, feeling the weight of it in my hands. I stare at the thick yellow hairs on Daryl's toes. The telly's going behind me. Some advert about nappies. Babies laughing. Like babies ever laugh in real life.

My finger runs around the rim of the can. I feel the ridge of it. Daryl looks down at me. The veins are up on his neck, gold earring swinging, mouth going, finger jabbing at Mam, or me. The same. I lean back, up on my knees, like I'm as small as that little kid hiding in the kitchen cupboard, too scared to breathe. The can slips in my hand. I hold tighter and watch the cider swill around his mouth.

'Are you stupid,' I say, to no one, seeing my can slam into that big black hole of his mouth, taking his teeth with it, jamming them down his throat.

I'm going to do it, beat the wickedness out of him. I bring the can up, cold against my cheek. Mam's there, at the edge of what I can see. She's staring at me, with her face blurring red and blue and green. Her head moves about a millimetre each side. She knows what I'm thinking. I nod, a millimetre up and down. Her eyes get wider. Her palm comes up beside her face, fingers stretched tight.

How, I think. *White man speak with forked tongue.*

I lift the can high over my head, and throw it at the wall.

'Ya cunt,' Daryl says.

The can bounces and lands on the crappy table. Beer sprays like piss onto the carpet. I don't even look at him, but I let my hand accidentally brush through Mam's crinkly hair. I walk past her, out of the room, and I know, I'm never going back. I look at Daryl's stupid photo for the last time, him sitting on that bike with his hair hanging down over his Sunderland shirt, like he thinks James Dean was a hairy Mackem. I laugh at that. It's only after I close the front door that I think of Benjy's Noddy pyjama-top, and all Dad's stuff, still up there under my bed. But so what? A kid I don't even know, and a load of old videos from some bloke who pissed off before I even knew him.

And anyway, Dads are for puffs.

The pavement's dark, but the rain's stopped, and there's a sort of heaviness in the air that gets into my head. I stare up at the blue clouds, and think of Mam's wide eyes talking to me, telling me not to hit him. Maybe she was right. He isn't worth it, but there's still that jittery feel of held back punches in my arms. I walk faster. The clouds turn orange over towards the town, like the colour of Emily Tiverton's hair, like the orangey smell of her.

It's two days before my sixteenth birthday and I'm bouncing over the pavement, feeling wired, but good, as if my body's made of air. Tonight, is going to be special, and nothing Daryl says is going to matter anymore.

My feet go on their own, like I'm crossing the plains and there's no one around, just the sand and the sun, and you don't even need to think, cos your horse knows the way. I don't know where I've come to till I'm there, up on Shields Road, staring in through the Raby's plate-glass window.

Hoola's behind the bar like always, with that half-smile scar curling up towards her shaved head. There's a few old boys down the long end of the bar, but just one on the short end. He's sat on his stool, leaning back against the pillar with his bottle of Brown and his half pint glass in front of him, and his pockets bulging with cellophane wraps. Maxi lifts his sweaty face towards me.

I'm well early, but he hooks his finger at me through the glass and smiles with his piggy mouth. I walk into the bar.

'Pint for the lad,' he says to Hoola.

'Cheers, Maxi,' I say. 'Alright, Hoola?'

'Alright, Flower?' She smiles at me with half her face. 'Carlsberg?'

'Probably,' I say, and she laughs like it's not the millionth time I've said it.

She pours the pint with just a thin froth on the top and puts a bag of nuts down on the soggy beer towel.

'On the house,' she says. 'Just so long as you eat them.'

'Thanks, Hoola,' I say, but she's already away to the other end of the bar with a flush of colour on the back of her neck.

'There you go, son,' Maxi hands me two plastic money bags bulging with home-grown Walker skunk.

'Ta.'

I put one in each pocket of my jeans. I don't need to look at them to know I've got five twenty quid deals in each bag. That's two hundred quid. A hundred and sixty for Maxi, and forty for me. But it's better than that. I've got another four empty coin bags in my back pocket. A little bit from each wrap gives me four more deals, one for me, and three for profit. All the lads do it. Maxi doesn't care, so long as he gets his money.

'Another one?' Hoola asks, nodding at Maxi's empty bottle.

'Later,' he says, putting both hands on the bar and heaving himself off the stool. 'I'm away for me dinner. If the other lads get in, I'm up at Maccy Dee's,' he waves a hand at me and Hoola. 'Back in a bit.'

'Aye,' she says. 'Just make sure you look out for Tommy.'

Maxi doesn't answer. It makes me think of what Mam was saying before, about Paul Conway, and that night in Maxi's kitchen after Conway got lifted, and I got promoted.

'You do the job,' he said, with his belly hanging over his

boxers and the sausages spitting in the pan. 'Anything goes wrong, mind; you don't know anything about me,' he pointed the spatula at me, grease flying. 'Nothing.'

'Right, Maxi. Nothing.'

'Nothing.' He grunted, and went back to prodding his sausages. 'If they ask, but only if they say my name, you can tell them I'm the bus driver from school.'

I take my time with the pint. The bar starts filling up, but none of the lads come in, so I guess I may as well go down to Jesmond and get started. I do this student bar they call The Lynch. Maxi reckons its perfect for me cos of my innocent face, and my lucky eye. That's what he calls it. It's weird up there, like walking into some different world. This massive bar full of crappy old shit they'd even have thrown out of here. Chairs made out of reeds, and tables like ours at home, and what's even weirder is there's these pictures on the wall of this lass that looks just like Mam before she started on the drink, when she could have had anyone she wanted, and she chose Daryl 'ya cunt' Boyle.

'Cheers, Hoola,' I say. 'Catch you later.'

'Aye. So long as they don't catch you first.'

I flash her a smile and this weird thought pops into my head. I wonder what it'd be like to have Hoola as a mam?

I turn away from the bar and see that they've re-covered the pool table since Gemma put the cue through the baize. The smile gets heavy on my face. I pull my eyes away from the perfect green surface, and step into the familiar smell of piss and disinfectant, trying to catch what's left of that buzzy feeling I had walking down here. Come on, Tommy, I tell myself, you've got the easiest job in the world, a hundred quid a night for sitting in a posh bar and having a pint. I just have to look out for the hairy students, ones with Rasta t-shirts, Bob Marley smoking a big fat joint, like they're just asking to get lifted. It really is a piece of piss. I smile to myself, watching my spray bounce off the porcelain. It doesn't make any sense that I feel like shit.

Chapter Eighteen

The Byker Wall

Both the cubicles are empty. There's just this one hippy kid over by the sinks, poncing about with his blue streaked hair; and there's me, staring at the chipped urinal with, *suck my plums*, scrawled across it in red felt tip. I'm zipping up by the time the kid goes out. The door doesn't close. I hear the noise from the bar, and this screechy, radgy voice that raises the hair under my collar.

'Haway man, ya blue-headed cunt. Fuckin move.'

The hippy kid mumbles something. The door swings shut, and Frogga's footsteps come slapping across the tiles. I stare at the red felt tip and wait for him to go into one of the cubicles, to start pissing, for someone to come in. For anything.

'Aye, aye,' he says, in a sing-song voice that bounces off the walls. 'Eye, eye, Bandit Boy,' and I can hear the grin in his voice, like every bastard day at school.

'What are yee deein in here then, puftah? Waiting for a shag?'

He comes round my blind side, a blur at the edge of my vision, so close I can feel his rancid breath on my hair.

'Look at me when I'm talking to yah, arse-Bandit.'

I'm not that kid anymore. That's finished. I'm working for Maxi now, doing a job, getting paid. I'm not scared of this lanky piece of shit. Move, I tell myself, but I can't turn around. My legs won't stop shaking. All I can do is stare at that red felt-tip.

'I said...' his knuckles jam in the back of my neck, jolting my face against the wall, clearing the blockage in my head.

I turn, keeping going, spinning like Billy friggin Elliot. There's no strength in my arm, but there's momentum. My fist cracks against his bony face, standing him up in a hot burst of blood. His eyes open wider. I swing back around. The door creaks. I catch a glimpse of Klepto's spindly legs, feet turning, running back out, and I bury my fist in Frogga's kidneys. He squeals and falls sideways into the open cubicle. I follow him in.

I can hear Klepto shouting out in the bar, but I don't give a toss. I've got a handful of Frogga's crappy wire wool hair, and this has been coming for too long to let go now. I smash his head into the shitty yellow toilet bowl, two, three times. And then I'm gone, out into the crowded bar, wiping my hands on my jeans.

I keep my back to the wall, edging past the lasses' toilets, heading for the open door. I'm just by Maxi's pillar when my face goes cold. Carl Burns is on the other side of the pool table. He's heading straight for the bogs, jaw pushed out in his square, bulldog face. I grab the pillar, not sure if I'm hiding or just holding myself up. He keeps coming, dragging this dark-haired lass behind him. I'm freezing cold, sweating, but I make myself wait. He passes so close I can smell him, see the dying dragon on his sovereign ring.

I get my head down, watching the cracks on the painted floor, edging across to the far wall. My hip bangs against a table. Some radgy snarls at me through sharp, yellow teeth. I look away, staring at the flashing lights on the bandit, stopped there like a moron with the white noise screaming in my head.

A gust of warm air blows in from the street, carrying the smell of petrol and freedom, bringing me back to life. It pulls me round the bandit and past these two baldy blokes in the doorway. I've got one foot on the step, and the other out on the pavement. I'm that close, when he reaches between the baldies and gets a grip on my collar. My t-shirt pulls tight against my throat. There's half a second before I turn around, screaming in my head, ready to puke all over him. But it's not Carl, it's the lass who was with him. Silver bangles jangle on her wrist.

'Haway, man,' one of the baldies grumbles, but he moves, and the lass is looking right at me, with eyes like the darkest chocolate you can get.

'Tommy Boyle.'

'Fuckin hell. Annie Cherani,' I'm dizzy, buzzing with fear. 'Look, I've gotta run. I've just bounced Frogga's head off the porcelain.'

'You mad bastard.' She smiles at me, that same dozy, dimpley smile, from years ago, that first time we ever went on the knock.

'That Flake was lush,' I say, but she's turned away, back through the bar.

I follow her eyes, over the top of the baldy heads, to Carl Burns' massive shoulders banging through the bog door.

'Get out of my fuckin way,' he shouts, and Frogga's bloody face comes leering out behind him.

'Aye, well. See yah,' and I'm out into the dusk, running across towards Tantastic.

I should keep going on down Shields Road, but I look back, just for half a second, cos I have to see if that dozy smile's still on her face. And it only is, right up close to mine.

'Haway, Tommy man, you soft get,' she grabs my hand and pulls me down Raby Street, laughing her mental head off.

She's fast as fuck, legging it over the cobbles and the zebra crossing. We cut through the Metro and onto this stone bridge, the whole thing shaking with all the lorries roaring along underneath.

We're nearly at the other side when there's a gap in the traffic, and I hear Frogga's voice behind us.

'Arse bandit,' he screams. 'You're fuckin dead.'

He runs across the cobbles with blood all down his face, and Carl Burns two steps behind him.

'Fuck you, Chester.'

I flick him the vees, but it's a mistake. My foot catches Annie's.

'Annie…'

She falls against me. Her sandal goes skidding across the stone. The breath stops in my throat. My legs start to go, but Annie doesn't give a toss. She bounces off me, running again, laughing and spluttering like that dodgy tap. She kicks out, sending her other sandal up into the air ahead of us. I watch it turn, silver and gold against the dark blue clouds. And another lorry comes roaring in.

We jump the metal barrier together. Her plaits whip my face. I catch the smell of peaches, and we're over the other side, through the Raby Gate, and away into the Byker Wall with my cheeks still tingling from the whip of her hair. We run close, breathing hard in the hot night. I feel the sweat between our palms, and the flimsy nothingness of her dress brushes against the back of my hand.

I know they're going to kill me, but they'll have to catch me first, and they never will, not in this maze. We're running down towards the river, past a wooden fence, when I hear Carl shout. It isn't even a word, but he's close. Annie lights up under a streetlight, dress high on her long brown legs. Then she disappears.

I stumble another step, alone.

'Fuckin Bandit,' I hear Frogga's panting voice, his feet thudding closer.

An arm jerks out of the darkness, grabbing my hair, pulling me through the broken fence. A hand clamps across my mouth, and Frogga's footsteps fade away down the hill.

Annie's breath is hot on my neck, her hair soft on my cheek, her body tight against mine. I hold her, searching for the smell at her throat. She pulls away, but her hand is on my shirt, tearing, dragging me off the fence. She walks backwards over this square of grass and stops. My hands go out around her, feeling the cracked bark of this massive tree behind. I press in.

'No,' she whispers, breath gushing in my ear.

Her hand slides inside my shirt, holding me back, drawing me forward. I can see the softness in her eyes, that fat line of concentration down her forehead, lit up under the orange streetlight. Her lip lifts, showing me a flash of teeth. I feel her heart hammer. Her lips are wet and sweet, her tongue hot and strong. Her knee presses in between my thighs. All that's left between us is her flimsy dress.

Her hand moves down, fingers scalding across my stomach, working the button on my jeans, pulling the zip. I groan. She laughs, holding me, rough and clumsy, guiding me up under that scrap of dress. Her body opens. My breath catches. Her arms fold around me, sending blue sparks up my spine.

I'm stoned, and pissed, and flying. I don't hear their feet pounding back up the slope. How could I? Her arms pull me closer. Her body draws me deeper. I don't know where I end, where she begins. I don't care.

Her eyes close and her nose wrinkles, like that time at her mam's, with her ten years old in her mam's red bra with that big knot tied at the back, and her hair sticking out like a chimney sweep, and me trying not to laugh.

I'm laughing now, sucking in that peachy smell, laughing at

myself for thinking I loved some red-haired girl I didn't even know. But I know this one. I know the things she's done, and the things they did to her. My hands slide high on her silky thighs, feeling the memory of those bruises, taking me back to her Mam's red duvet and secrets in the dark. Daryl and the finger game, and how he's back in the house, like always, and Mam's back on the vodka, and at the bottom of it all there's my baby brother, not saying a word while that hairy hand lifted him away from me. And I let him go.

I'm shaking now, like I might never stop, tasting my tears on her perfect throat.

'It's alright, Tommy, I've got you,' she says, strong and certain, with her arms tight around me.

The sob that bursts out of me is way too loud, but all I can hear is the rush and draw of her breath, and the blood beating in my ears. There's only the heat of her pulsing around me, and the salty sweet taste of her neck under that beautiful scrunched-up face. Frogga and Carl don't exist. They never did. Not even when their bodies slam against the fence behind me. Not even when their bright white trainers drop onto the spiky grass.

2008

Chapter Nineteen

Take It Easy

My hand tooled Lucchese cowboy boot squeezes down on the pedal and the boxy red Volvo hurtles on up the Coast Road with the sun bright on the windscreen and warm air blowing through the open window. The car might be an old wreck, but at least the colour hides the rust growing out of the wheel arches, and if the engine makes a bit of noise, so what? The sound system's louder, a pimped-up Sony XAV.

I'm far enough out of Walker to feel safe. No one's going to see me here, so I switch to my secret playlist, crank up the volume, and the best advice I ever heard comes belting out of the speakers.

'Take it eeeeasy, take it eeeeasy…'

I sing along with the Eagles, letting it go, screaming into the wind, and by the time I get back to town I've got Desperado croaking out around me, sad and slow and true. Maybe I should listen to the words, but I kill the music, roll up the window and take the Walker turnoff. There's work to do.

I'm looking for this blond kid they call Louis Solomon, wears a black hoody and jeans, which narrows it down to about every other kid in Walker. It helps that he hangs around outside the Black Boar. I come down Walker Road, crawling past the pub. There's three kids sitting on the fence, legs stretched out, passing a can between them. Sharing spit. They nudge each other, faces lifting. Two little dark-haired lads laughing like Ant and Dec, and this gangly kid on the end, with electric blond hair sprouting from under his black hoody.

He doesn't look much to me, but there's got to be a fair chance that this is the lad Peeler wants, and Peeler knows the score. I've been working with him for years, practically since I started with Maxi, and I don't take anything for granted, but he's never let me down yet. Plus, he still lives on Pottery Bank, where it all happens. So, if Peeler says we need this kid, that's good enough for me.

I pull up twenty yards down the road and reach across the passenger seat for my crumpled leather jacket, a genuine 1880's steersman with bone buttons, that came all the way from Colorado. I breathe in the smell of it. Twenty different shades move in the light, from soft chocolate to the same dark ruby as my Lucchese boots. I take my time getting out of the car, pull my jacket on and walk back towards them.

I don't need to look to know they're watching me.

Hips rolling, I fix my eyes on the pub's red-brick chimney stack and let my heels scrape on the road. The shoulder vamps are hidden in my jeans, but my burnished toecaps flash in the sunlight, my signature mark. Sure, the lads take the piss out of me, marching around Walker like Clint Eastwood, but there's a reason behind it. People remember red cowboy boots. They know who I am. I speak for Maxi Blair, with Eddie Burns' big angry shadow looming up behind us.

Ant drains the can. He crushes it and throws it down in front of me. I make out like I haven't noticed, like I'm going into the pub. The blond kid's foot is tapping in time to some tune in his head, shit-brand trainers drumming on the pavement. He lets his foot brush my ankle. I step past him, getting a good look at his white, freckled face, and I hear another sound beneath his drumming foot, the steady click-clack of his tongue.

'You Louis Solomon?'

'Maybe.'

I give him my innocent look. 'Don't you know?'

Dec snorts. 'Who are you, like?'

'That's Farrier,' Ant says. 'Works for Maxi Blair.'

'My name's Tommy,' I tell them, but I keep my eyes on Blondie. 'The talk is you've been dealing in The Boar.'

He ducks his head. His lip twitches.

'So, have you?'

'I can do what I want.'

I have to smile at that. That he doesn't even have the sense to deny it.

'Course you can't,' I tell him, leaning in with my hand on the wooden rail. 'Because my lads sell down there, and my lads are Maxi's lads, which means they're Eddie Burns' lads.'

He shrugs like he couldn't care less and steps up off the fence, this great lanky kid a head taller than me. I know what I should do now, what Maxi would say. "Give him a couple of slaps. Let him know what's what." But his lips are a tight white line, and his face is a shade whiter, with the freckles standing out across his nose. Anyone can see he's just a scared kid playing it cool in front of his mates.

'Look,' I turn sideways, giving him a good look at my dodgy eye. 'You know who Eddie Burns is?'

He doesn't answer, but then it's not really a question. I'm just giving him the chance to remember what he's heard. Eddie Burns who walked into The Grace last Christmas and stood everyone a pint, Eddie Burns who's done a lot of other things too.

'Well, Eddie wants you on the team.'

'What for?'

'What for? Don't be thick. To give you a bit of protection, the chance to make some real money. So come on, get in the car.'

He steps back, hands tight on the fence.

'We're not going to sort it out here. Get in the car, and I'll tell you the score.'

'Farrier's alright,' Ant says.

'That's the truth,' I say, getting an arm around Louis' shoulder, leading him up towards the car. 'Look man, Louis, Alan Sugar's not going to come looking for apprentices round here, but Eddie Burns wants to give you a chance.' I open the passenger door and ease him down into the seat. 'Do yourself a favour, don't fuck it up.'

'Eddie knows about me?'

'Sure, he does.'

I slam the door and get round my side, revving the engine and dropping the clutch before he gets any bright ideas.

'Eddie was pissed off,' I tell him, 'about you dealing in one of his bars.'

'I was just in the bar like, and this lass asked us–'

'Alright, I know how it goes. Nothing's going to happen. I'm not even asking who you were buying off. You did a deal for this lass, then there's a few of her mates, and then a load more. You're making a few quid and you're getting excited because you want it all today, so you can pay for your pills, and your X-box, and maybe get yourself some decent trainers.'

He gives me a look.

I shrug and give him one back.

'But you're going nowhere. So, listen. You can go on doing ten quid deals on your own, standing on people's toes, getting into bother with the likes of Eddie Burns. Or you can be part of something, get protection and still make the money, and maybe one day you'll have enough to get out of this shithole.'

That gets me thinking. Where does it all go? I mean, it's not like I'm lighting my own supply. Okay, the boots and the jacket, and the rent isn't cheap either, but mostly I don't even know. The money comes in, and it goes out, and I have a good time. Isn't that what it's for? Having a laugh, having fun. Whatever that is?

Problem is, I'm better at convincing other people that I am at believing my own bullshit.

'This is the easiest job you're ever going to get. We give you the gear. You go where we tell you. You sell what we tell you. You hand over the cash, and you keep your mouth shut. You start off working with a friend of mine, and if Peeler likes you, you're in, sorted, on the road to somewhere.'

I'm just driving anywhere, up past the Roman fort, switching my attention between Louis and the road. I can tell he's taking it in, but he still doesn't speak, just pushes his hood back off his hair and starts that clicking with his tongue. I look across at his freckly face and my fingers come up over my lips, hiding a smile.

'You're that little kid, always kicking your soggy ball against the wall on the corner of Sandy Crescent.'

'I know who you are,' he says. 'Used to hang out with that Paki lass.'

'Indian.'

'Eh?'

'Annie Cherani. She was Indian, well, half-Indian.'

'Yeh, okay,' he says, picking up on my tone. 'She was dead canny though, with the chocolate and that.'

'Yeh, she was.' The words come scratching up the back of my throat, angry enough to make him look, then he leans forward and turns on the sound system.

'Cheeky twat,' I say, but it's too late. Desperado comes blasting out of the speakers.

I turn it down.

'My mam's got this,' he says.

I roll my eyes up past the saggy sun visor, and think of Mam dancing in the kitchen, with this same song squeaking out of the tape-deck. She's still there, I suppose. With him. Not that she's dancing anymore. You need to be able to stand up before you can dance.

'So, what can you do for us?' I stretch out, pushing myself back in the seat. 'What are you good at?'

'I can tell if the gear's any good,' he says. 'A couple off any joint and I'll tell you what's in it.'

'Okay, what else?'

'I can tell when people are lying,' I look at him sideways and his lip twitches again, till there's half a lopsided smile. 'I can.'

'Alright, I believe you. So, open the glove box.' He looks at me. 'There, that thing in front of you,' I reach across and do it for him. 'Right. That's your work phone.'

'This,' he pulls out the ten-year-old Motorola, with the charger attached.

'Yes, that, and don't twist your face. It's not for downloading sounds or taking pictures, it's for work, and it's got my number in, and Peeler's. I'm TT and Peeler's PP. You leave it like that. You don't put anyone else in unless we tell you. You don't use it for anything but work. You don't lose it. And rule number one that you will always, always follow, is if that phone rings, you answer. I don't care if you're about to lose your cherry to Cheryl Tweedy, you answer that phone.'

'Alright, alright.'

'No. Not, "alright, alright". This is serious,' I spell it out, giving him the exact same shit Maxi gave me seven years ago. 'You take care of us, and we'll take care of you, but this isn't school.

You screw up, you don't get a rap on the knuckles,' I pull over so I can look him full in the face, let him see mine. 'I promise you. You don't want to piss off the Burns Gang.'

I turn the music off and we drive back down to Walker with just the sound of the tyres humming on the tarmac, and the engine grunting, and him clicking his tongue. We're past the Boar, and I know what's coming next, Atwal's big blue sign on the corner of Belmont Street, with the police camera that never works, and half bricks lying in the road, and all those mean-eyed bastards sitting on their front steps getting pissed, shouting the odds at anyone who looks at them.

No way I'm going down there. I'm out of that shit and I'm never going back, whatever happens at Eddie's place tomorrow.

'You alright,' Louis says, leaning into my space.

'Yes man, don't fuckin crowd me.' My hand comes up, pushing him away. His head bounces off the window. 'Shut up,' I tell him, even though he hasn't said anything. 'You just worry about the shit you're going to land yourself in if you're not very fuckin careful.'

Thing is, I'm really talking to myself.

I get past Belmont and turn down onto Evistone Gardens. Black iron railings run the length of the street, with new-ish red-brick houses set back behind squares of grass, every one the same. I pull up outside Peeler's flat, walk round, and open the passenger door.

'Alright, Louis, come and meet your boss.' He looks up at me like I'm a dog that bit him.

'Oh, come on.' I nudge some rust off the wheel arch, it's not really a kick. 'I'm sorry.'

Louis clicks his tongue and grins. 'Head-case,' he says, but he gets out of the car.

'Go on,' I point at Peeler's cracked plastic door. 'He's

expecting you.'

'Are you not...'

'Take it easy, Lou,' I tell him. 'You're going to be alright.'

I watch him up the path, till Peeler's door opens and I catch a glimpse of those sticky-out ears.

'I've got a good feeling about you, Louis,' I shout, then I pump up the volume and press my foot to the floor. And it's true, I really do have a good feeling about Louis Solomon. I've got a good feeling about everything. So long as I keep the music playing and the money coming, so long as I don't go back down Belmont Street, so long as I keep on flying and never look down.

Chapter Twenty

The Wedding Anniversary

Maxi and me are downstairs at The Hammer, this big open bar with a raised dancefloor and a marble staircase that curves up to an indoor balcony. The place is normally lit in this pinkish dusk with silk sheets hanging off the balcony rail, so it looks like the sort of boozer Aladdin might've bought after he found his genie. But Aladdin didn't buy it. Eddie Burns did. That's why we're sitting here, shitting ourselves, waiting to see exactly how pissed off Eddie's going to be, and what he's going to do about it.

The lights are way too bright, every one turned up full, all except the red ones on the dancefloor. They've taken the poles out too, which I suppose they would, Eddie's wedding anniversary being a family do. The thing is though, Eddie was married for years and there was never any big deal about it until his wife, Donna, died last September, run over right outside their house, and now there's this big party for their anniversary.

Make sense of that?

There's loads of people up on the balcony, looking down and laughing, making my neck itch. I risk a glance. Salim stares straight back at me, Frogga's little cutter with his child's body and his pretty girl's face. He gives me his wide, closed-mouth smile and pats the pocket on his made-to-measure jacket. He's telling me he's got his switchblade in there. I know that's just his idea of a laugh, but the kid creeps me out. I hold his look for three long seconds, take a mouthful of lager and squeeze my itchy eyes.

I've been awake since five this morning thinking about how Carl Burns is bound to be here, and if Carl is, then so is Frogga, with all his hangers-on. So what? It'll be just like all the other times. We'll look straight past each other like we've never met. No big deal. Business comes first. But my palms keep sweating and there's this burn high up in my stomach, and I don't even know if it's because of Carl and Frogga, or because of Maxi being such a screwup. Either way, all I want is to get out of here, back to the flat and down in the cellar, with my dark little secrets, and the hatch locked tight over the throbbing pain in my head.

'Tommy, man. Stop picking your fuckin leg,' Maxi says, rocking back on his bar stool just like the Raby in the old days, except this isn't the Raby, and it isn't the old days.

I clench my teeth and keep my mouth shut, smoothing down the leg on my new suit trousers, with one eye on the dark wool blend, and the other on Maxi. He's always liked his burgers, but the state of him now, arse spilling over the sides of his zebra-print bar stool. I've been carrying him for years, and the more I do for him, the nastier he gets.

"Don't get high on your own supply."

Maxi told me that seven years ago, but his hair's sticking up in sad grey tufts and his pink cracked eyes are buried somewhere in his puffy cheeks. He's wasted. It stands out like a dick on a stripper. God knows what's rattling around inside him. Pills to get up, green to chill out, and pills to get up again. He's like an alcoholic Alice in Wonderland sucking on his third pint in the last half an hour, just to stop himself from falling over. It's scary watching him, and for half a second, I almost understand. Maybe Maxi's right to hate me, because without me bringing in the cash, he'd never have been able to pack in driving that school bus, and he'd still have something to hold him together.

He came up short with Eddie's money twice last month, and then just on Friday a group of the lads heard him shouting his mouth off in Peggie Sue's Bar, trying to impress that gawky lass from the bank. Talking business, mentioning names. Eddie's pissed off. Everyone knows, even Maxi. That tells you how bad it is. And what's worse is, if Maxi goes down, he takes me with him.

I'm not really looking, just following Maxi's line of sight up to the balcony. Eddie Burns is up there with his mouth wide open in his big, bearded face. He's laughing.

'At least he seems in a good mood,' I say, like an idiot.

'Listen man, Tommy,' Maxi leans in. I can smell the sweat on him. 'You better hope he's not laughing when we get in there. Just keep your smart mouth shut,' he says, like I'm the one who's a liability, 'and let me do the talking.'

I should let it go, but I'm as edgy as he is.

'Do the whining more like.'

'Eh, what's that?'

'Chill out, Maxi, okay. You and Eddie are mates from way back. That's what counts,' I say, as much to myself as to Maxi.

'Way back,' Maxi says, nodding to no one. 'Way, way back.'

The door swings open behind us and this bloke, Frankie Morton, comes into the bar wearing a suit and a white bowtie. He's holding a little box wrapped in silver paper. The bar goes quiet. Frankie walks around the dance floor in these jerky steps, like he's on strings. He's trying not to show how much it hurts, but his jaw tightens every time his foot presses on the carpet. It's costing him this walk.

No one says a word, no one except wasted, off-his-tits Maxi. 'That's what you get for messing with Eddie's wife,' he mutters into his pint.

Maxi's getting off on scaring himself, but the rest of us are just willing Frankie to get on with it, to get away up the stairs so we don't have to look at him. He takes forever, walking towards the staircase with that red rope on brass hooks across the bottom.

Strangler, the bouncer, is practically standing to attention. He's about seven feet tall with this big grey moustache, like the guy in that old army poster, but there's something not quite right about the Strangler. Even from here I can see a little bit more of his cropped grey hair that I should, because there's a ragged, half-moon gap where the top of his ear ought to be.

Frankie gets to the rope. I think it's nearly over, but Strangler shakes his head. He hardly moves, maybe just twitches that moustache, but the message still comes blaring out. No chance, Frankie. You're not getting up those stairs.

Frankie's shoulders sag. He bends down like a broken puppet and puts his silver parcel on the bottom step, then we have to watch him do his clockwork walk all the way back across the bar.

'That's why they call it The Hammer,' Maxi says, pointlessly, and I wish he'd shut his stupid mouth.

I try to think about that story of some boxer's right hook, and the picture under the boarded-up window in the bogs, of him knocking Mohammed Ali on his arse. I've seen it a dozen times. But the only picture I can imagine now is the big claw hammer that Eddie keeps in his desk drawer, along with the screwdriver and the pliers, and how they say he still likes to do his own DIY when the mood takes him.

Henry Cooper. That's the one. I stare at my pint and think about his gentle, ugly face, so I don't have to watch Frankie Morton or think about why he's walking around like some kid's toy with the batteries running down, and all that's left of Donna is a little pile of ash in a box, and how she's getting the first anniversary party she ever had.

The day's already turned to shit when the door swings shut behind Frankie Morton and the bar comes back to life.

'He's ready for you.'

My heart jumps out of my chest, but I keep a smile on my face, looking up at this anorexic glam-gran type with outsize breasts and a giant silver cross balanced in between them.

'Alright, Patricia,' Maxi grins, like a big, stoned puppy.

Patricia scowls. Her mouth puckers in her skeleton face.

'Upstairs,' she says, to the space between us.

Patricia leads us round the dance floor and my eyes lock on to the half-moon gap in Strangler's ear. Up close I can see the shape of four pointy, overlapping teeth, like a dentist's cast, and I can't help wondering where those teeth are now, and if they're still attached to someone's head.

Strangler sees me looking, and there's just a tiny suicidal moment when I want to ask.

I bite my lip and get my head down and watch him lift that fat red rope. I'm sure it's too thick to really strangle anyone. Pretty sure.

'Evening all,' he says, like someone from the good old days when everyone left their doors open, and I step over Frankie's silver parcel.

So, this is it. I'm going upstairs at The Hammer. I'm going to actually meet Eddie Burns instead of just nodding at him across a bar, except it's probably only to get my head kicked in because of Maxi and his stupid mouth.

I watch the shiny brass rods running across every step and follow Patricia up the curved staircase with Maxi panting beside me, ogling her bony, sequined arse. God knows what he finds to fancy there. Maybe it's just wanting what you can't have, because even an idiot like Maxi wouldn't mess with the Burns' women.

There's this weird light at the top of the stairs, like the whole room's coming towards me. I grab for the rail and stare into a blur of colour. The wall in front of me is covered in mirrors, some as big as car windscreens, others small and round, framed in gold and silver. The wall behind is the same. That's what's making me dizzy, watching the room reflected back on its own reflection, with streaks of rainbow from my dodgy eye.

'Come on,' Patricia snaps.

I follow her over a carpet so thick I can't hear my own steps.

I put my hand over my eye, giving it a rest from the glare and the heat, but even with one eye open I can see that every bloke up here is dressed like Maxi, in one of those black suits with a bow tie, as if we're at some kind of bouncer's meeting. The women are wearing big flouncy dresses, or else little frilly things that stop about an inch below their arse. I'm not interested. There's nothing sexy about any of them. The weird light has set the fuzziness going behind my eye, that stale cheesy taste that tells me there's a monster migraine on its way.

I jam my finger under my collar, take a breath, and remember Maxi's stupid laughter. How was I supposed to know that 'black tie' meant bowtie? At least I wish I'd got a normal suit, but the bloke in the shop said that collarless jackets were the cutting edge, whatever that is. So now I just look like a twat.

We stop outside these two wood-panelled doors set into a dark red wall. The carpet hardens beneath my feet. I'm standing on this dark stain. Maybe it's coffee?

'Wait there,' Patricia says.

'I'm away for a piss,' Maxi says, fishing in his pocket for his pills, or his Ket, or another one of his crappy ready-rolled joints.

'Wait,' Patricia snaps through her tight little arse of a mouth, and totters away on her five-inch heels.

Even Maxi gets the message. He mumbles something to the swirly carpet, but he doesn't move.

The far door is marked, "Management", in big white capitals. The only sign on the near door is this squashed-down Japanese looking guy standing outside with a bulge in the shoulder of his jacket. He's got deep black ridges running down his cheeks and an expression that tells you he hates the whole world. Smiler, they call him. At least Eddie does.

So that's got to be Eddie's office, and it sets all this shit churning around, repeating on me like a bad curry. How Maxi's really screwed up, and Eddie isn't exactly Jesus Christ when it comes to forgiveness, but then they do go back a long way so maybe we will get one more chance, except one look at Maxi's pale, bloated eyes tell me the answer to that.

I could do a runner, leg it down that curved staircase in five giant strides. And meet Strangler at the bottom.

I look back anyway.

This scrawny, bulgy-eyed bloke is at the top of the stairs, with a nasty goatee and slicked back hair copied from Eddie Burns. Frogga. So what? I've seen him half a dozen times in the last few years, and even in a suit he still looks like a slimy, bulgy-eyed bastard. He isn't what bothers me.

The girl's one step ahead of him, turning away towards the bar. Dark hair sways across her blue silk dress. Frogga catches me looking, and flashes me his sick, lizard smile. His fingers graze the small of her back. She reaches behind her and flicks at his hand. I glimpse her arm, one shade darker than a suntan, and the hairs prickle along my neck.

'Annie,' my lips move, but no sound comes.

There's no way it can be her, not here, after all this time. Not with him. It's the pressure, that's all, making me see things that aren't there. Maybe Maxi isn't the only one who's losing it.

She smooths her dress and sits at the end of the bar, facing away from me with that dark hair hanging down her back. I watch the stillness of her shoulders. Her head lifts and falls, swaying left and right. Frogga rubs his hand across his nose and walks away from her. But that circular motion keeps turning in my stomach, carrying me over the swirling carpet.

Her face is blank and distant, reflected in the mirrored wall. She's wearing a gold earring with a matching ring in her nose. A fine gold chain runs between them, swaying against her cheek.

'Annie Cherani,' I croak, and I swear, I can smell peaches.

A frown creases her forehead, and then she bursts into this big fake smile. But somewhere between the frown and the smile, I get a glimpse of the truth. Her eyes widen in something that might be fright.

Tommy, she says. 'Tommy Boy...'

'Farrier,' I tell her. 'Boyle was his name.'

'Good. Good for you.'

She sips her champagne and looks at me over the top of her glass.

My tongue sticks to the roof of my mouth.

'Your eye?' he mouths the question.

I'm desperate to say something, but not about that, and there's all these pat phrases running through my head, limp and pointless.

A dry cough comes out of my mouth.

Someone edges in behind me.

My hand brushes her arm.

She doesn't smell of peaches. I can't say that.

She sips her drink. The smile sets on my face. Her hand comes up, flicking her hair back. One of those super-trendy cuts with her fringe down practically in her eyes.

'Your hair looks good.'

She flicks it again, and this time the smile is almost real.

'You didn't like the chimney-sweep look?' she says.

'The plaits weren't bad,' I say, and I remember the whip of them in my face, sharp enough to raise the colour in my cheeks, even now.

'Oh God,' she says, closing her eyes, opening them. 'Pocahontas.'

I glance down, like I'm going to see those silver sandals or the grey-green bruises on her legs from years before, but there's only the silky blue of her dress.

'You lost something,' she says.

'Just thinking.'

'Well, there's a first time for everything, cowboy,' she laughs at me with her eyes, and I know I'm going to ruin everything, but I have to ask.

'Annie. What happened to you... in the Wall?'

Her teeth creep over her bottom lip. I think she's going to tell me, but then her face changes back into that faraway frown.

'You gotta go,' she says.

'Why?'

'Chez is coming back.'

'Chez?'

'Chester. He's just come out of the office.'

'Frogga. So what?'

'I'm sorry,' she says, touching my chest. 'Go. Please.'

She pushes me away, and this time I don't need to hear his

footsteps beating on the road, scrambling over that fence behind me. My body tenses, ready for that first punch against the side of my head, spinning me around for the second to come up under my chin and lay me out on that tiny square of lawn.

My jaw tightens.

Annie snatches her hand away. She presses herself back against the bar.

'I'm sorry, Tommy,' she whispers. 'I let you down.'

'Too fuckin right you did.'

She says something else, but all I can hear is the white noise in my head.

I stare at the big fat diamond in the hollow of her throat, but what I see is that single star shining through the clouds, and Carl and Frogga standing over me, filling the space where Annie should've been.

Frogga's trainer comes swinging at my face. I get my hands up and deflect that first kick past my head, but they keep on coming, hard and fast, until I curl into a ball with the taste of mud in my mouth and their feet battering in. I try to protect my face and pull my pants up from my knees, and I scream for Annie, while they kick and punch and spit on me.

The hitting stops.

Frogga looms above me like a ghoul in the orange light, with a long thin blade shining in front of his face.

'I'm going to do you. I'm going to fuckin cut you up.' He's so excited he looks like he's going to wet his pants.

But it isn't him that does.

'Annie,' I scream, but Annie's gone.

There's a crash of breaking glass.

'Please, Annie, help me,' but she left me there, and you don't forget a betrayal like that.

I look from the diamond at her throat to the blue and grey BMW remote on the bar in front of her, and I understand a whole lot more than I want to.

'Frogga getting what he's paying for, is he?'

She flinches like I've slapped her.

'Fuck you,' she says, and her gaze lifts to the presence at my shoulder.

Frogga slides a twitchy hand around her waist, and flashes me that lizard smile.

'Yeh?' I say. 'Fuck you, too. I should never have got you those Caramels. You're not worth it. You're not even worth a bar of fuckin chocolate,' I know I'm talking shit, but I can't help it, like I'm still that pathetic little boy pushing chocolate bars through the letterbox of an empty house, except that now, I don't want her back. I want to hurt her, like she hurt me.

'Like mother…' like daughter, I'm going to say, but Patricia's torpedo tits come diving in between us.

'Shut the fuck up and get in there,' Patricia tells me.

She makes a grab for me, but I get past her, to Eddie's wood-panelled door.

I look back at Annie Cherani and send her the hatred she deserves. Her face is tight with anger, nose scrunched into her forehead. I don't care. Rumplefuckinstiltskin. I'm not thinking about her. I'm getting my head together because this is business and Smiler is opening the door, and the first thing I see behind it is Eddie Burns' big meaty face.

Chapter Twenty-One

A Drink with Eddie

Smiler gives us the nod, but Maxi just stands there, so I walk on through into this shadowy room with blue lights shining in dusty spirals, up from the floor. There's a leather-topped desk, totally clear except for a tiny mobile phone. The wall behind is covered in photos, each with their own little light. I'm aware of a waitress with a silver tray, Maxi's panting breath, and Eddie Burns filling the space behind his desk.

He leans towards me.

I step back and stumble on Maxi's foot.

'Twat,' Maxi says, and Eddie lifts his huge head and laughs.

His lips are pink against his thick beard, one of those Muslim types with no tash, cut low on his face so you can see his big saggy cheeks. His nose is squashed flat, and his hair slicked back and tied in a ponytail. I can tell he's looking right at me even though he doesn't seem to have any eyes, just these points of glittering darkness under his forehead.

'Have a drink, lads,' he says.

Maxi snatches a glass of champagne off the tray.

I shake my head.

Eddie stretches. He brings his hands out of this black suit jacket that's too big, even for him, and clasps his fingers, showing me the gold sovereign ring on his index finger, setting the pain pulsing behind my eye.

I've seen that design before. A man on a charging horse, his spear in the dragon's throat.

'You won't have a drink with me?' Eddie's voice is hurt, like a kid's, like a grumpy, twenty-stone toddler.

There's no sign of a glass anywhere near him, but I take the hint. I lift one off the tray and take a fizzy gulp.

The waitress's shoulder brushes my arm. She walks out through the open doorway, leaving a spicy smell behind her.

The door closes. The room darkens. Eddie's face turns a dull blue.

Smiler stands close at my back, and there's something else moving against my leg.

I look down. Christallfuckinmighty.

Two rows of sharp yellow teeth are about six inches from my balls. Kylie looks up at me over her curling black lip. She knows the score. Eddie'd kill me before he'd hurt one hair on her velvety head. Eddie's bitch they call her, and sometimes I think they're joking.

'Right, lads,' Eddie says. 'Good of you to turn up, Maxi.' He grins, and then the smile falls off his face. 'What the fuck is wrong with you? Shouting your mouth off, stealing my money?'

'Eddie man, haway. It was a couple of hundred. Just the once like…'

'It was fuckin twice.'

'Aye well, you see that first time didn't count cos there'd been that bit of bother with those lads down Pottery Bank. The Bronx, that's what they call it. Like in New York,' Maxi forces this wheezy laugh. 'There's some mental fuckin kids down there. I mean, we both know that, Eddie, but I swear it's getting worse…'

Eddie looks down at his phone. His fist opens and closes, but Maxi just goes driveling on in his squeaky stoned voice, turning the atmosphere to shit.

I have to do something.

'Maxi didn't steal from you,' I say. 'I mean, he wouldn't. They were mistakes. He paid them back on the next collection, and there was that other time after Christmas when he paid too much. A grand over.

'That's it,' Maxi says, finally clicking on. 'Just mistakes, right?'

'Mistakes, just mistakes,' Eddie copies his squeaky voice. 'Course they're fuckin mistakes, else you'd be in the ground, you fat cunt.'

'Ah, haway, man, Eddie.'

Maxi puts his hands flat on the desk and Eddie's up out of his chair, peering at Maxi. I know what he's looking at, those bloated red balloons behind Maxi's eyelids.

'You stupid fat fucka.'

'He's not so well,' I say. 'We've been up at the factory all night, sorting those crappy lamps.'

'Ha, ha, ha.' This slow, false laugh comes at me from the far end of the office.

The room's bigger than I thought. Longer. There's someone there. I can sense him over by the shuttered window, but Eddie's watching me with those glittery eyes, nodding his head like we all know this story about the lamps is bullshit.

I wait for Maxi to back me up, but there's just this long slurp while he empties his glass, puts it on Eddie's desk, and belches. Only a little sound, but I can hear my life gurgling down the tubes.

'I mean, yeh okay, Eddie,' I say. 'So, then we had a smoke, afterwards.' I know how messed-up this is, but I've got to say something. 'Just a couple of J's, to chill out.'

'Did we,' Eddie says, 'so how come there's only one of you off your face?'

'Well, cos, because…'

'That's enough.' He waves the back of his hand at me.

'Look, Eddie. Mr. Burns…'

'Are you fuckin deaf? Shut up.'

Smiler steps closer.

I press my hand over my mouth and stare at the photos on the wall, pictures of Eddie Burns shaking hands with a load of different guys. There's one, bigger than the rest, of Eddie hugging this bloke with blood on his face and a gold boxing belt in one bandaged hand. My eyes fall to the yellowing certificate below it.

Viking Motors, Salesman of the Year, 1988 – Mr. Edward Burns.

'You stupid fat fucka man, Maxi. Did I not give you enough chances?'

'It's the lad man Eddie, he cannot fuckin count.'

I look at Maxi's sweating jelly face, and I can't even be arsed to hate him. I edge away and press harder on my lips.

'You're out, Maxi.'

'Ah, Eddie man. What about them deals we did with Kingsley at school? It was me taught you to roll your first spliff. Eh, you got to remember that. Titcha's remedial maths?' Maxi tries to laugh, but it's just this wheezy sound that makes me want to throw up on Eddie's clean, green desk. 'I mean we've been mates-'

'You let me down. You're not reliable. If I can't trust you to do the job, I may as well do it myself. Is that what you want? Me, running round collecting grubby tenners off those poxy kids?'

'Nah, Eddie it's not…'

'You're taking the piss out of me. Ripping me off. Turning up here stoned on my gear. It's a fuckin insult.'

Eddie's arm juts forward, grabbing Maxi's throat. He follows it with a right cross. His fist flashes past my face and cracks into Maxi's mouth.

Shit.

The vibration drums through the pain in my head.

Kylie growls, down by my bollocks.

Maxi's body slams back against the marble fireplace with the blood streaming from his face. And I know, if the desk wasn't between them Eddie'd be round to finish the job.

'Call yourself a fuckin mate,' he shouts, leaning over the desk, finger jutting at Maxi's body. 'I trusted you, you fat prick, and you turn up at my wedding anniversary to insult me. I should be having a drink with the family, but now I've got to find some cunt to run the business in Walker, cos of you. You let me down, you bastard.' He takes a breath and looks at the rings on his fingers. 'Donna'd be going mental, if she was still with us.'

Maybe it's him saying her name that makes me look, makes me see that silver urn up on the mantelpiece with their names engraved on the front, *Eddie and Donna - eternal love*, in a big black heart.

That's what I'm looking at, but what I see is that diamond glinting at Annie's throat, and Frogga's lizard grin.

'I ought to break your fat fuckin legs,' Eddie says. 'Take your fuckin eyes out,' but that touch of Annie's arm is more real than Eddie Burns' anniversary wish list.

That's why I do it.

'I won't let you down.'

Smiler moves behind me, but Eddie lifts his hand.

'I'm reliable.'

I lean across the desk and hold my hand out, two inches from the swell of Eddie's stomach.

He looks at me, then down at the spray of blood on his phone.

I concentrate on my hand, keeping it relaxed, keeping the tension out of my face.

The door opens behind me.

I stare at Eddie Burns, through him, to those photos on the wall.

The door closes. A mobile phone beeps, and it's like the thing's connected to Eddie's shoulder, cos his arm shoots forward and he takes my hand in his hairy paw.

'Well, you've got some balls,' he says. 'I'll give you that,' and he sits back in the chair, taking my hand with him, so I'm bent over the desk with the dog sniffing my arse.

'I won't let you down.'

'Make sure you fuckin don't,' Eddie says, squeezing the bones in my fingers.

I'm keeping it cool, controlling the expression on my face, but I can't stop my hand from sweating. I feel the slipperiness between our palms, and I can see that Eddie does too, because he grins, showing two rows of pointy, overlapping teeth. They remind me of this programme I saw, about how people get to look like their dogs.

And then they remind me of something else.

'Mr. Riley?' Eddie looks to the shuttered window.

I twist my neck to see.

Michael Riley's sitting at a low table with his legs stretched out in front of him, and what looks like a fat plastic pen clamped under his big hawk nose.

'Michael,' I give him a nod, at least the best I can with my head twisted halfway off my shoulders.

Riley smiles like the Devil and tilts his leathery head.

'Alright,' Eddie says, pulling my hand closer. 'You can work with our Carlo. I know you're old mates, so there'll not be any problems. Alright with you?'

'Carl?' I look down at the sovereign ring on Eddie's index finger.

'That alright, son?'

'Right, Eddie.'

'Right, Eddie,' he says, and lets go of my hand.

'Mr. Riley'll keep an eye on you. He'll be in touch with the wheres and whens, the usual shite. And while you're here, you can meet our new best mate,' Eddie points a fat finger at Smiler. 'Get him in here.'

I look past Maxi, dabbing his mouth with this scratty bit of tissue, and watch a trickle of blood darken on that big black heart behind him.

Eddie checks his phone.

Riley sucks on his vape.

The door opens and Smiler comes back in, with this little bloke hovering behind him in the doorway.

'Haway, man,' Eddie says. 'Move.'

The little bloke steps towards us in a neat grey suit. His hair's combed back, so thin that you can see the pinkness of his scalp, and his lips are a fat red bow on his baby face. He looks like some weird Pampers advert.

'This is Mr. Linthorpe,' Eddie grins again. 'Our personal bent copper.'

Pampers Linthorpe, I think, but then I see the scowl flash across Linthorpe's face. Dark lines, like brackets, cut in around his mouth. He still looks like a baby, maybe Smiler's bastard child.

'And this is Mini,' Eddie laughs at his own crap joke. 'He's going to make us lots of money, and you're going to help him.'

I nod at Linthorpe.

'Alright,' he says, his flat, almost-Yorkshire accent, totally wrong for his baby face.

'Go on then,' Eddie sighs, like he's suddenly bored. 'Piss off, the pair of you. And you,' he says to Maxi. 'I won't see you again. You stay out of my town, away from my business. You don't call anyone. You don't speak to anyone. You don't exist. Okay. Pack up and fuck off. I'll give you till…' he looks at his watch, and I do the same. It's gone half-four. 'Let's say, five o'clock.'

Maxi keeps dabbing at his mouth, but Eddie isn't looking. He stretches back in his chair.

'And stick to the lager,' he grins at me. 'I didn't buy Bolli at thirty quid a bottle for charver scum like you.' He grins again, and I try to smile. 'It's a fuckin joke.'

I hold his glittery eyes, stretch my smile wider, and back out of the room. He laughs. I laugh back. We're both roaring like lunatics, till Smiler slams the door in my face. But I can still hear Eddie, even through that thick door, even when I'm looking down over the balcony rail, at the sharp, overlapping little teeth marks in Strangler's ear. I wipe the cold sweat off my forehead and I know I've screwed-up. I just don't know how badly.

Chapter Twenty-Two

Peeler's Plan

That stupid collarless jacket is locked in the boot, along with the black tie and shiny shoes. I've got my boots on, my leather jacket with the silk lining smooth against my skin, and Kurt Cobain on the stereo telling me it's less dangerous with the lights out. I crank up the volume, let the sound blow the doubts out of my stomach, and I start to feel like me, the person I want to be.

I can make this happen.

Two point two pounds a kilo, sixteen ounces a pound, thirty-five ounces in a kilo. You want it the other way around? No problem. Twenty-eight grams an ounce, four hundred and fifty-three make a pound. I can remember that, and I can add up. I'm where I need to be when I need to be there. I play it straight down the line with everyone, keep smiling, and don't let anyone get too close. That's why it works. That's why I'm good for business, and business is good for me. And if I do that, then I don't see why Riley should be a problem. Or anyone else come to that.

All I have to do is tell the lads. Maxi's out, I'm in. Maybe give them a little bonus and carry on like nothing's changed. And it hasn't, not really. Maxi's been no use to anyone for years. Me and Peeler have been holding everything together, and it might sound stupid in this business, but I trust Peeler Kaminsky. I mean, we go way, way back.

Just like Maxi and Eddie. The thought pops into my head, as

welcome as a turd in a swimming pool.

I'm past the Black Boar, and there's Atwal's on the left. I should go straight on to Peeler's like always, take the next turn onto Evistone, but I don't. Maybe it's the day for making stupid decisions, or maybe I just need to prove that I'm not scared of Daryl Boyle, any more than I'm scared of Eddie or Carl, or any of them. I take the Belmont turn.

I drive down the street feeling for the wad of cash in my wallet, and thinking how Daryl hasn't got a pot to piss in. He's a total loser, and I'm winning all the way. I could get him done over for a hundred quid. I don't know why I haven't, except maybe deep down I know it won't change a thing. The tyres hum on the tarmac and I'm doing it, driving past that peeling green door and not giving a shit. It's the van that fucks it up, dirty dark blue, with one bald tyre up on the curb. My foot comes off the gas. The Volvo judders to a stop and Daryl's transit sucks the moisture out of my mouth.

My hand closes around my middle finger, and Daryl's brown-toothed face merges and shifts through Carl's and Frogga's and Eddie's until the fear's so strong in my stomach that the music doesn't make any difference. I turn it off and hide in the echoing silence.

Half a lifetime in that crappy house. Not anymore. I haven't been back there in seven years, and I never will. I'm out of that shite and I've done it myself, and if I have to work for the Burns Gang to stay out, then that's fine by me.

A car horn blares, and I practically jump through the Volvo's window.

There's some bloke behind me in a giant four by four, shouting the odds. If he gets any closer, he'll be in my back seat.

I hold up my hand, but he just keeps leaning on the horn.

Twat. I give him the finger and wheel-spin away down the hill, screeching up onto Evistone Gardens, and skidding to a stop outside Peeler's flat.

The woman in next door's yard gives me the evil-eye, this bleach-blond Buddha with a plastic bottle in her hand, thighs sagging over the sides of her deckchair. She makes Maxi look good. I give her a nod and walk up between the two scrawny patches of grass, telling myself that nothing can touch me. I'm in control.

Except that's bullshit. Maxi's gone, and there's nothing left between Eddie and me except Carl and Frogga, and Michael bloody Riley. The thought pushes me closer to the edge, which I suppose is why I'm acting like a tit.

'Police,' I bang on the plastic door. 'Police, open up.'

Buddha scowls at me over her bottle, and the door opens.

'You're going to get in trouble doing that,' Peeler tells me, eyes wide between his big, sticky-out ears. He doesn't make a big deal of it though, just turns back into the flat and I follow him down the corridor, past a bike with one wheel, outside a closed bedroom door.

'Maxi's out,' I tell him.

Peeler keeps walking, through his little living room and into the kitchen.

'Maxi's out,' I say again. 'Gone, finished.'

Peeler slides this tray out of the oven, then he stands in the kitchen doorway in that crumpled stripy shirt he never takes off. Peeler doesn't care what he looks like, which is sort of cool. The flat's a mess as well, but there's a great smell wafting out around him, meaty with loads of garlic.

'You want some lasagna,' he says.

So, we sit in Peeler's living room with his massive DVD

collection and giant T.V., and we eat lasagna while I tell him how it is.

Maybe the tips of those big ears go a shade pinker when I tell him how Eddie knocked Maxi on his arse, and he raises an eyebrow when I tell him about shaking Eddie's hand, but that's it. He doesn't say much, just acts like it's no big deal, which is exactly what I need.

'So, what do we do next, boss?' he says, taking the piss.

'Haway and fuck off,' I tell him.

'Yes sir, whatever the gaffer says.'

'You're asking for a slap, you,' I tell him, but we're both laughing, and by the time I walk out of there we've got a plan, and I'm feeling good again.

Peeler's going round the bars, making sure the lads know the score, and I'm away up to the factory to tell the gardeners how things are. No more freebees for Maxi, not that even he would be stupid enough to try.

I tell them they're getting a bonus and everything's going to be sweet, then I get back in the car, crank up the stereo, and think about how this is going to be.

There's two and a half grand a week for Eddie, a cut for Peeler and the lads, and the rest gets split between me and Maxi. At least it did. I made a grand, easy, on a good week. Eddie never cared what we took, so long as he got his money. So, I don't see why I shouldn't make twice that now, even allowing a bit extra for Peeler. I could save some, get out of the business before I end up like Maxi. Poor bastard.

I'm still ten miles from Newcastle when the phone rings. I pull it out of my pocket and stare at my home number on the display.

'You're late,' Clara's voice is crisp and posh, and even before I look at my watch, I know I've screwed-up, again.

'You're in my flat?'

The line goes dead, and I drop the phone like it's on fire. Shit. I put my foot on the floor, but all I can do is think about Clara, opening cupboards and hatches, poking around in my private business with that smug smile on her face.

'Bitch', I say, and like always with Clara, I don't know if I'm angry or excited, but at least she pushes the Burns gang out of my mind.

I haven't seen Clara in months, and if I'm honest, I missed her at first, all that clever talk and hysteria. Clara's made-up tantrums to distract us from the real shit going on in our heads. We had some fun, me and Clara, but I'm not stupid. I know I was just her bit of rough, an optional extra to her student rebellion. The thing is, it's August, and Clara's not a student anymore. So, what I don't understand is why she got back in touch last week? Why she invited herself over, why she's waiting for me now, back at the flat? Maybe I could work it out, if I could just stop and think, but there's way too much shit swirling through my head already, and my mind drifts back to that first night, a year and a half ago.

I heard her before I saw her, pissed and angry, screaming at someone in her high, posh voice. I came out of White's bar expecting tousled hair and Uggs, instead, I found Clara. She was flat on her arse in the snow, a throwback to the nineties in blue dungarees and Doctor Martin's boots, with her woolly hat in her hand and her hair shaved within an inch of her skull.

'You okay?'

'Clumsy facking oaf,' she screamed, like it was my fault.

I could hear the vodka slur even through her stretched out vowels. Like Peeler says, any normal person would've left her there, so I suppose that proves I'm not normal. He reckons she's a mother substitute. Whatever. I'd never seen anything like her.

'Let me give you a hand.'

'Fack orf.'

'Right.'

I gave her both hands, hers small and hot in mine, even though it was freezing. I lifted her towards me. Her frail, bald head tilted back, showing me her delicate face, eyes hidden behind blotches of black make-up. Baby bondage; with a line of studs up each ear, and a drop of clear liquid shining on her nose-ring.

'Want a drink then?' I said.

'That's the least you can do,' she told me, running her sleeve across her nose, but she kept tight hold of my hand all the way back into the bar, and after that, I couldn't let her go.

She sat with her legs tucked underneath her, gulping vodka and tonic and telling me this rambling story about how her dad was such a bastard for leaving her up here on her own all Christmas.

'He keeps hassling me to go to St Vincent.'

I thought she meant that church in Shieldfield, but for once, thank God, I kept my mouth shut.

I was tempted to tell her about Mam, but I could see that Clara wasn't the sharing kind. In her life, she was the main event, the only show in town, and to be fair, it wasn't a bad one. So, I shut up and listened while she knocked back her Absolut vodka and assassinated her family, then they called time and kicked us out.

'Careful you don't fall,' I told her, watching her totter down the path.

Her laugh was loud enough to bring the loose snow tumbling off the roof.

'You're funny, Goldeneye,' she said, and slapped me hard across the face. 'You simply must come back to the flat.'

Chapter Twenty-Three

Clara

I pull up behind Clara's pearly white Golf GTI and see through the hanging branches of the cherry blossom, that my front door is standing open. I grab my leather jacket off the back seat and try for that slow rolling walk up the path, but my heart's beating too hard. I move like I'm on springs, bouncing under the faded pink branches and the stone gargoyle over my open door.

I follow the wide corridor past my bedroom with its luxury en-suite bathroom, and into the living room. The rest of the flat is open plan, which means it's one big room. The kitchen's at the far end with what the estate agent called a picture window over the sink. Three steps lead back up from the kitchen area to my forty-inch plasma, opposite an 'L' shaped leather sofa. There's a sheepskin rug, and an iron-mesh coffee table with an open bottle on top and a pair of shiny high-heeled shoes leaning against each other underneath.

The shoes aren't mine.

Clara's sitting on the short end of the 'L', with her long legs curled underneath her and a faraway smile on her face. Her dark blond hair has grown out, a stylish slash, angled across her face. She's still going heavy on the eye make-up, but the rest of it has gone. All those piercings replaced by a subtle gold swirl in each ear. The woolly dress and dungarees have gone too. I can see the shape of her under a thin white blouse, and what could almost be a business suit, if it wasn't quite so soft and silky.

This is the final product, the new Clara who's been appearing in stages since the spring, shedding her poor little rich girl personality like a caterpillar in a story, starting on her next incarnation. I'd like to ask her which version is nearer to the truth, but she wouldn't understand the question. She certainly wouldn't answer it. This is who Clara is today, so this is what's real, what's always been real, and I do sort of get it, because underneath all the bullshit Clara's world is the same as mine. It's about getting out from under, breaking free from the past, and you don't need a fine-art degree to see that the sexy businesswoman act is going to get you a lot further than the angry Goth. The only thing I can't make sense of is why she's here, after all this time, wasting her glossy smile on a low-life chancer like me.

'Hola.' She holds up one of my glasses with a little gold puddle shining in the bottom, and smiles like butter wouldn't melt.

I can't help smiling back.

'Hola, Bella,' I say, using up two thirds of my Spanish in one grand gesture.

'Congratulate me,' she says, patting the sofa and rattling off something about bellas artes.

'Congratulations,' I sit, and she hands me a glass of wine.

'Salud,' she says.

'Salud,' I throw in my last word.

She takes a sip, and her face relaxes. Mouth open, she stares blankly at the iron mesh table with one shiny nail tapping on the glass, setting off this tinkling echo inside my head. Maybe it's that sound, or something in her expression that triggers the black tension inside me. I need to put that smile back on her face. And with Clara, it's easy.

'So,' I clink my glass against hers, and take another drink.' You've got the degree. You've got the job, and you're away to Barcelona. You're a genius.'

Her face lights up. Red lips part over white teeth, and even if I don't really believe that smile any more than I believe in this sexy businesswoman or the spoiled little rich girl that came before, what I believe has nothing to do with how I feel. I put that smile back on her face and the anxiety washes out of my stomach.

'That may be true,' she says, 'but there's more.'

'Oh yeh? So, what else am I congratulating you for?'

She presses one long finger to my lips and takes her time, dragging a shiny nail down across my throat.

'I'm going to make your dreams come true,' she whispers, in her husky, twenty-a-day voice.

So that's why she's here. She wants a victory shag. One last night with her bit of rough before she moves on to better things.

My body stirs in anticipation, but there's a part of me that's not so sure. Maybe it's an ego thing? Or that I've finally got over her and I'm scared of going back? Or maybe there's another reason? A scrunched-up face spitting insults at me across the bar.

I'm excited and confused. My hands are on her cheeks, but I don't know if I'm pulling her towards me or holding her away, and that about sums up me and Clara.

I make a dash for the kitchen and flick the kettle on.

'Can't beat a good cup of tea,' I tell her, with a big fake smile of my own.

Clara isn't bothered, she purrs at me over the work-top, in that breathless way that's supposed to tell me there's something exciting coming.

'I want to move you,' she says, talking like one of her cryptic crosswords. 'Out of the cellar and into the viaduct.' She touches one polished nail to the tip of her nose. 'El Viaducto.'

I narrow my eyes, but I know better than to ask her what she's on about because that would be gauche and simple, so I smile and nod and let her go on. And she does. She leans across the work-top, talking at me in a mixture of English and Spanish. Her top button pops open. I try to make sense of what she's saying, but I can't help seeing the press of flesh at the top of her blouse. She catches me looking and laughs, just a little like Michael Riley.

'So that's what we'll do,' she says, and for all she might look like a different person, even an idiot like me can see that she's just as far from planet Earth as she was that first night in the snow.

It turned out my place was closer to White's Bar than hers, so we slid back here on the icy road and picked up where we left off, with her curled on the sofa like an exotic cat, knocking back my vodka and ranting on about some 'menial' holiday job her dad had found her in a gallery.

'Nailing bloody frames, with a facking hammer.'

The word thuds through my memory. But back then The Hammer was just a bar I'd been in a couple of times, the place Maxi went to sort things out with Eddie.

What hit me was the anger in her voice, and the way it set the guilt churning in my stomach. I lit a Marlboro and took a long draw, concentrating on the grainy rush in my throat, the hit in my lungs, breathing a long, faded stream with the rest of it left inside me, like they always leave something inside you. No way, I told myself. This isn't real. Just a dead reflex left over from another world. There's no way Clara's shit is my fault. No way Mam's shit was my fault.

I took another drag, sinking into the silence, before I realized Clara had stopped talking. She walked straight past me into the bedroom, dropped her clothes on the carpet and slid under the duvet. I was in beside her, fast as a greyhound after the hare.

She pressed her lips hard against mine. Her studded tongue took one sweet turn round my mouth, and then she rolled over and slept like a baby for ten hours straight. Clara. She was as clear as the darkness. But wasn't that what made her interesting? Our endless game of hide and seek.

We were lying in bed the next morning, sharing four Codeine and a can of Coke, and what turned out to be my last Marlboro.

'I'll go to the shop,' she said, fishing the keys out of my jeans and pulling her dungarees on over my Johnny Cash t-shirt.

I should have known something was up, but I was just pleased to drift back to sleep with that image of her running through my mind. If she took twenty minutes instead of five, so what? Who was counting? And anyway, what possible harm could she do?

I found out pretty quick.

That night, she let herself in.

I never heard the door, wasn't listening for it. No one had a key, I thought, and anyway, I was down in the cellar with my mind racing, and my hand scrambling to keep up. How could I know how long she'd been up there, watching me?

'Wow,' she said, and I practically jumped up through the open hatch.

'What the fuck?' I spread my arms in a feeble attempt to block the opening.

'Well, well,' she said, looking down on my darkest and most private self, with her false, knowing smile, 'you've got to watch the quiet ones.'

The heat came surging through my body, but this was something different. Not guilt. Humiliation.

'Piss off, Clara,' I pulled myself up the ladder two steps at a time and slammed the hatch behind me. 'How did you get in here?'

'You gave me a key.'

'I fuckin didn't.'

'Of course you did. To go to the shop, this morning.'

'Eh, you borrowed it.'

'Eh,' she said, letting her jaw drop, mimicking me in a way that made me want to punch her. 'Yes, and I had it copied. I mean you can't want to leave me standing out in the street all night, freezing my pert little tits off.' She wiggled her shoulders, setting them jiggling inside her dungarees. 'While you play monsters in your deep, dark dungeon,' And she leant back against the wall, and laughed.

I looked from her open mouth to the hatch behind me. No one had been down there but me in three years. That was my place, and even if Clara was happy to show me her spoiled silly madness, I wasn't happy to show her mine. I was comfortable playing the suffering silent type, putting up with her drunken tantrums, like I had with Mam, feeding my fantasy that I was sorted, and sane, and whole.

Of course, I wasn't and I'm not and I know it, at least some of the time. So maybe her seeing me down there should have cut through some of the bullshit, brought us closer together. And it might have done, except that wasn't what either of us wanted. You see, it doesn't pay to get too close. Not for me. I don't need other people's screwed up reality, and I don't want to share mine. But you know Clara.

She knelt down, running her fingertips over the hatch, and then she snatched at the iron ring and pulled. I stood on the hatch, snapping the ring out of her hand.

'Bastard.' She lifted it again.

'No, Clara,' I stamped down.

'I'm not your facking dog.'

'Leave it.'

'Alright, alright,' she said, rounding her eyes at me, 'sit down. I'll get us a drink.'

'Okay,' I watched her take a step towards the kitchen and let myself fall back on the sofa.

'Ha,' she grabbed the iron ring, and swung the hatch back on its hinges.

'Bitch.' My hand fell on her throat, pinning her against the wall, not even feeling her fists on my face.

I let her go, kicking the hatch shut, and she launched herself at me, pulling my hair, tearing my shirt. Her nails drew three red lines across my chest.

'Hit me,' she screamed, with her face close against mine and grey tears running down her cheeks. 'Hit me, you ignorant bastard.'

Her nails came up again, tearing down my cheek, and I did it. I slapped her across the mouth.

'That's enough, Clara,' I shouted, but it wasn't. Not nearly.

Her dress was up over her head, falling in a crumpled heap on the floor. She punched me, full on the jaw, pulling her clothes off, and mine, straddling me on the wooden floor, fuckin me, with us still battering at each other and the blood running in little rivers from her burst lip, down over those tight rose-bud tits.

I didn't hear what she was screaming, just shapeless sounds behind her bloody nails, sobbing and broken.

'Daddy.'

I heard that. And Mam's name was there, blaring in my head. I could have shouted it right back, driving myself up inside her with my cock hard as the iron mesh on the coffee table. Mam. You sad, selfish, alky, bitch. But I held it in. I'm not that sick.

Trust me. There's nothing so real or so false as being screwed by a girl like Clara. The rest of her was one big lie, or maybe lots of little lies piled on top of each other. But the sex was real. You can't fake that.

'*Oh, for God's sake, Tom,*' Clara laughs in my head, '*that's the easiest thing of all.*'

'Right, Clara,' I say, but I don't believe her.

The kettle clicked ages ago. Clara's still rattling on about her flash new job, dropping a bit of Spanish in at every opportunity. All I drop is a couple of teabags. I make two cups that nobody wants and watch the water darken. I don't bother with milk. I just walk up those three steps to the living room, put the cups on the iron-mesh table, and sit down with six clear inches of sofa between us.

We didn't see each other for a while after that night, like we'd both given too much of ourselves away. But she turned up a couple of weeks later, when the clubs kicked out, slipping into the flat, and the bed. That was how it went. She'd turn up in the middle of the night, pissed and looking for a shag. Or a fight. Usually both. I told her I didn't want her just letting herself in, but we both knew that was a lie.

There was always something not quite true about me and Clara, but God love her, the anger was true enough. Maybe that's what did it for me, all the screaming and shouting that I didn't know how to do, lighting me up inside. Or maybe it was just that her endless self-obsession suited me, because the other great thing about Clara was that she never asked any questions. Okay, sure; "What's your problem? Who do you think you are?" That sort of shit. But not real questions, ones with answers, like, "where were you at four o'clock this morning?" - when I was out doing business.

I suppose the truth was that while our secrets pushed us apart; they held us together, too. The same anger burning inside us. Hers waving like a flag, mine folded tight and close and hidden inside me, while I pretended to be someone else. Don't get me wrong. She's as big a fake as I am, but she's learned something at college, or maybe she just knew it all along. Little Miss Anarchy, getting her hair done, finding a job, and sanitizing her rebellion, so all that's left is turning her daddy down and working for the competition, not seeing that it's all the same. He's still pulling the strings, getting her in with one of his mates, popping the champagne for his arty daughter. Anything goes in the art world. Isn't that the way it is?

'We're booked up all winter,' she's saying. 'Right through till May. Christ, Tom, they're practically beating the door down. The thing is though,' she presses her finger to my lips. 'There was some contract thing with this guy, Claudio Jensen. He pulled out at the last minute, and Jose-Luis says I can have the place for the first week in September. Do what I want.' She touches her hand to my chest, nails pressing through my t-shirt. 'You know what that means.'

'Do I?' And I honestly don't know if I've been dreaming and missed it, or if she's still playing her cryptic games.

'Don't give me that working-class humility shit,' she says, 'just come here and show your appreciation.'

She leans across in her silky black suit and runs the tip of her tongue around my lips. But I've looked into those blank panda eyes one time too many, and I turn my face away.

Chapter Twenty-Four

The Black Boar

I walk into The Black Boar and order my fifth pint of the night. I haven't drunk any of them. That's not why I'm staring around like an idiot. It's this place, an oblong box with a line of battered tables down the middle, like a broken body in a coffin. Nothing's changed in here for about a thousand years, except there's maybe a few more tab burns on the carpet. And there's still that feeling, something like the hall at Nana's church, with Mam's hand on my shoulder and the top button so tight on my throat that I can hear my own breath.

'Three quid, exactly.'

The landlord puts my pint on the bar. He looks at me like he's trying to remember who I am, but I was a kid the last time I was in here and he hasn't got a clue. I know him though, Mickey Cassidy, with those pock-mark scars and his cheesy grin, and his couple of cans for Mam.

'Thanks,' I say, and get away before he's got time to work it out.

I shuffle round behind the blokes lined up along the bar to the safety of the furthest table, down by the tab machine.

There are two old girls at the next table, pink rinse heads together, gypsy earrings swinging, whispering like God's just told them about the numbers for next week's lottery. One of them looks at me, sips something out of a tiny glass and puckers her orange lips. I nod and get my head down, peering out from behind my pint and the Daily Mirror.

There's a bloke with a beard rustling his paper over by the window, but the rest of the tables are empty, leaving me a clear view of the full length of the pub.

I fix both eyes on the door, ready to wait for as long as it takes for Louis Solomon to walk in and tell me what's going on. That's why I'm here, why I've spent the last two hours on my drink-free pub crawl. I've been in half the bars in Byker and Walker, seeing the lads and being seen, buying pints I don't want, trying to suss out what's going on.

I was over at Howdon Metro before that, making the drop for Michael Riley on the old stone platform, three grand in a green Fenwicks carrier bag, in the second bin on the left. They were watching me as soon as I came through the barrier, but I kept my eyes on the bin till I heard the train coming, then I made the drop and got out of there. But I looked back, like they say you never should, and I saw Justine doing the pickup.

The last time I'd seen her was months ago, up at The Hammer, wrapped around a metal pole, shaking her arse. But it was her, doing collections for Michael Riley, clicking through the station in three-inch heels and a business suit. She grabbed the bag and stepped onto the metro, just as the doors hissed shut. Three grand, gone. Three grand, when the total take was less than two.

I lift the pint halfway to my lips and lay it back on the table. My phone vibrates against my thigh. I pull it out.

C.T. comes up on the display, reminding me of the shiny rows of bubble-wrap she made me buy, still untouched in the back of the car.

"I've looked at your stuff, and it's good."

"Good," that's what he said. That one word way back in another life, but what did he mean? Nice? Pretty? Or really good enough?

I watch Clara's initials flash on the screen and put the phone back in my pocket.

We paid two and a half grand, me and Maxi, and there were weeks when we took double that. Riley rounded it up to three. He called me that night, after Eddie's, told me where and when, and how much, just like Eddie said, and that Carlo and Chez would be in touch.

I told him we paid two and a half, and all I got back was that slow, false laugh.

'I'm rounding it up to three,' he said, again, and sucked on his vape.

What was I supposed to do?

'No problem,' I told him, trying to make myself believe it. I was thinking that if we could take five it would hardly make any difference, but I should have known then, that without Maxi's connection to Eddie, I was screwed.

That was less than a week ago, although it feels like a month, before Peeler came back with a handful of grubby notes and a load of green the lads couldn't sell. Half their regulars hadn't turned up. The next night was worse. And then Louis Solomon disappeared.

Louis, who spent half his life kicking that ball against the corner of Sandy Crescent. He was going to be the next Alan Shearer. Everyone said. A nailed-on certainty to get a fat professional contract with Newcastle United, but he never did. They let him go in the June. He was dealing on his own by July and working with us in August.

The door swings open and this group of lads come into the bar, half-pissed and shouting, practically filling the place. Anyone can tell, it'll be years till any of them see eighteen. The tallest one, with spiky hair and a wispy tash, lays a twenty on the bar. Mickey Cassidy tells them to settle down, but he takes the money and gives them their fizzy blue bottles.

Orange Lips looks at me and rolls her eyes to the ceiling. It's the first time I've smiled all day.

I have another go at my pint, and this time it goes down, but then I stare at my Daily Mirror, looking at Laura from Lincoln's grey tits, and up to her blank face. She looks like she's watching repeats of Emmerdale, a lot less sexy than Justine looked stepping onto that metro with three grand, twelve hundred quid of it straight out of the whisky box in the cellar. There's eight hundred quid left in there. I don't even know what's in the bank, but not much. No way will it carry me through next Saturday, not unless some money comes in.

Maybe Riley'll give me a pass and let it ride? I think of his slow, vicious laugh and I know the answer to that. I need to find out what's going on, and fast.

I turn the page, but I'm not reading. Truth is, once you've read the football the rest of the paper's crap. I pull the phone out of my jeans, push one for messages, and listen to Clara Tate's demanding voice.

'Pick up the phone. I've set this up for you, put my reputation on the line, risked my own money,' by which she means her dad's. 'Answer me, you little shit, because…' I press the red button.

Skid was in The Butchers Arms, over by the bar. He was looking sharp with a good view of the door, but his head went down as soon as he saw me.

'How's it going,' I said.

'Alright,' he told me, with his eyes on his Nike Airs.

I bought him a drink, but the chat didn't get any better. No, he hadn't seen anything. No, there was no problem, just the regulars weren't buying. They weren't even coming in.

There was no one in Jacksons or The Raby, but there was this kid slipping out the side door of The Grace, as I came in the front. He could've been anyone, just some lad in a green hoody. But there was something about him, the way he moved, weirdly calm with his little hand patting at his chest.

I ran out after him, staring down the street at a group of girls in matching pink t-shirts and sparkly hats. Nah. It was hardly pretty boy's style. Sharp-dressed man in a dirty hoody?

The door opens and another couple of old lads shuffle into the Boar. The pub's filling up with that motley selection you get in a place like this. '*Community Pub*,' it says on the sign outside. Star Wars café more like.

I stand up to watch another stranger fight their way through the door. My shoulder bangs against a picture and I sit back down. Stupid, sitting at the back of this place on a Saturday night, like it's not going to end up heaving.

Paul wouldn't look at me in Peggie Sue's. The rest of the bars were dead, and there was still no sign of Louis Solomon. Peeler's been up to his gaff a few times, and so have I. He's not there. We got in the back window the last time. Clothes in the wardrobe, milk you can drink in the fridge. No sign of Louis.

The Boar's his local, the place he meets his mates to go into Newcastle, where he does his deals. But Ant and Dec haven't seen him, and he's not answering his phone. That's the first thing we tell them. Answer your phone, no matter what. Sure, they're only kids. They lose the things, get sick, do a runner. Maybe? But sooner or later Louis Solomon is going to turn up, and when he does, I want to hear what he's got to say.

Except I'm not really sure that I do, or that he's even going to turn up at all. Because however much I try to pretend that everything's okay, the dull ache in my balls tells me there's something bad going on.

'*This is the easiest money you're ever going to make.*' That's what I told him, along with all the usual bullshit, looking up into that same freckled face that used to be about four feet nearer the ground. What an arsehole I am, saying that, doing whatever it takes to keep business ticking along.

I turn another page and stare at Posh Spice's spindly body. Poor cow. A zillion quid and nothing to eat. I look at my full pint and try to remember when I last ate something, but all I can think about is the thump and scrape of Louis's ball against the wall, and Michael Riley's stupid monotone voice telling me about the drop for another three grand next Saturday.

I'll be cleaned out. I'll get my face stoved in and end up back down here in some crappy damp flat, waiting for giro day, so I can put a few quid on the gas and score enough pills to get me through to the next one.

I grab for my pint, like that's going to help, and some twat bangs against the table sending beer splashing onto my shirt.

'Haway man,' I shout at the kid with spiky hair, eyeing daggers into the back of his head. He doesn't even turn round.

'Your lass in again, Moocher,' Spiky says, to one of his kiddy mates.

'Aw, the state of that,' Moocher grins, flashing big tombstone teeth, and points his alco-pop at the door. 'I wouldn't touch her with yours.'

I shouldn't look. The hairs are already up, prickling along my arm, even before I hear her shrill voice through the buzz of the bar.

'Go on, pet, buy us a drink.'

I open the paper in front of my face and try to focus on Laura's round grey nipples. I can't. My head comes up. I catch a glimpse of hunched shoulders under black and yellow hair.

'Get yourself home, love,' some old boy says, but the lads are laughing, pushing each other towards her. Spiky's got his arm across Moocher's neck, holding him.

'A couple of vodkas,' she says, her voice falling to a husky slur. 'Just to get us in the mood.'

She presses herself against Moocher's chest in this shapeless green coat with her witch's hair, like some spiteful kid's drawing of the person she used to be. Her hand comes up, orange carrier bag bumping against her leg. I want to look away even more than I want to be free of Michael Riley, but I can't. I see the blue veins across the back of her hand, one long red nail, the rest snapped short, sliding inside her open coat and down between her stick thin thighs.

'Fuck off,' Moocher breaks Spiky's grip. He pushes her away.

The smile fixes on Mam's face. She turns to the next table. Mine. Her mouth opens, too wide for her hollowed-out face, showing me brown, shrivelled teeth. She leans in, stinking of wet dog and piss, and stares right through me.

'Aw go on, pet,' she says, 'just a couple.'

Her hand slips back through her coat, and the stool slides out from under me. My shoulder bounces off the wall. There's a brush of balding fur under my hand. A dim light flickers in her eyes, and I'm up and past her.

'Tommy.'

I push through the crowds, but she won't give up.

Spiky gets in my way, then he moves back, laughing, and lets her through.

'Please. Tom-Bomb.'

Her hand touches my face.

I shake her off and fight my way to the door. There's a wall of staring faces behind me, those pinch-faced old cows with their pink-rinse hair and orange lips.

'Fuck you,' I tell them, all of them, digging in my pocket and slapping a clatter of coins on the bar. 'Give her whatever she wants,' I scream in Mickey Cassidy's face, and I'm out into the cold air, running hard, screaming down the empty streets, letting the wind blow her filth off my skin.

I get to the corner of Belmont, panting, with my hands on my knees, swearing at those smug old cows in the pub, at Mickey Cassidy, and at her, and then I take the long way back, up Eastcote Terrace, to the car. I get the door shut and the engine on. That's when the guilt kicks in. I'm driving home to my posh Jesmond flat and leaving her behind. The burn tells me that my hand is down between my thighs, pinching and twisting, and even that reminds me of her, the veins on her hand, that one red nail sliding down. I snatch my hand away. No more. She's been blaming me since I was five years old. That's long enough. I've got problems of my own. I'm a couple of weeks from ending up in the foundations of some office block.

I could just as easy go back to the Boar, get a bottle of vodka and sit there with her, blaming the world for everything. I laugh at the windscreen. Why not? I might as well, except the thought makes me want to puke. But I need something. I could go up to Clara's, get wasted, get fucked. But my heart's still hammering, and the last thing I want is some other screwup, if she's even still in the country.

I know who I really need. I picture her face through the blurring streetlights. Bullshit. The bitch let me down. She betrayed me. All that's left is to roll that rug away and get down in the cellar with my cold, sick dreams. I'm already there in my mind, braking hard outside the flat, when the phone goes. M.R. comes up on the display, in ugly grey letters.

Chapter Twenty-Five

Faustino's

I run up the metal staircase at Faustino's restaurant, thinking about Riley's voice on the phone, and wondering what it means. Eddie wants to see me, "right now, at Faustino's." All Riley's ever done is tell me the drop off, a bin or a back-lane, every word in that same deadpan monotone, like a machine. Till now.

"Right now."

I remember the tension in his voice, and the sweat comes again, burning under my arms. This isn't right. He's setting me up.

Oh, come on, Tommy. If they were setting you up it'd be in a field in the middle of nowhere, not the busiest place in town. And why would he want to? Riley's had his money, with the extra that goes straight in his pocket when it should be in mine, and I haven't breathed a word to anyone. I keep on at myself, being reasonable, making sense, but I can't shake the hollow feeling in my stomach, the sense that Riley was lying.

Either way, Eddie isn't here. I walk around the restaurant, just to be sure. The place is crammed with posh students eating pizza at red and white check tables. It's not exactly Eddie's scene. The sweat dries, sticky on my forehead, and I'm fishing in my pocket for my mobile when I spot another set of stairs. I put my foot on the step, and a hand grabs the back of my neck.

'Can I help you, Sir?' A real Italian voice, but even with the accent I can tell helping me isn't what he's got in mind.

I turn around, looking down at the three chins rolling away

off his stubbly face. He's short, but his shoulders fill the space between the wall and the banister in a way that tells me I'm not getting past unless he says so.

'I'm looking for Eddie Burns,' I say.

'And who are you,' he says, rubbing his fat chin, enjoying himself.

I tell him, and his hand tightens on my neck. He puts one shiny shoe on the step beside me and shouts up the stairs.

'Faustino,' I get a face full of garlic. 'Faustino.'

An old man appears at the top of the stairs, sort of dignified, with silver hair.

'Tommy Fairr,' Fat Face says, like my name isn't even worth finishing. 'Looking for Mr. Burns.'

The old man disappears, and I stare at Fat Face, breathing his aftershave and his dinner, until Faustino comes back.

'Okay, Toolio,' Faustino calls down.

Fat Face raises an eyebrow. His hand lifts off my neck and I walk away from him, up towards Faustino.

The staircase is one of those mesh things that looks like it should be in a prison. I'm halfway up when I see about twenty pairs of feet, black leather boots and women's heels with smooth stocking legs, all together round one big oval table.

'Ah fuckin love this Chianti.'

Eddie's voice echoes through my stomach. I get my shoulders back, and my head up, and I'm ready for him, I swear. But the first face I see is Annie Cherani's. She peers out under her fringe, with that gold chain across her milk chocolate cheek.

Frogga's beside her, sneering at me like he's something more than a bulgy-eyed piece of shit. Carl's there too with his big white hands folded in front of him, and that vacant stare. And I guess the girl sat next to him, with big tits and fast eyes must be his fiancé, Kelly.

I turn round the head of the stairs, and there's Eddie Burns' red meaty face. His mouth's wide open and there's something alive in there, long white worms slithering between his shiny lips. He sees me and his mouth opens wider. He spits a load of spaghetti back onto the mountain on his plate. He's going to say something, but Michael Riley beats him to it.

'Thirteen minutes and change,' Riley says.

Eddie frowns. He makes a show of checking his chunky, gold Rolex.

'Nah man, Michael,' he says, spraying mince across the table. 'Fourteen, dead.'

'Right. Fourteen it is,' Riley nods like he laughs, slow and false. 'That'll do.'

The lines deepen on Eddie's forehead. His hands come up over his face, sliding into his hair, and then he grins.

'Unlucky, Chester, son,' he says.

Eddie's head goes back. He laughs at the ceiling, and the rest of the table laugh with him.

I smile too, like I've got any clue what's going on, but Frogga doesn't seem to get the joke. He's still trying to stare me out, but it's Annie that takes the smile off my face. Her eyes are wide and frightened, head turning a fraction left, then right, so slowly that the gold chain never moves against her cheek.

'The lads don't think you're up to much,' Eddie says, waving a hairy paw at Carl and Frogga, cutting off the laughter.

The only sound now is the glug of a drink being poured at the far end of the table.

Eddie clears his throat.

The sound stops.

'But Michael says you're alright. And you stood by my mate,

Maxi, even when he was going down the pan. I won't forget that.' He says it like Maxi had a disease or something, like it wasn't him that got Maxi a one-way ticket to God knows where, and a warning not to come back.

'You wanted to see me?'

'You're right,' he says, 'and you got here in fourteen minutes.' He laughs again, and I force another smile.

'Should I, eh,' I shrug. 'What should I do?'

'I'll tell you,' Frogga leans across the table. 'Fuck off.'

'Chez,' Annie touches his shoulder.

'What?' Frogga shakes her off.

'Don't, please.'

'You want me to pack it in?'

He's shouting at her, working himself up.

Annie doesn't say a word. She stares at the crystal chandeliers.

I move towards them, close enough to see the heat in her cheeks, and the hooded anger in her eyes.

'Pack it in, eh. Pack, Packi–'

'Cheer up, Chester, you miserable bastard,' Eddie shouts down the table, and this sickly grimace crosses Frogga's face.

'Yeh, cheer up,' I mouth at him, and the tightening in his jaw tells me he understands.

'Looks like you're getting the bill, Chester,' Riley says.

Frogga nods, but he never takes his eyes off me.

'Eye, eye, Bandit,' he says, winking like we're still at school. Sad bastard. He mouths something else through that stupid goatee. Something like, "seen you," except not quite.

What do I care? I make out like I don't even notice. I laugh with the rest of them and edge around behind Annie, so she's directly between me and Eddie.

'Right,' Eddie says, rubbing his hands together. 'I'll have one of them sticky toffee things and a nice warm glass of brandy, something expensive, eh, Faustino?'

He waves to the silver-haired waiter and about five of them come out of the walls, swarming around the table. The men order whisky and brandy, the women vodka and coffee. I take my chance and lean across the table, stretching my hand towards Eddie with my cheek so close to Annie's that I can feel the heat in hers.

'Cheers then Eddie,' I shout. 'Polo's,' I whisper into her hair. 'Now.'

My eyes close for half a second. Less. I open them to see Eddie Burns watching me through those glittering points of darkness, my face against Annie's, my hand hovering over the table.

'Piss off,' he says.

I take the stairs three at a time, pushing past waiters and chairs, out into the drizzle. Taxis flash past, headlights trailing rainbows of light. All I need to do is stick my hand out, get myself home. Maybe see if Peeler's up for a pint. That's a normal thing to be doing on a Saturday night. But I turn back, past Faustino's, and look through a set of big glass doors into Polo's bar, next-door.

Pretty faces stare back at me under messed-up, blond-streaked hair. They remind me of Laura from Lincoln. I open the door and the music comes thumping through me, some bassy house shit that the students think is cool. Different people, different drinks, even a different name. They wouldn't call this place a community pub. But there's one thing it's got in common with the Black Boar. The drug. This is Saturday night and people are out to get pissed. Laughing, fighting or fucking, they're out to escape from themselves.

I push past these student types with cocktails and rugby shirts and give up. The place is packed tight with pushy blokes waving twenties in the air. It'd take an hour to get to the bar, and probably the same again to get served, and all I really care about is if Annie's looking in through those glass doors, wondering where the hell I am.

I edge my way back through the crowd, scanning the bar and the street outside. There's no sign of Annie. All I can do is wait, for a girl who probably isn't coming. And why should I care? I should hate her after what she did, running away and leaving me, to them. But all I hate is the fear on her face, and that bulgy-eyed bastard up there with her.

I mean, what was she going to do, kick the shit out of Carl Burns for me? It wasn't her fault. It was them. So, I make excuses for her and try not to hate her, and it works because those angry eyes shining under Faustino's chandelier make a lot more sense than anything that happened back in the Byker Wall.

'Excuse me,' this snooty, blond girl pushes past me, and slides in around the table with her gorilla boyfriend.

He looks at me from under thick black eyebrows, staring at me like I'm some kind of freak, and I don't really blame him. I've been standing here for ages, jammed between the door and the edge of the table with my dodgy eye, and not even a drink in my hand. I want to say something normal, but there's nothing normal left in me, just Frogga's thin, white lips moving behind my eyes, and his stupid goatee scratching at my brain.

'*Seen you.*'

That was what it looked like, his mouth opening, pouting, goatee lips pushing towards me. I step outside and let the door swing shut behind me. The cool air hits me, and I know.

'Seen Lou?'

I get that feeling like my stomach's dropped through my balls.

I remember Salim's little body slipping out of The Grace under that green hoody, and somewhere deep down, I realise, I already knew. Salim's the reason that Louis disappeared. He's the reason the regulars aren't showing. Frogga's fuckin me over, and Riley's screwing me too. The spit-roast from hell. I picture Eddie's spaghetti-filled face laughing at the ceiling, and I'd bet ten-to-one he knows what's going on, and a hundred-to-one he doesn't give a toss.

I make out like I'm staring at the road, but I can feel the bouncers watching me from Faustino's door. This bearded guy steps out between them and my stomach flips, but he's about six stone lighter than Eddie. The door hasn't even closed behind him when she slips through, into the street, with her thin purple shirt blowing out around her. And I have to smile, because Annie Cherani and Eddie Burns have exactly the same effect on my stomach.

'Hi, Annie.'

'What do you want?' She pushes her jaw out, arms tight across her chest. 'And what are you grinning at?'

'Nothing. Come on,' I reach out, almost touching her arm through the thin material. 'It's safer in the crowd.'

That gets her moving. She nods and follows me into Polo's. I find a piece of wall to stand against, back beside snooty girl's table, with Annie facing me, and the press of people forcing us together. She has to uncross her arms to hold her balance.

'What was all that about?' I ask her, not that I really care.

'Riley and Chez were arguing about whether you were any good.' Her breath is warm on my neck. I concentrate on her gold chain and try to pick her voice out through the noise. 'Eddie was egging them on, like he does. So, it ended up with this bet, whether you'd get there in quarter of an hour.'

That, more than anything brings it home to me, how totally screwed I am. The bastards are playing with me. Annie must see it in my face.

'Sorry, Tommy,' she says. She turns her head and the warm breeze dies. She's looking at my eye, just like she did in The Hammer.

'What happened?' she says.

'It's no big deal.'

'What happened, Tommy? I know it's from ages ago. The colour rises in her cheeks. 'I saw it that night in the Wall.'

She lifts her hand to my face and my head jerks back, fast, before I realise how much I want that touch. Her hand darts away. Something breaks between us, and the frustration makes angry.

'That why you're here? To see the freak show?'

'You know me better than that.'

'So, what do you want?'

'To warn you,' she says.

A group of lads come through the glass doors behind her. She edges towards me, and her hand comes up, hot on my shoulder.

'Chez hates you.'

'Chez?' I say, half to myself.

'He heard you at The Hammer, least he thinks he did. Calling me a whore.'

'Annie. No, I didn't...'

'I told him we were talking about the Beamer, that you were jealous. He liked that, but he still hates you. He's got Carl under his thumb, and he knows the business. Even Eddie listens to him.'

Snooty's gorilla boyfriend is on his feet. He's about eight feet tall, pushing between us, staring down at Annie with those horrible eyebrows nuzzling each other across his forehead. Eventually, he gets out of the way, but I can feel him hovering behind me.

'So be careful,' Annie says.

She leans in. Her chest brushes against mine. I glance down, just for a moment, at the silk shirt open at her throat, and what looks like a tiny gold shield hanging from the chain at her neck. She turns away.

'Don't go,' I grab her wrist.

'Tommy, let go.'

Gorilla boy sneers at me. He steps back to let her through. *She's out of your league.* He might as well have said it out loud. I know it's true. That's what sets the spike of pain searing down behind my eye.

'Yeh. So run away again, leave me in the shit.'

'That's not how it was.'

'No? Seemed like it to me, Annie. I didn't see you while your boyfriend was kicking shit out of me. Watching were you, having a good laugh?'

She snaps something back, but I'm not listening.

I let the anger come, not knowing if it's right or wrong, only that it's been pent up for too long. I can't even hear my own voice, just the blood roaring in my ears, and I feel like I'm caught in this loop of her and Carl and Frogga fuckin up my life, and Gorilla boy's still there, watching us, listening, so I have to make Annie repeat herself before I can make sense of what she's saying.

'Who do you think broke that window?'

She's shouting at me, and I'm gasping for breath, feeling their feet thud against me, hearing that shattering crash that might've been inside my head, thinking this is it, they're going to cut me. But they didn't. I'm not even sure if I'm imagining that broken window now, because I want so much to believe it. But the light was real, flooding out onto the grass, and that old bloke in his doorway, with a stick in one hand, and the phone in the other, outlined against the yellow light like a miserable bloody angel, shouting the odds about how he's calling the polis.

'I smashed this rock right through it, then I waited till the old guy came out, till Carl and Frogga ran away up the bank. But I was scared, Tommy. I thought you'd be angry with me.'

'Course I was fuckin angry.' But it's not true. I wasn't, not then, but I can feel the tears welling in my eyes, and that makes me furious.

'Right. Fine.' Her faces scrunches. She snatches her wrist away. 'I saw you were alright,' she hisses at me over her shoulder. 'I watched you go down towards home, away from them.' She opens Polo's big glass door. Gorilla boy steps between us, and she marches away from me for another seven years. I duck under his arm.

'Annie, no,' I spin her round, holding her against me.

'I'm sorry,' I tell her. 'I'm sorry.'

'Alright, Tommy. You're sorry. We're all bloody sorry.'

'I need to see you, to talk to you.'

'No.'

I don't know if it's a raindrop or what, but I wipe my eye and she pulls away again. The bouncer opens Faustino's door for her, and Eddie Burns' laughter comes booming out from the lobby.

'Go.'

'Annie, please.'

I want to grab her again, but I know one of these monkeys

is just waiting to break my arm. What is it about her, makes everyone want to be a hero?

'Five minutes, Annie.'

'Very nice, Faustino. Very fuckin nice,' Eddie's voice is on the other side of the open door.

'Lacey's gym. Me and Kelly'll be there tomorrow morning.'

And for the second time that night I get told to piss off. So, I do. I leg it up Pilgrim Street, with Eddie and Riley, and Frogga and Annie, all chasing each other round my head. I'm neck deep in the shit, so God knows why I'm grinning. But I am, until I pass this old alky throwing up in a doorway, and think of Mam.

Chapter Twenty-Six

Running

The cellar door is closed and bolted, invisible under the smoothed down sheepskin rug, and the bottle of wine is still three-quarters full on the table between us, smudged at the lip where we've both taken a token sip. Red Bordeaux, that's what the bloke in the shop recommended. Full-bodied he said, which sounded sexy and sophisticated. You don't put it in the fridge, you let it breath. So, it's been out on the table, breathing. The stuff still tastes bloody horrible, but then I didn't buy it for me.

The gold chain has gone, and that wispy purple shirt. There's just this stranger with Annie's face, sitting at the far end of the sofa, in jeans and a baggy sweatshirt. She's two steps from the door, but she's here, and she's finally sitting down.

'Chez is out with Carl. Boys' night,' she says, staring at the bits of fluff in the rug. 'And Kelly's alright. She'll cover for me. So long as she thinks I'm with Gav.'

So, call me Gav, I want to say. I try the words in my head, but they feel naff. I take another sip of wine. The bitterness makes me think of that four hundred quid, collarless suit in the wardrobe. I should stop listening to posh blokes in shops.

'He's my personal trainer,' she says.

'Yeh, I saw him. Leonardo Di Caprio's face on Peter Andre's body.'

Annie's brown eyes flick towards me.

'Wanker,' I say, and her lips open, flashing teeth and dimples.

'Course Kelly'll want the details,' she shrugs. 'Only fair, I suppose.'

I smile at that, but there's still too many thoughts rushing round my head.

Boys' night out. Does that mean he's going clubbing? Out all night? I want to ask, but the moment's passed, and anyway, it's a cheap question. All I can do is sit here, and watch her dimples fade away.

'She saw you in the gym. Kelly, I mean. Just from the back, walking out of reception, but she knows it was you. Least she thinks she does. I told her it wasn't, but if she mentions your name to Carl. If they work out where I am.' Her teeth creep out, biting down on her lip. 'You know what they'll do.'

'I know, Annie,' I say. I go to take her hand, but she pulls away, and I'm left holding one little finger. I let it go and she pushes her fists down into her lap.

'You've stopped then,' I say.

'What?'

'Biting your nails.'

'Hmm,' she says, and the dimples flash. 'Forty quid, these nails cost.' She smiles, round eyed through waggling fingers, then her phone beeps, four even pulses, and she practically jumps off the sofa. She stares at the handbag between her feet, and her fear sends a surge of anger burning through my head.

'For fuck's sake, Annie. What are you doing with that sick bastard?'

'What?' she looks at me like she's asking a question, but she's not. 'Same as you're doing, selling shit for Eddie Burns.' Her nose wrinkles into her forehead and she snatches at her handbag.

'Annie,' I scramble round the table, standing between her and the door, both of us holding the bag's long leather strap.

'Piss off, Tommy.'

'Don't go.'

'So, I'm a fuckin whore. Fine, but I'm not staying to hear it.' She snatches the strap away.

'Please.' I want to touch her, but the scowl on her face holds me back. 'I don't think you're a whore. I think you're the best person I know, the toughest and the sweetest.' I reach for the strap again, slowly, holding her eyes.

'You think I'm tough, Tommy?' Her head tilts back, showing me the smoothness of her throat. 'You haven't got a bloody clue.'

'Okay, so you're soft as clarts, but me, I'm an idiot, a raving bloody moron.'

She sighs, a long breath that ruffles her fringe. 'Well, there's definitely something wrong with you.'

'Maybe I've got Tourettes?'

She falls back into the sofa, but she doesn't smile. 'Sit down, Tommy.' She takes a long drink that puts the scowl back on her face.

'Bordeaux,' I say, 'full-bodied, for the more sophisticated palate.'

'Shut up, Tommy.'

'You see. There I go again...'

She doesn't answer, just fixes me with her dark-brown eyes, making me feel like a stupid kid, which is exactly what I'm being. I sit down and press my fingers to my lips. I only let them move when I know what I'm going to say.

'What happened to you, Annie? Why did you disappear?'

'Why did I disappear?' she says. 'More like you did.'

'Right,' I say. I'm scared to say anymore, but I don't know what she means, and I suppose she must see it on my face.

'I came looking for you,' she says, 'after that night in the wall. I watched the house, but you never came. I rang the bell in the end, but your mam didn't even know who I was, kept asking if I was from the social. Me, just turned sixteen, in those sorry plaits. I didn't know who else to ask.'

She stops. The only movement is her hand in her lap, one long nail scratching at the inside of her thumb.

'Maxi got me working over the west end, till things died down.'

'Well, you could have told me.'

'But I thought...' I shut my mouth, ashamed of what I thought.

'I went back a couple of days later. Daryl opened the door. I was already backing down the path. I should have just kept going, but he smiled at me, remembered my name. He made me come in, sat me on that sofa. "Take a load off," he said, like it was 1977 or something, and he told me this story. He said you'd met someone. A whirlwind romance he called it.'

'No, Annie,' I touch her sleeve.

'It doesn't matter now.' The nail scratches faster.

'Please, Annie,' I say, 'it does.' I should shut up and let it go, but the truth is I've never been able to keep my mouth shut. 'Tell me,' I say, 'what happened,' then, when it's too late, I press my hand to my mouth and listen to the tick-tick-tick of her nail.

'He gave me a drink and sat beside me on the sofa, and then, y'know.' Her voice falls to a flat monotone, and she tells it to the blank T.V. screen.

'He was grinning at me, with his face right up close and that snake tattoo pushed up under my skirt. I was screaming. Least there was this voice screaming in my head, telling me to spit in his face, to scratch his beady eyes out, but I could hear water running in the bathroom, your mam moving about upstairs, and…' her voice cracks.

'His hand was moving between my legs. There was too much going on. The scream got further away, till there was just this one thought, that he's doing this with your mam in the house. Like he knew who I was, what I was. I heard her come down. The stairs creaked. He could hear them too. He must of, but his hand never stopped. The door swung open, and I was up, pushing past your mam, out into the street with him shouting behind me, telling me you'd found a proper white lass and you didn't need any dirty Paki.'

I think of Daryl's sly, lying face, and my fingers press harder into my lips, like I'm holding in the hatred. And I know I'm a shit for putting her through this, and I should have stopped her, but that's how it is, when there's something useful to say, all I can think of is myself.

'So, you never came back.'

'I never came back.'

'I did,' I say. 'Just before Christmas, I was in and out of every bar in Walker doing…' I shrug. 'Working for Maxi Blair.'

'I was in London by then.' She shakes her head and laughs like breaking glass. 'I wanted to be a model, like every other stupid kid in the world, and amazingly, I actually got some work. This agent, Clive Declaire, spoke like Prince bloody Charles, said he was going to make me famous. Paid my train fare, hotel room, the works. Eight hundred quid I got for that first job, sneezing into a Kleenex for about half a second. Turned out that was about the worst thing could've happened. There were other bits of work, catalogues, things like that, but it wasn't enough to live on, especially not down there.

'That Christmas, when you came back, I was washing dishes

at this curry house in Kilburn. I did that for years, on and off, waiting for jobs to come up. I was sick, Tommy, by the end.' The nail scratches faster against her thumb.

'There was this guy, called himself a producer, talked the talk, said my look was just right for this project. Two hundred quid a day. Of course, he never really told me what it was.'

'You don't have to…'

'Glamour.' That shattered laugh comes again. 'Stupid fuckin word. Like there's anything glamorous about it. But it kept me out of that curry house, for a while.' She snatches at the glass and takes a mouthful of wine. A red drop spills onto her chin. 'In the end, it's like everything.' She wipes her sleeve across her chin. 'How far will you go? Well, maybe it'll surprise you, but there were things I wouldn't do. So that was that. It was either the curry house or coming back here.'

'Jesus, Annie.'

My fists clench so tight my nails cut into my palms, and I'm looking at her saying all this stuff, spelling it out, and I know one thing for certain, I couldn't do it. All I can do is hide myself away and blame other people. Maybe that's why my own selfish shit comes slithering back to the surface.

'But Frogga?'

'Fuckin hell, Tommy. I tried so hard, but it didn't work out and I'm not spending my life living on the dole, and maybe turning a few tricks on the side when the money runs out. I've seen that life, Tommy. I'm not going to live it.'

'I'm sorry, Annie. I know.' And this, at least, is true.

'I went back to the house, waited for your mam, but…' she shrugs. 'She was worse than before. Said she hadn't seen you for years.'

'I know,' I say. 'I know.'

'I'd been away so long. I didn't know anyone anymore. I ended up down the Raby. Sat there all day, asking people for Tommy Boyle, but no one seemed to know you.'

'Boyle is…'

'His name,' she finishes for me. 'But I thought you'd got out. I hoped it was true, for your sake.'

She stares at the glass and her hand opens, sharp nail picking at soft red skin, like there's one thin layer of protection left between her flesh and the world.

I can't stand it. My hand closes over hers.

She pulls away, but this time, I hold on.

'I went back to my mam's, but I didn't last the night, with the door slamming and the bedsprings going, and the noise of Mam's performance. I had to get out of there, but there was nowhere left to go. Ended up just walking round in circles. It was up on the Byker Bank where I saw Wendy Callaghan. You've got to remember her. She was in your year at Heaton Manor. The spit of Angelina Jolie, but better looking.'

'Yeh, I remember,' I say, trying not to sound too enthusiastic. 'Always in those black leather trousers.'

Annie isn't fooled. Her eyebrows rise, just a shade.

'Anyway,' she says, 'this sad cow comes walking down towards me with her saggy trackies hanging so low you could see the crack of her arse. She had a fag in her mouth, and I swear the ash was an inch long, dropping into the buggy in front of her, with this screaming kid in her other hand and her belly bulging with the third. But what freaked me out was the way she was staring, with these cold eyes and a mouth like she was sucking lemons. Then I realised who she was.'

'Wendy?' I say, but it isn't her I'm thinking of, it's Mam, begging for vodka, with her hand sliding down inside her worn out coat. Miss Evening Chronicle, after twenty years of scraping by, with Daryl 'ya cunt' Boyle. Who am I to say that Annie Cherani shouldn't have more than that?

'So then I met Carl. I mean I tracked him down. Wandered into The Hammer like I was just passing through, cos like I say, no one had heard of Tommy Boyle, but they all knew about Carl Burns, and the Merc and money, and the house on the river. And that was what I wanted.' A silvery drop swells on Annie's eyelash. 'Of course, he was with Kelly. So, I got second prize.' She blinks, and the drop spills down her cheek. 'I've got my Beamer and my membership at Lacey's. I get my hair cut at Friars, tailored, they call it. I get my hair fuckin tailored.' She laughs, with the tears rolling down her face.

'What does that make me, Tommy?' Her whole body's shaking. I hold her, pressing my face to hers. A tear runs from her cheek to mine, sweet and salty in my mouth.

'What does that make me?'

I hold my breath, a silent coward, and listen to the thudding in my chest.

'I'm not just a stupid cow, Tommy.' The sob bursts out from way down in her stomach, shuddering through me, and all I can think of is the power of her. She's so real, so strong, like I need to be. I want to tell her so much, right back, even from before our beginning. But the words don't come.

'I'm a whore, Tommy, like my mam. Cos you can't escape where you come from. You can try, but you can't escape who you are.'

She stands up, but I throw my arms back around her and I cling on. My face is pressed to the tiny swell of her stomach, and I won't let her go, because this is my Annie. I know she's with Frogga now, like she was with Carl then, because she's scared and trapped, and she doesn't know what else to do. I press my head deeper. Her fingers turn, coiling in my hair, pulling, hurting me until it eases the pain, and I'm sorry, and I'm sorry and I'm sorry.

We stay like that, me kneeling on the floor with my arms around her, feeling the vibration of her body through my chest, and I want to cry with her, to let it all go, for Annie, and for me and for Mam. For all the things that might've been. I try, but I can't. I don't know how. I've been clamped down, too tight for too long. I look down at the mess we've made of the rug, its ruffled fur stirred up by the Devil's own footprints, and all I can do is cling to her with my mouth tight shut, and feel us moving apart again, like always.

I should have banged on that door till she answered and pressed those Caramels into her angry little fists. But I didn't. I waited until it was too late because I was a coward. And the knowledge is like a dead thing in my chest. This is how I will spend my life, watching the world through a screen, seeing other people cry and love, while I just get to fight and fake.

I have to break the spell. I know that, but I can't even think it, not clearly and honestly, because then I'd run and hide like always. And that's what I do. I run and hide inside myself, but at least this one time, I look back. I peek at myself through the hinge of a closing door, this cold, lifeless creature a moment from eternal darkness. Panic screams through me.

I feel the burn in my finger, and Daryl's face up close to mine. The dead skin in his yellow tash, his mouth moving, telling me I don't have a brother. And the Devil's dancing in that thick brown rug in my Belmont Street bedroom, and here, on this rug beneath my knees, because this is the third time and if I say it again then he's got me forever, so I don't understand how the force of Annie's sobs jolt the words out of my throat.

'I have a brother.'

'What?'

'I have a brother.'

Terror dries my tongue in my mouth, and when that phone rings it's like the best hit you ever had, a numbing rush of freedom.

'I'm sorry, I have to,' I mumble, snatching the phone out of my jeans, jabbing at the green button.

'Peeler?' I say, seeing Annie's mascara-lined face go up and round, watching me with slanting eyes that tell me she knows.

I have to make Peeler repeat what he's saying, yelling at me down the phone. I finally get it.

'Lock the door,' I tell him, and grab my car keys off the windowsill, safe in a world I hate, but understand. 'Make him tea, with loads of sugar. Keep him warm. Don't speak to anyone. Don't answer the door till I get there.'

'I'm sorry, Annie,' I tell her from the doorway. 'Really, I'm sorry,' and I don't know if I'm lying or hiding, but I'm out and running for the car.

Chapter Twenty-Seven

Slide Away

'*Slide away, slide away...*'

I get the sound up full, shaking the windows, and I'm shouting along with the Gallaghers, buzzing with music and fear, blocking out the rest, till I pull up outside Peeler's flat and it's time to get out of the car and face what's inside.

The street is still and dark. Even Bleach-Blond Buddha is tucked up in bed. I walk between the two squares of grass and press the bell. There are footsteps in the hallway, and Peeler's voice.

'Who's that?'

'Open the door.'

The bolts go, and I'm looking at Peeler's jug-eared outline in the corridor.

He leads me through to the living room, past that wall of DVDs. The smell stops me in the bedroom doorway. The sharp metal tang of blood, and the acid stink of shit and fear.

I peer in through blue lamplight. There's a strip of carpet between a stack of boxes and a sagging single bed. Louis' body is laid out on the bed, with a blanket tight beneath his throat.

I take a breath through my mouth and edge between the boxes. My eyes fix on the blanket, stained dark across his chest.

'Louis,' I kneel down, scared to touch him. 'Louis.'

A sound comes out of him, somewhere between a groan and a sigh. His face turns, shiny with sweat, and I get a sudden image of him in the sunshine, six years old, kicking that ball against the wall, with Annie laying out chocolate buttons in a neat little row on the gatepost, and him clicking his tongue, starring in his own private match, lips moving, telling himself the score. Just like he's telling me now.

'Salim,' he says, and fresh sweat bursts onto his forehead.

'Salim?' I watch the light in his eyes. 'He did this?'

He wanted a d-deal,' Louis stutters, with his body shaking under the blanket, and that dark stain spreading in the blue light. 'He grabbed a bag and legged it into the car park. I caught him under the b-back wall.'

'Sure, Louis. You caught him.'

'H-Hold, hold my hand,' he says.

I don't want to, but I take his hand, feeling the strength in his grip, the stickiness of blood on his palm, and the warm wetness seeping through the blanket. I fold it back, and a lump rises in my throat. He's naked from the waist up, his skinny white body is black with blood, still oozing from the open wounds across his chest.

'You'll be alright,' I say, squeezing his hand. And I remember Eddie Burns' hand against mine when I got us all into this.

'That's where they jumped me,' he says. 'Three of them. They locked me in this van. Left me there for ages. Days. Then they came back.' He starts to cry, big heavy thuds that set the blood pumping out of him. 'Two of them held me. Salim did the cutting.'

'I'm sorry,' I say. I lift his hand to my cheek and this great flap of flesh falls open at his shoulder. Vomit burns in my throat. I swallow it back down. 'Take it easy, Lou,' I say, letting my voice drop to a whisper, as if that makes the lie less bad. 'You're going to be alright.'

'You told me,' he croaks something else, but all I hear is a rush of air. I lean in, feeling his cracked lips against my ear. 'You told me that before.'

I drop his hand, and my head swings back against Peeler's legs. 'Jesus, man, Peeler, will you not stand on top of me.' He clatters back against the boxes. 'Get an ambulance,' Peeler's mouth opens. 'Peeler.' I jam my elbow into his thigh. 'Nine, nine, nine.' He fumbles for his phone, drops it on the sodden carpet.

I snatch it up and make the call myself, give them Peeler's name, his address.

'You're going to the hospital,' I say to Louis. 'They're going to look after you, but this is important, for all of us,' I lean back over him, holding his face, looking for some spark in his cloudy eyes.

'They jumped you right,' I tell him, running my hands through his pockets, checking for wraps and pills, doing what I have to do, while the song screams in my head. *Slide Away, Slide Away.* 'You didn't see anything. You don't know anything,' I spell it out, not wanting to remember where I've heard those words before, or how it can possibly be me that's saying them now.

'I'm sorry,' I say, for what seems like the hundredth time, and push Peeler out into the living room and close the door behind us.

'Salim-fuckin-Iqbal,' Peeler says.

'Yeh, Salim Iqbal,' I say, 'but I've got more to worry about than that little shit. I need to sort this, Peeler, like right now. I mean there's no point in me hanging around here.'

Peeler nods, but I can see he doesn't want me to go. And maybe it's true, what I just told him, but deep down we both know that I'm running away. Again.

'You'll be okay, Peeler,' I say, trying to make it true, like I can make everything okay by saying it. 'You found him outside The Boar, right. He'd been jumped. Nobody saw anything.'

He nods again, this time with a shade more conviction.

'Good. Now go back in there and talk to Louis. Stay with him in the ambulance.' I push Peeler back towards the bedroom and get out of there, slamming the door behind me, feeling like a piece of shit.

I sit in the car and turn the engine on, and the stereo off. I need to think, whether I want to or not. If I'd stopped to think before, this shit wouldn't be happening. Because I knew. I knew it was Salim in The Grace, and I went up to Faustino's and wound Frogga up. I opened my mouth when I should have kept it shut, just so I could feel good.

My hand slips down, fingers twisting inside my thigh. I need the pain. The punishment. I don't even care what kind of nutcase that makes me. But it doesn't work.

I wish I'd left Louis dealing on his own, maybe getting a slap from one of Eddie's lads, a few bruises. But there's nothing I can do about that now. He'll be okay in the hospital, maybe, and there's other lads to think about. None of them'll be working till this gets sorted, and I can't hardly blame them, with Frogga's pretty-boy, nutcase on the loose.

I get my hands up where I can see them, and my mind turns, like always, to what's best for Tommy Farrier.

Michael Riley won't give a shit about any of this. He'll be coming for his three grand on Saturday, ringing with the drop-off in that stupid monotone voice. And Eddie's hardly going to take my side against him. Right, so think. That leaves Carl and Frogga. My hands tighten on the wheel. If I can see Carl on his own, tell him Eddie's pissed off about Louis, maybe he'll get Frogga to back off? It's a chance. I don't see there's anything else I can do.

The warning sirens blare, flashing lights come screaming

down the road. I don't react. I'm too busy trying to kid myself that my stupid plans are going to work. The police car pulls up in front of me. Doors open, voices shout, before I finally put the car into gear and get out of there.

I wait till I'm up on Walker Road before I make the call.

'Theeyammer,' this Brummie barman answers.

First time lucky. Carl Burns is in.

Brummie passes the phone across the bar.

'Yeh,' Carl tells me, 'we can have a chat any time you like.'

'Just between us,' I say, keeping my voice light, like the old mates we are.

'Sure,' he says, 'whatever.'

Twenty minutes later I'm standing at the bar, squinting through red flashing lights at Justine, winding herself around a silver pole on the dance floor, not half as sexy as she was stepping onto that Metro at Howdon. I get to the bar, shouting through bad, bassy music for a bottle of beer, and scanning the place for Carl Burns. There's a few faces I know, but I don't meet anyone's eye. I work my way around the dancefloor to that thick red rope at the bottom of the stairs. That's where he'll be. Up there.

'Evening,' Strangler's tash twitches.

'Carlo around?'

'Eh?'

I step around him to shout in his whole ear, and he lifts his little brass hook.

I walk up that curved staircase with the music and the flashing lights fading behind me, but it's already too late. Between the noise and the lights, and everything else, the damage is done. That stale taste creeps round my mouth. The needle digs in behind my eye, and the next thing I see is that wall of mirrors glaring back at me with a blur of colours streaming out around them.

Maybe I catch a glimpse of him in the mirror, but I know, a moment before I turn, that Carl Burns is there, watching me with his arms folded and his jaw pushed forward. The needle burns deeper. Not because of Carl. I look at him standing there, wooden as Pinocchio with the same fake hard-case expression he's been hiding behind since school. It doesn't impress me anymore. Anyone can see that he's trying to live up to his uncle. I almost feel sorry for him.

Sorry, Carl, but you'll never be a real boy.

Frogga's the one who sets the needle digging deeper. I can tell it's him, facing away from me, leaning on the bar in his shiny suit, with his slimy, slicked-back hair. He half turns and flashes his lizard smile.

'Alright,' I give him a nod like nothing's happened.

I need to hold it together. There's no point starting a fight I can't win. I need to be wise for once in my life. Move on. Get this sorted and let it go.

'Is now okay?' I say to Carl.

'I'm listening,' he says, but his eyes flick questioningly at Frogga, and that should be enough to tell me I'm wasting my time.

'Just us,' I say.

Carl opens his mouth, but Frogga's faster.

'There is just us,' he says, putting his bottle on the bar.

'Yeh, just us,' Carl laughs. 'You got a problem?'

'Look, Carlo. We're on the same team, right?' The music thuds up the stairs. 'You do the coke, we do green. That's good for business. I mean I'm not trying to tell you what to do, but that's how Eddie wants it.'

'Does he,' Frogga says.

'Yeh,' I say. 'He does.'

'Well, so,' Carl says.

'So, my lads are getting scared off. Louis Solomon got cut up.'

'You accusing Mr. Burns?' Frogga says, which is obviously bullshit. But then I'm not sure if he means Eddie or Carl.

'I'm not accusing anyone.'

'I wouldn't if I was you,' Frogga says.

'I'm not. I just want to know that you're gonna have a word with Salim. That this is the end.'

'He's crazy, that Fat-Boy. Fat Boy, Salim,' Frogga snorts, and a big purple drop swells out of his nose.

I close my eyes and see the tear balanced on Annie's eyelash, and I'm dizzy with anger.

'Look, Carl,' I get a grip on the bar's brass rail. 'I'm not looking for trouble. I just want to know where I stand.'

'You're standing in our fuckin bar,' Frogga says, and Carl laughs again.

'The organ-grinder and his monkey,' I whisper.

Maybe they hear me.

Carl's fist closes across his chest.

Frogga's sleeve comes up, wiping that drop off his nose. He sniffs and stares at the smear on his sharp silver suit, then he looks up at me, with his lips shut tight behind that nasty little beard.

'Right,' I say. 'Okay.'

I can't leave it like this, but when I look at Louis's bloodstains on my hand, I know if I stay another moment, I'll smash my beer into Frogga's ugly face, and get myself killed, right here and now.

I clench my teeth and walk away from them, keeping my

eyes down, away from the screaming mirrors, and take the stairs one cold step at a time. I'm halfway down when I hear the rush of footsteps behind me. I tense for the impact, but he barely touches me.

'Sorry lad,' he mumbles in his almost-Yorkshire accent, and slides his hand across my jacket.

'What?'

'Think about where you're going,' he says, looking at me with his bright blue eyes and those pouty, baby lips right up close to mine. And then he's gone.

I stand there watching him walk away from me, past Strangler's rope, stopping to jam a fiver into Justine's tiny knickers. Goes to show, I don't know a damn thing, especially now, with that bass beating in my head. I take another step and stop.

Someone's calling me back.

I look up at Frogga, and I'm thinking right, it'll be okay. They were just taking the piss. We can still sort it out. And then the music drops, and I hear what he's shouting.

'Tough shit, Bandit.'

I take the rest of the stairs in two giant steps and I'm out in the night with my heart beating in my throat. The key scrapes around the ignition, and I'm away, tyres screaming, with one hand switching between the wheel and the gearstick, and the other twisting at the flesh on my thigh.

This is fucked, and it's all my own stupid fault. If I'd kept my mouth shut, Louis wouldn't be dying. There's no point kidding myself. That's what's going to happen. It'll be me next, or Peeler, and they'll keep going till we're finished, and the only certainty is Riley ringing every bloody Saturday, for three grand I haven't got. I'm screwed. I'm a moron for getting involved with these bastards, for thinking I could do it without Maxi's protection. And of course, Eddie'll have given the nod. Now it's all family, what's the need for me?

I should cut my losses and do a runner, get on a flight, and never come back. But that's not going to happen. I'm not running away anymore, and even if I won't admit it, Annie Cherani is the reason why. I should stop and think of her, but all I can think about is how every shit thing in my life is down to that bulgy-eyed bastard and his thick fuckin mate, and whatever happens, they're never going to leave me alone.

So, like always, all that's left is the cellar. I'm hungry for it. To get down there and pin him down with those fine steel ropes, to scrape the poison off his slimy green skin and feed it back, drop by drop into his bulging eyes.

Chapter Twenty-Eight

My Brother

That's what I'm thinking about when I get back to the flat, getting my sick fix in the cellar. I've pulled my jacket off and got both hands clenched around the sheepskin rug when my breath stops. Hairs prickle along my neck. Someone is watching me.

I drop the rug. The thud of cloth drowns the sound of breathing. I catch a flicker of movement in the yellow light from the street and wait for the cold burn of Salim's knife in my back.

'Annie.'

She's there, where I left her about a hundred years ago, perched on the edge of the sofa opposite the blank T.V. There's only the shine of her eyes and the shape of her body in that baggy sweatshirt, standing, raising the wineglass to her lips. I watch the movement of her throat, listen to the small sounds of swallowing. She holds the glass towards me, red wine, black in the glass.

My fingers brush against hers, the force of her prickling up my arm. I hold the glass to my lips. My throat tightens. The iron taste is bitter in my mouth. I throw it back, gagging, but swallowing, draining the glass, lowering it back to the table.

Annie steps closer. I feel the softness of her hair on my face. My arms come up around her, and we hold each other, still and close, safe from the world. Cars roll by on the street outside. We move in fractions. Her cheek against mine, nuzzling like animals, babies, hungry for comfort. Our lips touch, soft and closed. I hear the screech of an ugly gear change, the ratchet of a handbrake. I press harder, piercing her with my tongue. A car door slams, and already some innocent part of us is lost.

We fall back on the Devil's rug, hands clutching, greedy, and angry. I rip her sweatshirt over her head.

Cloth tears.

Our jeans are loose and open.

I grab two full handfuls of her body, and drive myself inside her, hard and furious. She meets me with an anger of her own. Thighs tight around my waist, her hips beat against mine, while my twisted secrets lie still and silent, a floor-board's width below us. The memories drive me deeper. Faster. Running through the dusk. That silver shoe turning above us. Bodies slamming into the fence. Feet and fists pummeling in.

The selfish bitch. The whore. What the fuck is wrong with her, giving herself to Frogga. I should kick her out into the street right now, with her knickers round her ankles and her tits swinging in the breeze. I want to punish her, to hurt her, like she's hurt me. But I can't. She's the only decent thing in my life, and I have to forgive her. Is that love, or desperation? I don't know. I let go of judgments and anger and hold tight to my sweet brown girl until the smell of peaches and Louis Solomon's blood draw a strangled scream from my throat.

Later, when the sweat is dry and cold on our skin, I take Annie's hand and guide her through to the bedroom, where we lay, separate and alone beneath the deep feather duvet, with the weight of nameless defeat heavy in my stomach.

Her eyes close. Her breath falls to a regular rhythm, and with Annie gone there is no one to hold back the fear, the pictures spinning through my mind. The glint of Carl's sovereign ring, and the flash of Salim's knife. I see the shock on Louis

Solomon's face, and I open my eyes, blocking it out, but Eddie Burns' face is there, laughing in the darkness.

Annie stirs beside me, a sound too small to be called a snore, but it banishes Eddie back to hell. I watch her open mouth, the arch of her throat, and the tight swell of her breasts against the duvet. One pink nipple peaks out towards me. I smile, remembering the last time we slept together, on her Mam's silk duvet. That bed, that seemed so enormous and exotic, with Annie's head on my arm and our legs coiled together, as if she was somebody else. And even now, half a lifetime later, I feel the shame burn in my cheeks, for that terrified boy, running away with his clothes in his hands, and I wonder, can I really love anyone at all, apart from my lost little brother?

'Benjy,' I say his name out loud for the first time in a long, long time, and listen to its strange childish sound.

'Tommy,' Annie's head turns on the pillow, eyes looking into mine, reading my thoughts. 'You had a brother,' she says, and the fear burns through my finger, while the Devil dances his final jig.

Okay, Daryl, you mean spirited bastard. So let him dance.

'His name is Benjy.'

I try to be brave, but the lump swells in my throat. I lower my eyes, glad of the darkness. My hand slides across Annie's stomach. She draws me to her. The only sound is the beat of her heart, and I tell my secret to the soft curve of her throat.

'He was four, when they took him.'

The words spill out of me, about the World Cup and the shiny wetness of Daryl's lip, and how all those tiny bits of glass jumped out of the whisky bottle. I tell her about the angle of Benjy's arm, not like an arm at all. I even tell her how we curled together under the Rainbow Blanket with Benjy's cheek inside my elbow, and Mam's feet squealing up the stairs. I keep going, not caring how much sense I make, only getting it out.

"'Boyle,' he said. "Your name's Boyle. And you haven't got a fuckin brother.'"

I even tell how Benjy was burrowing in like Buster when they opened the door. Only I don't tell that it was my fault. How it was me that screamed when that board came squeezing down, but Benjy was the one they took. I don't tell her that because I'm too ashamed.

But I tell about Mam taking us to the station, sending those cards to Mrs. Abuto Palacios every year, on Benjy's birthday. 'Till the drinking got too bad,' I say, seeing that spray of copper coins clatter on the station tiles, and the worn-down stumps in the old soldier's open mouth.

'We never got a reply. I mean to the cards, and I never went back with Mam. Not after that. But I went on my own, sometimes. That was where I went that night, after you broke the old bloke's window. I followed the river, and my feet just took me up to the station. I wanted to be near him. Slept on those crappy plastic seats, waited for the first train to Sunderland.

'I could hardly move when I woke up, but I staggered up to that yellow line and watched the train come in, remembering those little bits of card fluttering onto the track. And I felt bad, Annie,' I'm crying, forcing words out. 'You have to understand. It was the day before my sixteenth birthday, and there was nothing. Nothing good. I thought you'd set me up, that there was just Daryl and Carl, and my useless, pissed Mam, and all those letters that never got a reply, like they'd just been thrown onto the track, too.

'The rush of air was humming in my head. I swayed forward.

Way too far to stop. The pain was gone, like Nirvana or something, but there was this hand on my shoulder, holding me back. So strong, for such a little hand.'

Annie squeezes me in, burying my face in the soft nest of her hair. She keeps me close till I stop crying.

'That was when I went up there. Got the next train. Hid in the toilets all the way to Sunderland. Blagged a taxi to Elliot Terrace. That was the address on all those cards. The place they'd taken Benjy.

'I'd been more scared of it than anything. Like I thought that was where the child-catcher lived, the guy off Chitty Chitty Bang Bang with the big nose and the net,' I laugh, a single syllable that catches in my throat. 'I mean, I was too old to really believe it, but I was still scared, terrified, but excited, walking through the big glass doors, and thinking, this is it. I'm going to see Abuto Palacios. I'm going to find Benjy. It seemed crazy that I hadn't come before. A few minutes on the train and I was there, in this place that just existed to look after kids.

'There was a long desk with plastic windows, and these two blonde women behind it, like soldiers in a fort. The younger one had a stud in her nose, that made it easier. I asked her. Told her I needed to speak to Mrs Abuto Palacios. She made me say the name three times, and it came out different every one. I'd said her name so often in my head, but never out loud. And God knows what I looked like, hobbling around with blood all over me, and my blank shark's eye.'

'No,' Annie lifts my head, holding me back away from her. 'Your eye's beautiful,' she says. 'You are beautiful.' She kisses my eyelid and draws me back in to the safety of her throat.

'The woman told me to wait, so I sat on the end of this row of plastic seats, and I waited. I waited ages, with the blond women looking daggers at me through their plastic windows. Eventually this pissed-off bloke with a tash came out wanting to know who I was. Carl Burns, I told him. He told me Mrs. Palacios wasn't there, but that he could help me. That turned out to be a load of shite. I told him Benjy's name, that I needed to find him, and he started snapping at me about all these rules and regulations. He wouldn't even tell me where Mrs. Palacios had gone.

'I hung around for a while, asking all these people walking in and out, until the woman with the stud said I had to stop bothering everyone. I went outside then and asked on the steps. No one even answered me. Not till they were closing reception and this woman came round with a giant hoover. She was the one who told me Mrs. Abuto had retired. Moved to Birmingham or somewhere. By then I was tired and hungry and sick of it all. I went back to Maxi's and carried on like nothing happened.

'But Benjy saved me. He held me back off those tracks and I just walked out of there and pretended he wasn't even real.

'But he is real,' she says. 'Benjy is real.'

'Yes,' I say, and it's so strange to hear his name on her lips.

'You'll find him, Tommy,' she kisses my forehead. 'We'll find him,' she says, and it's like the prison gates are open because I'm not alone anymore.

'It was my fault,' I tell her. 'I screamed when the board came down. That was why they found us, why they took him away,' I clutch her to me, getting the last of it out while she shushes me like a baby. And when at last I lift my head, there's a thin blue light around her chimney-sweep's hair.

'That Cadbury's Caramel,' I say, 'you getting caught by Mrs. Atwal. That was the best thing in my life.'

She kisses me again, warm lips working open, her mouth wet, with the sweet taste of morning. I feel the heat of her thighs, the soft swell of her stomach, so unlike Clara's jutting edges. I lean away and look down at her body. I don't need to possess it. I want to, but all I really need is just for her to be. To know that she exists, safe and warm, somewhere in the world. Her hands come up around my neck, turning circles on the back of my skull.

'She's with me,' Annie says. 'That was what you told her. You saved me, Tommy.'

We coil together.

There are no more words. Only the birds chattering in the cherry blossom. Her palm is warm at the base of my spine. Slick and hot, fraction by fraction, her body draws me in. Her eyes widen. We are still. The pulse of her blood beats against me, holding and releasing, taking me deeper.

'Tommy,' she whispers, holding me with her eyes. 'You saved me, Tommy.'

I feel the broken pieces of myself drawn together, washed clean, part of something more. We are one complete creature. Fingers locked, arms held out across the dark sheet in perfect crucifixion.

Her body pulses around me, more than a background to my own throbbing beat. She is the centre. I watch her face, the flush of her cheeks, mouth moving, sounds that have more meaning than words. She echoes through me, and I offer her the seed of my own new self.

I lie cradled in her arms with the tears wet on my face, not understanding the feeling growing inside me until it bursts out of my mouth, and I shake with near silent convulsions.

'What's so funny,' she wants to know.

That pink balloon comes floating down, and Mam's tickling us till we scream, till the whisky falls and the laughter dies. But it doesn't matter because this isn't about Daryl or Mam or Benjy. This is about Annie and me. My life might be falling apart, but I feel great. I land a clumsy kiss on her beautiful mouth and press my hands to my aching stomach.

'Mental case,' she says.

There's a bright white light slicing through the curtains when Annie rolls away from me with the promise of coffee and, 'whatever I can find in your manky fridge.' My blue check shirt has never looked so good, riding up over Annie's smooth little cheeks.

I lie back, stretched across the bed, and listen to the slap of her bare feet on the wooden floor, the tap running, cupboards opening. Cars go by, reminding me that there's a world out there, but I'm not thinking about that, not yet. I pull on my trackie bottoms and go looking for Annie.

I kneel on the sofa, facing back over the kitchen counter. She flashes me a smile and slides the coffee cup across. The bitter-sweet smell reminds me that I'm starving.

'You can have green furry bread,' she says, 'or a block of yellow plastic that might once have been cheese.'

I shrug and smile.

'Didn't anyone tell you about shops,' she says.

'Da-dah,' I say, pulling a brown-spotted banana off the windowsill.

Annie rolls her eyes, but she comes round to sit beside me on the sofa. We pass it back and forth between us, taking smaller and smaller bites, until she jams the last lump of soggy flesh in my mouth.

'Cheeky cow,' I say, through a spray of banana, and grab a

handful of hair.

I pull her face towards me, tongues fighting over that last, chewed mouthful. She squeals and beats at my chest, then she pushes me hard, sending me back the length of the sofa, warm thighs straddling my stomach.

'Right,' she says, and then four even pulses suck the smile off her face.

She looks down at the sheepskin rug, the iPhone sticking out of her handbag, half-hidden under her crumpled jeans. The phone lights up, and beeps again. Her eyes turn to the clock over the fridge.

'I need to get going,' she says, lifting herself away from me. 'Kelly's booked us a facial for nine-thirty.'

'A facial,' I say, stupidly, watching her pick through the mess of clothes on the rug, turning my face to the kitchen while she pulls on her sensible white knickers, and swaps my shirt for hers.

'Tommy, please. I wish it was different,' she says, and I turn back to see her sitting on the far side of the sofa.

The sunlight falls across her face in shades of honey and caramel, raising auburn tints in her tatty hair. I watch her, watching me, the two of us, cowards, facing each other over the coffee-table with its crappy bottle of wine, and still too many unsaid words.

'I better get ready. It's safer if I call him from there,' she says, walking away from me. The bathroom door closes behind her.

I stare at my clothes, crumpled and pathetic on the floor, jeans inside out with my boxers still attached like some stupid Superman costume, loose change fallen onto the rug. I think of the trapdoor below. Goose bumps come up along my arms. No more.

I snatch my shirt off the floor, feeling the warmth of her body fade between my fingers, the smell of her. I throw it back down and stamp across to my leather jacket under the T.V. and pull it on. The lining is cold against my skin. I jam my hands in the pockets, feeling car keys and my Zippo, and something else. Something thin and light with one sharp corner digging into my thumb. A blank white card. I turn it over and remember that rush of footsteps on the stairs behind me. The feel of his hand sliding across my jacket.

"Watch where you're going," he said, through those pouty, baby lips, and jammed a fiver into Justine's knickers on his way out.

'You alright?'

Annie walks back through with her wet hair tied back and that BMW key fob in her hand, reminding me who she's going back to. My teeth clench in frustration, but the fear is stronger, the fear that she will leave and never come back.

'Sure, Annie. Alright.'

I open my hand, surprised to see the crushed card in my palm. I flick the crumpled ball away from me, watching it bounce and roll under the sofa.

'Bye, then,' she says, standing in the doorway.

She steps away down the corridor, opens the front door, and looks back over her shoulder. There's just that moment of hesitation, but it's enough. I rush towards her, tripping over the coffee table. The bottle falls behind me. I squeeze her to me, pressing my cheek against hers.

'Tommy.' She pushes me back, one strong shove, like she did that day at The Hammer, but not until I've felt her chest shudder against me.

'Find him, Tommy. Find Benjy. If you can't do it for yourself, do it for me.' She backs out, onto the path.

'I won't let us down again,' I say, not even sure who I mean. Maybe feeling in some strange way that finding Benjy will lead me to Annie, or she will lead me to him. Not understanding, only knowing that I need to be strong now, more than ever.

'And I'll call you,' I shout through the open door.

'It's not safe, Tommy. He checks everything.'

'Wait. Wait there,' I say, scrabbling in the sideboard and getting the last of those crappy Motorola's out of the drawer, then I run back down the corridor and press it in her hand. 'I'll call you,' I say again.

'Okay, Tommy, okay.'

'I'm going to get us out of this,' I say, lifting her jaw, holding her eyes. 'I'm going to do it.'

She reaches up and takes my hand from her face, and then she kisses my mouth and walks away beneath the cherry blossom, to her shiny new car.

Chapter Twenty-Nine

The Phone Box

I walk over the dancefloor with my head high and my red Lucchese boots clicking on the springy pine boards. I look at Strangler's hairy face like I own the place, give him a fraction of a nod, and watch his manicured fingers close around the rope. He lets me pass. I take the stairs three at a time with the white noise crackling in my head, blocking out the thoughts, and the fear. I feel strong because I've got someone to be strong for.

The mirrors don't bother me. I keep my eyes on the carpet, lifting them to the blank panelled door of Eddie's office. Smiler's not at his desk, and Kylie's not here either, but I can hear muffled sounds inside. Eddie's growling voice.

The handle is cool in my palm. I turn it and push. The door opens, a finger's width. I look in through a sliver of light, at the big black urn on the mantelpiece. Eddie's chair is empty, but his voice stops me cold.

'I saw him with my-own-fuckin-eyes,' he spells it out like he's talking to an idiot. 'On the Fossway. Smiling. Fuckin waving at me out the window of that Kike gold Ferrari. He pulled over, right beside me, grinning like a cunt. "Alright, Eddie? How you doing, Eddie? Hope we haven't got a problem." Well, I've got a problem. The cunt's supposed to be inside, out of my fuckin way. That's why I gave you the fuckin photos, the names, the crate number, the fuckin bill of fuckin lading. I mean you've got some cheek you, you cunt, taking my fuckin money.'

'Ah dern't take your money,' the voice answers, in that flat, almost-Yorkshire accent.

'What, man? I cannot understand you; you doss Yorkshire twat.'

'Ah said, I dern't…'

'Don't get smart with me, you bent cunt. Those filthy fuckin photos cost me money, and when you've earned them, you'll fuckin get them, and the way you're going we'll all be living on the Starship fuckin Enterprise by then.'

Someone laughs, slow and false.

I edge the door a fraction further, peering in at the three of them, Eddie and Riley standing either side of Linthorpe against the bay window. Linthorpe's turning his pink face between them like some weird little kid, sucking his cheeks in behind those pouty lips.

'It takes time, Eddie, to put a case-'

'Not you though, you limp-wristed fudge-packer. No Captain Kirk for you, cos you'll be down under one of them new windmills at Wallsend, doing your bit for the environment. And what the fuck are you doing in here,' he says in the same breath, with his black eyes burning through me.

I let the door go and step into the room, but the white noise has stopped. The certainty and the bravery turn to water in my guts. All that's left is the memory of those words running through my mind all the way up here.

'I need to get away.'

'Fuckin right,' Eddie says. 'Piss off.'

There's a low rumble from behind the desk, and Kylie stands up to meet me, her shoulder as high as the green leather top.

'No.'

'What the fuck,' Eddie says.

'I mean I need to leave. Carlo and Frogga - I mean Chester. They can have it. The whole set up. St Anthony's, Pottery Bank,' I shrug, 'all of it.'

'You need to leave?' Eddie says, like he's no idea what the words mean.

'I don't want anything. I'll just disappear. No bother. Out of Newcastle. Gone.'

'I gave you that job,' Eddie says. 'For fuck's sake you fuckin asked for it, and you promised Mr. Riley here two and a half grand a week.'

I look at Riley, telegraphing the extra five hundred quid, wondering, again, if Eddie even cares. Riley stares back at me like I'm a tiny piece of shit floating in his coco-pops, with dead eyes and his mouth turned down.

'Right, Eddie. Two and a half grand,' I look from Riley to the urn on the mantelpiece, reading Donna's name in that black heart, but all I can see is those windmills they're going to build on the river, arms turning like big white flowers. 'I mean, I'm really grateful, Eddie, that you gave me the chance, but I just can't do it. I've got half my buyers disappeared, and one lad in hospital. The rest of them are shitting it. They know Chester wants them working for him. I'm not complaining or anything,' I hold my hands up. I'm talking too fast, but I can't stop. 'I'm just saying, Carlo and Chester want the business. I get it. That's family. I'm not getting in anyone's way.'

I stop, breathing hard. Eddie leans back against the window. His expression softens.

'Well fair enough. Every man has the right to change his mind. Or is that every woman?' He slaps Linthorpe's back, jolting him forward, and a light flares in Linthorpe's baby blue eyes.

'Thanks, Eddie,' I cross the room and hold out my hand. 'I understand. It's better, keeping the business in the family. I mean I'll pay Mr. Riley this Saturday. Give Chester time to get things moving,' Eddie's head nods. He isn't listening. 'No one's going to lose out.'

'Alright, son. I get it,' Eddie takes my hand. 'You've changed your mind.'

'No, it's not -'

'And now you can change it back.'

His voice is so soft that I don't get what he means, or maybe I just don't want to. Linthorpe does. His face drops to his shiny shoes, showing me his scalp, pink through slicked back hair. Riley leans in, resting his weight on the back of a gold-framed chair. The wood creaks. His eyes narrow over that big hawk nose, and somewhere behind them I can see there's a grin, trying to get out.

'But Eddie, Mr. Burns,' I look at his hand folded around mine, the sovereign ring on his index finger.

'Two and a half grand every Saturday, until I say different. Alright with you?'

'But the lads'll work for Chester. I mean once they know it's safe. He'll take twice the money I can,' I stumble through words that seemed so good in the car. Then I scream.

Smiler's hand is clamped on my neck. The pain burns down through my back. Eddie nods. Smiler's grip eases. The pain falls to an aching throb. I shut my mouth and try not to move.

'What the fuck is this prick doing in here?'

'Right, sorry, Eddie,' Smiler says, 'just went for a jimmy.'

His hand tightens, making me scream again.

'Shut the fuck up,' Eddie says, and I press my fingers over my mouth.

'Good.' His voice falls back to that soft tone. 'Now listen to me, son, because you know I won't tell you again. I own you. You're fuckin mine, right. Like this fuckin puff. This fuckin cigar,' he picks one out of the box on the table, and crushes it in his hand. 'And I want my two and a half grand every Saturday till you learn some fuckin manners. Right?'

'Right. Yes, Eddie. Mr. Burns.'

'What's that?' He bellows.

I'm walking backwards out the door, with Smiler's hand tight on my shoulder and that bitch, Kylie, showing me her long yellow teeth. I know that I'm a moron. That all I can do is agree with Eddie and walk out of here, or argue and get my head kicked in, but I still hate the whining tone in my voice, nearly as much as I hate Eddie Burns.

'Yes, Mr. Burns. Every Saturday. Till I learn some manners.'

'Doesn't any cunt knock anymore,' Eddie says, and the last thing I hear is Riley's false laughter, then the door closes behind me, and Smiler's fist thuds into my stomach.

My knees are up against my chin. A low squeal comes from my throat, straining for a breath that won't come. The world gets darker. I don't care about anything except getting that breath, and when at last it comes, I look up at Strangler with something like gratitude.

'That's for making me look like a cunt,' he says. 'Do it again and you won't be walking away,' he walks back to the racing pages laid out on his corner table and picks up his sawn-off bookie's pen in his big fat fingers.

I stumble towards the blur of mirrors. I'm at the head of the stairs with one hand on the rail when I see Carl and Frogga back at their posts, on their zebra print barstools. Frogga wipes the back of his hand under his nose and flashes his lizard smile.

Even Carl manages a sly nod, like he knows what I've come for, and what I've got. But what stays with me, after I get downstairs and out into the cold fresh air isn't the look on Frogga's face, or Eddie's, or any of them, but Eddie's hand slapping down on Linthorpe's back, and the flare of light in those baby blue eyes. Not just anger. Hatred.

I'm still thinking about that look when I get back to the flat, double lock the door and fall back onto the sofa. Pain burns through my bruised stomach. I clench my teeth and wait till it falls to a distant ache, then I reach under the sofa for that crumpled white card and rub it flat on the wine-stained table. The card fits exactly into the purple ring left by Annie's glass. Each of its four corners touches the edge of the circle.

Northumbria Police
Inspector 3648 Peter Linthorpe
Area Command

There's an address in Ponteland, with a mobile number scrawled underneath in green biro.

I remember his footsteps behind me on the stairs, and those pink pouty lips, moving, up close against mine.

"Watch where you're going."

No, he didn't say that. Not exactly. I picture his tongue pushing out towards me.

"Think about where you're going." That's what he said.

I take my mobile out of my pocket, put it on the table and try to follow Linthorpe's advice. Think. I remember the look in his eyes today, and the last time, when I first met, "our bent copper". That was for real.

Linthorpe hates Eddie Burns as much as I do, but then so

does half of Newcastle. I'm trying to make-believe Linthorpe is on my side, and part of me almost believes it, but there's a wiser part that knows the truth. In this business, no one's on your side but you. It might suit Linthorpe to use me today, but if he's really willing to betray Eddie Burns then I can bet my life, he won't think twice about betraying me.

I get a couple of beers from the fridge and take a long cold pull, then I flick the iPod to random play, pull my boots off and sit back down, carefully, with Eminem thudding through my head.

At least Louis is going to be okay, if you don't count the scars, and the fear. The beer slides down. And Maxi sent me a text from Bulgaria. I mean Bulgaria, for Christ's sake.

I crack the other beer and let everything drift away. I haven't slept in thirty-six hours. I'm three beers in, with my head back the sofa's arm, staring at the words on Linthorpe's card until they move and blur. My head turns and my eyes close, with one last thought floating through my mind. What kind of weirdo uses green biro?

Eddie Burns growls at me across his office, but the fear is dull now, and I can see past his glittering eyes, past Riley, to Linthorpe. He's the one who matters. I feel Smiler's hand on my neck, and I'm there, yelping in pain, watching those soft baby lips that never moved, but there's a smile or a nod or some damn thing. Some message in his eyes. But what?

Other faces come. Frogga's leering smile, his scabby hand clutching at Annie's waist. Annie's eyes, wide and frightened, staring at the mobile in her handbag, and Frankie Morton jerking across the bar like a broken puppet.

My mind lurches. I sit up with that panicky feeling of waking up when I've barely been asleep, and I know, we have to get out. I can't let Annie down like I let down Benjy. We should do a runner, get on a flight, and never come back. Spain, that's where everyone goes. But I've got less than a grand. That might last us a month. What then? And what if they come looking for us?

Fear chews through my stomach, but the beer holds it back, helping me to think. So, okay, I don't know what Linthorpe wants from me, but whatever it is, he put that card in my pocket, so he wants something. Plus, he's a copper, an Inspector, which means he can find things out. So, there's three things I know for sure. Linthorpe hates Eddie Burns. He wants me to call him. And I've got fuck all left to lose.

There's some gravelly old singer meeting up with a gambler on the iPod. They share a bottle of whisky, reminding me that my mouth feels like shit. I take another pull of beer and punch six numbers into my phone and cancel. I jam the phone back in my jeans, and I'm up and pulling at the sideboard drawer. There's a paperclip and a biro, and a pile of pizza menus. Shit. I gave the last of the Motorola's to Annie.

'You got to know when to walk away, know when to run,' the iPod tells me, and I pull my boots on, and I'm out and running, with the car keys in one hand and Linthorpe's card in the other.

I drive down Osborne Road into Sandyford, wishing I'd brought the iPod and trying to remember where I saw that phone-box. The exhaust clunks over speedbumps about a mile high. There's an Italian café, painted raspberry pink. Ti Amo, it's called, whatever that means, and the phone-box is right outside.

I lay the card on the black metal shelf, lift the receiver, and listen for the dial-tone, breathing cold metal and twenty years of stale cigarettes. It's the smell that stops me, like I'm there in that other phone-box on Belmont Street, where we went when they cut ours off.

Mam sits me on the shelf and holds the phone to my ear. I can hear Nana's voice. She tells me how she'll always love me, and how I've to look after Mam and Benjy. She says my name and coughs, and all the time I'm breathing this sickly smell of tabs and metal.

'Yes, Nana,' I say, and she tells me she loves me, over and over, and then I wait while she coughs some more. It sounds like she's being sick.

'Say goodbye to Nana,' Mam says. So, I do.

I listen for her answer, but the sound can't get through. There's just this long flat dial-tone, and Linthorpe's card on the thin metal shelf. I slide a pound coin in the slot and press the numbers into the clunky keypad. Three rings, and I'm listening to Linthorpe's Yorkshire voice, harder than I remember, more certain. He says his name, so I say mine. I ask him why his card was in my pocket and that's it. He does the talking. And when he's finished, I tell him what I want. My impossible dream.

'I'll sort it,' he says. 'Call me on this number, same time tomorrow.'

'Tomorrow?'

I think of that desk with its plastic windows, and those blond women looking daggers at me like soldiers in a fort, and that pissed-off bloke snapping at me through his tash about rules and regulations, not even telling me where Mrs. Palacios had gone. I feel the echo of my fear and frustration, and I know what Linthorpe's saying can't be true.

'I'll have it for you tomorrow,' Linthorpe says, then he tells me the price. He rattles off all this stuff about a hotel on the Quayside, some guy called Haywood, times, and amounts. 'You got that,' he says.

'Yeh, enough.'

He laughs, 'Right. Call me again. One o'clock tomorrow afternoon and bring a notebook and a pen. One that works. Because, Tommy,' the laugh drops out of his voice, 'this is one job you've got to do right.'

'Okay, Linthorpe,' I say, and I wonder if he realises how much he sounds like Eddie Burns. 'One o'clock tomorrow,' but the line's dead.

I'm scared and buzzing, with way too many thoughts bouncing round my head. I find Annie's number on my mobile but dial on the fat metal keypad. I get the answer-machine. Not even her voice. I call four times. For fuck's sake. I need to speak to her. I'm trapped in this crappy phone-box and she's not here, not anywhere. I slam the phone back in its cradle and check the number on my mobile. That's when I see the two-day old, missed call from Clara.

'*I put my reputation on the line... answer me you little shit.*'

I remember her posh voice shouting through my voicemail in the Black Boar, as if Clara would ever set one high-heeled Mule down in a place like that. You'd sooner see an Arabian leopard bolting out of trap six at the dogs. Sure, Clara's off her head, but there's a good heart under all that bullshit, and there was always a kind of fit between us. Anyway, I need to talk to someone. Just talk, that's all.

I press call-back. The phone rings forever.

'Hi there, Lover Boy,' Clara answers. She's had a drink.

'You're still here then, not off to the style and the sunshine?'

'Not until tomorrow,' she says, and I can hear other voices in the background.

'Look, I need to see you before you go.'

She laughs again. 'So come over.'

'No. It has to be at my place.'

There's just her breath down the line, and those voices in the background.

'Come on, Clara. I've got a bottle open, and something interesting to show you. A bit of work,' I tell her that much, cos I know her well enough. Underneath that party girl front, it's work that counts with Clara. She's Daddy's little girl right down her shiny shoes.

'Come on. For old time's sake.'

'Give me an hour,' she says, and I hit the red button before she can change her mind.

The iPod's still going when I get back to the flat, one of Clara's Spanish things. I open a bottle of wine, take a sip, then I get another beer and watch the ancient Kings of Country clock over the fridge tick its way round from Willie Nelson to Johnny Cash.

I pull the sheepskin rug towards me, and my fingers tighten, remembering Annie's body laid out across it in the darkness. I take a breath and roll up the rug. I need to keep calm, think of one thing at a time. I lay the rug against the wall and fish in my condom pocket for the padlock key. I swing the hatch up, pull the light switch, and look down at my evil little treasures.

The doorbell makes me jump, one long demanding ring. Bob Dylan's croaking away, telling me that times are changing, like I don't already know. Clara's going to hate it. The bell rings again. I leave the music and go and let her in.

'My dad listens to this,' she says, making me think of Louis Solomon.

Chapter Thirty

Mrs. Julia Harper

The train rattles past jagged stone walls that cut the fields into brown and yellow oblongs, like the patchwork of lines on the woman's face. I watch her knitting needles duck and click, until she coughs and looks up at me across the plastic table. Her eyes are big and watery, behind giant coffee-coloured glasses, and she's got this whitish fuzz of hair around her head, like a negative of Jimi Hendrix. Like Nana. She catches my eye and smiles. I don't know what she's got to smile about, but I make myself smile back, and it feels good, because I know it's the right thing.

I let my cheek rest against the window, and I could be back on the train to Sunderland with those furry blue seats and wine gums sticky in my mouth, and Benjy's card open on the table between Mam and me. But I'm not. I'm on my own, on my way to see Mrs. Julia Harper.

"She's expecting your call," Linthorpe told me, just a couple of hours ago.

I was standing in that phone box, with the big plastic phone clutched in my slippery fist and my heart battering in my chest. I stared at the clumpy metal keypad, not really taking it in, what he was saying, what it meant. My eyes itched. I'd been awake since God knows when, too wired to sleep, climbing up and down those cellar steps, dragging everything out of there, looking at it ranged around me. My black soul exposed in the rising daylight for anyone to see.

"Well, well. You've got to watch the quiet ones."

That was what Clara said that first time, looking down at me through the open hatch with her knowing smile. I felt that surge of humiliation come rushing into my face, just like it had then, with my arms stretched pathetically across my dirty treasures. I wanted to throw them back down the cellar steps, set light to the lot of it. I felt the silver Zippo, smooth in my pocket. I drew it out, watching the fat yellow flame, and I lit a Marlboro, as if I could kid myself that was what I'd meant all along. It was too late to back out. Clara was on her way.

I stare through the train's big square window at the patchwork fields, a handful of freshly shaved sheep cluster around an old stone cottage, not a beanie's worth between them. She'll be there now. Clara, in my flat with her high-class removal men, judging and packing, with that thin smile on her pink lips.

The sun was up by the time I walked out under the cherry blossom and unloaded a mountain of bubble-wrap from the back of the car. My stomach was growling, but my mouth was too dry to eat. I forced down half a cup of coffee and got back to work, slicing through masking tape, hiding my secrets in a bubble-wrapped fog. I felt safer, calmer, with each job done, and I realised that in the end, this might be all there was left. Maybe it was better for Clara to have them?

I checked my watch, staring at the black face until the second hand clicked on, proving that the thing hadn't stopped. I put it in my pocket and went on wrapping, taping my endless bundles, until finally it was just a job, an unthinking task that helped me forget what Linthorpe had told me yesterday, and stopped me thinking about what he might say to me at one o'clock this afternoon. I hid in the rhythm of my work; from

Linthorpe and Eddie, and Mam and Clara, the past and the future, until there were forty, neat bubble-wrapped packages stacked between the T.V. and the sofa, marching out along the corridor.

I reached across them, for a pack of Paracetamol from the drawer. I swallowed them dry and massaged my temples, then I fished my watch out of my pocket, turning it round to make sense of the single fat pointer. My cheeks went numb. It was five-past-one. My instinct was to call him on the mobile, but I knew that would only make it worse. Like Linthorpe said, "you can't expect to screw this up and walk away".

I ran for the car, screeching out onto Osborne Road, nearly colliding with a white Golf coming the other way. Clara's face was sharp through the windscreen, with the green removal van trundling along behind her. I got to the phone-box in about ninety seconds, booting the Volvo up to sixty between traffic lights, taking off over speed bumps, slamming back down with the impact juddering through my head.

You idiot, Tommy. You stupid, bloody moron. I left the car angled across a junction, two long steps from the phone box door.

Linthorpe answered on the first ring.

'Call when I tell you,' he said.

'Yeh, sorry, I didn't realise.'

'You got a pad?'

'Sure,' I lied, digging through my pockets with the big receiver jammed against my ear.

'Right. Mr. Haywood is staying at the Mal Maison Hotel, room 309. Got it?'

'Sure, sure,' I said, finding one of Maxi's chewed biros, writing the numbers on my palm.

'Twelve o'clock tomorrow. Noon, right. Not before, not after. You go to reception, tell them your name is Charlie Brogan, and you ask to see Mr. Haywood. They'll send you up to the room. You go. Third floor. The door will be open. There'll be a black guy in an orange shirt. That's Haywood. He'll give you the plan, and you'll do exactly what he tells you. Right?'

'Okay.'

'Right. So, after you've seen Haywood, get yourself sorted. Go for a walk, whatever, but no booze, and no drugs. You wait till six o'clock. Not before, not after. You go up to The Hammer at exactly six and ask for Eddie. Make a big deal of it. Tell them you have to see Eddie. He won't be there.'

'So, why-'

'Shut up. Eddie won't be there, but Carl and Chester will...'

Linthorpe spelled it all out. He didn't let me speak, not until he'd finished, and then he spelled it out again, while I bit my lip and scribbled up my arm.

'Right,' he said, when he was done.

'Okay.'

'So, tell me.'

'Mr. Haywood. Charlie Brogan. Tomorrow. Twelve o'clock. Room 309,' I read it back to him, making sense of the jumble of words on my skin, fixing them in my mind. 'Then I go up to The Hammer at six, but Eddie...'

'At exactly six.'

'At exactly six,' I repeated back. 'I ask for Eddie. He won't be there, but Carl will, and Chester.'

'You're going to be fine,' he told me. Just like I told Louis Solomon.

He sounded like he really knew, but when I closed my eyes all I saw was Frankie Morton jerking across The Hammer like a Thunderbird, and I knew Linthorpe didn't have a clue how this was going to pan out, any more than I did. He was bluffing like the rest of them. Lying his head off because that's the way the world is. Doctors, lawyers, the prime-fuckin-minister, all telling us everything's going to be alright, when the truth is nobody really knows what they're doing. Except maybe Eddie Burns.

The sweat was running hot between my ear and that clunky phone, even before he told me Julia Harper's name. I pulled my jacket off, leaving it hanging from one arm, while I wrote her phone number up the other, with the pen digging in like I was tattooing it their forever.

I read it back to him afterwards, like I did with Haywood.

'Good,' he said, then he coughed, and his voice dropped. 'I'm sorry there's no better news.'

I waited for him to say something else, but there was just the grey noise of passing cars, and the scrape of an exhaust on a speedbump. Why be sorry? My jacket fell off my other arm, lying in a pool of leather and shiny chocolate lining, while the question slithered around me in that little oblong box. I swallowed, but I couldn't speak, and it seemed like Linthorpe couldn't either. Or maybe he just had nothing else to say.

'But, but so-'

The phone clicked and I was left with Julia Harper's number scrawled up my arm, and this terrible fear thumping in my chest.

I wanted to run, to go screaming up the street, take the car into wall and spend a peaceful, painful month in hospital with Louis Solomon. I wiped my hand down the front of my t-shirt and opened the door. The air dried the sweat on my face, cold and clear, and I knew that if I failed him now, if I made my excuses and ran away, that I'd never come back. I'd never be the person I wanted to be, just some squirming, faking thing. There would be no more chances. I had to be strong, for Benjy.

I stayed where I was and punched in the numbers. The phone rang three times, each empty silence like a little death.

'Julia Harper.'

I said my name and forced out the question, listening to her ludicrous, impossible answer.

'Yes,' she said, this crystal-voiced stranger, 'I am Benjamin's mother,' but at least her voice was gentle when she told me.

I lock my fingers together and watch them turn white in front of me, swaying with the rhythm of the slowing train. The brakes squeal and the tannoy starts. I hold back the panic, picking the word Hexham out of that nasal, Martian drawl. Such a short journey. He was half an hour away all the time.

The train stops. The old lady watches me through her giant glasses. She leans across and presses a tissue into my hand. She asks if I'm okay. I tell her yes, I'm fine, and we smile again, then she walks away from me with her big black handbag tight across her chest.

She leaves me with her clean lemony smell, and the empty churning in my stomach. I'm so used to the fear that I hardly know what I'm scared of anymore, only that I'm tired of it. Exhausted. I want to lay my head on this plastic table, and sleep and never wake up. A whistle blows somewhere out in the station, and I remember. I have to be strong, for Benjy.

My legs carry me out under the arches, like Newcastle Central Station, only in miniature, without the noise and the people. There's an old man perched on the step. He's looking at the platform like its nine feet down, instead of nine inches.

I'm close enough to smell his tobacco, old man smell. He looks at me over the grey bags under his eyes, a lifetime's luggage hanging on his stubbly cheeks. What choice have I got? I offer him my arm.

'Bless you,' he says, like a priest, and a woman with a buggy looks me full in the face and smiles.

'Dad,' she says, and her smile goes past me, hands clasped behind his broad, bent back.

I watch them walk away from me and realise that her smile was never meant for me. I feel ashamed. The train pulls away. I take out the tiny pad I bought at Newcastle and follow Julia Harper's careful directions. It isn't far.

The station opens onto a wide path with trees on either side, branches touching, high over my head, under a dirty sheet of cloud. I blink and see a swirl of colours that I know cannot be there.

This is where Benjy walked. His feet turn with mine, down onto a cobbled high street. We walk together, me and Benjy, with his golden curls and cherub face, through this land of tea and scones.

I turn off the High Street, up a narrow lane. A slow sloping corner leads me onto a wide gravel drive. My mouth's dry. My chest aches. I forget to breathe, then take a giant gulp and feel the Devil's rug in the stones beneath my feet.

There's a wide door with an old-fashioned bell and an iron ring that you pull. I feel like I'm up in my room at Belmont Street, dreaming another fantasy. I grip the ring. The door opens before I can pull the bell. I stare at my arm, embarrassed by the washed-out ink stains, and lift my eyes to the woman in the doorway.

She steps close, hugging me, holding me tight, and when the

talking and the crying are done, we walk together down the quiet cobbled street, with the wind blustering around us and fine pointed needles of rain blowing in our eyes. We hold each other one last time, before she kisses my cheek and leaves me at my brother's gate.

Chapter Thirty-One

Coming Home

I'm back in the Black Boar, edging my way between the lads drinking bottles at the bar and the old blokes hunched over their dark, flat pints. The place is heaving, thick with sweat and shouting voices that I cannot understand. They could be talking a foreign language, but it's not them, it's me. I feel like an alien, dropped into this dark-brown coffin from some nameless, far away planet.

This old girl looks up at me with gypsy earrings dangling under her pink rinse hair. Her orange lips twitch in what might have been a smile, but then she remembers, and her eyes shift past my shoulder. I keep going, past the scowls and the elbows, checking every face.

I've been in Newcastle for a couple of hours; down The Raby, The Foss and The Turbinia, kidding myself that I'm looking for the lads, like any of them are even out. Like I still care. I don't, not anymore, but I have to keep pretending because even with half a dozen pints inside me I can't admit who I'm really looking for. I need her. But I'm terrified that I'll find her, and she'll shrug and nod at me with her blank, stupid face. Or worse, she'll hold me close and fake it, cry her sly crocodile tears, and beg for a couple of drinks to settle her nerves.

I finish my tour of the bar and stand with my shoulder on the doorframe, getting a gust of cold air every time, the door opens, and first sight of everyone coming into the bar. I won't look at my watch, but I know that time's running out. What I don't know is where the hell she is. A fuckin alky you can't even trust to be in the bar. What kind of loser is that?

The bell rings for last orders. I give up and push in towards the bar. I need a drink.

The door swings open. I catch a glimpse of long dark hair. It's not her. This Russell Brand lookalike walks past me. Bodies move to let him through, like the Red Sea parting for Moses. Mickey Cassidy lays a perfect pint in front of him, and then he calls time.

There's a rumble through the bar, like a heavy animal growling, and some bloke with a Yorkshire accent shouts how he's been waiting ages. It makes me think of Linthorpe, telling me what I have to do, the price I have to pay for this knowledge he's given me. I don't even know what it is that I've agreed to, not really, only that there's no going back, and if I screw it up, they won't even find the bits of me. And so, what?

The Yorkshire bloke doesn't get served. He stamps out the door, muttering to himself in a voice so low only I can hear.

'You can stick your pissy, Geordie, watered-down beer up your arse.'

If I smile, it's only a reflex.

They follow him out in groups of twos and threes, then a huge crowd together, like cattle on the plains.

'Many buffalo,' a small voice whispers in my head.

I watch them go until I'm looking at the line of tables surrounded by a jagged ring of empty chairs.

'Pull the wagons into a circle.' Maybe I say it out loud.

Mickey Cassidy looks at me with a tight line running down his forehead.

'Get yourself home,' he says. 'I'm locking up.'

But I can't go home now.

'Give us a couple of bottles.'

'No chance.'

'Haway, do us a favour.' I put a twenty on the bar. 'Two bottles.'

He shrugs, and the money's gone.

I get two bottles of cheap lager, one in each pocket, and step out into the darkness, stone cold sober with six pints sloshing about in my stomach. And I'm lost. Sure, I've been in all those bars, but like I say, I was just hiding, delaying, like a scared little kid on his way to get a bollocking. Because deep down, I knew she'd be at the Boar. At least I thought I did. But she's not, because she's never there when I need her.

The door closes and I laugh at the sound of the bolts banging across behind me. Maybe I'm laughing with relief, that I don't have to face her lying bullshit, or the truth and the tears that would set the guilt burning through my chest. Like Mickey Cassidy said, I should go home, but even the cellar wouldn't be enough tonight, and anyway, there's nothing there, because Clara has stolen it all away.

So, I go where I have to.

Mam always said it was half a mile from The Boar back to ours, and it was for her, zig-zagging across the pavement. I let my feet follow hers, from one side of the pavement to the other, along past Pottery Bank under the orange streetlights.

'Yer fuckin bastard,' a kid's voice floats down from St Anthony's Road.

No one answers. There's just the sound of my shoes slapping on the pavement, and the smell of late-night chips wafting out of nowhere. Maybe it's that I'm following her footsteps, or the smell of the chips, but this picture flashes into my mind, a memory so old I hardly knew it existed.

There's me and Mam, with Benjy in the middle, all of us wrapped in our duvets on this square of grass, with the back door open behind us. Mam's got this cone of home-made chips. They're all gold and salty and zingy with vinegar, and she's feeding us, one then the other, with aeroplane noises, like babies. I think Benjy might get the last chip, but then he starts snoring, and Mam gives it to me, and it's the best chip of all, cos now there's just me and Mam staring at the starlit Sunderland sky.

'Snug as a bug in a rug,' Mam says.

'No Mam, snug as three bugs.'

'Yes,' she laughs, 'snug as three bugs,' but then she goes quiet.

'You see that star, Tommy?' Mam points, 'at the end of the upside-down pan.'

I follow where she's pointing.

'That's the star that'll bring your dad back home,' she says, and she tells me this story about monsters and shipwrecks and mermaids with emerald eyes, and Dad, building a raft. 'He'll be setting sail soon, Tommy. Coming back to us, singing all the way.'

The story makes me smile, and I feel that I'm drifting, like I'm there with Dad on his raft. And the last thing I hear is Mam sort of laugh and sort of cry. 'You know Tommy,' she whispers, 'your mam's full of shit,' and she holds me so tight I can hardly breathe.

'I know, Mam,' I say to the empty street, 'I know,' and then it's there in front of me, Atwal's blue sign, on the corner of Belmont Street.

Annie's old place is dark and still, on the other side, and I turn up our path for the first time since that night in the Byker Wall.

I press the plastic button. The bell jangles in my head.

There's no answer, just a faint yellow light through the glass panel above the door. She doesn't come. I kick the door, feeling the pain through my crappy shoes. But like always, she isn't here, the useless pisshead, and I don't understand how I can need and love and hate the same person so much.

A shadow moves across the light. I take a breath and try to make myself strong, but I'm not strong, I'm desperate, and that's why I have to believe. She's our mam, the only one who can understand. The door swings back, catching tight on the chain, and maybe it's the fall of his footsteps or the sound of his yellow fingers on the lock, but even before the door opens, I know it's him.

'Alright, Daryl,' I say through clenched teeth.

This wizened bloke squints up at me through the gap in the chain. His face is as grey as his tash, and he's got a nasty little goatee on his chin, just like Frogga's, which makes sense because they're both a pair of bastards. Only his skull is white under the bulb in the corridor, shining through his swept back hair. It's the same old Daryl, only boil-washed and bleached out. His red-veined eyes are the only colour in his face, widening while his mouth opens, making this "O" around the stumps of his teeth.

'I need to see Mam.'

'Ah don't think…'

His sulky lip starts to slide, sending a surge of anger crackling up my spine. Maybe he sees it on my face. Either way, his tone changes.

'I mean she's not here.' He stutters on the last word, and his fear makes me stronger. Keeps me calm.

'So, we'll wait,' I say.

'But nah, because…'

'It's alright, Daryl,' I tilt my pockets, showing him the bottles, and I smile. The falseness makes my mouth ache, but it's enough to fool Daryl.

He grins at me. The door closes, but there's never any doubt. I hear the chain rattle and fall. The door swings wide and I step back into the land that time forgot.

The place is the same as always, except smaller, seedier, and smellier. Daryl's pictures are still there, up along the stairs. Sunderland's hairy cup winning team from some time in ancient history, and Daryl beside them on his motorbike, grinning out from that silver frame just like I remember. Except younger. Young as I am now. Young as when he broke my Benjy's arm.

I take a long breath and follow the new washed-out Daryl into the living room with my fists clenched tight by my sides. He is the reason it's taken twenty years to find my brother, the reason Mam's a useless drunk, the reason for every shit thing in my shitty, shitty life. I'm fighting to hold myself together, but Daryl hasn't got a clue. Every bit of his tiny mind is focused on the bottles in my pockets, and the cash he can smell coming off me, that he thinks might buy him some more.

That crappy brown table is still in the living room, and the slime green sofa sagging in the middle, where I so nearly smashed that can of Strongbow into his mouth. I look at the wall, where I threw it. The stain's gone, faded away, but Mam's chair's still there, and the T.V. in the corner, that same giant box playing some ancient cop show.

'Who loves ya baby?' An American voice wants to know.

I stick my head in the kitchen, like I'm going to see her dancing to one of those old reggae tunes, stumbling and laughing with a little kid hanging off each leg. There's just a load of crusty pans, and the stink of something rotten.

That numb feeling creeps back over me, but then I look at

Daryl with the snake-bitch tattoo stretched along his arm, and his thin rat-face pointed at the T.V. And the memories keep me strong. I step around Mam's chair and pull the plug out of the wall. The T.V. pops.

'She in here? Upstairs?'

His lip pushes forward. He shakes his head at my feet.

'So, where is she?'

He doesn't answer, just starts fishing about in his pockets, brings out this fat red penknife and opens a tiny, clawed blade.

'I'm well parched,' he says, with that stupid grin back on his face.

I give him a slow nod, take out both bottles and pass one over.

'Alright,' he says, snatching it and popping the top. He lets it fall between the crushed cans and overflowing ashtrays on the floor, and then he drops the knife back in his pocket and takes a long drink, while I stand there looking from the lift and fall of his scrawny throat to the unopened bottle in my hand.

'Cheers, man,' he says, belching poison through the gaps in his brown stump-teeth.

'Jesus, man, Daryl,' I tilt my bottle towards him, but he still doesn't get it. 'Give me the fuckin knife.'

'Right,' he says, and hands it over.

'You're unbelievable, you,' I tell him, popping the bottle, taking the froth off the top. 'So, where is she?'

He shrugs and sucks on his ten quid beer.

'Where is she?' I step in closer, risking that breath.

'I dunno. In the town, having a drink.'

'So she'll be back in a bit?'

'Depends.' He takes another pull, staring hard into his empty bottle. 'If she meets someone, you know.'

I know, but I won't say.

'She'll be in Offshore, or The Quilted Camel,' he says, sly eyes sliding across my face. 'One of them late bars along the Quayside.'

'Right, so we'd better have a look,' I take another pull and put my bottle down on top of the T.V. 'Haway then. I'm buying.'

He looks at me like he can't quite believe I've fallen for it. I haven't really, but I need to find Mam, and some chance is better than no chance at all, and if I have to buy Daryl Boyle a couple of drinks to do it, well that's the way it is. Anything's better than staying here. Daryl must think so too, cos he's away and past me. A draft of air blows through from the open front door, and by the time I get into the lobby he's already pulling on this shapeless brown anorak that the old Daryl would never have been seen dead in.

'We'll track her down, mate,' he says. 'Trust your uncle Daz,' and I've got nothing to say to that.

We follow the long, long curve of Walker Road, what's left of it anyway, broken rows of terraced houses. There's one on the corner with scraps of wallpaper flapping on the wall and a chest of drawers standing against it, like one of those bomb pictures from Iraq.

'Investing in the Future Together,' the billboard says, except the government's investing in their banker mates, and the rest of us are investing in beer and ten quid deals.

Anyone in Walker who's really thinking about the future is only thinking about one thing. Getting out. And that's what we're doing, heading west, towards the city. I can see the Baltic Gallery, and the silver slug of the Sage Music Centre on the south side of the river. The lights on the Millennium Bridge change through red and blue and green, lighting up the quayside with its swirly roofed offices, and flats with balconies over the river. We come off the main road, down St Anne's, past the tall glass windows of the Pitcher and Piano, and the Mal Maison hotel. I look up at the scraps of curtain blowing through the hotel's high windows and imagine Haywood all tucked up safe and warm under his luxury duvet, waiting for me to come and see him in the morning.

Daryl stops beside me, tash twitching hopefully, over that stupid goatee. As if I would take him in there for a drink. As if they'd let us through the door.

'Haway, man Daryl.'

'Ah, but I'm knackered,' he says.

I clench my teeth and keep walking, along the quay, under the old Tyne Bridge and up towards the noise, with Daryl scuttling behind me. We turn past Chase onto this busy cobbled street and it's like we've just stepped into some big party. Practically every building is a bar, and they're all thumping with sound and rammed with people, drinking and shouting, and spilling into the street.

I shove my way into the Quilted Camel and spend ten sweaty minutes forcing my way from one end to the other. I do the same in Bob Trollope's with Daryl at my back whining about when we're going to get a drink. In Offshore 44 I leave him in an alcove, staring at the flashing lights on the ceiling while I push on through hot fleshy bodies. It feels like half of Newcastle's in here, and half of London going by the accents. I'm sweating hard in my leather jacket, and not just from the heat, from the hope and the fear, because I want to find her, but I'm scared too, because what I need is the old Mam who can make everything alright, not some greedy-eyed drunk with her hand sliding inside her coat.

There's a woman at the bar, head back, laughing. I slip past a student type with a handful of glasses, getting close enough to see. It isn't her, but I'm here now, hemmed in by the press of bodies, and the barman wants to know what I'm having. I give in and get some drinks. It must be half an hour by the time I get back to Daryl with four bottles of lager. He's exactly where I left him, staring up at the lights like the oldest space cadet on the planet. I give him two bottles and the lager brings him to life. He takes a long pull and leans in close with his deadly breath.

'Did they not have any cider?'

I have a vision of smashing both my bottles into either side of his face, but I don't. I drop a bottle into each pocket, get a grip on his minging anorak and drag him through the bar to the courtyard out the back. It's rammed here too, but at least you can breathe. He slides out his pink pet lip and mumbles something. I push him back against the stone wall and lean back beside him, watching the people, and drinking the beer.

Some part of me knows she isn't here, but I could be wrong, and anyway, the beer does its job, holding everything away from me, warm and out of focus. The trouble is, two half-pint bottles don't last very long. I can't be arsed to go back in. I could send Daryl, but I know, if I gave him money he wouldn't come back. So, I give in. I fight my way back to the bar, keeping one eye out for Mam, desperate to see her and desperate not to, and I know that I'm just like the rest of them, because all I really want is the beer.

Daryl's still in the courtyard, only now he's leaning over these two girls sat at a barrel table. I don't know what he says to them, but they're up and away, and he's laughing, sitting down, pointing me to the still warm seat opposite.

'Take a load off,' he says, like we're back in the seventies, like he said to Annie on that saggy green sofa, before he put his hand up her skirt.

I look at his grinning face and wonder why I'm spending my money buying beer for Daryl Boyle, why I'm drinking with this piece of shit when we both know that wherever Mam is, she's not here. But scum as he is, he's a link to her, to all of it. That's what I tell myself. I suck at my beer and watch him talk, staring at that tash until I can see each individual hair, yellow and grey over colourless skin, like some horrible hairy insect.

'Trevor reckoned he knew the score... worked the sewers for years...'

I can't hear more than every other word. Daryl's reedy voice rises and falls through the noise around us, and the roaring in my head.

'I've found Benjy,' I say, to shut him up.

He doesn't hear, or he doesn't care, just keeps going on, telling me these stories about people I've never heard of, pausing long enough to gulp down his beer while I sit here with my heart thudding halfway out of my chest.

'Sammy went straight over backwards, splat into the shit. We were pissing ourselves. Came up looking like a drowned rat, stinking like one too...'

'Right,' I stand up, looking down at his twitching face. 'Like a drowned rat, sure,' I say, and push myself away from him.

'Going to the bar? Good lad,' he shouts after me.

And where else is there to go? They've got triples for two quid. Some nameless, dragon's piss whisky. I get us each a couple and take them back out through the thinning crowds. The stuff burns like the fires of hell, and what's worse is it seems to sharpen my hearing. I can't help but hear Daryl rattling on.

'I'm mashing the Honda up this hill... huge wagon coming

right at us… some cunt in Jag overtaking…'

He keeps talking, and I keep buying the whisky, until two o'clock comes around and they throw us into the street.

It's quieter now, apart from a couple of lads kicking off in the taxi rank. We walk away from them, back along the river, under the arch of the old Tyne Bridge and up towards its flashy new cousin. Daryl's still mumbling on about back when I was a kid, stuff I don't want to hear. He staggers against me with his spindly nine stone body. I don't care. I'm looking up at The Millennium Bridge, those rainbow colours flashing against the sky, and I don't exactly mean to, but my feet find their own way, following the lights, up onto the bridge. I lean over the rail and look down at their reflection on the river, turning the water from brown to red and purple, blue and gold, like our Rainbow Blanket come to life.

'Ah nah you were pissed off with me,' Daryl says, his face close beside mine. 'But it wasn't easy for me like, neither.' He smiles behind his goatee, but his eyes are scared and small, telling me his wheedling excuses. His lies.

'I was the one stayed around when your dad fucked off. Another man's kids. There was plenty said I was a mug, but I took care of you like you were my own.'

'Sure, Daryl. Sure, you did.'

'Aye. I did my best. I'm not perfect like, but there's none of us are. I mean look at you, all the advantages and you're a drug dealer. Well, you are. And it's not surprising like, I mean your mam's no angel neither.'

'But she was,' I say to myself as much as to him, looking down at the wind ruffling the water like the fur on the Devil's rug, and I think about all those Sundays, lying in bed too wired to sleep, watching the rug, and waiting for Daryl, or the Devil, and hardly knowing the difference. But he never came again. And I wonder if maybe he forgot, or just got bored with his game? But deep down, I know the truth. He did it on purpose, because me and Daryl both know that the waiting is the worst thing of all.

'She was an angel once,' I say, 'and so was Benjy.'

Him,' Daryl says, 'I did you a favour there.'

I look at him, this pathetic drunk under the rainbow lights, and I see the sincerity on his rat-like face. Pins and needles spread along my jaw. He really believes it; this deluded shite he's telling me. Like if he keeps on talking, that'll make it true.

It all started with this bastard here, and he got away with it, like he gets away with everything. He doesn't even get to feel guilty because he rewrites the past as he goes along. My heart pounds in my throat. Not with fear or guilt, but with a deep and satisfying hatred. Daryl "ya cunt" Boyle, the fantasist of the fuckin century. Blood roars around my body. I'm scalding hot, strong enough to embrace my anger.

'Shut up,' I tell him. 'Shut your stinking, lying mouth,' but he doesn't.

He keeps rambling on, pulling a home-rolled fag from a battered Marlboro box, holding up that long gold lighter with the red triangle shining like a ruby on the back, just like that time in our doorway, with him shouting at us about the football, and Benjy's pink balloon drifting down, and me running, and the bottle falling, shattering in an explosion of glass and whisky.

Chapter Thirty-Two

The Point of No Return

Six o'clock must be too early for The Strangler, because there's no one to stop me lifting that brass hook and walking up The Hammer's marble staircase with my head still throbbing from last night's dragon's piss whisky. The last thing I need is that glaring wall of mirrors, or the sight of my own sickly face. Or Smiler's, come to that. He's sitting at his table, chewing on his biro with the racing pages spread out in front of him, and that big black and tan dog curled around the table leg.

Like Linthorpe said, Carl and Frogga are the only other people in the place, perched on their zebra print bar stools, like always. I'm pleased to see them. That's how weird things are, but I make out I haven't even noticed. I walk up to Eddie's office door and give it three hard knocks. Smiler puts his pen down. Kylie stretches her neck. Both of them watch me with the same stillness. I can feel Frogga's eyes on me too, from across the bar.

"Eddie won't be there, but Carl and Chester will…"

I knock again, thinking about the certainty in Linthorpe's voice, and hoping to God he's right. I imagine Eddie's black eyes glittering on the other side of the door, the fury on his huge, flat face when I go barging into his office, my body set rigid under a silent white windmill. I swallow and turn the brass handle. It rattles in my hand. The door is locked.

'Does he never fuckin learn?' Smiler comes lumbering

towards me with Kylie at his heels.

'What the fuck are you doing?'

'Where's Eddie?'

'Not here.'

'Look Sm…' I stop, not knowing what else to call him. 'It's important. I need to see Eddie.'

'Well, he's not here, so you can't.'

'Okay then,' I say, trying to sound pissed off, rather than shit scared. 'I'll wait,' and I stride away towards the bar.

There's a low rumble behind me, one stop short of a growl. I think it's from the dog, but there's no way I'm looking back to check, so I fix my eyes on Carl Burns' bland, stupid face.

'Vodka,' I say, leaning on the bar. 'Make it a double.'

The Brummie barman doesn't ask, just gives me the cheap shit from the optic and steps back through the kitchen door. Even he knows I don't matter.

'Cheers,' I say to no one, and take a burning mouthful. I let my elbow hit Carl's arm.

'What's your fuckin problem?' Carl wants to know.

'Nothing.'

'Well, fuck off.'

Frogga laughs like it's the funniest thing he's ever heard.

'Look. Do you know where Eddie is? When he's getting back?'

'What's it to you?'

'Don't waste your fuckin breath on that loser,' Frogga says, and heads for the gents.

Carl stares up at the ceiling fan, eyes narrowed to dark slits, jaw pushed forward. He sips his drink, so I sip mine, and follow his gaze up to those copper-coloured blades. The things aren't even turning. It's pretty clear Carl doesn't want to speak to me, so I keep my mouth shut and wait. The vodka isn't doing anything for my head, just echoing the bitter taste of last night's whisky, bringing that familiar, sticky-sweet taste creeping over the roof of my mouth, trailing another monster migraine.

I drop my gaze to Carl's big white hands, that sovereign ring, an exact copy of Eddie's, and I wonder if Carl can possibly be as thick as he seems. Maybe he is? His eyes turn towards the gents, waiting for Frogga to come back and tell him what to do. And suddenly, I understand. Sure, Carl's not the sharpest tool in the box, but what's really holding him back is the fear of looking weak. I stare at that gold ring, and it's weird to even think it about Carl, but he's just not bad enough. An innocent, that's what Carl is.

I wait until I see Frogga come sniffing towards us, rubbing his nose like the original Cocaine Kid.

'Alright, Carl, I'll tell you,' I say, 'but you've got to tell me where Eddie is. Give me his mobile number.'

'Eh,' Carl looks at me like I'm mental, which I probably am.

'I've seen this bloke,' I say, 'just this morning. This black Dutch guy they call Haywood. Says his boss used to know Eddie from way back. He's got this deal.'

'You want to get into town, Carlo,' Frogga says like I'm not there. 'Get some action.' He pouts and shows his fist, so I can't tell if he means fuckin or fighting.

'Four keys of coke,' I say.

'Four ounces,' Frogga says, still looking at Carl.

'Four keys,' I say again, pausing just long enough to hear the silence, 'for a hundred grand.'

'Bullshit,' Frogga says. 'No one sells a key for twenty-five grand. Not even if it's bashed to shit, and least of all to a low-life loser like you.'

'Not to me.' I grab my chance. 'To Eddie. And it's not one key, it's all four or nothing. Haywood was definite about that.'

'Who the fuck is Haywood?'

'The black Dutch guy,' Carl says.

'What?'

'Listen.'

Frogga cuts me a look, but he shuts his mouth.

'This guy Haywood came looking for Maxi.' The sweat prickles under my arms. 'He found me.' There's no one anywhere near us but I drop my voice anyway, telling it just like Haywood told me in that flashy hotel room, seeing the words in his big, toothy mouth.

'They were moving these four keys through Amsterdam to London, over to Shields on the ferry, driving down south. The bag man got ideas; thought he'd do a deal of his own.' I shrug like these things happen. 'That's sorted, but things got messy. When they find him, and Haywood reckons it won't be long, there'll be a murder investigation on the go. Police all over the place, not ideal for a black foreigner with a record, and four keys of coke.

'That's why he wants out. He'll take a hundred grand for all of it, but it has to be quick. Like tonight.' I hold out my hands. 'So I need to see Eddie.'

'For this bullshit scam,' Frogga blows through his horrible goatee, but his twitching hands give him away. Now Linthorpe's pointed it out, it's obvious. Frogga's way out there, coked-up halfway to hell.

'Eddie knows this guy Haywood?' Carl says, like he's still caught up in the last conversation.

'No, Carl. He knows his boss, Ludwig Van den Berg.' I take the card that Haywood gave me and press it into Frogga's hand.

Big square letters, just Van den Berg's name, and a number.

Frogga laughs at the ceiling fan, so loud that Smiler puts his pen down. Smiler's face splits into a sort of grimace, stretching the creases on his cheeks. I drop my head, but it's not me he's looking at. Michael Riley is coming up the stairs with a gold vape clamped under his long hawk nose. He takes his time, walking over towards us.

'Ludwig Vandango,' Frogga says, forcing a laugh, and slides the card into his pocket. 'Fuck off, prick,' then he leans in, hissing in my ear. 'Keep your mouth shut, and your phone on.' He pushes me in the chest. 'Alright, Michael,' he says, flicking his forehead in a mock salute.

Michael Riley takes the vape out of his mouth and gives Frogga a thin smile. 'Alright lads. Black coffee with a drop of Remy Martin,' he calls through to the kitchen, while I get myself away, three steps at a time down that marble staircase.

The Volvo starts first time, and I rev that big old engine setting my tyres spinning on the loose gravel. I try to keep it cool, but I'm sweating through my t-shirt and all I can think about is Frankie Morton walking into the bar like some fucked-up Thunderbird, and Maxi telling me that's how The Hammer got its name. I grip the wheel and try to imagine living Frankie Morton's life, working for the guy who did that to him, and it sets another thought flaring behind my eye. I'm already fuckin living it. Cos Frankie and Eddie aren't so different from me and Carl.

'This bullshit scam,' I say out loud, and see the tiny drops of spit spraying through Frogga's goatee, merging with Daryl's in my mind. "I did my best... took care of you like you were my own."

'Well screw the both of you,' I think of Frogga's fingers

twitching on the bar, and the big greedy shine in his eyes. Just like those lights on the Millennium Bridge. 'Keep your mouth shut, and your phone on,' I say to the windscreen, and it's my turn to smile. Frogga'll be calling. And like Linthorpe said, there's no way he can get his hands on a hundred grand that fast. Way too much has already gone up his nose.

I'm driving fast, dropping a gear on the bends, flogging the old wreck like there's anywhere to go like I can outrun the fear in my stomach or the pain behind my eye. The smile fixes on my lips, tight as Smiler's Plasticine face. I shouldn't have drunk that vodka, not after all that shit last night. But there are a lot of things I shouldn't have done and setting this deal up with Frogga has to be up there in the all-time top three.

There's codeine in the glove box, but it won't touch this. I check my pockets for some real pills, but I know they're back in the flat. All I can do is keep driving and try to think.

The answer's so simple. Don't go back. If Frogga calls, or Linthorpe, or Haywood, just don't answer. Or tell them it was a mistake, a wind-up. Sure, Frogga, like you said, there were just four ounces. And keep on driving, forever, to someplace where the sun shines and none of those bastards are ever going to find me.

I'm on the A69, heading west on this crappy two-lane road with all these cars flashing their lights at me. It takes half a dozen till I realise it's practically dark and I'm driving with my lights off. I flick the switch and see the petrol gauge wavering into the red. At least that gives me something to do, keeping an eye out for a petrol station, pulling in, breaking my paranoid rhythm. I stand at the pump with the cool air on my face and I know, I've got to stop dreaming. I've started this, and I have to see it through. I'm screwed if I don't. The pump clicks. A few drops of greasy petrol splash on my sleeve. The truth is I was always screwed. From the moment I shook Eddie's hand across that green leather desk.

Or from the moment Daryl Boyle came grinning into our lives.

I keep driving, following the road. I never set out to come here, but somehow, I've driven all the way to Hexham, as if I could just take the turn off and visit my brother. I drive on past, thinking back, trying to get in touch with little Tommy Boyle. Not with the guilt and the blame, but with the fight. The kid that made Daryl break his finger before he'd say he didn't have a brother. The one that went up to Heaton Park to face the hardest kid in school, and the one that smashed Frogga's face into that shitty yellow toilet bowl.

I'm at Carlisle by the time I've sorted myself out, sitting in behind a line of trucks. I take a U-turn at the roundabout and head back to Newcastle at a steady fifty, calm and focused all the way. I'm going to face them again. Except this time, I'm going to make it different.

I'm going to get through this the way I've got through everything else. Face the truth. Deal with it. Take the bastards on. Maybe I'm wrong, but at least I've decided, and by the time I get back to Newcastle even my headache is down to a pulsing throb.

I turn the stereo up, wind the window down, and listen to Johnny Cash telling me about the prettiest girl in town. And I'm singing along, waiting for my phone to ring, ready for whatever comes.

There's a space right outside the flat, which is a little miracle of its own, and I take that slow, easy walk under the cherry tree with The Cash still singing in my head. I've got the key in the door and one foot on my antique pine floorboards, when I hear the creak of moving weight, branches waving in the breeze.

A hand falls on the back of my head. Strong fingers twist in my hair, turning my head.

Her lips press against mine. I hold on tight. The air comes out of her in a frantic rush. I feel the heat of her through my t-shirt and I know what this is all for, why I can't run away. I have to do this right. Set us free forever.

I take a few clumsy steps, drawing her into the living room. My body beats with need. Let them all burn in hell. I want her. Here on the Devil's rug. I kiss her, hard. My hand runs down the length of her spine. Her back stiffens. There's a tension in her that has nothing to do with sex. I kiss her again, more gently, and let her go.

'Chez found the phone.'

'Jesus, Annie.'

'I couldn't help it,' she says, like I'm blaming her. 'I told him I'd never seen it before. He laughed for about ten minutes, then he found a missed call from a Jesmond number.'

'A call box,' I say.

A draft of cool air blows down the corridor. Annie shivers, standing above my empty cellar in her thin white shirt, with the pink flush high on her cheeks.

'He's going to catch us, Tommy. We have to get out of here.'

'Yes, Annie, we will,' but even I can hear the doubt in my voice.

'Now,' she says.

'Soon. One more day.'

'It's this Dutch coke deal, isn't it?'

My heart skips. Now I know for definite. Frogga's in.

'I've got to finish this, Annie. We've got to sort things properly or we'll never get out. Not for real, forever, out.'

'Don't do it, Tommy.'

'We need the money.'

'No,' she presses her hot hands on my chest and looks into my face. 'We need each other.'

I want more than anything to tell her the truth, all of it. But the less she knows the safer she is.

'We will need it,' I tell her. 'In a month, or a year. Do you want to spend your life cleaning up other people's shit? I don't think so.'

Her hands tighten into fists on my chest, pulling back away from me.

'My passport's in the car. There's enough cash to fly us anywhere you want to go.'

She smiles at me, but only with her mouth, and it's already too late, like there's some wall I've built between us. She senses that I'm lying, holding something back. I try to pretend, reaching out, touching her cheek, but she turns her face and leaves my hand lost in the air.

'One more day,' I say, dropping my hand, feeling stupid, angry, stubborn as a kid.

'There isn't one more day, Tommy. We need to go now.'

And I want it to be true, like Frogga wants his coke, like Mam wants her vodka. I think of the passport in the bedroom drawer, purple and gold with that terrible picture. It's so right, so easy. Just go, and never come back.

I can't do it. I might have, an hour ago, but I can't now. I know that, but I can't explain it. I hardly know myself, so I stand here like an idiot with that acid syringe sliding back in behind my eyes, and my mobile phone pulsing, unanswered in my jeans.

'There's a flight to Rome at eleven. Or Paris, or New York. Yeh, maybe New York's better cos at least they speak English. Sort of.' She's laughing, burbling on like we're going on a weekend break, but I can hear the desperation, see the fear he's put in her eyes, and I'm as angry as I've ever been. 'No. Rome's best. The Colosseum. The… whatever you call it.'

'Alright.' I hold up my hands. 'So you go.'

She steps back, mouth open. I see the hurt in her eyes and I'm sorry. God, Annie, I'm so sorry.

I want to tell her, but the words don't come, only the old terror, and my thigh burning between my finger and thumb, balancing the pain in my head.

'Fuck the money, Tommy. Don't do this deal. Chez is sly and clever, and he's going to screw you over just like…'

Her voice trails away, but I know what she's saying. He's a better man. He'll beat me every time.

Maybe it's the memory of his feet pounding into my face, or his hands on my back, pushing me over that rail in the park. Or maybe it's the knowledge of his hands on her?

'Screw me?'

We look and each other, both realising what a terrible, stupid, wicked thing I've said.

Her face closes against me.

'I'm sorry.' I mouth the words, but like always, I'm too late.

Her fist swings up towards me, sending a new pain searing through my eye, and she's past me, down the corridor, and out through the open door.

'Annie,' I shout, running up the path with one hand clamped over my eye.

'Fuck off.' She doesn't look back.

'Soon, Annie. I'll call you; I promise.'

The lights flash on the BMW.

'How?' She opens the car door, and I see her face, angry and crumpled as that very first time. 'Liar,' she screams.

'No, Annie, please. Call me. Please, call me.' The car door slams. 'And stay away from Frogga,' I plead into the roar of the BMW.

An upstairs light goes on in the house across the street. A woman's face looks out, white in her bedroom light. I give her the finger, go back inside, and slam the door.

'Silly bloody cow,' I whisper to myself, pulling the rug back, ignoring the rhythmic buzz of the phone in my pocket.

I get the hatch open and I'm two steps down before I remember that there's nothing there. Just a low cold space, like an empty grave. I stand on the step, alone, when I should be with Annie, and the hate surges through me, for all of them. Sure, Frogga and Carl and Eddie, but Haywood and Linthorpe too. I'd call him now, tell him to stuff it up his arse, but it's way too late for that. Like Frogga's not going to want to know what happened to the biggest deal of his life. I pull the phone out. Two missed calls from the same number. I step out of the cellar and press call back.

Chapter Thirty-Three

Frogga's Deal

Frogga answers on the first ring, with all his usual charm.

'Where the fuck have you been?'

With your girlfriend, I think, but I press my hand to my mouth and count to three.

'Alright, Frogga,' I say.

'I told you to keep a hold of your fuckin phone.'

'I'm on it, aren't I?'

'Cunt,' he says. 'Where are you?'

'What?' I play for time, looking round the room for traces of Annie, staring at my sheepskin rug and remembering the flush of her cheeks, pink on gold. 'You mean now?'

'No, last fuckin Christmas. Of course, fuckin now.'

'Billabongs,' I say, talking fast, over the silence. 'It's my local, in Jesmond, about halfway along Osborne Road. You go past-'

'I know where it is. Stay the fuck there.'

The line goes dead. I look at the phone, then up at the clock over the fridge. Quarter to Kris Kristofferson, and I don't even know where Frogga is, how close, or even what he wants. Not for sure. Annie could have called him from the car, told him anything. No way. I block out the thought, but I can't stop the goose bumps from lifting along my arm.

Either way, I haven't time to hang about. I grab my leather jacket off the door, drive the three minutes to Billabongs and dump the car in the taxi rank outside.

'A bottle of Becks,' I tell Robby, the barman, and take a quick walk between the silver tables.

There's no sign of Frogga, and by the time I get back, Robby's poured my Becks into a glass. I don't see why. I've told him before to leave it in the bottle.

'Four pounds,' he says.

Four keys, I think.

'Keep the change.' I give him a fiver and take a long drink, then I lean back with my elbow on the bar and look out across a sea of shiny furniture.

There's a few student types clustered around an American Football game on the T.V. in the far alcove, but it's summer now, and most of them have gone back to the Home Counties, wherever that is? The place is dead. There's no one at this end of the bar, just a girl on her own, running her finger around the rim of her glass.

A silver chain runs across her throat, with a tiny pendant glinting from the top of her dark velvet dress. She catches me watching. I look past her, like I care about the Denver Broncos, but not before I've seen her pretty, elfy face, shaded lilac under the purple wall light. There's something familiar about that look. I glance back, and her mouth flickers in something too weak to be called a smile. It's about the saddest thing I've ever seen, her, dressed up like that, for some selfish bastard to leave her there.

Same old story, but I've got troubles of my own. I fix my eyes on the door, but I can feel her watching me, at least I imagine I can. I'm too warm in my leather jacket. The glass slides in my hand, and I feel that strange déjà vu stirring of a memory, watching the girl out of the corner of my eye.

It's alright, I want to tell her. You're a good person, not a lying,

low-life drug dealer who's too scared to get close to anyone.
I want to comfort her, to hear her sadness so I don't have to
think about my own. Or maybe I just want to ease her out of
that velvet dress, use her to punish Annie, to push her away
before she gives up on me, if she hasn't already. I don't know
what I want, but I lift my elbow off the bar and step towards
her.

Someone walks into the bar behind me. They're moving fast,
making the hair prickle on my neck.

I keep my eyes on her silver chain, with the words running
through my mind.

It's alright. I'm an artist now, Emily.

I ignore the presence at my back, willing him to disappear.

The girl looks up. Her green eyes open wider. *Being a ref didn't
work out. I got sick of being called a bastard.* I smile, imagining
that she's laughing back at me with that long red hair blowing
out behind her.

Honey and moonlight, she's saying, *like the gods spilt a tiny jar…*

'Bandit,' the voice hisses in my ear.

Frogga grabs my shoulder. He spins me round, so close that I
feel the tiny balls of spit spraying from his long white face. Carl
Burns is standing behind him, both of them looking about
as friendly as ever. Maybe I should be scared, but all I feel is
disappointed, like they've woken me from a dream.

'You want a drink,' I ask them.

'Alright,' Carl says.

'Shut up,' Frogga says.

I catch Carl's eye, and in that moment we're both thinking
the same thing. Which one of us is he talking to?

'We're here to do business, not fuck about with scum like you,'
Frogga spits at me. 'So, this is how it's going to be. You bring

Haywood and this Vandalberg bloke to us.'

The girl walks towards me. She's tall, running her palms down over her hips.

'To my place. Tonight,' Carl says.

She passes close enough for me to see there isn't a freckle on her face. Her hair is as brown as mine. She's no more a doctor than I am.

'He's in The Hague,' I say, watching her walk out the door, hips swaying just enough to show me what I've missed.

'Eh,' Carl says.

'Holland,' Frogga snaps, and Carl's bulldog jaw drops open. He catches himself and fixes his face back into its slit-eyed wooden pose.

Frogga doesn't notice, he's too busy shouting the odds at me.

'Don't be fuckin smart. Do as you're told, there's five grand in it for you. Or you can piss about and get another kicking.'

'Fuck you, Frogga.'

'Don't you fuckin call me that.' His hand comes up around my throat, pinning me back against the bar. 'This is my deal okay. You got that?'

A couple of students look over.

Robby the barman moves towards us in slow, shrinking steps, like he doesn't ever want to arrive.

'Excuse me,' Robby says. He looks at Frogga and runs out of words.

Frogga lets me go.

'It's alright,' I say, running my hand around my throat. 'It's okay, Robby, we're old mates.' I give Robby a nod and hold his look, until he shrugs and gets back to work, emptying beer trays, taking the nozzles off the pumps.

'Look, I'll do this any way you want,' I tell Frogga, 'but there's no way a bloke like Van den Berg's going to fly over here. We're dealing with Haywood, and at a hundred grand for four keys, Haywood sets the rules. He wants to deal with Eddie. He wants me there and he wants the deal done quick, or else he'll take it up to Glasgow. That's how it is.'

I take a step away from him.

'And I'm not doing it for any poxy five grand.'

'You think anyone's going to give a cunt like you a hundred grand?'

'That's up to Eddie. All I want is a fair cut.'

'You want your cut? I swear, you fuck me about and you'll get your fuckin cut. Want me to send Salim round to your place? Or I can get him down here right now, slit you open like the cunt you are.'

'I'm not fuckin you about. Just telling you how Haywood wants it. I have to be there. For fuck's sake Frogga, there's half a million quid in this. That's enough for everyone.'

I don't realise what I've called him till it's out, but he doesn't notice. His pinpoint eyes are bulging at the thought of it.

'No,' he says, 'I'll tell you how it's going to be. You're coming to Eddie's, right now. You keep your mouth shut and remember this is my fuckin deal. And you'll get what Eddie gives you. Now get in the fuckin car.'

'Cheers, but I'll follow you in mine.'

'You fuckin piss me about…'

'I'll be there, Frogga.' I walk past him, into the night.

'You fuckin better be,' he shouts, 'cos if you're not -'

I slam the car door.

Half an hour later Strangler lifts his thick red rope and the three of us walk up that marble staircase. My boots stamp on every step. Frogga's coke-fuelled confidence is running through me, and that old theme tune is playing in my head, like we're back there in the cemetery with guns on our hips, and a fortune in gold buried just a few yards away.

I'm ready for the glare of mirrors, and even Smiler's vicious face. He sits up and pulls his shoulders back. Kylie stretches too, muscles tight along her neck. She walks over to the top of the stairs and puts her nose in my crotch. She knows. The bitch.

'Alright, Kylie,' I say, 'good girl,' but I keep my hands well clear of that velvet skin.

I'm not a total idiot.

I think.

'He's expecting you,' Smiler says, which is about the nicest thing he's ever said to me. I'm tempted to tell him, but then he opens the door to Eddie's office and Kylie follows us in.

Pills rattle in the desk drawer, and Eddie scowls up at us, shoulders hunched like an angry bear. Michael Riley's in his usual place with his legs stretched out at the side of the desk, wearing a dark silk suit and an evil smile.

'This better be fuckin good,' Eddie growls into the desk, and Frogga pushes Carl in ahead of us.

'Alright, Uncle Eddie,' he says, bobbing his head.

'Shut up,' Eddie says. 'You sound like a fuckin retard.'

'Sit down lads,' Riley tells us.

There are three green canvass chairs laid out in an arc between the fireplace and the desk. Frogga takes the middle one. I sit nearest the door as if that's going to give me a chance. I don't realise how low they are until we're all sitting, like Riley, with our legs out in front of us, and our faces level with the green leather desktop. I look up at Eddie feeling like a little kid.

'What's this cunt doing here?' Eddie points a ringed finger at me.

'He's the link-man,' Frogga says.

'The fuckin what?'

'He's alright,' Frogga says, and I feel a rush of warmth through my stomach.

Eddie grunts. 'So, what's this crap about?'

He looks along the line of us, stopping at me. I can sense Riley's eyes on me too, and Kylie's panting breath, her black mouth level with mine.

I stare at the pictures above Eddie's head and do what Frogga told me, keep my mouth shut. There's Eddie on a boat, Eddie holding some football trophy. I fix on that boxer's gold belt, trying not to see the urn on the mantelpiece, while I replay Eddie's question in my head.

What is this crap about? I don't know, not really, only that there's a pretty good chance I won't see tomorrow morning.

'Like I said…' Frogga clears his throat and starts again. 'I told Michael everything on the phone.'

'So, now you can tell me. That a problem?'

'No, Eddie. No problem.' Frogga's Adam's Apple bobs like a dinghy in a storm, but give the bastard credit, he keeps going. 'This guy Haywood's desperate to off-load. They were moving these four keys over from Amsterdam, Haywood, and his boss. Some Dutch bloke called Vandalberg.'

Van den Berg, I want to say. I bite my tongue till it stings.

'But the bag man got greedy.' Frogga says, just like I told him, like Haywood told me, except that Frogga's too coked-up to stick to the script. 'He's in a skip now, in bits, in Byker. They're going to find him, and when they do there'll be filth all over. And this guy Haywood, he's foreign, doesn't know shit. He's black for fuck's sake, might as well have a sign on his head saying catch the fuckin darkie.' Frogga's snort of laughter echoes round the room.

'He wants out. He'll take a hundred grand for it. All of it. Fuckin hell, Eddie, I could offload it tomorrow for twice that, but give me a few days, get it cut and bagged and moved out there,' he jabs a dirty finger at the curtains, 'and we can take half a million fuckin quid.'

Eddie nods like he doesn't believe a word of it. 'You're standing behind this are you, Chester,' he says, opening a drawer in his desk. He lays a red-handled claw hammer and a matching pair of pliers on the desk. 'Giving me your guarantee?'

Frogga swallows, but he comes back fast. 'It's a peach, Eddie, but it has to be quick, like tonight, or tomorrow, or else-'

'Your caste-iron certain fuckin guarantee?'

Eddie looks at Riley. I'd give my left bollock to know what he's thinking, but then it might come to that. He's an angry, twenty stone toddler with a pair of pliers, and nothing he does makes any sense.

'I guarantee it,' Frogga says, but I can tell he's thinking pretty much the same as me.

'Alright,' Eddie says. 'So, what are you putting up?'

'Eh?'

'How much money you putting in?'

'I can get thirty grand,' Carl says, 'cash.'

'You think he'd take a fuckin cheque?' Eddie says. 'And you?'

Frogga sniffs and rubs the back of his hand across his nose.

'Fuckin junkie,' Eddie says. He doesn't bother asking me.

'Right. If this is going to happen, and I'm not saying it is, then I want forty grand from you lads by tomorrow morning.' Eddie rubs his chin through his beard. 'And I'll take that piece of shit Porsche as collateral for another ten. Alright with you, Chester?'

Frogga's eyes bulge like Eddie's just suggested selling his sister, although who knows, that probably wouldn't bother him.

'Alright, Chester?'

'Eddie, man, I paid forty grand for it.'

'You'll get it back.'

'Why don't we just take the gear? Rip this Dutch cunt off?'

'Wanker,' Eddie says. 'You know who Ludwig Van den Berg is?'

'No.'

'No.' Eddie opens the pliers. 'Well, I do.' He nods at Riley and squeezes them shut. 'It's forty grand and that fuckin car, here, bright and early in the morning.'

'Have a drink,' Riley says. I look around me but there's nothing there, just Kylie's panting face. 'In the bar. All of you.'

'What for,' Frogga says.

'We've got a couple of calls to make,' Riley says.

'Yeh, and you look fuckin thirsty to me,' Eddie says, and I'm up and heading for the door with my tongue stuck to the roof of my mouth.

I'm halfway down a bottle of Budweiser before I realise how bad it tastes, mixed with that staleness at the back of my mouth, last night's whisky, and tonight's vodka, and the almost migraine still lingering behind my eye. I'd go to the gents, get my face under the cold tap, but Frogga's already in there getting his own refreshments, so I lean back on the bar with the music from downstairs pounding in my head, and watch the side of Carl's blank face reflecting back from the wall of mirrors. Poor bastard.

Jesus. I've got Frogga giving me a warm feeling, and now I'm feeling sorry for Carl bloody Burns. Carl looks at me, and his forehead creases as if he's read my mind. But it's not me he's looking at, it's Frogga, walking back towards us, still sniffing, with his thumb pressed to his nose.

I don't hear Smiler's mobile go, but I see the lines tighten on his face. He looks at the screen then hooks a finger at us and opens

Eddie's brown panelled door. We file in and take our places.

'Nothing else you want to tell me,' Eddie says, fingers dancing over the red rubber handles on his desk.

No one speaks. There's just the suck of Riley's lips and the beat of the music from below, and the dog weaving round between us, soft paws padding on the carpet, reminding me of the last time I was in here, bent over the desk.

"I won't let you down, Eddie," I told him.

"Make sure you fuckin don't," he said, and I can still feel the ache in my knuckles.

'Right.' Eddie stands up. 'Set it up. Twelve o'clock tomorrow morning,' he tells Frogga. 'That'll give you time to get to the Porsche to my place. Like I say, you lads are in for forty grand. Keep you honest.'

A stream of fake smoke rises from Riley's vape. Eddie blinks. He looks down at Riley.

'And you can go forty grand en all, seeing as you're so keen.' The plastic tube cracks between Riley's teeth. 'So that leaves twenty for me, which is a fuck of a lot better than a hundred.' Eddie laughs. 'I can even trust you bunch of monkeys with that.' The vape glows bright in Riley's mouth, while the rest of us try to smile.

That's when it dawns on me.

Eddie isn't coming.

'You'll be here at eleven with the cash, and back at one, with the gear boxed up in Nescafe's finest and locked in the safe at old man Cooper's. Right.' He claps his hands.

I look across the desk with the sound echoing in my head, and I know I can't leave it like this.

Eddie's hands are pressed together. His lips are pink and shiny wet, like Daryl, standing in the doorway with a fag in his mouth, and Dolly Parton singing, and that wrinkly balloon floating down. That moment before I panicked and ran, before Daryl ruined Benjy's life, before he ruined Mam's life too, and mine. Except I won't let him. I won't give in, not again. Because if I lose, then Daryl wins.

'He's expecting *us*, Eddie. You and me, to do the deal.'

'Fuck off,' Eddie says. The hammer bangs like a judge's gavel sending a stab of fear through my stomach, so sharp and fast that all I really feel is the echo of it, throbbing in my balls.

'Van den Berg thinks I'm the man in Walker.'

'Well, he's not as smart as everyone reckons.'

'He told Haywood to deal with you. There's no way he'll do the business if you're not there.'

Eddie weighs the hammer in his hand.

'You lads aren't fuckin me about now, are you?'

Chapter Thirty-Four

Easy Money

Frogga takes the lead, hungry for the deal. He pushes through the glass doors of the Mal Maison Hotel, a proper little businessman with his dark grey suit and briefcase. Eddie lumbers after him, jeans hanging off his arse and a red Nike hold-all dangling from his hairy paw. Carl's got Eddie's back, and then there's me, taking it all in.

The place is almost dark after the sunlight outside, done up in purple and black with sofas and cushions scattered over the carpet, like one of those glass-fronted brothels in Amsterdam. I suppose that's what rich people want, to be reminded of sex, just like everyone else.

Reception is a big shiny smile of a desk opposite a winding silver staircase. Frogga pauses, ready with his story, but there's no one on the desk. His hand creeps towards the bell, and that's when I make my move, edging past Carl and Eddie, whispering in Frogga's ear.

'Don't do it.'

'Eh?'

'The switch.'

'What man? Fuck off.' Frogga twists his ugly face at me and stamps up the soft carpeted staircase.

I drop my head, but I can feel the break in Eddie's stride, his eyes boring through the top of my baseball cap.'

'Fuckin switch,' he mumbles, and I'm thinking, shit I've gone too soon, screwed the whole thing up.

Except I haven't, because we're all way past the point of no return, and Eddie comes plodding up the stairs, his big bear head fizzing with the promise of four kilos of cocaine.

He doesn't know what I'm talking about, but that's okay. He will.

I drop back along the corridor rubbing my sweaty hands on my jeans and think about Michael Riley. He's at The Hammer, holding the fort till Eddie gets back. That's what he said, leaning back in his chair beside Eddie's desk, sneering up at us. "I'll hold the fort." But let's face it, if Michael Riley had been at the Alamo, he'd have been slithering out the side gate long before Santa Anna's Mexicans came marching up to the front.

And me, what would I be doing? Creeping out in the night to open it?

Frogga knocks on the door of room 309, three slow raps, like a copper.

The door opens and we troop in.

The room's the same as yesterday, massive, about the size of my flat. There's a low oval coffee table and a pair of fat leather chairs by the near wall. The bed's over towards the window, and everything from the shiny wallpaper to the coffee table are done up in shades of silvery grey, like the whole place was designed to match Frogga's suit.

Haywood is standing, facing the charcoal curtains, showing us his shaved brown head. Class I, free-range, I think. One solid tap would crack it open. He looks like a Buddhist monk with the breeze blowing through the curtains, setting his bright orange shirt billowing around his skinny ribs. What's that shirt about? He's selling half a million quid's worth of coke for a hundred grand, just so he can get out of here before anyone notices there's a dead Dutchman somewhere in Byker, and another one here with a shitload of drugs and a criminal record, and he's got that shirt blowing around him like one of those flags at the World Cup.

No one else seems to notice. They're all clustered round the bed, staring at the open suitcase on the duvet, bulging with a load of polythene bags of what definitely looks like cocaine.

My impulse is to move closer, get a good look, but I do as I was told. I pull my baseball cap low over my eyes and step sideways, into the alcove.

'Hello, my friends.' Haywood turns towards us, flashing about a hundred shiny tombstone teeth. 'It is good you are here.'

He doesn't even glance at me, but I can tell straight off there's something weird going on, like that stupid grin, and the fact that his near-perfect English seems to have changed into this comedy African. I mean for Christ's sake, is that the best he can do?

'Haywood?' Eddie barks.

Haywood grins and nods his frail head. 'Mr. Eddie Burns.' He slaps a hand on Eddie's arm.

Eddie looks at it until Haywood lets go, but the grin only slips for a moment.

'What is this?' Haywood says, opening his palm towards the case.

'Eh?' Eddie looks from him to Frogga. 'Who the fuck is this prick?'

'What could it be?' Haywood says again, like a magician.

'Coke, I fuckin hope,' Frogga says, flashing his lizard sneer. 'Blow, toot, snow, flake, Charlie. Colombian marching powder. The Devil's fuckin dandruff.' He slides a pearl handle from his inside pocket. 'Least it better be.' The blade flicks out against

Haywood's cheek, glinting under the chandelier.

Haywood stops grinning. He backs against the billowing curtains while Frogga kneels at the foot of the bed and draws the blade across a polythene bag. He touches a fingertip to the powder and rubs it on his gum, grinning through his goatee like the mutant child of Kermit and D'artagnan.

'Hmmm,' he says, pouting and smacking his lips, making me think of Linthorpe's voice echoing down that big clunky phone, telling me how sometimes things can take a walk, from the evidence room.

Frogga brings the bag over to my side of the room and tips a messy handful onto the coffee table. He stands between the fat leather chairs with that blade slicing up and down in a blur of silver and white, a racing certainty for Hell's Kitchen, coke chef of the year.

Alright,' he says, chanting under his breath like a witch-doctor; 'blow, toot, snow, flake; blow toot, snow, flake.'

The freak.

He scrapes his knife across the table and piles up something about the size of a powdery finger of Twix.

'Don't fuck about,' Eddie says.

Frogga scowls, but scrapes half the coke off, bending to take the rest of it in one long snort. He stays very still then his head comes up, staring into the jewel-studded mirror in front of him.

'Fuckin, yes,' he says, nodding to himself, grinning, turning around. His fists clench. 'Fuckin yes,' he's going like he's just scored the winner at Wembley. Except that there's a five-inch blade sticking out of his fist, and I can't see your modern ref letting that go. Not even if Frogga played for Chelsea.

Eddie isn't impressed either.

'Do it properly,' he says, picking Frogga's briefcase up off the floor and throwing it at him.

Frogga catches the case and lays it on the desk. He turns the combination, probably to six, six, six, and clicks it open. He's got something like a kid's chemistry set in there, vials and test tubes all tucked up in red velvet. The first thing he takes out is a black frame about as big as his hand. He sets it on the table and lays a roll of velvet down beside it, with a tiny silver spoon, a test tube, and a plastic vial.

We're all watching now, Haywood, Eddie and Carl clustered round the bed, and me in my alcove by the bathroom door, with my head itching under this stupid cap. Frogga's loving it. He cracks his knuckles, tips a tiny spoonful of coke into the test tube, and rests it on the frame. The vial snaps in his hand. He empties a colourless liquid into the tube, swirling it around until the mixture turns this light turquoise colour.

Eddie grunts and digs another pack from the bottom of the case. He brings it over and drops it on the table.

Frogga slices through the cellophane and takes another vial from his case, blinding us with science.

'It's good,' he says, 'like really shit-hot gear. Ninety percent, like there's a half a mill…' he looks at Haywood and stops. 'It's good.'

'This cocaine is what you want? What you buy?' Haywood says, holding out his hand.

'Yes, man.' Eddie says. 'Shut up.' He gives the red hold-all to Haywood.

The room's bright enough already, but Haywood pulls the string, opening the curtains so the sun comes slanting through the window. He sits back on the windowsill with the sun shining through his shirt and unzips the bag.

I know what he's looking at because I saw them this morning, a hundred grand in twenty tight wrapped bundles.

Haywood pulls a note from one of the bundles and holds it up to the light. A gust of wind blows through the open window, ruffling the crisp purple paper. Haywood shakes his head.

Eddie's fingers flex.

The itch under my cap is unbearable, and that stupid Nike catchphrase keeps repeating in my mind.

'No,' Haywood says.

Eddie growls.

'No good.' Haywood says.

'That's a hundred grand of my fuckin money,' Eddie says. His eyebrows come together across the flat bridge of his nose, and I can see that big bad penny about to drop.

'Is not real.'

Haywood steps to the side of the window.

'Is, how you would say, fuckin forgery.'

Eddie's mouth opens. He stares from Haywood's delicate black face to Frogga's white one. His chest heaves and his nostrils flare, like a bull between two toreadors.

'You lying, black, fuckin darkie, cunt.'

He rushes Haywood and takes a wild swing. But he's given him a warning, and Haywood's ready. He squats under the arc of Eddie's fist, and swings the bag up over his head, between the curtains, and out through the open window.

There's a moment when it's there, that red bag hanging in the air with Eddie stretching out across the windowsill. Then it's gone. A hundred grand for the first lucky bastard strolling along the quay.

'Cunt,' Eddie roars.

He gets one good boot into Haywood, then he's jamming down the suitcase and hoofing it past me, into the corridor.

Carl's one step ahead of him, and Frogga's one step behind, with his flashy science kit forgotten on the silver table, and a bag of coke clutched in his fist.

That's my cue. I slide the bathroom door open and bang it shut behind me, except it doesn't close. The thing bounces back on its runners, just a crack, but it's wide enough for me to see Frogga's bony fingers come out around the bedroom door. He's going to pull it shut behind him, leave me here. His knuckles whiten, but then he lets it go.

'Police.'

The shout comes from out in the corridor, and Frogga and Carl burst back into the room.

Eddie runs through them, with that suitcase still clutched across his chest. He gets about two steps from the window when the call comes again, this time from outside.

'Armed Police.'

This guy drops down outside the window like Batman, covered in black plastic, with a big black gun pointing at Eddie's chest.

'Fucka.' Eddie screams, and another copper comes running through the open door.

Carl, the moron, takes a swing, laying the copper out on the carpet.

The next one slams the butt of his gun into Carl's mouth, sending a spray of blood across Frogga's chemistry set. Then he grabs the top of Carl's head and smashes his face into the jewelled mirror, with Carl's arms still windmilling around him.

Frogga darts behind them, going for the door, but more coppers come running in. One of them grabs his collar and jerks him round. For a moment those big ugly eyes look straight into mine. They twist one hand up behind his back. He screams, and swings with the other, still holding the bag of coke. There's a silent explosion of white powder, and by the time the cloud settles the four of them are cuffed and laid out face down on the floor.

There's a copper sitting across Eddie's back. He pulls his helmet off and points his gun at Eddie's head. But even that doesn't stop him bellowing abuse at Haywood.

'I'm going to tie you to a fuckin a cross and burn your stinking black balls off-'

'It's the fuckin Bandit,' Frogga hisses, his mouth up close against Eddie's ear.

'You cunt,' Eddie's head swings back, butting down into Frogga's face. 'You switched my fuckin money. You thieving, cunting, coked-up junkie.'

The copper jabs his gun into Eddie's neck, but that just attracts his attention.

'I know your face. You ginger copper cunt. And I'll find you, and your horrible ginger bairns, and I'll fuckin -'

'Having a good day, are we?' That flat almost-Yorkshire accent couldn't belong to anyone else.

'You fuckin bent bastard,' Eddie roars, and they press his face down into the carpet. He keeps going, but the words are too muffled to hear.

'Not so good then, Mr. Burns,' Linthorpe says, setting Eddie off again. They let him go on, roaring at the carpet till he runs out of steam.

'Turn them over.' Linthorpe says. He clears his throat.

'Edward Burns, Carl Burns, Chester Temperley and Daniel Haywood, I am arresting you on suspicion of conspiracy to supply class A drugs. You do not have to say anything, but it may harm your defence if you do not mention when questioned something which you later rely on in court. Anything you do say may be given in evidence.'

'Fuck you,' Eddie says. 'This is fuckin entrapment. I was lured here on false pretences. That black cunt there asked me to carry his bag. And you'll find no prints of mine on that cash.'

'What cash is that then,' Linthorpe says. 'Those forgeries?'

Eddie stops. His eyes narrow and his nostrils flare, and I swear, handcuffs or not it's about the scariest thing I've ever seen.

'You thieving fuckin Yorkshire arse bandit. You gayboy, fuckin cunt-'

'Blah, fuckin blah,' Linthorpe says. 'So, I'm gay, and now everyone knows.' He shrugs, dropping onto his haunches. 'Well okay, Eddie, it's true. But it's not 1967 anymore, and no one gives a shit, except you, and you're a murdering, racist, homophobic drug dealing scumbag. And you'll do thirty years for this.'

Linthorpe taps Eddie's cheek and lifts his middle finger towards the bathroom door.

The bastard's pointing at me.

Except he isn't, he's pointing at the wall lamp in my alcove, at the tiny chrome blob swivelling back and forth above it. He steps across, takes the camera out of the lamp, and drops it into a clear plastic bag.

'That's sorted,' Linthorpe says, standing with his back between me and the rest of the room. 'You're on film, Eddie. The next time you're walking the streets it'll be with a Zimmer frame, if your heart doesn't give out first.'

That sets Eddie off again, and maybe it's meant to, because I do what I should have done ages ago, and ease the door along on its runners, till it clicks shut.

'Take them down to the vans,' Linthorpe says. 'Seal the room for forensics.'

There's a rattle of handcuffs, but no one seems to have anything left to say, except Frogga.

'Bandit's in the bathroom.'

I stop breathing. I stare at the sliver of light under the door and wait for it to slide back in my face.

'You're the bandit,' Linthorpe tells him.

To be fair, Carl and Eddie don't say a word. Only Frogga keeps bleating on.

'Look, man, open the fuckin door. Just open it.'

His voice fades down the hall, and one by one, the rest of the coppers follow him out. I feel the vibration of their footsteps, the click of the light, and finally, the door slams shut.

I stand there in darkness with my cheek pressed to the cool tiles, and I wait like I waited in that cupboard a million years ago. A sharp ridge digs into my cheek. The pain makes it better, helping me think about everything I've done since then, and whether any of its worth a damn. Clara thinks so. At least she says she does. But she's the craziest bitch I've ever met, so what sense does it make to trust her? Or Annie? Or Linthorpe? Or any of the bastards?

The door doesn't open, it comes crashing off its runners. The room floods with stinging light. A hand presses my face into the tiles. Someone pulls my cap off and a rough canvass bag comes down over my eyes, shutting me back into darkness. The bag pulls tight around my throat. Panic drums in my chest. I lash out, and a fist lands in my kidneys, knocking the breath out of me, sending pain flaring through my stomach. Plastic handcuffs cut into my wrists.

'Shut the fuck up.' It's a posh voice I don't know. 'Walk.'

I take a small breath through the bag, and like always, I do as I'm told.

This is it. This is fuckin it. I know too much.

We're in a lift. I can feel it in my stomach, hear the clash of metal. The door opens into wet heat and food smells that make me want to puke, and then I'm out in the cold with my face to the wall and my hands locked behind me.

'Don't you move. Don't you fuckin dare.'

An arm comes around my side. I think he's going to hit me again, but he's not. His hand goes in my jacket pocket. It's my cap, he's putting my cap in there, then his boots click away over the tarmac.

I stand there, shivering, knowing I'm a fool, and I bloody deserve this because if there's one thing I should've learned from Daryl and Mam, and Maxi, and a lifetime living in Walker, it's that you don't trust people. The one truth worth knowing, the one obvious simple dead-eyed certainty in this life is that if you lie there with your legs in the air, you're going to get fucked. I bang my head against the wall. It's like I'm some awkward little kid who just won't learn. Well, I'm going to learn now.

There's a car coming, fast.

An accident.

They'll say I was wandering about in the back lane, probably pissed. So, they're going to run me down. Well, fuck it. I don't care. Let the bastards do it. But I do care, and now, finally, I know. It's because of her. She's the only one who matters. My fingers are itching to twist the soft flesh of my thigh, but I can't even do that. I should have listened to her, but there's so many things I should've done.

The car comes roaring in. I open my mouth and howl into the wall. At least now it'll be over.

The door opens before the car stops.

He grabs my jacket and pulls me in, with that tell-tale hand on the back of my head. A copper. He forces me down, flat along the back seat, and the car revs away up the lane.

I can feel that we're going up a steep bank then we stop, turning, maybe to the left, but I can't really tell, and if I am going to die then I don't want to waste my last minutes playing soldiers.

I think about her. I want to remember us together in my bed, but what I see is her standing on my sheepskin rug with her arms crossed over her thin white shirt and that pink flush high on her cheeks. She's screaming at me, but her voice is tiny. I press in close, desperate to hear, but I can't. I've made the wrong choices too many times.

Her fist swings up into my eye, and that BMW goes roaring down the street.

Brakes squeal. The car stops. The handbrake crunches, and the engine dies.

There's a gust of fresh air when the copper opens the back door. He leans across me and pulls the bag off my head.

I blink up at soft pink lips half an inch from mine.

'Linthorpe.'

'Shut up,' he says, and turns me over so my face is pressed against the leather seat. He lifts my hands, pushing my face down further with the cuffs tight against my wrists.

'You fuckin bastard,' I say, then the cuffs come away, and he pulls me feet first out of the car.

'You're not on the camera. You were never there,' he snaps, while I stand and stare at the cobbled street. 'This was Frogga's deal, Frogga's and Carl's. They set it up.'

The words keep coming but all I really understand is that I'm not going to die, not yet anyway, and I'm not going to do thirty years in Durham or Belmarsh, or some other living death.

'If it comes to it, you saw Frogga with a red Nike bag this morning, switching the cash right beside Eddie's desk. But it probably never will. Haywood and Van den Berg are in too far to back out.'

He holds something up in front of me, this plastic Thomas the Tank Engine backpack, and presses it into my chest. 'You alright?'

'Erm, yeh.' I look up.

'Thanks, Tommy,' he says. 'That was one bastard I really wanted,' and his hand rubs up along my arm, squeezing my shoulder.

His blue eyes look straight into mine, locked on in a way that makes me feel the charge of something between us. He holds out his hand, but I ignore it, and fold my arms around him, then my face turns, and I press my lips to his. What can I tell you? In the moment, it feels right.

'Thanks,' I tell him.

'Thank you,' he says. 'Now go on, and don't come back.' He nods at the big black M across the cobbles.

'I'll be on the next stage out of Dodge.' I smile and turn away, with that jagged moment bright as lightning behind my eyes.

Linthorpe watches me go. His eyes follow me to the Metro steps, and it feels okay.

I half turn and raise my hand, then I walk down into the station just in time to see the big yellow train come rumbling in. I check my empty pockets and take my chances, jumping the barrier and sitting, ticketless on the orange plush.

I pull my phone out of my pocket and scroll through the address book. I press the green button and listen to a foreign ringtone.

'Come on, woman, answer the damn thing.'

She does, at last, and my toes clench with frustration.

'Hi there. Welcome to Clara's voicemail. So sorry I can't get to the phone right now, but I'd love to hear from you, so-'

'Shit.' I click the phone off and hunch over my plastic backpack, feeling like I'm ten years old, watching for a black-uniformed ticket inspector to come marching up the aisle, with a gun in his hand, and Michael Riley's long, leather face.

Chapter Thirty-Five

The Viaduct

The Metro took forever, with no ticket and twenty-five grand in my Thomas the Tank Engine backpack. I feel calmer in the airport, weaving through the Friday afternoon crowds, past the information desk, to left luggage. I hand over my ticket and get a small tartan suitcase, not so different from Haywood's, just uglier. I chose tartan because I thought it would blend in. Another stupid idea. I feel like some kind of comedy criminal, with my child's back-back on my shoulder, and my green tartan case trundling along behind.

The toilets are empty. I lock the cubicle door, balance the case on the cistern, and open it up. The first thing I pull out is a little box not much bigger than my mobile, wrapped in gold paper and tied with a purple bow. I slip it into my jacket pocket with my iPod and slide my passport and ticket into the back pocket of my jeans. All that's left in the case is a week's worth of clothes and a handful of photos, jumbled together on the black nylon base.

I unzip my Thomas bag and unpack Eddie's money. The five tight packs of twenties make a neat little tower on the toilet seat. I wrap each one in a t-shirt and pack it away in my tartan case. The case is still half-empty, even after I smooth my backpack over the top. I zip the case shut and lock the tiny padlock like that's going to make any difference, then I swear and open it up again, and jam a thin wad of twenties into my jeans.

That's it. I check-in, hand luggage only, and buy a paper, some sweets, normal stuff. I get a strong black coffee, take about two scalding sips, then I leave my coffee and my baseball cap on the table and wheel my tartan case over to the escalator, and up to security. I stand in the long snaking line with the Clash screaming in my earphones, and shuffle forward, trying not to see the two black-dressed coppers with weird, futuristic guns held across their chests. I get to the front of the line, put my twenty-five grand bag on the little conveyor belt, and watch it slide away from me.

By the time I've got it back and put my shoes on there's less than thirty minutes to take off. I take a fast walk to gate fourteen with the black plastic handle slick in my hand, and the Clash breaking rocks in my head.

The flight's boarding. I turn the iPod off. They call priority first; families and kids, and people who pay extra, so I don't know why everyone gets up at once. Like it's going to get us there any quicker. Still, it leaves plenty of seats free in the lounge.

I sit down and make my call, and this time, she answers.

'Clara, where the hell have you been?'

'Oh, busy, busy, getting ready for you.'

'Well, I'm on my way.'

'Of course you are,' she says, with that rich people's certainty, like she can make things come true just by saying them in her posh, high-pitched voice. And who knows, maybe she can?

'We're landing at ten to five.'

'Don't worry, baby. I'll be there. I can't wait to show you what I've done,' and crazy as she is, I'm left grinning at the phone, then I turn it off and wheel my tartan case to the back of the shrinking queue.

I end up in an aisle seat beside some bloke whose thigh bulges halfway across my seat. I suppose that's the price you pay for getting on last, but who cares. I'm two hours from Barcelona.

I unfold the paper and see that Newcastle United are two points off the drop zone with their star striker saying how much he loves the club, but how flattered he is by the interest from Arsenal. Same old shite. There's no such thing as loyalty anymore, just money ripping the soul out of football, same as it does with everything else. I try to follow the story, but I don't really care. I flip the paper.

There's a small grainy picture on the bottom of page one, a man on a motorbike, long hair hanging round his face. The picture should be familiar, but the adrenalin's leaking out of me. My eyes are rolling, and the print blurs on the page.

I'm desperate for sleep, but the loudspeaker keeps shouting at me about safety procedures, and snacks and perfume, and a load of other shite I don't want. Eventually, it stops, and I close my eyes, trying not to think about all the stuff rumbling around in my mind.

How Van den Berg'll get a word in the judge's ear for his trial in Holland. He'll get off easy like rich guys do, but it's a shame about Haywood. He seemed alright, in a fake, flimsy sort of way. Maybe he'll get some credit too, for helping out, but even so, he's not the sort of bloke you can imagine lasting long inside.

The main thing is that it was Frogga's deal. That's all anyone needs to know. That's what Frogga told Eddie, so I don't see what else he can say now, especially with Eddie trying to rip his throat out. The thought comforts me. My head falls onto my chest. I drift into a very real dream.

I'm standing in Eddie's office, but he isn't there. There's a presence looking up at me from Eddie's black leather chair, with all those photos on the wall behind him. They're the same as Eddie's photos, the boat, the football trophy, and the boxer, except that Eddie's face has been torn out and someone else's stuck clumsily in its place, on grainy grey paper.

'It was Frogga's deal,' I say.

He doesn't answer, but nicotine vapour clouds my eyes.

'It was his deal. He told you himself.'

There's still no answer, only a long slow laugh.

Liar.

He doesn't speak, just puts the thought into my head. The vape burns bright under his long hawk nose, and a pair of red-handled pliers come walking across the desk in Frankie Morton's juddering steps.

I'm frantic now, feeling that dog's breath hot on my neck, searching the photos for Eddie's face. And it is there, real, and close against mine, with his nostrils flaring and two shiny horns curving out of his head. He charges.

I run for the window but there's nowhere left to go. Eddie's roaring in. I see the orange billow of my shirt and I'm Haywood, ducking down towards that grey hotel carpet, throwing my green tartan bag out the window. But like always, I'm too late. Eddie's horns pierce my chest. He tosses me into the air. I scramble away, to a place on the edge of my dream.

Eddie roars again, but this time I know it's only the engines. There's a hand shaking me awake. The fat man beside me, desperate to get off.

'I get claustrophobic,' he says, standing over me, making me think of Maxi, and that message from Bulgaria.

The plane's jammed full. There's nowhere either of us can possibly go.

'It's a medical condition.'

Clara's there to meet me, looking stylishly Mediterranean with her dark-blond bob and little white dress, light years away from that bristle-headed Goth snarling in the snow. She kisses me full on the mouth, and she smells good too.

'No luggage?'

I shrug and nod at my tartan bag.

'That's gorgeous.'

Clara smiles at me like I'm a psychiatric patient and leads me out into the warm afternoon with the bright sunlight showing every curve of her body through that loose white dress. The taxi driver wants to take my bag. No chance. Clara shakes her head and shoots off a few words of Spanish.

We climb into the back of the taxi together, and as we pull away, out of the airport and onto the motorway, I begin to believe that I'm really here.

'Did you call…'

'Shush. 'She pats my thigh, leaving her hand there like she's forgotten it's attached to her. 'Don't worry,' she says, then her nose crinkles and she takes her hand away. 'Don't they have showers in Newcastle anymore?'

I sniff at my armpit and see what she means.

'You should try mine,' she says, opening the window. 'Stephan designed it. Hundreds of tiny, mirrored tiles, so we can watch you in pieces while you wash.'

She smiles this big open smile that doesn't belong on her face, no doubt one of Clara's new accessories practiced in front of those mirrored tiles a thousand times, to hit just the right ambiguous nuance. It works. I've no idea whether she's serious or not.

'Sure,' I say, looking out the window, with Clara laughing to herself beside me.

The hum of the tyres is vaguely soothing, until it makes me think of the Volvo still parked outside the flat. That reminds me. I need to ring Peeler, tell him what's going on, and that he can have the car and whatever he wants from the flat. Try and pretend that makes up for leaving him to deal with the fall-out.

I'll send him some money, tell him to get out of Newcastle, but he won't. Those big ears start to ring if he goes a mile out of Walker. He's in for the duration. But he'll be alright. The good thing about Peeler is he lacks ambition. That stops him getting into all the shit I get into. He'll do a few little deals, get by, and when the fighting's done, somebody'll take over dealing green in Walker and Peeler'll slot right in there, helping them out, keeping his head down, and making the best lasagna north of Naples.

The taxi slows, bumping past a row of warehouses, grass sprouting between clusters of acro-props on the half-built plots between them. It reminds me of home. The signs that the builders have been and gone, and there's not much chance they'll come back.

We pull up outside what looks like a sealed railway tunnel. There's a huge arch bricked up with pale grey breezeblocks and battered double doors that seem tiny inside that great closed brick mouth. Clara says something in Spanish and hands the driver a crisp green note. The door clicks open. I step out onto a road strewn with white dust and rubble, and the taxi pulls away.

There are four paint-splattered steps leading up to the double doors, and a brass plaque bolted to the wall. I walk up the steps and lay my hand on the plaque.

'El Viaducto,' I say out loud, remembering the name in Clara's flexible mouth, her long legs curled along my sofa.

'Not yet,' Clara says, taking my hand and leading me across the street towards a row of dusky orange buildings.

Up close I can see that they're old houses, converted to something between shops and market stalls. There's maybe a dozen of them, each with baskets outside, selling beads and herbs and pottery and paintings, and at the top of the row, a glass-fronted café.

The place is pretty dead, just an old guy standing behind the counter with narrow eyes dug into his leathery face, and two younger ones sitting opposite him on high stools, eating something off tiny plates. Clara tells me to get a table and leans in between them to order.

There are only three tables, but they're all empty. I choose the one closest to the open door, put my case on the chair beside me and hold my face up to the warm draft from outside. The worst of the heat is fading, but I'm still sweating inside my Colorado jacket. I shrug it off, over the back of my chair. I check the zipped pocket, feeling for my gold-wrapped parcel with its purple bow, and a folded newspaper falls out of the other side. The *Newcastle Evening Chronicle*.

I pick the paper up and drop it on the table, staring at those words from far away, with that grainy picture in the bottom corner. A man on a motorbike, striped football shirt showing through his open jacket.

'We have ten days from tomorrow,' Clara says, putting two tiny cups of coffee on the table. 'After that, we've got to start setting up for Pedro Hernandez.' She takes a sip, and gives me a toothy smile.

'That's brilliant, Clara,' I tell her. 'But will you sit down. I need a minute, you know, to chill out.'

'No, no, no,' she shakes her head. 'Still setting up. Loads to do.

The publicity's gone brilliantly, given that we've had no time to work with. She widens her eyes at me like the sweetest girl you could ever meet, and it amazes me that a creature like her exists.

'We got a piece in *La Gamberra*, written by yours truly, with just a bit of help from Jose-Luis on the translation. I'll show you. There's a great picture.'

My eyes fall back to the grainy picture in front of me. *Full story page nine*. My hand creeps across the table, lifting the corners; three, five, seven.

Clara snatches it away from me.

'For God's sake, Tom. You won't find it in the *Evening Chronicle*,' she throws the paper into her empty chair.

'They're thinking about a piece in *La Imagen* next week, but I can't get any sense out of them about whether they're going to run it. They keep hassling us to pay for advertising and you wouldn't believe what that costs, but Jose-Luis knows the editor, so there's a chance.'

'That's great, Clara,' I say, and it should be, but all I want is to get my hands on that paper.

'He says if we get any real interest we can have the last week in October, but it's not definite. Jose-Luis doesn't really like young guys. He says you need to live before you can work. You need to have a story before you can tell it. Something like that anyway, it doesn't translate.'

'Right,' I say, 'I'll remember that.'

I make myself look up at her, and I realize she's more on edge than I've ever seen her, if you don't count her fake tantrums, which I don't. Or maybe it's just me "projecting", like Clara would say.

My leg's going, bobbing under the table. I'm willing her to get out of here, and finally, the message gets through.

'Like I say. Gotta go. Loads to do,' she presses her lips to mine. 'Chill out here if you want.'

'Thanks, Clara.'

I squeeze her hand, and watch her hips sway down the narrow lane, past the warehouses, and up those four paint-splattered steps. The double-doors swing closed behind her, and I make a grab for the paper, knocking Clara's coffee cup over and sending a brown pool spreading across the table. But I get to page nine.

They've printed the same picture, only bigger. A man on a motorbike with one foot up on the foot-peg and the other stretching down to the road.

I try to read the expression on his face, but the picture's blurred and dark with coffee, so I have to remember it. Him, squinting up through the camera, with a tight-lipped smile, and a wispy tash fighting for attention on his ratty face.

Local Man Drowned, the headline booms.

The body of a man later identified as forty-nine-year-old Daryl Boyle was dredged from the Tyne in the early hours of this morning. Preliminary indications are that Mr. Boyle may have fallen from the Millennium Bridge whilst under the influence of alcohol. He had been dead for approximately thirty-six hours.

Mr. Boyle of Belmont St, Walker was known to social services, and had endured a long-running battle with alcohol addiction. Police report no suspicious circumstances at the scene.

The body was discovered by Mrs. Margaret O'Hara of Ropery Drive in Newcastle. "I was walking along the quay with Betsy, my Poodle, when I spotted a strange shape floating in the river. At first, I thought it was a piece of driftwood, something fallen off a boat…"

I go back a few lines.

Police report no suspicious circumstances…

I turn the paper over and press it down over Clara's spilt coffee, and then I drink mine in one strong, tepid mouthful.

The sun ducks behind the café, casting a shadow over the buildings across the street. The two young guys walk out into the street, and the barman follows them. He disappears into the shop next door, leaving me alone in his café. Cooler now, I pull my jacket back on and stare across at the battered double doors in that huge grey wall, as if they might give me some clue as to what's inside.

Deep down, I know already. But I can't face that now. Not alone. Not without her.

So, I stare, and I wait, and I hope.

The car comes down from the far end of the lane. That's why it doesn't register, not even when the yellow bonnet juts into the periphery of my vision, and the tyres crunch to a stop. The door opens and closes.

I look into my empty coffee cup and slide the palms of my hands along my jeans.

Lilac sandshoes, pale blue jeans, and that same loose white shirt. She walks down towards the cafe, head high, leaning back against the slope.

I stand up. The table scrapes across the floor.

Her hair is tied back, her face clear as a girl's.

I'm in the doorway when the light of recognition softens her dark brown eyes. Her face bursts into that huge dimply smile, and I'm holding her warm body tight against me for a long time. Not moving, not until I'm sure she's real.

My eyes open to the leather-faced barman, waiting to get into his café. I draw her to one side, and he goes past, taking his time, studying Annie as if she's a piece of sculpture. He smiles approval, showing us the gap between his splayed front teeth.

We look back at him, still clinging to each other, and giggle like kids. I feel the tension fall away from me, only realizing the weight of it now that it's gone. There won't be a better time than this.

I unzip the pocket on my leather jacket, and I don't know why, maybe it's just that I'm so excited, but I go down on one knee holding the slim gold box up towards her, with its silky purple bow.

She stops laughing, and takes the box with her delicate, tentative fingers. Her teeth creep over her lip, and a stone digs into my knee.

'So? Open it.'

Her head sways, lifting and turning, dancing to its secret song. She pulls the bow.

'Go on.'

She holds the parcel in her palm, about the length of her hand from wrist to polished fingernails. She lifts the lid. Her lips part and she stares at me through shining eyes.

I stand up and draw her towards me.

Her fingers trace a line around my eye.

'Beautiful,' she says.

I kiss her.

She shudders against my chest and pushes me away.

'I suppose you'll be wanting to share it then, will you?'

She sniffs, and runs her sleeve across her cheek, leaving a grey smudge of eyeliner. Her nose wrinkles and I see the merest hint of Rumpelstiltskin on her gorgeous face.

'Well,' she says, peeling the purple and gold wrapper off her Cadbury's Caramel. 'How about it, cowboy?'

I snatch the chocolate out of her hand, and get a good mouthful, gloopy as a brown banana.

'Hey, that's mine.'

She grabs for the chocolate, but she's way too slow. I catch her wrist and draw her close, and I whisper those three terrifying words through a mouthful of soft milk chocolate. Then I lead her up the four paint-splattered steps of El Viaducto.

We're on the top step when I practically have a heart attack. Old leather face is shouting across from the door of his café, and he's holding up my nasty, tartan, twenty-five grand suitcase.

Chapter Thirty-Six

The Benjamin Exhibition

I don't know what I expected, but this isn't it. I stand on a marble floor looking up at what might once have been some sort of tunnel, and I feel as if I've stepped into some vast and strange, and utterly familiar world. Bright white walls curve around great arched windows, with a row of skylights twenty feet above. The walls are hung with iron chains like some futuristic dungeon, and even in the dusk, the air is filled with light. Orange tinted beams falling through the glass roof, crisscrossing the polished floor.

There's a picture beside me, hanging loose off the curve of the wall, moving minutely on its short chain. The frame is a dusky grey, blending with the painted sky. There's a red-brick house and a figure in the foreground, an elf or pixie with its fists clenched, and one pointed boot stamping on the cracked paving. You can feel the anger. Chin thrust forward, face as wrinkled as the creature's green felt hat. What gives it away isn't her caramel skin, or the wire-wool hair jutting from under her hat, but that she's standing outside the cracked red door of number six Belmont Street, with that silver mermaid knocker suspended over her head.

'Thanks a bunch.' Annie jabs a finger in my stomach.

'What,' I say, spreading both hands and trying not to smile, but Annie isn't looking at me.

The next picture is similar, but here, a pair of huge flowery shorts flare out over her stick-thin legs. There are half a dozen more, variations on a theme, the last of them with Rumpelstiltskin grinning through a face full of chocolate.

'Bastard,' she says.

'Don't be angry,' I say, taking her cheeks in my hand, whispering in her ear.

'You haven't changed a bit.'

She punches me in the chest.

I catch her fist and try to kiss her, but she spins away, hair flicking across my face.

'Even those damn shorts,' she mumbles, stomping past the *Pixies furiosas*, as Clara has labelled them.

Chica en un puente, the next label reads, over a teenage girl running across a bridge, plaits flying, one silver sandal turning high against a deep blue sky.

There is only one *Chica en un jardín*, and that is unfinished, the girl's head thrown back against a tree's green-grey ridges, tinged to yellow where the light falls through the leaves. Her front teeth bite down, squeezing the colour from her lip, brown eyes wide, focused beyond the artist.

I feel Annie's intake of breath, but I walk on, to the bent figure of an old man in a doorway, a shadow against a bright yellow light.

El hombre sombrío, the label says, but I am not interested in Clara's labels. He's my miserable angel, and it's way too late to change now. I stare at him, this old friend in an unfamiliar place, and the crash of broken glass echoes in my ears.

'I saw him,' Annie says, her voice small and distant, and I feel a rush of sadness for the girl who broke that window.

The last rays of sunlight come slicing through the skylights, shading the curved white walls to peach, lighting an arc of copper coins in shades of gold. I watch the frozen fountain spray into a cold blue sky, and I hear them clatter on the station tiles, beyond a woolly outstretched hand. I feel the pain in my foot where I kicked his metal cup and the sharper twist of guilt in my stomach. I walk away from him, still pretending, refusing to look back. I don't care. I'm not scared. But the picture holds me, repeating itself. Canvas after canvas of falling coins, each painfully imperfect. My pitiful, spiteful life laid bare for the world to see.

An alcove is cut out of the curved wall, like a niche in a church. I duck inside, coming face to face with a bright grinning devil, dancing by a child's bed. The figure blurs as if there is not one, but three, overlaid, tails high and poised as scorpions'. I stumble back with the fear burning under my arms, and the blood thundering round my head.

The same slit eyes look in at me from both sides. Blue tattoos slither up knotted forearms. Pink lips glisten and hands press together, praying, for what? Daryl, when he was a god, or a devil, before he became a victim like the rest of us. I hold his blue-painted eyes, and I see him falling away from me, justifying, and excusing to the last, splashing into the shiny brown water.

I feel no guilt, only the strength to face my anger, and to let it go.

I step out of the alcove and look instead at a red-haired girl in a dimly lit bar, her freckled face tinted lilac in the lamplight. She looks across, as if at the next canvass, a blond bare-chested boy kicking a ball against a crumbling wall, his face dripping fat red drops.

A second boy is laid out on a rotting cross, a nail through his eye. He is chained to the cellar's stone floor, cold and defiant, wooden as Pinocchio, even as the hammer comes swinging down.

Carl at least is brave, in his dull-witted way.

Frogga is different, pinned down by a web of tiny threads, flat against a board, just like we did in biology, slicing our subject open to see what was inside.

I reach up to the canvass and touch his slimy green skin, his swollen, blood-filled eyes, and I feel that tingle in my head, the buzz of when I'm really getting there, out of my head and into my work, mixing my paints and my pain.

'Aye, aye,' I whisper, sucking in the dank smell of the cellar. 'Eye, eye,' and I hear him answering, pleading, and begging me for pity.

'You don't know what it's like to be me. To have these bulging eyes, this slimy, rotten soul.'

'It'll be alright,' I tell him. 'I can help you,' and I reach in with my middle finger locked straight, and drive down the side of his nose, into the socket. Pop goes the weasel.

His canvasses cover the whole back wall, each lit by a tiny spotlight, too bright and stark, away from the cellar's gloom. The tingling fades. Meaning drifts away from me, like a lover lost and gone. There is only confusion, and shame. Annie is silent at my side. Her eyes open wide, following mine to his bloodied green skin pinned out on the concrete floor.

I want to run from the sight of my own grotesque rage, to deny these twisted horrors. Let the world gawp, what does that matter, but not Annie. How can I explain?

This is not my work, only what is left after I go searching inside myself, through paths lit in raging scarlet. There can be no control, no decency. I can no more change what I see than I can change God. I am a visitor, a spy, a thief inside myself, struggling against forces far greater than will or belief. And while the light shines in the darkness there can be no pretence, only seeing what is there and getting it out, purging myself of bitterness and rage, laying it on the canvass in that damp, cold hole.

And that is where it should have stayed. Dreams of torture and vengeance left to rot in the cellar, leaving me free to rise from the darkness, pure and clean and fit for the world.

But I know the truth. Each fix is temporary, fluttering and fading like a candle in a storm. Already the peace is draining out of me, the darkness building. I am a criminal on the run from myself, and my destiny is to be jumping at shadows forever.

The high walls close in, trapping me in my childhood fears with the stink of the cellar turning my stomach, it's dull light casting a shadow over these bright walls, stirring me to begin. To rest a fresh canvass on the easel and mix my ochre and umber and viridian green, to search again for the ash grey pallor of honest defeat, that might set me free of myself for a few hours more.

I turn my back on Frogga, and on that darkness in myself, and in the notched alcove opposite Daryl, I find Mam, tall and proud in her long velvet coat. Her eyes are bright with laughter, mischievous as a child's. A small hand reaches up, holding hers. Benjy's or mine.

The same.

There is no child's hand in the next picture, only the legend *Vlad*, half displayed on a too big bottle bulging through her fingers. Her shoulders hunch as if against the weight, with that same long coat stained close to black against her dyed blond hair. I look at the next canvass, watching her shrink away from me; eyes dulled, hair darkened to a witch's nest, brown teeth rotted to stumps.

I walk faster now, past letters tied with fraying string,

edges black and curling on an open fire. My childish, unread handwriting still visible, grey on darkening grey.

Come back Benjy… please…

And on beyond the faceless, crouching children, without eyes, without features, only mouths howling, clinging together in terror of some unseen horror, until at last, I come to the beginning.

Rainbow colours flood through the darkness of older cheaper canvasses, some no bigger than my hand. I see a cabinet tipping, whisky falling, a blond boy in mismatched pyjamas with the light playing on his golden hair. His mouth closed. Eyes wide in terror.

And the last, a pale hand, black hairs thick as grass around a thin gold band, lifting him away from me. His face stretches in a silent scream, saving me, and condemning me.

'Terrible,' Annie whispers.

Her fingers creep into my hand. Her lips close and part in an expression I cannot read, and then her hand is gone. She turns her back, and standing between me and Benjy, she lifts a canvass off its chain.

'This belongs to you,' she says, and hands me the picture.

I look at the small canvass backed in blue and red, green and gold, with the sunlight shining behind. The boys lie in the foreground, on an uncovered duvet. My arm is stretched out, with Benjy's blond head in the crook of my neck, his knee between mine, our hands held tight between us.

I feel the old hopeless pity, and I realise that my anguish isn't only for Benjy, but for me as well. For the child who was left with Daryl Boyle, let down by his mam, while shagged out social services looked on, safe behind their plastic screens.

But even through the pain, my heart lifts, because these are the true stories. In telling them, stark and brutal as they are, I am right. That is the purpose of my work. To take the pain of love and hate, guilt and fear and rage, all the truth of life, and compress it onto canvass. To create a pathway through others' eyes, into their souls, where that truth can again be opened up to its full agonizing magnitude.

That is my purpose. To hold fast to my truth. To harness it in my work, but also to understand that if the message is altered on its journey, that is right and fitting, because we're surely all permitted to struggle for survival with the weapons of our choice. To fight our pain on our chosen field.

Living with all of the truth all of the time is too hard for anyone, and if people have been telling stories since we could speak, it is because every one of us needs our fiction. I must allow the world its deceptions and accept that I will be misunderstood, that the past may be as flexible as the future. And even if all the message is lost, is that my failure?

Perhaps? But perhaps there are some who wish only to gawp and walk away, insulated from the pain. Numb, and half-dead, but safe in their emptiness. I know I cannot reach them all, but to truly touch a single soul is ambition enough.

We must all find our purpose. Mine is to hold to my truth, to harness it in my work, and if it changes on the canvass that is how it should be. The most fundamental truth of all is that truth is malleable, evolving over time, as I myself am Tommy Farrier and Tommy Boyle, Benjy's brother, and Annie's lover. A drug dealer, an artist, and a murderer. The same person I was, and utterly different.

So, what am I left with? Colours and textures and shifting sand.

I shrug and laugh at the darkened skylights.

'It's alright, Tommy,' Annie says, taking Benjy's weight from my hands and laying him down on the marble floor. She holds me to her chest, and I cling on against the suck of quicksand beneath me.

When it comes, her voice is husky in the darkening hall.

'I love you, Tommy.'

I burrow deeper, sucking in the sweet smell of her neck, until she lifts my face and kisses me, releasing the lump in my throat.

'So, this is the Tommy Farrier Exhibition,' she says.

'No,' I say, looking up through blurring eyes. 'Not that.'

Chapter Thirty-Seven

St Andrews Gate

A young hippo is trampolining on my bed. She rolls over, and with her arm warm on my neck and her thigh heavy on mine, she snores in my ear. I kiss her cheek and turn away, in careful, sleep preserving stages. I love her, though maybe things are different now. Less intense, less selfish, like my work.

I've learnt the hard way, which Annie says is the only way I learn anything. If I want to sell paintings, then I have to give the people what they want. The tourists like golden coins and pixies, so for two years, that's what they got. I sold my work in the calles and mercados around Barcelona. Sometimes I made enough money to pay for my oils and canvasses, sometimes not, but still, I got that buzz every time a stranger bought a fragment of my memory.

Eddie's twenty-five grand is long gone. Five went to Peeler, and there had to be five for Lou. I took the train up over the French border to post the money from Marseille, with Annie close beside me, holding back the memories.

The rest of the money stretched over a year, but we've had too many weeks since then, living on bread and olives, running out the back when our prune-faced landlady came wheezing up the stairs to swear at us in Catalan and broken English. She threatened to change the locks a dozen times, but she never did, so now that things are finally coming together, Gorgelina Arroyo Lopez, aka. Prune-face will be first in line for a crate of medicinal brandy, and a fat wad of cash. Well, second, after Clara, who tells me that agents always get paid first.

I make out like Clara's ripping me off, but the truth is, she made it happen. If some of my work is good, I don't kid myself that I could have done it without her. She might have her issues, but then don't we all. And whatever else you say about Clara, she knows her business.

We're in Valencia next month, for a three-week show, with two canvasses already sold for bizarre and unlikely amounts. There's talk of Malaga, and even Madrid, and plenty more enquiries from what Clara calls the "clever money". That means investors. People who don't even look at the canvass.

The art business. She makes it sound seedy and corrupt, and maybe it is, but I can't help believing that someone out there must genuinely like my work.

The mattress lifts, bouncing me out of my thoughts, and Annie stumbles to the bathroom with the future cradled in her big belly. Benjamin Surinder Farrier de Catalunya, our little European. A citizen of the world.

He's due any day. The cot's made up, and all those tiny clothes are waiting for him in the cupboard. We're all set, ready as can be, though other parents laugh out loud when I tell them.

Maybe one day his beautiful nana will come and visit, when she takes a break from drinking herself to death.

"I've been dry for ages," she tells me, slurring her lies down the phone.

I won't pretend it doesn't hurt, but I accept that it is her choice. She won't harm Annie and me, or little Benjy. I won't let her bring us down. I'm finished with all of that, the booze and the drugs, the dodgy deals and stolen money, because that's the one thing Annie was wrong about.

Sure, you can't change where you're from, but you can change where you're going. And if you do, then you *can* change who you are.

The future is calling us forward. I only need to let go of the past, but I'm too wired to sleep, too tired to hold back the memory, and I drift away from our apartment on the sunny Mediterranean coast to that blustery day at St Andrew's gate, with the wind blowing fine needles of rain into my eyes.

I leave Julia Harper and walk through the open gate with my feet scraping on the long gravel drive and my head bent against the weather, and the future. The rain slants down, darkening an old sandstone building. Cold streams run down my neck. I turn my collar up and press on towards a distant line of trees, counting off the rows, and then the columns.

Six has fallen forward, grass growing tall around it.

Seven is a low grey stone, the inscription worn away.

Eight is clearer, *Arthur Rycraft*, on black marble. *Loving husband, father, and grandfather, 4th September 1885 - 12th December 1969.*

Nine is *Betty Jones*, on crumbling grey, *1894 – 1947. Taken too soon. Fifty-three years, she got.*

I step off the path, weaving between the headstones, head turning left and right, compulsively calculating ages.

Maude Cryer, seventy-three.

Mel Davis, eighty-one.

Jenny Archer, ninety.

Every grave is clean and tended, and the dead are getting older. Lives lived, children grown, making way for those who come next. There is no tragedy in their loss.

Eric Cole sucks the strength from my legs.

In loving memory of our little man, 5th of July 1995 - 1st of

December 1999.

A plastic windmill lies face down on the grass. I shake it clean and plant it, deep, beside teddy's outstretched leg. Watery sunlight plays on wet red petals, turning in the breeze. All these blustery days, the seasons, and the years, and still, someone is bringing Eric his toys.

I walk on, faster, striding over buried bodies, bones picked clean by worms, jigsaws unmade, thrown back in their boxes. Stones blur, merging in grey and marble and crumbling sandstone. Their owners stare up at me through hollow, sightless eyes.

Benjamin Harper 1986 – 2001, on a small white stone, no higher than my knees.

Mary Dawn Matthews, 1940-1996.

I move on, and back. It is the age that stops me, not the name. There are too many of those. Farrier. Boyle. Harper.

Benjamin Harper, 1st August 1986 – 22nd August 2001, beloved son of Julia and Peter, brother of Thomas.

I touch the coolness of the stone, tracing his name and mine, kneeling, as close to my brother as I have been in twenty years.

'Benjy.' I fold my arms around him and press my face to his stony cheek.

I loved him and I missed him for all these years, and I am ready for the pain, but not for this confusion. The surges of love and jealousy burning through my chest, and this strange truth that comes to me only now. I loved Benjy, and I wanted him back, but not for his sake, not really, not even to ease my guilt. What I really wanted was to soften Mam's pain, to bring her back to me, because it was always her that I missed the most. All those nights I cried into our Rainbow Blanket and prayed to God and Nana to bring Benjy home, it was Mam I wanted.

The old Mam, mouthing to me over Daryl's leathery shoulder, with her hips swaying, and her feet tip-tapping on the lino.

'Mop with a tash,' she says, winking at me with that sparkle in her eyes.

That was what you took, Benjy. Because from the very beginning, we both knew it was you that Mam loved best. I was always second prize. I loved her, but she loved you.

That's how it was.

I'm old enough to understand the vagaries of love, how little say we have in that cruel, silly, merry-go-round. But still, I feel my shoulders shaking, neither crying nor laughing, but releasing some nameless emotion, for Benjy, for Mam, and for me.

'Your name's Boyle,' Daryl's face is close up against mine. 'Boyle. Say it. And you haven't got a brother.'

'I do,' I scream into his brown-stained teeth. 'I do. I have a brother,' I shout at the stone and the swollen sky. 'And I always will.'

'Love Tommy,' he answers.

His voice is husky with the morning, his head warm on my chest. He watches me with wide green eyes.

I kiss his cheek, and my hand finds the sticky sweetness in the crook of his elbow. Arms and legs entwine. His fingers clutch at the neck of my pyjamas, and that husky voice comes again, from so very far away.

'It's alright, Tom-Bomb,' he says, forgiving me for loving Mam most, for needing her when she wasn't there. 'You were only five.'

I hold tight to the white marble, and I remember what Julia Harper told me, how when he first came to her, he cried every night. Not for Mam, but for me.

Realisation raises the hair along my neck.

As I loved Mam, and she loved Benjy, so Benjy loved me. I was his King and his clown, and his protector.

"I'm so sorry," she said, "but Social Services couldn't find you."

'Well, I've found you, Benjy, and I won't let them take you. Not ever again. Not ever.'

The old anger burns through my chest. I see those sullen women behind their plastic windows, and Mr. Pissed-off, with his rules and regulations. None of them caring enough to even wipe the crusted blood off my face.

I sit on the wet grass and stare at Benjy's stone, and those absurd, impossible dates, *1st August 1986 – 22nd August 2001*, and the anger drains away as fast as it came.

I'm not looking at the years. I'm looking at the 22nd of August, the day before my sixteenth birthday. The day I went to Elliot Terrace. The day I stood on that platform at Central Station and leaned into the roaring train.

The rush of air hummed in my head. I swayed forward, way too far to stop. The pain was gone like it was never there at all. Like nirvana.

But there was this hand on my shoulder. So strong, for such a little hand.

Benjy held me back.

He gave me another chance and if I don't take it, that will be the betrayal. I have a brother who loves me. There is no need to fake my way through life, separate and alone in my sealed glass jar. I can love, and be loved, because Benjy knows I am worthy.

'Thank you, my brother.' I close my eyes and kiss his marble face, watching a younger sunrise, blue and red and gold through the stripes on our Rainbow Blanket.

'Sleep, Benjy, sleep for as long as you want.'

I press my hand to the damp grass above him and turn

back towards St Andrew's gate with my head held high. The sun glints through a broken cloud, but the rain keeps falling, running in streams down my face, leaving me safe to cry.

If you enjoyed *The Silent Brother*, you might also enjoy our other northern novels, available now at Northodox.co.uk

Author's Note

Dear Reader,

Thank you for trusting me with your time, and your heart.

I hope you enjoyed Tommy and Annie's journey, and that they have left you feeling fulfilled, perhaps even a little heartbroken? That's my aim, at least - for us to reach out through this strangely distant and intimate relationship of reader and writer, and touch.

If you did feel some connection, then please, do me, and other potential readers a favour, and pop a review on Amazon. https://amzn.to/37LznvA It doesn't have to be long. A simple 'worth a read' is great, though if you've got more to say, that's even better. The fact is that readers are more likely to trust independent reviews that a publisher's sales pitch.

Of course, if you hated this book, please don't tell anyone – except me. I need to know, because it's only through your feedback that I can learn to make my writing better. So whatever you think of The Silent Brother, I'd be very happy to hear from you on Twitter @SimonVdVwriter, or via my website at www.SimonVanderVelde.com where you can sign up for free news and stories.

And if you would like to read more of my work; the good news is that my next novel, Dogwood is in the planning – while my award winning short-story collection Backstories is available now from Amazon, (https://amzn.to/3j8D2Hp), and all good bookshops, with Backstories II due out in the autumn of 2022.

Wishing you contented and peaceful reading, now and in the future, because whatever anyone says, there's nothing so meditative, mind broadening and healing as a good book

Simon Van der Velde

Victims or Perpetrators?

The Inspiration Behind
The Silent Brother

Working in the east end of Newcastle could be pretty dispiriting. Hard as we tried to make things better, there was always someone, plenty of someones, ready to tear it down. Drug and alcohol abuse was everywhere – as was anger and frustration, vented in seemingly pointless, and often vicious violence.

Put in a new central heating system, they'd rip it out to sell the copper pipe. Give them double-glazing, they'd put a brick through it. During the riots of 1999, local people set fire to their neighbour's homes. In the end, it was hard to avoid feeling that these people deserved what they got.

They didn't.

There was a time, in living memory for some, when fully half the world's shipping was built on the Tyne, and people would joke about the obvious foolishness of bringing coals to Newcastle. Not anymore.

These days, when a major employer closes down, special teams are brought into the area to help with retraining and to attract new employers. But in Thatcher's Britain, when the unions, heavy industry and even the north itself was the enemy – closing down the mines and the decline of the shipyards was an end in itself. A victory. Something like the *victory* in Iraq, with no plan beyond winning the 'war'.

The effect on these communities was devastating. Generations of skilled workers lost their jobs. More than that, they lost their identity and their union, and often their families. How could they teach their children the meaning of a hard day's work for a fair day's pay? - in this new world of every man for himself. And why would their children listen to these old mens' stories? - when both father and children were signing on at the same dole office.

Abandoned and useless, these once proud men faded away. Worse still, their children grew up without hope or direction. The old order was gone, and there was nothing to replace it and nothing to do, except anaesthetize yourself from day to day, until the hopelessness got too much - and erupted into violence. Ambition meant getting a few quid together, enough to score a deal to get you through the emptiness, until next week's giro. Dignity and community were replaced by crime and booze and drugs.

We're on the third generation now. For them, the glory days are something the history teacher drones on about. It has nothing to do with their lives.

In a community with so little hope, overstretched social services and policing priorities elsewhere, it's easy for the gangsters to take over – and anyway, no one likes a grass. Some, heroically, stay and fight for their community. But the truth is that most of the time, those who can, get out.

This is the world our hero, Tommy grows up in. So if *The Silent Brother* is dark in places, it's because my aim is to tell it how it is. To highlight the link between victim and perpetrator, and show you that often, they are one and the same.

In writing this book, I asked myself – if I had grown up in this world, what, if I was brave enough, might I have done to survive?

The Silent Brother is my answer.

Simon Van der Velde
March 2022

Acknowledgements

Heartfelt thanks to everyone who helped make this book all it could be. In particular:

To the late Dave Robson. An old-school gentleman whose decency and optimism showed me that there was more to Walker than bad news headlines, and when a local gangster blew up his car, he was happy to explain that it was just a misunderstanding.

To my publishers, James and Ted, and all the team at Northodox Press. Thank you for your faith and support, and for your expertise in bringing The Silent Brother to the world.

To my friends at Gosforth Writers; Karon Alderman, Ben Appleby-Dean, John Hickman and Trevor Wood for their invaluable insights, advice and encouragement – with particular thanks to Trevor, for lending me the benefits of his experience.

To my many readers and reviewers. Thank you for your guidance and reassurance, and for helping me iron out those nasty glitches. I'm grateful to you all, and whilst there isn't room to mention everyone, I would like to give special thanks to: Kate Horsley, for awarding a prize to my little short story back in the mists of time, and nurturing the seed that became

The Silent Brother. Alli Davies, for taking the time to read and advise on the earliest and roughest drafts of this story. Natalie Wortley for her expert legal advice, (any errors are my own), Dr Reshma Ruia and Davina Banner for their sensitivity guidance, (again, any insensitivity falls at my door), and to Julia Douglas, Adam Clarke, Katie Turnbull, Patricia Calef, Grace Smith, Deanne Wallace, Sarah Faichney, Diane Clarke, the Tsundoku squad and all the great people of book-Twitter, for your unbridled enthusiasm and encouragement, because that kind of support really is a jewel beyond value.

To my dog, Barney, for taking me on those long walks, listening patiently to my worst ideas, and allowing me room to think. Good dog, Barney.

To my boys, Charlie & Tom, for your inspiration.

And most of all, to my wife Nicola, for her psychological insights, her patience and her love, without which The Silent Brother would never have been written.

Simon Van der Velde
April 2022

NORTHODOX
PRESS

HOME OF NORTHERN VOICES

 FACEBOOK.COM/NORTHODOXPRESS

 TWITER.COM/NORTHODOXPRESS

 INSTAGRAM.COM/NORTHODOXPRESS

 NORTHODOX.CO.UK

SUBMISSIONS ARE OPEN!

WRITER &
DEBUT AUTHOR   [ ]

NOVELS &
SHORT FICTION   [ ]

FROM OR LIVING
IN THE NORTH   [ ]

CLOCKWORK MAGPIES

EMMA WHITEHALL